HER SALVATION

Lesbian Romance

Ellen E.

DEDICATION

To my wife Teresa, without whom this book would not exist.
You are my muse and inspiration every day.

A modern love story that takes you through a painful life of poverty, immigration and being lesbian in South America, finding the inner strength to fight against the love turning into dark obsession.

A clash of Latin and Scandinavian cultures where the heat meets the cool water, but who will save whom after all?

Inspired by a real-life events.

CONTENTS

I never knew my father and the first male figure in my life was a man who had my mum on her knees in front of him in our small flat in Germany. I had never been called someone's special girl and I was never my mum's favourite child – that's what she told me when she left me behind to chase her dreams in Peru.

Life had knocked me down more times than I could remember, and being attracted to the same sex didn't exactly make my life any easier. So when our eyes met for the first time in Madrid, I knew I should have tied her up and left, but I didn't.

I wasn't capable of love, she and I were never going to be a normal type of love and she would break my heart more times than a heart could break, unless I stopped her. We were like oil and wine: she sophisticated and expensive, and I explosive and cheap.

Little did I know that destiny would find its way to unite us again giving me another chance, giving her a chance to save me.

I just hope the demons inside me won't burn her trying, she might be my only chance.

Read our story, I dare you.

Love xxx, Lupe.

PART I

Chapter 1

The rain hit hard on the concrete pavement outside the hospital. The sound of the emergency vehicle sirens travelled to the closest underground station in Central London. The echo of the sirens made the newly recruited kindergarten teacher ask the children to cover their ears for protection. The first emergency vehicle arrived at the emergency area of St George's Hospital. The first emergency room doctor jogged to the scene.

"What do we have here?" the doctor asked, covering his face from the icy rain while assisting the emergency team to remove the patient from the vehicle.

"Code yellow, doctor," the senior nurse responded.

The doctor nodded silently, "ABC checked?"

"Yes doctor," the nurse hurried to reply. "29 years old, white female, serious hypothermia. According to eye-witnesses she jumped into water of 10°C; no identification determined, not carrying any medical information indicating medical condition."

The doctor sighed and checked the pulse. "Estimated time in the water?"

"According to the emergency team, up to 20 minutes. She was partly conscious before she was lifted into the rescue boat."

"I see," the doctor said and carefully parted the patient's eye, pointing a lamp towards it for light reaction. "Good reaction to light. Any reported or visible injuries?"

"No doctor."

"OK, cubicle seven, set up cardiac monitoring, pulse oximetry, and cerebral oximetry. I want vitals every four minutes. Move it people," he said and clapped his hands to make the care team jump and hurry inside.

"Jumped you said, eh?" the doctor asked and looked at the nurse on his way inside.

The nurse shook her head. "Yes, doctor, that's what the witnesses say," she said before running after the care team to obey the doctor's orders.

The doctor stopped at the entrance and thoughtfully eyed the care team as they rushed the unconscious woman through the Accident and Emergency Department's automatic doors.

The patient was approximately five foot two, blonde and petite, wearing a plain black suit with a curve-hugging pencil skirt and a waist-length blazer with golden buttons down the front, probably custom made. She was missing one shoe: black shiny leather stiletto.

Even with deadly cold and blue lips, anyone could see she was simply gorgeous, the doctor thought and sighed again as another two emergency vehicles pulled into the emergency area. He glanced up and could hear more vehicles arriving. He knew already it was going to be a long night.

It was the busiest time in the hospital. Extra staff, including nurses and doctors, had been pulled in from on-call rooms as well as their homes. The renovation of the Accident and Emergency department had only finished some weeks ago, allowing the medical team to fully use the facilities. Old medical equipment had been left as it was, but walls and floors were all re-made for the first time since the hospital had started its operations twenty years ago. The hospital had also got fourteen new cubicles as a result of the renovation, which meant the medical teams were able to serve more patients, which would eventually increase the bed turnover and bring more money to the common Trust's pot.

The hospital would finally be able to invest in the Maternity Ward and Post-Natal Unit, the doctor thought as he followed the team to the closest available cubicle in the new A&E majors.

The doctor grabbed the corner of the white plastic sheet. "On count of three. One, two, three." The team lifted the patient onto the hospital bed in the cubicle. The ambulance team who had assisted in the delivery process took the emergency trolley and disappeared.

"Nurse, vitals," the doctor hurried.

"BT 32°C, pulse 45 BPM, respiratory rate 15 and 115/75 mmHg. "

"Bring me white counterpanes and prepare an adrenaline shot, we need to bring the body temperature up and fast," the doctor yelled.

*

Lupe was running.

She had received the news from Giuliana only a couple of minutes earlier. Giuliana had seen the emergency vehicle being unloaded when she had arrived at the hospital on late shift. She said there was no question about it, it had been *her* on the emergency trolley. Lupe hadn't waited for further information, instead, she rushed through the Emergency X-ray and Scanning Department, shortcutting directly to A&E majors. She saw an incoming patient in her wheelchair cutting her path unexpectedly and hit her leg on the wheel, almost making them both fall down.

"*Mierda!*" she cried and felt a sharp pain on her injured knee and pushed her curly hair back. The ponytail from the morning had loosened almost to nonexistence letting her wild hair run freely. Suddenly, a picture of her appeared in her mind: laughing softly and running her fingers in her curls like she always did. She could almost hear her voice.

Lupe looked to the right before touching her identification badge on the card reader to open the door. They were not supposed to use shortcuts unless they were performing hospital duties. She knew it but this time she couldn't care less as she entered A&E majors and started peaking inside the cubicles.

"*Ma'am,* you can't enter here, we have a medical operation in progress," a nurse said and tried to push her back behind the curtain but Lupe resisted. "No, please, let me go, I need to see her!"

"*Ma'am,* back off, now!" the nurse said and signalled to the nearby security. "Security, a little help here!"

Two of the security officers jogged to the scene and hooked their arms under Lupe's armpits.

"Let me pass, please," she panted and desperately gasped air into her lungs. "Let me go. You don't understand, I know her!"

The loud noises attracted the doctor's attention and he lifted his gaze. "Get her friend out of here!" the doctor yelled, annoyed. "We are trying to treat a critical patient here."

Lupe tried again, tearing her limbs from the security officers' grip, but it was pointless: two against one, there was no competition. "No, she is not my friend! You don't understand. Please let me see her."

Suddenly, the cardiac and pulse monitor came to life and an alarm went off.

The nurse quickly placed her fingers under the patient's jaw looking for a pulse. "Doctor, I can't feel a pulse, we're losing her."

"Fuck, bring the defibrillator, now," the doctor said and turned around ready to receive the defibrillator machine. "On three. Get another adrenaline shot ready," he said and charged the defibrillator. "Clear!" the doctor said and gave the first electric shock.

"Noooooo!" Lupe cried out loud as she helplessly watched the doctor trying desperately to shock life back into the unconscious woman's body. When the defibrillator went off and her body jolted up from the bed, the physical pain ran through her, bringing stomach acids up to her throat.

The cardiac and pulse monitor continued alarming.

"Doctor, still nothing."

The doctor nodded. "Reload again and… clear!" The doctor gave a second shock on the patient's chest.

Her body lifted from the bed like a rag doll.

The doctor motioned one of the nurses to wipe the dripping sweat from his forehead and looked up to see the security officers and Lupe frozen in their places watching them.

"For fuck's sake, get the friend out of the operation room, now!" he yelled and angrily swung his hand toward them.

His outburst brought life back to them all and Lupe fought back fearlessly. "You don't understand, she is my life. I have nothing else!"

The nurse came to her: "I understand *ma'am*, but we need to let the doctors do their best now without distractions. Everything else is in the hands of God," she said and squeezed her hand before closing the cubicle curtain and leaving the security officers to escort Lupe out of A&E majors.

When the door light turned red again signalling it had been locked, the security officers let go of Lupe's hands before a bleep on the radios attached to their uniform belt told them another emergency required their attention and they left Lupe in the corridor.

She stood in silence for a moment listening to the sound of her own heart pumping quickly against her rib cage as if trying to escape. If she could, she would gift it to her, she thought as tears emerged in her eyes. She hardly ever cried as she saw it as a sign of weakness, something that had never been allowed in her world, but this time she couldn't stop it.

She gently touched the door separating her from the unconscious patient lying inside the operating room. They were only ten feet apart, but somehow it felt like an ocean. She looked at the light above the door, which was lit up red: *Occupied.*

It meant there was an emergency operation in progress and no one was allowed to enter except medical staff. Lupe knew it, but she had never expected the room to be occupied by someone who held this much importance in her life, it felt too personal.

What if she hadn't gone to work today? What if she hadn't heard the conversation? What if she hadn't let her go? she thought as the pool of questions occupied her mind. Letting the anger get the best of her, she punched her fist to the wall so hard her knuckles burst open and left a trail of blood on the white wall.

Lupe started wandering the hospital corridors and soon, without realising, she was standing in front of the chapel door on the lower ground floor of the hospital. She noticed the construction team equipment nearby and quickly snatched the "work in progress" signage and placed it in front of the chapel door before entering. She didn't want to be disturbed.

She hesitated for a moment before sitting down on the bench crossing her hands for a prayer. "God, I know we haven't been in touch for a while," she started, "I know I lost my hope at some point, because I couldn't understand why you put me through so much *shit.*" She winced as her hard words echoed in the small chapel. "I still don't, but it doesn't matter anymore because when I was in a thousand pieces you sent *her* to put me in one." Lupe felt tears surfacing again and sobbed out loud. "But I can't understand why you are taking her away from me now. It doesn't make any sense, haven't I suffered enough?"

She heard someone trying the handle of the chapel door and waited in silence until she heard footsteps walking away from the door before continuing. "But I tell you this, if you take her away from me, I swear I will take my own life and I will hunt her down, I will travel through hell and heaven to find her if I have to because she is the blue heart in my flames. She belongs to me."

Chapter 2

Kiel, Germany 1982

"Lupe, for heaven's sake, let your sister alone, now!" Altagracia yelled and pointed her finger painted with red nail polish towards the younger one of her two children. Lupe was laughing and hid herself behind the brown sofa where she would pick and pull her sister's long, black braided hair until five-year-old Reina would complain and whine.

Although Reina was a year older, Lupe had already outgrown her physically. She was a delicate child with the physique of a ballerina whereas Lupe could have been part of an American football team.

Altagracia looked at her children: *how the hell could they be so far apart?* she wondered and poured herself another glass of cheap wine in a plastic cup and lit a cigarette, adjusting herself comfortably on the brown armchair next to the sofa crossing her arms. Usually, she preferred beer over wine, but this was a special occasion and German wine cost nothing and contained more alcohol, which meant she would reach her euphoric point faster. Altagracia took another sip of her cup and smiled to her children, watching them play; she was, most of all, a practical person.

She had to admit the fathers of her two children had been quite different. She had named her first daughter Reina, "the queen", after learning she was pregnant and Reina's father, whose name she couldn't really remember, had promised her a ring and a house at the beach. In reality, Reina had been the result of a very drunken night at a nightclub in 1977. He had been a tall, dark Venezuelan stud with a good sense of humour. However, the good sense of humour hadn't lasted even through the pregnancy. He had left her before Reina had even been born without leaving any contact details of him or his family.

"Cabrones, todos," Altagracia snorted and took a long inhale on her cigarette, watching the red tip burn.

Altagracia had never been shy about her conquests with men; in fact, she was proud of them all. But she had to admit that having two children who didn't share a father in the 1980s was something she wasn't exactly keen on sharing, even though she was quite sure people knew it already. It was quite obvious – whereas Reina had olive skin with black straight hair, one could almost see blue veins through Lupe's fair skin during the cold winter months, and in summer the sun would create red shades on her curly hair so strong people often asked Altagracia if she dyed her daughter's hair. *Like she would have the time or money for that kind of thing,* Altagracia snorted again and pulled her own black locks looking for split ends.

Lupe was kind of a counter image of her father: whereas he had been slender and charismatic, Lupe was bulkily built and had a temperament from hell. They both shared the same curly hair with reddish shades and the pale skin with freckles, only Lupe's hair, if not groomed, made her look like Mowgli from *The Jungle Book*. Her father had been *stunning* in all aspects, Altagracia remembered, and she therefore couldn't hide her disappointment when looking at her younger daughter.

Despite the superficial aspect, with her character and temperament, Altagracia had no doubt Lupe would survive well in this world and take care of her older sister. Deep down, she could see her daughter had a very strong sense of rightfulness and honour, something that Altagracia lacked totally. A rude person would probably even go as far as classifying her as a selfish person, but truth be told, Altagracia didn't care what people thought of her. *It doesn't matter in the end*, she thought and finally dragged herself up from the armchair, sucking the final blows from the joint before finishing it in the ashtray. She didn't want to be late tonight.

Altagracia was a beautiful, exotic-looking Spanish woman with black eyes living in Germany where people hadn't seen anything exotic for decades. After the Second World War, Germany had really kept its borders closed, increasing its prosperity in isolation from other parts of the world.

At first, Altagracia hadn't intended to migrate anywhere, but considering the economic situation in Spain, she had been forced to look for job opportunities in other countries. Knowing her mother and sister lived in Germany with their families, it had been a natural choice in the first place. She had left Spain with a heavy heart, swearing she would come back to her home country one day.

Altagracia didn't consider herself particularly patriotic but it was the culture and people she missed, her friends and family. She felt alone and isolated from the small circle she had grown to love and hate, for better or worse.

She took a deep breath and picked up a white dress from the dirty laundry basket, smelling the fabric. *This will have to do tonight,* she thought and strutted to the bathroom.

*

Altagracia looked at herself in the mirror hanging on the bathroom wall. She had left the bathroom door open, replacing the poorly functioning ventilation with a practical solution to prevent the steam from building up small water works on the ceiling that would frizz her hair into an Afro at the ends and leave it dirty and flat at the roots. It was something that didn't suit Altagracia's plan for tonight.

She placed her hand in front of her mouth to cough. She had been suffering from a cough for a long time, which she refused to blame heavy smoking for and instead, kept looking for signs of dust and mould in every corner of the house.

The children were still playing in the living room, this time peacefully, as she heard Reina's giggles through the bathroom door. Altagracia peeked a quick look at them in the modest living room. She was waiting for her mother who was going to babysit the girls tonight.

Altagracia hadn't had money to buy furniture so she had rented the flat furnished. It was a one-bedroom flat, and she shared the tiny bedroom with her two children. She hadn't bothered to buy them separate beds and instead, they all slept in the same bed. *There wouldn't have been any space for bunk beds anyway*, she had thought. The ugly brown sofa was taking most of the space in the living room and the wooden coffee table was so scratched by a previous tenant that guests needed to watch where they put their coffee mugs as if misplaced, the deep scratches would cause the mug to fall over, spilling the coffee everywhere. Altagracia had removed all the curtains and washed the windows in the hope that would allow more natural light to enter the flat, but so far, she couldn't see any significant change. The kitchenette was plain with cupboards that had been white once upon time, and they were forced to dine in the living room on the brown coffee table, sitting on the floor just like the Japanese. The children loved it though and asked every time when they would visit Japan.

Like I would have money to even pay my bills because of you two, Altagracia thought but gave her normal "one day" response and a smile to her children.

A long silence grew in the living room making Altagracia suspicious and she peeked into the living room again, frowning; Reina had started drawing on the food wrappers from last night and Lupe was sucking her thumb and watching carefully while her sister worked. Lupe would soon take the pencils from Reina's hand and ruin the drawing or break the pencils, Altagracia knew it but she didn't have time to care and instead, closed the bathroom door.

She wanted to look ravishing for the evening, which required her undivided concentration; it was especially important because she knew the marine crew would land on the shore once again for their monthly visit.

The marine crew was scheduled to land once a month in the small German harbour in Kiel. They would land and group themselves in the local bar for beers and later hit the only nightclub in the town. Every single girl in town would put on their finest dresses and groom themselves from head to toe, trying their luck with the handsome *marineros,* and she wanted to be one of the lucky ones.

She pouted her lips to the mirror and added one more layer of red lipstick, kicking the bathroom door open when the tiny light attached to the bathroom ceiling started blinking. She didn't have a proper light in the bathroom as the landlord Samuel, or *Sam* for friends, hadn't had time to come and fix it.

Altagracia frowned her thick eyebrows in annoyance when the light blinked again causing the red lip liner to cross her lip line. She sighed and rolled a piece of toilet paper around her fist to remove the excess colour. She always had to wait for him to do maintenance around the house. *Clearly*, it was his job, but ever since she had kindly declined his dinner invitation, she had to wait for days for small things to be fixed in the house, which irritated her.

Sam was a small Turkish guy whose hairline was quickly disappearing and whose skin was covered in scars from teenage acne. He had poor posture, which he blamed on stress and lack of time to do any exercise, which made him look shorter than he actually was. He was a complete bore and the biggest complainer Altagracia had ever met, hence she had no intention of meeting him outside of her tenancy agreement to hear him whine about the German Social Security System and the lack of understanding and compassion the country provided to its refugees. He often told her that his life had been so much better in Turkey, ignoring the fact that he had immigrated to Germany in the 1960s and never considered returning to his beloved homeland, Altagracia thought. He was such an extreme as a person, which was entertaining, but not enough to go out with him, she thought sadly. She took one last look in the mirror, adjusting her skintight white dress to push her full pair of breasts almost out of her cleavage.

She loved wearing white because it suited her olive skin, long black hair and the five foot five body she was so proud of, *which no doubt Reina will inherit one day*, she thought and blinked her clumpy eyelashes, covered with so much mascara she could hardly lift them. It wouldn't matter anyway – *marineros* were not there to stare at her eyes. She smiled at her reflection and for a second, an image of Sam's sad face crossed her mind, but she quickly shook the image away. She had higher standards.

*

"Mamá, Lupe is picking her nose and wiping her hands on my *camiseta*!" Altagracia could hear Reina's protest.

"In a minute, I'm coming!" she responded and finished her make-up, adding some perfume on her neck and wrists before pushing the bathroom door open.

Her mother, *Doña* Margaret, had arrived and used her own keys to enter the house. *No doubt checking up on me*, Altagracia thought and followed the noises to the tiny kitchenette to find her mother fully occupied in feeding the children.

"*Ma*, don't give Lupe more milk!" she said and hurried to take the milk carton away from Lupe's chubby hands.

"She is going to feel sick and it's going to be you who is taking care of her during the night," Altagracia warned her mother. She opened the fridge door and hid the milk carton behind the soon-to-be-gone vegetables she had bought last week in the hopes of having inspiration to cook.

"Don't worry *hija*, we are going to be just fine," her mother said and lifted Reina into her arms to wave goodbye.

Lupe looked up at her grandmother expectantly and lifted her small hands up in the air, asking to be picked up too. *Doña* Margaret looked at her youngest grandchild in silence but didn't make any gesture to pick her up.

"Not now *cariño*, I've got Reina here," she said and pushed Lupe aside to walk her daughter to the entrance.

Lupe lowered her hands to her sides in silence and let her eyes follow the three of them walking towards the entrance door where she saw her mother pick up her coat and slam the front door closed behind her.

Chapter 3

Encarni arrived just in time in the local pub – the party was just about to start.

The pub was full of enthusiasm and testosterone in the form of sailors dressed in white uniforms from head to toe. The air smelled of beers and a mix of sweat and musk.

She nodded approvingly, scanned the menu of the day and felt her spirits speeding sky high. *Tonight is my night*, she thought silently.

The decoration of the pub was modest and very German. The wooden chairs and tables had been moved to the sides to create a dance floor for later evening and the mass of people were all packed around the bar cheerfully chatting and laughing. All ketchup and other condiments, heavily used in food culture in Germany, had been removed from the bar and tables as a precaution by the owner of the pub, wanting to prevent any overreaction by his dear customers that would mean having to pay additional cleaning costs after the party. *Not that he wasn't doing it already*, Altagracia thought, looking around and seeing broken pint glasses everywhere and feeling the sticky floor under her high-heeled shoes.

She entered the pub and took her coat off. As soon as she opened the front buttons of her coat and let it slide down her shoulders, she heard loud approving screams around her. She smiled coyly and pushed her chest up and let the coat fall off her shoulders down to her arms and onto the floor. It didn't take long for the first sailor in his white uniform to pick up her coat from the floor and offer her a seat in the bar. Altagracia smiled politely and took a seat.

"Are you alone here, *sugar*?" the sailor asked.

"Not anymore," Altagracia responded in German with a smile and took a first sip from the beer the sailor had offered her.

She had found the German language easy to learn. It had been much easier than English at school and a reason for her family to migrate to the country. *Not that the generous social security system had anything to do with their decision*, she thought sceptically.

The night turned out to be a success for Altagracia; she danced until her feet hurt and drank free beers until her head felt dizzy. She was a very skilled dancer and born with rhythm in her blood – so much so that the sailors had been queuing up to dance with her. Eventually she locked her eyes on one of them to go home with – her mother had promised to stay overnight, so she was free to go and enjoy her time.

"Wanna go home with me, *sugar*?" asked the sailor she had danced most of the night with.

"Well, if you insist…" Altagracia said coyly and tilted her head flirtatiously.

"After dancing with you all night, I think your body calls for me, *sugar*," he said and patted Altagracia on her buttocks. She laughed and stretched her round buttocks to offer a better view for him as they started walking towards the harbour.

When Altagracia was about to make a turn towards the harbour accommodation offered to the marine crew once a month for free, the sailor stopped her. "Oh look *sugar*, I'm sure you are aware that we are not allowed to bring any damsels to the accommodation area and we are not allowed to go on board drunk," he said and eyed Altagracia knowingly. "And I think we both know I can't fulfil either of those orders," he purred in her ear and eagerly awaited Altagracia's response.

She was fully aware of the rules for the sailors and understood clearly the sailor's hint of being invited to her house instead. *This wasn't her first night out*, she wanted to remind him but stayed quiet, weighing her options.

"That's OK, you can come to my place," she said softly and turned around to navigate her way home. *The children will be sleeping anyway*, she thought silently.

It didn't take long to arrive at Altagracia's doorstep.

"No screaming then, I've got very annoying neighbours," she said before turning the key and opening the door.

"If you say so, *madam*," the sailor said and lightly touched the visor of his uniform hat making Altagracia giggle.

She knew her neighbours couldn't care less what she did in the flat, in fact, she was quite sure the people living next door were hardly ever there, judging by the lack of complaints she had received when the girls had been smaller and much louder.

They entered the flat silently and Altagracia hurried towards the tiny kitchenette. "Do you fancy a drink?"

"Indeed *sugar*, yes please if not sooner," the sailor said and took his coat off, placing it on the brown sofa before looking around the flat and sitting on the sofa, straightening his long legs under the wooden table.

Altagracia followed his gaze and was secretly happy her mother had cleaned up the mess the girls usually made. The flat looked impeccable, *at least the best it could be*, she thought and shifted her gaze back to the white-clad giant on her sofa.

She couldn't stop glancing at him from the tiny kitchenette whilst looking for anything alcoholic she could find in the cupboards.

He was truly a stunning man; tall and handsome. His short brown hair had outgrown slightly from its original shape and he could have used a haircut, probably one of the highlights for every sailor during their monthly visits on the shore, she thought, examining her view further. He had mild highlights in his hair probably from the sun, and seawater had roughened the skin around his face, or maybe it was just the black, one-day beard growing, she wondered. She couldn't decide without touching his jaw, Altagracia thought and licked her lower lip approvingly before shifting her gaze from him to the drinks at hand.

She had found one unopened beer in the fridge and an almost-finished bottle of red wine in the sink, which she must have left in the bathroom meaning to throw away but had forgotten –her mother must have found it.

The girls must have required her attention full time, Altagracia thought with slight bitterness on her tongue. She loved her girls dearly, but she couldn't help feeling annoyance at times towards them for their lousy fathers. She also still felt so young herself and sometimes let the feeling overrule every single motherly instinct in her body. If only the girls would behave normally and stay quiet from time to time, especially Lupe, who was causing trouble all the time. Altagracia sighed.

"*Sugar*, are you ready? I'm losing my buzz," the sailor hooted from the living room, cutting Altagracia's further thoughts.

"In a minute, *amorcito*!" she responded and quickly threw beer in a glass for him and decided to finish the wine herself, adding a bit of water and cinnamon to her glass. She looked at her drink in disgust. Hopefully, she would be able to hold it down at least for tonight. She could suffer the hangover tomorrow whilst her mother took care of the children she thought and put a smile back on her face before returning to the living room.

"Here you go *amorcito*, bottoms up!" she said and sat next to him.

"It's about time *sugar*, took you ages to pour a can of beer in a glass eh?" he said with a heavy Irish accent, taking a long sip from the glass and moving his hands to her waist. He gave out a long approving burp.

Altagracia laughed: "You pig!" she said and placed her drink on the coffee table, where she could still see poorly wiped-up dinner leftovers stained on the wooden surface. She took a sip of her drink before placing the glass on the table shivering with nausea. It wasn't as bad as she had thought; it was even *worse*.

"Come here *sugar* and give me some love," the sailor said and placed a wet kiss first on her bare shoulder and then up her neck before reaching her mouth and covering it with his lips.

She replied eagerly. He tasted like beer, alcohol and cigarettes, leaving a hint of masculinity and sweat in the air.

"Mmm, *sugar*, you taste divine," he purred and caressed her hair giving it a slight tug. Altagracia smiled and moved quickly to his lap to hurry up the foreplay part as she was afraid of waking up the girls – she didn't want them to ruin her fun. After all, she *needed to feel like a woman* as well, she thought, which was her most common justification for dragging a man home.

She started rubbing her soft behind against his crotch and biting the sensitive area around his neck until she could feel him tense under her. "Oh, *baby* yes, keep going," the sailor murmured, letting his head fall back onto the back of the sofa.

Altagracia smiled. Despite the heavy drinking, she could feel him harden against her.

"Let's get rid of these clothes, eh?" he said and clumsily started peeling off Altagracia's dress.

Altagracia stood up from his lap to give him easy access to her clothing while helping him to unbutton his shirt and trousers. She placed his uniform hat on her head and gave him a quick twirl.

He laughed. "Oh *baby*, you look like a sexy goddess, come on here will you," he said and opened his arms for her. She laughed herself and leaned back onto his lap. He touched her between her legs. "Oh, *baby*, you are as wet and sweet as *sugar*," he said and touched her again.

Altagracia wasn't sure if she was even wet for him, as truth being told she was so drunk she couldn't even feel much of his touch, but as she was more after the attention and having someone close to her, she let it go.

"Oh yes, *amorcito*, feels so good, give me more," she raised her voice and threw her hair back, touching her own naked breast, closing her eyes, urging him to move his fingers lower and vigorously swirl them around her sex.

Altagracia's moans kept growing louder and soon she forgot her better intention of being quiet for the sake of her sleeping girls in the bedroom.

The sailor groaned and let his head fall again onto the back of sofa as if falling asleep. "Ah, *sugar,* take me in your mouth will you, just for a second, I'm so close," he said and Altagracia quickly changed her position and went on her knees in front of him, taking his full length in her mouth.

"Ah, that's right *baby*, take it deep, deeper!" he said and grabbed a big chunk of her hair in his fist as he pressed himself deeper down into her throat. She groaned but allowed him to enter deeper, hitting the gag reflex in her throat and sending the stomach acids and the cheap old wine to the surface from her stomach, bringing tears to her eyes.

"Just like that *baby*, you are going to make me come," he mumbled and moved his hips against Altagracia's mouth.

As they kept going, neither of them noticed a little girl at the entrance holding tightly against her chest the *peluche* she had got from her older sister to help her sleep at nights, watching them.

Her eyes were fixed on the strange man and her mother. Their moans reminded her of her mother sleeping on the sofa after her long nights out, a bucket placed in front of her on the floor if she felt sick. They would usually pick up the bucket and wash it in the tiny bathroom as otherwise, the smell of dried vomit and partly digested food would stay in the apartment forever.

"*Mamá!*" Lupe screamed and stormed into the living room, waking up Reina who rushed from the bedroom to see the reason for her little sister's screams.

The screams of her grandchildren woke up *Doña* Margaret who stood up from the bed immediately as she always slept very lightly when not in her own bed and, truth being told, she wasn't a big fan of her daughter's apartment either.

She quickly wrapped her morning gown around her shoulders and lifted the crying Reina into her arms to comfort her, following the sounds to the entrance of the bedroom where she could see her other grandchild screaming in the living room.

"Let go of *mi mamá*! Let go!" Lupe screamed until her voice turned into stammering, pushing her little four-year-old hands with all the force she had against the big naked man's leg.

The sailor was almost asleep but winced wide awake due to the sudden change of events.

"What the hell…?" he opened his eyes and pushed Altagracia from his lap, landing her on her bare buttocks on the floor.

She took a quick look at her younger daughter before turning back to the sailor, smiling. "Oh, it's OK, she's not mine. She's my friend's child, I'm babysitting them for the night," she said and casually shoved Lupe away on the floor.

The sailor eyed her with disgust. "What the hell, you leave your friend's child at your place unattended and then push him around too?" He raised his voice angrily.

The alcohol and lack of food and sleep reddened Altagracia's face in anger. "Well, first of all she is not a boy as you can clearly see and secondly…"

"Altagracia, what the hell do you think you are doing, *hija*?"

She could hear her mother's nagging voice over her shoulder before she even turned her head. *Great, just perfect*, she thought as she saw her mother coming from the bedroom door carrying Reina in her arms.

"*Ma*, don't..." Altagracia raised her hand in the air as a sign of defeat but her mother interrupted her with a fast Spanish earful and then turned her attention to her daughter's guest. "Firstly, let me tell you, young man, that both these girls are my grandchildren and she is my daughter, so these *are* her children," she huffed like a bull. "Secondly, your actions in this house are extremely disrespectful and disgusting, especially in front of little children, I'm sure you realise that too," she bridled and lifted her nose arrogantly.

The sailor looked defeated and awkward. It was clear he was caught off guard with a one-night stand he was having on his first night out after a long month at sea and he wasn't happy. He looked at the angry old lady holding a small girl protectively in her arms and at the other younger girl at his side with angry tears on her face.

He moved his eyes from the angry little girl to his planned entertainment for the night. She was a beautiful woman and one couldn't tell immediately that she had given birth to two children, but then again, how could he know? So far, she had only sucked him off, he thought.

She was a beautiful and exotic woman, but after today's episode he had no intentions of ever seeing her again.

If he had been any more in his senses, he would have got dressed and left the tiny apartment in a matter of seconds, but heavy drinking and being up over 24 hours took its toll and he didn't say anything. He just sat down on the sofa and fell asleep.

He would deal with the catastrophe in the morning.

*

Altagracia took a last look at her sailor.

She couldn't really understand his problem. She did regret the way he had found out about her children, and the way she intended lying to him, but in her defence, the situation hadn't really left much of a choice for her.

She still blushed under her make-up when she recalled the night's events. In the bright morning light and without the courage fuelled by alcohol, the sailor had been mortified. He had dressed quickly, apologised to her mother for the inconvenience he had caused during the night and left the flat. He hadn't said much to the children either, even though Lupe had been rather curious about him in the morning with his clothes on and had followed him with her eyes when he had prepared to leave.

Altagracia sighed and massaged the spot in between her eyes. Her mother was still not talking to her and gave her the silent treatment and shot her judgemental looks every time she could. On better days, Altagracia would have gone to her mother and made amends but today, with the splitting hangover, it had to wait.

She took one last look at the strong back of her sailor when he took the right turn from the street corner and disappeared behind the convenience store.

He didn't look back.

The wind blew strongly from the seaside and Altagracia shivered, wrapping herself deeply into her white dress, which she had thrown on in the morning to walk the sailor out. It was the worst hangover of her life and she really could have used some cuddling and proper food but didn't want to ask the sailor to stay. *Not that he would have either, the damage was already done,* she thought and crossed her arms on her chest and turned around to walk into the building. She took a deep breath and was just about to enter the flat when she heard a door opening next to her.

"Altagracia, what a pleasant surprise!" Sam, her landlord, said with a big smile on his face. "I can't believe it, I was just thinking about you!" he continued, exposing a full set of teeth, which had probably never seen dental floss.

Altagracia eyed him and muffled a polite greeting whilst looking for her keys but Sam didn't seem to mind the awkward silence. "Anyway, I'm on my way to fix *Frau* Fruscher's window, she can't close it apparently, but first I have to finish cooking my famous *menemen,*" he said and waved a kitchen cloth towards the entrance of his flat.

Altagracia smiled at him but didn't say a word, narrowing her eyes and letting him chat alone in the corridor. "I'm not sure if you know, but it's a traditional Turkish breakfast – scrambled eggs cooked with sautéed vegetables and served with bread. Turkish spices originally from Turkey of course. You can't really find the real stuff in this country, am I right eh?" he said and winked.

Altagracia looked at him, completely oblivious to the joke, only smelling the divine flavours coming out of the door he still held open. She was hesitant about whether she should just smile nicely and wish him good day and enter the flat or if she should give him a hard time about not answering her calls to fix her lighting.

She chose the first option. "Nice to see you again, Sam. I'm glad you are having a good day. Food usually lifts my spirits as well," Altagracia said and was about to enter her flat when she heard the girls fighting again. "Lupe stop it, don't jump on me, my leg hurts, stop it! *Mamá!!* Lupe doesn't let me be in peace!! *Mamá*, do something *por favor!*"

Altagracia heard her older daughter whining followed by the sound of breaking glass. The good thing with her children was that they didn't seem to hold grudges too long, like her mother, she thought ironically.

"*Mamá*, Lupe broke the vase for the flowers *abuela* brought us, the water is everywhere!"

Altagracia closed the door abruptly and made a choice. "Sam, are you busy? I would like to invite you for a coffee. It has been a long time since I last saw you," Altagracia smiled flirtatiously and moved her hair from her face, exposing her collar bone and cleavage.

He seemed to be totally surprised at her friendliness and his face lit up immediately. "Oh, Altagracia, I would love to, but please, let me offer you a taste of my famous *menemen*, it will be ready in just a couple of minutes and I'm sure the girls are hungry too," he said, almost stumbling over his feet when entering his flat.

Altagracia kept an innocent smile on her face but inside, she was smiling gleefully. She turned to return her flat when she heard his door opening again.

"Altagracia, now that I think about it, I remember you mentioned some time ago about your lighting not working? Maybe I should have a look at that too now that I'm here?"

"What about *Frau* Fruscher and her window?" Altagracia asked with poorly hidden fake concern widely spread on her face.

"*Frau* Fruscher's window can wait," Sam said and entered his flat again. She could soon hear the banging of dishes and him rushing to put together the breakfast plates for her and the girls.

She smiled viciously; it hadn't been her first choice, but it was definitely convenient for her and that was the most important thing for now.

Chapter 4

"Hello, anyone home?" Altagracia yelled and entered the flat. She had had a rough day at work and was secretly hoping Sam would have taken the girls out for dinner.

The little clothing store she worked in was run by a Turkish couple, but the workplace Sam had nicely organised for her was breaking into pieces. The old couple who used to run the shop had decided to retire from the business and had called their daughter to manage the store on a daily basis.

The daughter was over forty years old, born and raised in Germany, yet she spoke German with a heavy unrecognisable accent, which caused numerous misunderstandings between them. She had lived most of her life in South Germany and had inherited her mother's long black straight hair, brown skin and chubby appearance. Unfortunately, the similarities ended there, as her character wasn't even comparable to her mother's kindness and sense of humour. She usually arrived at work late, breathing heavily, and struggled just to open the front door lock, breaking into a sweat so bad that Altagracia could smell it under her cheap Turkish perfume.

But it wasn't the language barrier nor the personal hygiene issue that had started to break the relationship Altagracia had built up with the owners of the shop for the past months, it was simply the fact that the daughter couldn't stand her existence.

She had tried everything she could to please her, but Altagracia wasn't going to take her attitude and offensive way of talking to her much longer. She could feel her Spanish blood boiling in her veins every time she heard her nagging voice from the tiny office space they had created in the back of the shop.

On the contrary, her husband, as ugly as she was, had always been nice to her. In fact, Altagracia was convinced the husband only visited the store to have his coffee made by his wife and to stare at Altagracia as much as he liked. Altagracia wasn't offended by his behaviour at all: *That's the whole point of dressing sexily*, she thought and would usually give him a full backside view while organising the lower shelves in the shop.

She had thought about sleeping with him just to pay back his wife for her awful behaviour and the hard time she was putting her through, but in the end, she didn't think she could have slept with him. He reminded her of a potato with his bold round face and nose so big it could barely fit in his face. His belly was so much pushed and stretched upfront, Altagracia could almost think he was having triplets.

Despite the troubled relationship with the owners, the shop itself was the best place Altagracia had worked in her lifetime. She loved to leave the house early in the morning and have a quick coffee and breakfast outside the house on the way to the shop. She felt she was doing something important for the first time in her life, something which was recognised by someone else than her mother. Something she was even good at to her own surprise.

The shop was located close to the harbour, which wasn't too far away from the house allowing Altagracia to walk instead of taking a bus every morning. It was the only clothing shop in the area, which made the days busy, especially during lunchtime as people would pop in and out during their break. The street view of the shop was covered with glass and inside, they had three mannequins, which Altagracia made sure to dress differently every Friday for the weekend shoppers. She would plan the outfits at home whilst Sam watched the children, making sure she didn't use the same style repeatedly, to attract a whole variety of different customers.

Inside the shop, there was only one big room for the clothing and a tiny kitchenette in the back, which was now used as storage and office space at the same time from where all the administration and material orders were managed on a weekly basis. Normally, Altagracia would avoid the tiny office space at all costs, not only because of the owner's daughter, but also for the dysfunctionality of the space itself. It was a dusty and disorganised place as the clothes would remain in their original boxes waiting to be hung in the main shop area.

The daughter of the owner would sit on the only office chair and run the whole shop from the brown kitchen table that had been brought in when the office next door had closed its operations just before Altagracia had started working in the shop. All mandatory documentation had been stuffed away anywhere possible in the kitchen cabinets and under the table; even though Altagracia never went to college, she was sure any governmental body visiting the shop would disapprove of their filing practices. In general, the whole space wasn't used as originally intended and it tended to get very hot during the summer months due to insufficient ventilation – the only relief during hot weather was a tiny electronic fan that would provide small relief in the small space, in addition to the small rooftop window that they were able to crack open when needed.

The main room where all the clothes were hung and sold was the heart of the whole shop and where Altagracia tended to spend most of her working hours serving the customers. Unlike the messy office, the main shop area was well organised and ventilated as the fresh sea breeze from the harbour would enter the shop every time the door was opened. As her first task, when Altagracia had started working in the shop, she had reorganised the whole layout of the shop and now all the clothes were displayed neatly on the white rails by size and colours. Originally, there hadn't been any fitting room space and customers had been advised to buy and try the clothes at home and then return later if they didn't fit properly, but since Altagracia had started, she had quickly had the owner install a round curtain rail and a green curtain with a flower pattern to separate off a small space for fitting. During peak times in the shop, she would simply open the curtain fully and lift it on top of the rail to allow the whole space to be used. The owner had thought it an excellent idea and so had the customers.

Altagracia had felt valued for her efforts and in her wildest dreams had seen the owners hand over the shop management to her once they had decided to retire. Unluckily, she hadn't had enough time to prove herself.

*

Altagracia sighed while hanging her coat and scarf on the clothing hooks at the entrance. The weather in the small harbour town was unpredictable and changed dramatically from warm to icy in a matter of hours, which made it impossible to plan her clothing as chances were she would get it wrong anyway, she thought and rubbed her arms.

She had high hopes Sam would be able to do something about the unfortunate situation at work as she really liked her job. She decided to have a chat with him later as he might be able to change the owner's mind, Altagracia thought as she sat down on the brown sofa and lifted her legs onto the coffee table.

"*Darling*, don't put your legs on the table, you set a bad example for the children."

Sam appeared from the bedroom.

She rolled her eyes at him and slowly lifted her legs down from the table without saying a word.

As always, he was dressed well in a clean and fresh white dress shirt and brown straight trousers, which he washed and ironed himself as Altagracia couldn't be bothered. He looked overdressed for everyday life with small children and running his engineering work duties,

Altagracia thought. For the past week, he hadn't shaved his beard and it had started to look like an untidy hairy mess covering his top lip and uniting on the sides with his black hair like a true Amish man. It was annoying and looked ugly and every time he tried to kiss her, she would turn her face away as she despised the feeling of his hairy lips on her.

"Thank you *darling*. I just put the girls to sleep. I don't want them to have a bad example. Do you have any idea how hard it is to change behavioural issues, which are started by the careless parents in the first place?" he asked and sat down next to her, giving her a light kiss on the forehead. The beard tickled and she fought back the desire to scratch her forehead, and instead she took the remote control to turn on the TV. She didn't want to say anything and start an argument with him.

They hadn't been together long but Altagracia felt they were already having a crisis in the relationship. To be fair, she hadn't bothered to get to know him before moving in together as he had clicked so well with the children. They had fallen in love with him during the first breakfast over six months ago where Altagracia had shed crocodile tears about her unfortunate life, explaining that she was barely able to pay the rent due to being a single mother raising two children alone without any help. Sam had listened tentatively and simply suggested she find a roommate to share the housing cost. Altagracia had smiled viciously and moved her hand on his thigh. "Sam *darling*, would you consider living with an unlucky woman like myself?" she had said and tilted her head, looking to the ground. "I mean, we could share the housing cost and you could even rent your own flat for extra cash and later who knows what might happen between us…"

There had been a silent promise in her words that Sam had followed – he had swallowed the hook like a fish, losing sight of reason. "Altagracia, this is very sudden, but I think you make complete sense," he had said eagerly, lifting Reina and Lupe onto his lap. "We would be just fine, wouldn't we girls?"

The girls had been overjoyed and had welcomed him with open arms and after a couple of days, when they had finished moving all his belongings to their home, Altagracia had invited him to her bedroom and during the late hours of the night when the girls had been sleeping, she had allowed him to undress her and make love to her quietly. His breath had caressed her ear from behind like a train chimney as he had humped her at the speed of a rabbit, and when she had closed her eyes, she had almost been able to enjoy herself.

Altagracia couldn't blame her children for liking him as he was a tender and trustworthy father figure to them. She had to admit, however, that relationship-wise, they couldn't be more dysfunctional.

As a boyfriend, Sam was very whiny and annoying, which made Altagracia's temper tick more than once a day. He was a *know-it-all* type of person who carried a large package of confidence issues from his childhood; he had been put down all of his life, which led him to continuously compete with her about everything, trying to prove his superiority every chance he got. He didn't have children of his own, yet he acted like he knew more about parenting than she did. She had to admit she was never going to be mother of the year, but hell, she didn't want a middle-aged, bold, Turkish guy with too much hair on his face telling her how to raise her children. After all, they were smart, they would know not to follow their mother's example in everything and if they did, *well good luck to them*, she thought and shrugged her shoulders.

Unfortunately, her mother, *Doña* Margaret, loved him too much to pay any attention to her daughter's suffering and complaints. She would always brush aside any of her remarks by simply stating it was normal in a long-term relationship that the honeymoon period would fade away eventually.

Altagracia couldn't decide if her mother loved Sam for himself or for the stability he was able to offer her grandchildren, but she was sure there hadn't even been a honeymoon period in this relationship. There had never been the butterfly effect in her stomach for seeing him or excitement of their date nights, not to mention her lack of interest in any sexual activity in the bedroom. *Luckily, she was able to blame the children most of the time*, she thought ironically.

Truth being told, it wasn't all bad staying in a stable relationship: having a nice and cosy home for the children and sharing the parenting responsibility after a long day at work, not to mention the financial benefits it brought. However, the weekends were pure torture and seemed to go by slowly as her Latin blood craved *fiesta* and action.

Joy in her life.

But Sam was extremely talented in organising the weekly routines for the girls: he cooked all their meals, played with them and took care of the household work in between his work duties from the apartments he owned. It was a good stable life they had, just like her mother had always wanted for her.

Chapter 5

"Is this seat taken?"

Altagracia looked up from the half-eaten sandwich she was enjoying during her lunch break sitting on a bench in the harbour.

From the start, she had adopted a healthy routine of eating her lunch outside the shop, not only to cool off her busy mind, but also to break the long day and rest her aching feet from standing all day in the shop. Unintentionally, she had developed a habit of wandering to her favourite place in the city, the harbour. On a normal day, she would sit down on the bench and admire the giant ships entering the tiny harbour. She had always wondered how the captains were able to guide the gigantic ships through the tiny entrance of the harbour of Kiel without any accidents or damage. The entrance was made of bricks and formed a barrier to prevent the waves destroying the ships in the harbour during the stormy weather. The waves would hit the brick barrier with all their power, but the barrier didn't give in, not even in the worst storms.

Altagracia had always been fascinated by the sea and ships. Her mind was triggered by the thought of absolute freedom and many times she pictured herself entering a ship and never coming back.

Glaring up, she was greeted by the smile of a gentleman around his mid-thirties. The gentleman had black hair, which he had casually brushed behind his ears, and he was wearing a white shirt and khaki-coloured trousers with a brown belt and pockets on both sides at knee level, like the army style, finished with black army boots. There was a small knife with a wooden handle hanging from his belt. He wasn't as tall as she liked, but his eyes captured her attention. He didn't look like a traditional German and there was something familiar about his accent. For once, Altagracia was speechless.

"Um, hi."

"Um, hi? Does that mean the seat is taken or available?" the gentleman broke into laughter. He had a beautiful smile, Altagracia thought, even though he was missing one tooth in the back of his mouth.

She smiled back and tapped the seat next to her and the stranger sat down.

They both stayed quiet for a while, watching the harbour. Just when Altagracia thought it would be safe to continue eating and took a massive bite of her sandwich, the stranger opened his mouth again. "You like ships?"

She coughed and pointed to her mouth as a sign she needed a couple of seconds to respond. The stranger waited patiently.

"I love ships." Altagracia gulped. "They remind me of hope and freedom."

The stranger nodded and looked longingly at the sea. "I know what you mean. I feel the same. I think it is quite common for people who grew up close to the ocean."

Altagracia nodded approvingly.

"I take it you're not a German?"

"God, no!" Altagracia laughed and shook her thick black hair. "Spanish."

The stranger turned to face her. "Oh, then it must be my lucky day as you don't often see Spanish-speaking people in this part of the country." He smiled and changed his language to fluent Spanish to

Altagracia's surprise.

"I knew your accent sounded foreign!" she smiled and playfully punched him on his shoulder. "Which part of Latin America are you from?"

The stranger laughed and massaged the shoulder she had hit. "Was it that obvious?"

She smiled coyly. "I just have a good ear for Spanish accents."

He laughed again and held out his hand. "Jorge, it's a pleasure to meet you."

"Likewise," Altagracia said and shook his hand.

And to her surprise, she actually meant it.

They started seeing each other casually then and there. He would come down to the harbour during Altagracia's lunch hour and they would talk about everything.

Altagracia learnt that he was Peruvian from Jaen, a small city close to Amazonas and approximately a fourteen-hour bus ride from the capital of Lima. He was the middle child of five and the only one who had immigrated to Europe. One of his sisters lived in the US but the rest of the family had remained in Peru. He was an ex-sailor but was now working on land in the exporting office due to a knee injury sustained when the heavy metal chain of an anchor had dropped on his leg some years back during a storm in the open seas.

At first, Altagracia had kept her distance and considered it a *pasa-tiempo*, but day after day, she started waiting for their time together. Sometimes, if there were no shipments due to arrive or leave, he would be waiting for her outside the shop to walk her home. From the start, the relationship had felt different and she had been brutally honest about her current relationship situation and children. He had not liked it and it had caused them to part for a couple of weeks before he had come back again.

During those lonely weeks, Altagracia had felt like the world had come to its end and for some reason, she had blamed Sam and the girls for it. She had been easily irritated and difficult even in her own opinion and, after the first week, Sam had started taking the girls to his mother for dinner and coming back late in the evening to put them to bed. During those lonely hours, Altagracia would go and buy a bottle of cheap wine and drown her sorrows in the bottle. By the time Sam and the girls came back, she was drunk and passed out on the sofa.

Altagracia had to admit that Sam's loyalty and patience were impressive. He wouldn't say a word, but instead would cover her with a blanket on the sofa and go to sleep in the bedroom with the girls. Altagracia wasn't even bothered anymore with the work situation, although she bet Sam's pity was feeding from the thought that she was going through a tough time at work. *Let him think whatever he wants*, Altagracia thought.

It was day fifteen when she went to her routine lunch place in the harbour that she found Jorge waiting on the same bench where they had first met with a bucket of red roses in his hands. She was barely able to hide her joy at seeing him and it had taken all her efforts to remain cool. Once Jorge had seen her arrive, he had gone on one knee in front of her. "Fifteen roses – one for each day we have been apart."

When Altagracia had remained silent, just watching him, he had tried again. "*Amor mio*, I'm so sorry for my bad reaction to what you told me. I should have appreciated your honesty instead of judging you. Please forgive me and marry me."

His words had made Altagracia nearly lose her balance in surprise and she had shot a quick look at him. "What?"

Jorge had blushed under his rough skin but hadn't lost eye contact with her. "I asked you to marry me, if you want. I love you."

It was quite a change of events and something she couldn't have expected, not in a million years, but she couldn't have been happier. "I love you too, *mi loco*," she had said and kissed him, whispering in his ear, "I will marry you."

That night she hadn't gone home for the night. Instead, they had found a small storage room in the harbour located at the end of the commanding office with a view to the open sea. He had quickly picked up tapas for dinner and she had gathered the ropes to be used as a temporary table and the old and broken sails to warm them up from the cold wind arising from the sea. They had dinner and later, during the late hours of the night when the sea was at its worst, they had made love until the sunrise.

As the morning had risen, Jorge had gone back to his work and Altagracia had returned home after calling in sick for work from Jorge's office.

On the way, she had stopped in a liquor store to pick up the cheapest wine and had gurgled the wine in her mouth and splashed drops around her neck and chest area. She had loved Jorge's proposal, but two failed relationships resulting in two children had taught her better. Jorge might be sincere but before amen from the priest, she wasn't going to take chances of ending up alone.

"Where the hell have you been for the night?" an angry Sam greeted her from the entrance. The girls were still in their pyjamas in the living room, eating cereal on the sofa. They didn't come to greet their mother and instead continued eating.

"Girls, aren't you happy to see mummy?" she said and approached the living room. Sam stopped and grabbed her by her arm. "I'm sorry, I think you might have missed my question. Where the hell have you been? I called the shop and they said you left around nine p.m. as usual."

The best response is to attack, Altagracia thought and raised her voice. "You don't talk to me like that in my own house, you hear me! I'm an independent woman and I can do what I want!" she said and flicked her long hair behind to spread the odour of alcohol.

Sam shook his head. "Absolutely not, you are an adult and you have responsibility for your children, Altagracia. This is not the first time I'm telling this to you, I'm not…" Sam's voice got quiet as he smelled the alcohol. "Have you been drinking?"

Altagracia weighed up her answer before responding. She wanted to tell him about Jorge, wishing him to the farthest end of the world so she could run to the hills with Jorge, but she needed to be smarter than that.

"Altagracia, I'm tired and I can't stay quiet anymore. I think you have a problem that needs to be taken care of before it gets worse," he said and took her hand in between his. "It's OK, you don't have to hide it anymore. And don't worry, I will be here supporting you all the way."

It wasn't exactly the reaction Altagracia had expected, so she remained quiet, waiting for him to continue. Sam sighed impatiently. "Altagracia, I know you are an alcoholic," he said and smoothed her hand. "But that's OK, *darling*, we will get through this," he promised and hugged her tightly.

Once again, Altagracia was amazed by his loyalty, or stupidity. Luckily for her, it seemed to work in her favour over and over again.

*

From that moment, Jorge and Altagracia were able to start planning their future together.

Altagracia had been brutally honest with him and said she wouldn't leave Sam before she had a ring on her finger and they were safely married and for the remaining time, she would still sleep with Sam if necessary. Jorge wasn't happy about it and during their heated arguments, he would even threaten to leave her but Altagracia didn't given in.

Luckily, Sam was a complete gentleman and treated her respectfully during her *illness*. He agreed to sleep on the sofa during her recovery period until she felt strong enough to take care of her wifely duties, as he referred to it. The situation suited Altagracia better than ever and it seemed that their relationship got even better as a result. At least the girls were happy.

They had been halfway through planning the upcoming wedding when Jorge had received a long-distance call informing him of his mother's first heart attack. Altagracia had been sympathetic and tried to support him the best she could but his family had been persistent about him returning to Jaen as soon as possible. He had booked his seat on the next ship over the Atlantic and would continue first to Peru by rail and then take a bus to Jaen. In total, the whole trip would take him seven days.

Altagracia couldn't believe her bad luck and she was desperate not to go back to her old life now that she had found joy. On the last evening, as they had wrapped their bodies together and made love fiercely as never before, and he kept whispering in her ear that he would be back for her, there was something in the air that wouldn't leave Altagracia's mind at ease and she had made a choice. "*Loco*, what do you say if I would come with you to Peru?" she asked and looked at him tentatively. When he had stayed quiet, looking at her thoughtfully, Altagracia had quickly added, "We could get married there and I would come back for the children later once everything is settled."

Jorge had been surprised by her decision and hesitated. "I don't know Altagracia. I love you but it is a hard trip and takes time. I don't know how long my mother will be in a fragile state, but as long as she is, I can't come back. You would need to leave your children maybe for a long time, months even."

Altagracia had weighed her options before responding slowly but firmly. "No Jorge, the children will be fine. We will come back for them."

When he still hadn't seemed to be convinced of her suggestion, she had lowered her voice and given the last shot to seal the deal for her. "Also, you should know," she had said intensely. "I'm pregnant."

The decision had been made.

*

On that evening, Altagracia returned home earlier than before. She had said she didn't feel well in the shop and the owners' daughter had shrugged her shoulders disapprovingly and said they would need to review her working hours again as she was taking an awfully long time to run her own errands each week and her sickness record had started to build up so much it wouldn't be sustainable soon.

Altagracia sighed silently. Naturally, she didn't really have any additional errands to run and was merely taking extra time off to spend with Jorge, so that she would be able to return home at the closing time of the shop in order not to draw attention to what she was really doing.

She had agreed to have a meeting first thing in the morning. *When I will be long gone, crossing the Atlantic Ocean with my future husband*, she thought as she arrived home to a ready-made dinner. They ate in silence before the girls started sparring at the table. Sam ordered them to stop if they wanted to play with their toys later and without any fuss, they did. He was such a good father figure, Altagracia thought longingly. He would take good care of her children.

After dinner, Sam went to put the girls to bed, allowing them to bathe and play a little bit before reading them a bedtime story. Altagracia looked at her children with sadness in her mind. Even though the girls were a pain in the buttocks most of the time and the main cause of her relationships falling apart, she still adored them in her own way. To be honest, she hadn't planned either of them and since the lousy fathers hadn't taken any responsibility for them ever, she felt entitled to run after her dreams now that the opportunity presented itself.

It felt only fair, she thought as she sat down to write a short letter to Sam to explain what she wanted him to do with the girls. She didn't feel the need to explain her reasons for leaving as she was sure he had noticed that their relationship had not been going anywhere for a long time, even a blind person would see it, she thought.

"*Mamá*, would you tuck me into bed tonight?" Lupe asked quietly, breaking Altagracia from her thoughts. She was immediately annoyed but smoothed her voice before replying.

"In a minute *cariño*, I will tuck you both into bed tonight," she said and squeezed Lupe's chubby cheek.

Lupe's feet started marching on the floor in excitement and she turned around, yelling at the top of her lungs, "Reina, don't sleep yet, *mamá* is going to come and tuck us into bed!"

Altagracia could hear the joyful screams from the bedroom and shook her head, *such sweethearts, my babies,* she thought.

Unfortunately, she completely lost track of time while drafting her last letter to Sam, forgetting her promise to her children and instead, packed some of her personal items into a small fabric shopper and placed the letter on the coffee table so that Sam would find it easily in the morning and left the house.

That night, she missed the faces of her two girls, holding hands and seeking comfort from each other in their sleep, eyelashes glued together as a result of dried tears for the broken last promise of their mother.

Chapter 6

Lupe didn't really understand why or where their mother had gone and that she wasn't coming back home.

They had both woken up in the morning and found Sam sitting on the sofa holding his hands against his face. Neither of them had ever seen him cry before.

"Your mother has left us," Sam said between sobs when they entered the living room. "She has decided to be a sailor's whore instead of your mother."

Reina and Lupe stayed quiet, observing him. Neither of them knew or understood what he was talking about, so they waited, staring at the hopeless sight in front of their eyes.

Reina was more naïve and lagged a little bit behind in understanding, but Lupe had learnt much from a very early age and was like a sponge; she absorbed everything. She understood something permanent had happened that was going to change their lives.

They went without breakfast that morning and Sam didn't go to work. He woke up from the sofa, poured a shot of bourbon and drank it at once.

Lupe had never seen him drink alcohol before.

Nausea went through his body when the taste of the alcohol hit his stomach, making him shiver and cough uncontrollably.

He wiped his mouth on the back of his sweater. "OK girls, in the kitchen, we have to start making lunch for all of us."

And just like that, the situation cleared, Lupe thought happily and gave Reina a pat on her shoulder to reassure her that everything was going to be fine.

*

Lupe wasn't entirely sure how long had passed since their mother had left before strange women started visiting the house. They would come in, sit on the sofa and entertain Lupe and Reina whilst waiting for Sam to prepare coffee in the kitchen.

At first, Lupe had been shy to answer all the questions about their life, but as they kept coming back, always bringing small gifts for them both, she started enjoying the attention and felt important, as if the visitors wanted to catch every single word she said. It made her feel special and occasionally they would entertain the guests with various different performances; when they asked about their mum and what they used to do together, she would throw herself on the sofa holding her tongue out as if she was sleeping with a bottle of wine and Reina would come and gently slap her cheeks to wake her up. Lupe would then mumble, waving her hands and turn around. Sometimes, she would start gasping for air as if she was vomiting on the floor and Reina would make cleaning gestures on the floor, holding her nose like a Cinderella.

They would both laugh, and even Sam found their performance hilarious.

Naturally, they missed their mum a lot. They had grown to love her with all her flaws and by now, they knew when to approach her and when to leave her completely alone. Lupe wasn't entirely sure if it was the way it should be as she had seen very different types of behaviour in the local park many times when Sam had taken them both out to play. She often saw other children running in to their mother's open arms before they would close them into a tight squeeze with a big smile on their face. These children were laughing and didn't seem to even consider that their mother might get angry at them or leave them in the playground as a practical joke. The situation seemed intimate to her and even when she looked away, she could still hear the happy laughter of the children.

Until now, neither Lupe nor Reina had been to kindergarten, which meant their social skills lagged slightly behind and they had shown no interest in learning to read or write. At home they were not offered many activities and mostly, what they were expected to do was play, draw or watch TV.

That was why Lupe was extremely happy whenever Sam took them both with him to run his errands or fix the houses. Reina didn't care much for the activities and would usually bring her only doll with her and play quietly in the corner whereas Lupe tentatively followed Sam everywhere.

First, she just followed him around, walking after him like a shadow, but quickly she learnt that she could be useful to him and started dragging the tool bag for him, giving out tools when needed. The tool bag was heavy but thanks to her heavy build, she was able to drag it around the floor.

The first time she had done it, Sam had looked at her with surprise on his face and laughed, "Well, well, well, look who is picking things up fast. If you want, you can start giving me the tools so that we can get out of here sooner, what do you say?"

Lupe didn't really want to get out faster as she dreaded the moment of returning home where time stood still, and they had nothing to do, but small gesture or not, she was happy to accept his offer. From that moment, she made sure she remembered at least the basic names of the tools in German that Sam usually needed and with careful concentration on her face, handed out tools as fast as she could.

Lupe learnt how to air a thermostat by watching Sam doing it and holding the flashlight for him. She learnt that the thermostat would make an airy noise before leaking water out and when the water started leaking, it was time to close the vent.

After a while, Sam started joking that she would make a good engineer one day as she was learning at such an early age. Lupe wasn't sure what that meant and raised her thick eyebrows when Sam pinched her in the stomach. "It means earn money my friend. A lot of it."

Since their mother had left them, they had formed new routines, which didn't really differ much from what they had been before she had left. They would have spent most of the day with Sam anyway, only seeing their mother late before going to bed.

They didn't shed tears with Sam; Lupe wanted to, but for some reason thinking about their mother made her feel nothing inside as she couldn't remember a single affectionate deed her mother had ever done for her, although with childlike innocence she was sure there must have been many. She kept thinking about her, but she couldn't really miss her. After all, she couldn't really miss something she never had.

Chapter 7

It was early November, exactly five months after their mother had left, when Lupe finally understood what was happening.

It had been an extremely difficult autumn.

The flats Sam owned seemed to have more problems than usual due to a cold wind pushing in from the North Sea and breaking the already sensitive plumbing and window seals. Many tenants were angry and requiring his attention more than usual. He had even lost some rent for it.

To make matters worse, Reina had picked up a cold that made her cough ugly green mucus from the top of her lungs and which required several visits to the local Accident and Emergency Department. Every time they visited the hospital, the doctor would pull Sam aside and have a long discussion with him behind closed doors whilst the nurses would keep an eye on Lupe and Reina. Afterwards, on their way home, Sam would be deeply lost in his thoughts, massaging his receding hairline with his fingers. The weather, sleepless nights and stress took their toll on him and his clothes started hanging freely on his hips, barely staying up, and his temples started showing more grey than before. The dinners changed into simple pasta and sausage meals and whenever either of them would ask him something, he would turn and snap at them.

Early one Tuesday morning, they heard the doorbell ring during breakfast and Lupe ran to open the door, Reina behind her.

A middle-aged blonde woman peeked around the door. "Hello little ladies, may I come in?"

Lupe and Reina eyed her curiously; she was wearing a long flowery skirt, red rainboots and a mismatching green jumper that had a giant cat on it with a red 3D bow and whiskers. The strange detail caught Lupe's attention and she had to work hard not to stretch out her hand to touch it. The hem of her skirt was dripping water on the corridor floor despite the red matching umbrella she carried with her which Sam would end up cleaning as he was in charge of the cleaning of the building.

They pushed the door open and let her in and she toddled in and shook her shoulders. "Good morning girls, my name is Elizabeth Von Houten," she said with a heavy German accent while bending down to look at them both at eye level. Her accent was so strong it made her spit in between words and Lupe quickly wiped her face.

She wasn't a pleasant-looking lady, Lupe thought, with her greyish skin tone and strong masculine body shape – especially compared to the slender and feminine mother figure they had once known, and when she leaned closer, Lupe could swear she saw a tiny black moustache on top of her lip. She was smiling but the smile looked more like a grimace with one yellow front tooth.

Lupe and Reina stayed quietly at the door, looking at her.

The woman, now known as Elizabeth, straightened her back and placed her hands on top of her belly which reminded Lupe of the Santa Claus she had seen in the German market where Sam had taken them to buy Christmas wreaths for his tenants.

The silence didn't seem cease her smile at all as she continued. "I'm looking for a man named Sam. Something tells me you two girls might know where to find him?" she winked.

"Sam is our friend and he is in the kitchen," Reina said and looked at her feet shyly. "We were having breakfast."

Lupe pinched her on her arm. "Ouch! Why did you do that? It

hurts!" Reina cried out loud and looked angrily at her sister, massaging the spot on her arm.

"Frau Von Houten, there you are and thank you for coming so quickly," Sam said and hurried from the kitchen. Lupe looked at their greeting, like they had known each other for years.

She observed Sam quietly; he had left the kitchen table as soon as he had heard her voice at the door she assumed. He had breadcrumbs on his jumper, which had previously been hanging casually but was now neatly tucked into his old blue jeans. Even his hair, which he usually kept neatly combed behind to cover his thinning hairline, was now left in front revealing the bald spot on his crown. *He looked older than before*, Lupe thought.

"Not at all Sam, I totally understand your dilemma and I'm sorry we meet in these sad circumstances," Elizabeth said and entered the house.

"We take our shoes off inside the house," Lupe said and stood with Reina behind her.

"Lupe, *cállate*! Don't be rude to the lady," Reina whispered fearfully in her ear.

Lupe looked the woman in the eye, straightening her body to its full four feet two inches as if she wanted to challenge her. She crossed her small arms on her chest and pushed her chest out as much as possible to create an illusion of a taller and bigger girl.

Elizabeth and Sam froze in their places and Sam glanced at Elizabeth apologetically before he turned to talk. "It is actually true, in this house we don't wear shoes inside. You know, rain, dirt and stuff like that," he said, eyeing the red furry socks he wore to protect his feet from the cold floors. He had bought a pair for each of the girls as well. *Three musketeers* he had called them, and the girls had danced around the brown coffee table.

Slowly, she bent down again to look Lupe in the eyes. "I'm sorry little lady, I didn't know there were such strict rules in this house, but

I'm glad to see you both obey and respect them, that's a good value," she said and took off her rainboots, exposing her bare big toe which had escaped through a hole in her tights.

Both girls stared at her feet.

Elizabeth laughed nervously. "If I had known the house rules, I would have made sure I was wearing my good pair of tights!" she said.

Lupe didn't say anything as Sam motioned Elizabeth to the living room where there was still evidence of yesterday's play on the floor, with colourful pencils, paper and plastic cars everywhere.

Lupe knew it was going to happen, even before she heard a small bump. "Auch, god dammit, girls. I have told you millions of times to clean up after yourself!" Sam growled and jumped on one leg, holding his other leg in the air.

Lupe giggled silently but Reina seemed to be too frightened to even respond.

The girls followed the adults to the living room.

"Sam, please tell me if I understood correctly. Your ex-partner left approximately five months ago and left *her* children with you?" Elizabeth asked, whilst sitting on the brown sofa and sipping tea that Sam had prepared for them.

Sam held his tea mug in the air without looking at either Elizabeth or the girls who were waiting tentatively, wanting to hear every word that was discussed. "Umm, yes, but they have been like my own children. It's just, it has been hard for the last month," he said and sighed quietly. "You see, the business is not flowing as it used to and one of them has been sick all the time," Sam said, spreading his hands.

He seemed very uncomfortable with the situation and kept drying his sweaty hands on his jeans and looking at the clock. Elizabeth nodded and kept writing notes on a piece of paper she had taken out of her briefcase as soon as she had sat down on the sofa. She hadn't paid any more attention to Lupe and Reina after the first introduction at the entrance and mainly focused on listening and nodding whilst Sam talked.

"It's OK, I understand. There's no need to be defensive about this," she said and patted Sam on his bony shoulder after he had finished the full sad story of how he had met Lupe and Reina's mother and how he had ended up taking care of the girls by himself.

"Can you please confirm that you have no blood relationship with these two children who are living with you?"

"Well no, not exactly," he said and writhed on his seat.

Elizabeth's hand paused over the paper and she eyed Sam over her glasses. "I'm sorry Sam, but we need to be very honest and specific here," she said and pushed the glasses up her nose. "Are they or are they not blood related to you?"

"Oh, sorry. I meant no, they are not," Sam quickly corrected and jerked forward on his seat, glancing nervously to Lupe and Reina who were now sitting on the floor carefully listening to what was said in the room, Reina still behind Lupe, holding her doll against her chest. Lupe had started sucking her thumb, a habit she had picked up after their mother had left. He didn't tell them off for listening or order them to go to the bedroom or kitchen as he usually did when they had guests. This time, he was too consumed with guilt and returned his attention to Elizabeth who was still talking. "Have you been able to contact their mother since she left?" she asked and waited for Sam to reply. When he didn't respond, she quickly added, "Have you tried to communicate to her that you will no longer be responsible for her children?"

"Well, it has been rather hard as I don't have any phone numbers to call. She only left this letter to me," he said and handed her a piece of creased paper. "I found it on the kitchen table the morning she left."

Lupe looked closer and saw that it was the same letter he had been reading the morning he had informed them their mother had left.

Elizabeth read the letter. "God, where do these mothers come from?" she said and placed the letter inside her briefcase. "I will keep this letter as confirmation that she had trusted the children into your care. Now, can you please confirm that you had no idea this would happen at all?"

"Absolutely no idea," Sam shook his head. "I mean, she had a problem with alcohol for months before she left but I thought it was because she was going through a tough time at her workplace," Sam said and brushed his thinning hair.

Lupe looked at his movement. She could see sweat breaking on his forehead and the greasy hair which he had not washed for days hanging on one side of his head. Now that she thought about it, he wasn't the biggest fan of showers and rather washed himself quickly at the sink: face, armpits and groin. Maybe that had been the real reason why their mother had left them?

"Yes, these are common problems with mothers who abandon their children, but don't worry, we have a big orphanage not far from here and from there we are hoping to place them in foster care. They will learn more and will be attending normal school as other children do," Elizabeth said reassuringly.

Sam nodded.

"Do you have any more questions at this point?"

"Ummm, not really, I just…" His voice cracked. "I just want to know if they will be together or if there is a chance they will be placed in different foster homes?"

Elizabeth didn't respond immediately, weighing her answer first. "Hmm, it is difficult to say and depends totally on the availability of families. Of course, we would take this into consideration, but to be honest, we have seen great results with siblings who have been assigned to different families. They are able to learn more independence that way and they have been able to stay in touch with each other by writing letters and so on." When none of them responded, she hurried to add, "Naturally, we prefer siblings to stay in the same city, but obviously we don't have much power after they are assigned to their families as you must understand," she said and returned to the forms she had been filling out.

Lupe felt her heart drop and she reached to hold Reina's hand.

"Now, this will require a little paperwork and some calls back and forth but I can take the girls with me now if you wish? I have Sister Agnes waiting for me. We will head straight out of the city tonight," she said and stood up abruptly to signal that the meeting had finished. "Also, I would like to collect all the girls' personal belongings such as toys and clothes so that they will adapt to the new environment faster."

Sam stood up nervously and started moving around the house, collecting their toys. This broke the trance that Lupe had been in whilst trying to understand as much as possible from the conversation and she broke into action. "Sam, don't, please don't send us away, we will be better, we won't fight, we won't cause you any problems, please Sam, let us stay!" Lupe cried, grabbing him on his jumper sleeve.

Reina hadn't understood it all but she knew something was going on and burst into hysterical tears.

Sam was crying too. He had picked up two black rubbish bags and started throwing their toys inside them.

There were not many conventional toys in the house as most of what they played with was made of normal household supplies and rocks, wood or anything they might have been able to find. They had used their imagination and made a herd of sheep out of empty toilet paper rolls and a small wooden fence out of matches their mother used for smoking. They had bent one corner of the roll to create a face for the sheep and drawn big eyes and a smiley mouth. Reina wasn't convinced that sheep could even smile but she was happy to let her sister be in charge of the drawing part. They had collected dead leaves and grass and placed them inside the fence to allow the sheep to eat. Reina had proved to be skilled and handy with her hands when she was not playing with her only doll, and she would sit for hours matching and gluing the pieces together. She had endless patience and vision for it. Lupe had no patience at all and always wondered how her sister could stay still that long and stay concentrated. She would watch her work or take out paper and her drawing pens and draw something. Sometimes she felt jealous of her work and dedication and tried to steal one leg or two from the sheep causing them to fall down.

One time, she had even gone so far as to urinate on the sheep herd, claiming that the sheep had encountered a rainstorm. Reina had screamed as her lovingly prepared sheep had become wet and flexible and in the end every one of them had collapsed on the ground. The smell of urine had been pungent and made the parts unusable again.

Sam and their mother had hurried to the living room after hearing Reina's scream. Giving one look at the mess, their mother had simply walked to Lupe and given her two slaps on both cheeks, so hard that each slap threw her head right and left. Then she had walked away. Sam had said nothing and walked behind her.

Reina had come to Lupe but Lupe hadn't cried. She hadn't said anything when Reina had hugged her tightly and together they had gone to the bathroom to pick up the cleaning equipment to clean up the mess she had caused.

*

"I suggest we collect only the real toys," Elizabeth said. "We can provide supplies so the girls can make their sheep again and have something to keep them occupied in the beginning," she said, pointing her finger towards the sheep Reina had built, sitting on the only shelving unit in the room, so high Lupe could not reach it.

Sam didn't move, and Lupe was still grabbing onto his thigh trying to stop him from moving. He looked like he had lost a battle.

Elizabeth noticed his reluctance. "Now, this is completely normal for these situations, but we must not let our emotions take over. We know what is best for the children."

Sam sighed. "Do you think you and Sister Agnes would be able to stay in a hotel for tonight and pick up the girls tomorrow? I would really like to talk to them and spend the last evening together," Sam said.

Lupe and Reina both went silent and looked at the woman tentatively as if the rest of their lives would depend on her decision, and strangely, it did.

Elizabeth scratched her head. "Well, this is highly unusual, but I guess that would be OK, as long as we are able to leave early in the morning."

The life returned to Sam's eyes at this short-lived reprieve and he hurried to agree, nodding his head. "Yes, of course, I will make sure to pack everything tonight so that they are both ready first thing tomorrow morning."

"Very well then," she said and bent down to close her briefcase. "I will leave the paperwork here so that you can fill it out by tomorrow. If there is anything you are unsure of, we can go through it tomorrow."

Sam walked her to the door. "Thank you so much Frau Von Houten, I really appreciate this," he said and closed the door, holding his head against its cold frame.

Lupe and Reina had followed him to the entrance. They were waiting for him to turn around and tell them he had changed his mind. They were praying for it.

When he slowly turned around, he looked at the girls but didn't say anything. Instead, he walked straight to the living room and picked up the phone. He waited and nervously drummed his foot on the carpet.

"Hello *Doña* Margaret, it is Sam. I would just like to inform you that I'm placing your grandchildren into foster care. They will leave tomorrow morning," he said and placed the phone back on the small living room table next to the sofa. He didn't turn around and instead, walked to the bedroom, closed the door and didn't come out for the rest of the evening and night.

That night, Reina and Lupe didn't wash or eat. Reina found white crackers in the kitchen cupboard and poured a glass of water for both of them for dinner. After they had eaten the crackers, they silently collected all their toys from the black rubbish bags and placed them around them as if to provide some comfort and safety to their world which was about to be changed forever.

*

The morning came quickly and Lupe was woken by the ringing doorbell. It was a cold morning and Lupe could feel the cool morning breeze pushing through the window seals. She was freezing and her legs were icy as she tried to wiggle warmth into them. Their mother had taught them this and it was the only piece of advice that seemed to work, Lupe thought. She looked at Reina by her side on the sofa and could hear her teeth clatter. She was still asleep.

The doorbell rang again.

Sam emerged from the bedroom, looking angry. He hadn't shaved his beard and the dirty hair hung on his forehead; he brushed it quickly away. The hair seemed to stay in place better when it was greasy, Lupe thought whilst watching him passing them.

"No, don't open the door, please Sam, don't, please don't!" Lupe cried but she was too weak from lack of sleep and energy due to the light dinner they had had last night so ended up crawling out from the sofa and following Sam to the entrance, weeping. He didn't say anything and instead pushed her back angrily. She ended up falling on the floor with a loud thump.

Sam opened the door. They were both surprised by the visitor. "Sam, let that be the last time that you threaten to put *my* grandchildren into foster care!"

It was *Doña* Margaret. *She has come to rescue us,* Lupe thought hopefully.

Reina ran into her arms. "*Abuela, abuela,* we missed you so much!" *Doña* Margaret opened her arms and grabbed her into a tight hug. Lupe stood up from the floor and ran to them as well. They all hugged.

Sam looked at the crowd silently. "It would have helped if you had answered any of my previous calls," he said sarcastically.

Doña Margaret glanced at him. "I have been busy, it's not like I don't have a life as well."

Sam rolled his eyes but didn't say anything. Instead, he turned around and started packing the toys from the sofa. *Doña* Margaret put Reina down on her feet and looked at them both. "I can already see, you haven't cared much for making sure my grandchildren are properly looked after," she said, directing her sharp words to Sam. "Look at them, they both look like they haven't been bathed for a week! And they look as though they are starving."

As proof, Lupe's stomach gave an approving rumble. They hadn't had dinner last night and she was very hungry. *Doña* Margaret was furious. "That's it. I will feed my grandchildren here before we go. Make sure you collect all of their things by the time we are ready and tell the awful social worker she won't be taking my grandchildren," she said dramatically and took Reina and Lupe by their hands and guided them to the kitchen. The hand hold was strong, and Lupe felt as though she was flying across the floor to the kitchen; she couldn't have been happier to see their *abuela* again. After all, she had come to their rescue, she thought and smiled.

Doña Margaret made them porridge for breakfast. Sam didn't come to the kitchen at all and while they were eating in silence, *Doña* Margaret went through the kitchen cupboards as if she was looking for something. Occasionally, she would look at the door as if ensuring no one was looking and would put items in her handbag. Lupe thought it was funny. She didn't understand why their grandmother would need an old silver candle holder or the small salt and pepper holders Sam had given their mother as a gift, or the coins Sam used to leave on the kitchen counter for milk and bread.

When they finished eating, *Doña* Margaret asked them to wash their hands and faces. Meanwhile, she laid clothes on the kitchen stools for both of them. Reina would wear dark blue leggings and a pink tunic with Winnie-the-Pooh on the front. *Doña* Margaret asked her to sit on one of the kitchen stools and separate her hair into two sections which she braided. For Lupe, she had left light jeans and a simple dark red sweater. Lupe had inherited the jeans from Reina, but they barely fit her due to her heavy build compared to Reina's delicate figure. Luckily, their grandmother had been able to sew an elastic waistband on them and now Lupe couldn't have been happier to wear them every day. *Doña* Margaret decided to leave Lupe's curly hair as it was and made a mental note to cut it at some point. They finished dressing with matching jackets and hats.

Once they were ready to go, they saw the two black rubbish bags waiting for them at the entrance. One of them was open and Lupe could see Reina's favourite doll's head hanging out of the bag. Reina quickly picked it up and hugged it tightly. *Doña* Margaret picked up the bags and guided the girls out of the door. Lupe glanced behind her to catch a sight of Sam, but she didn't see him. That morning was the last time she saw him.

Chapter 8

They walked quickly to the green Fiat Punto their grandmother had driven for as long as Lupe could remember. It was a cold November morning and the ground was hard and icy. Lupe felt her shoes slipping on the ground as she tried to keep up with her grandmother and Reina. Her coordination was good considering her young age, but she still found it difficult sometimes to keep up with her big sister.

The door handle of their grandmother's car was hard to open, and it seemed to be even harder with the cold weather, even if Lupe tried to use both hands. *Doña* Margaret gave an irritated look and opened the door for them. "Get in both of you and remember your seat belts. No fighting or the one who fights gets left behind," she said and slammed the car door closed. Reina and Lupe both stayed quiet for the whole trip. The only sound was Reina's coughing every now and then, which made their grandmother shoot worried looks at her back-seat travellers through the front mirror.

Lupe felt like they had been driving for hours when they finally stopped, and their grandmother killed the engine. Lupe felt sleepy. The car had warmed quickly, and the rhythmic purring of the engine had made her relax for the first time in a long time. Reina had fallen asleep as soon as they had reached the motorway.

"Ok *niñas*, get in the house. Your *Tia* Carmen is waiting for you with your *Primo* Christian."

Lupe looked at their *abuela*. She had never heard of *Tia* Carmen and wasn't even aware they had cousins. She glanced at her side and grabbed Reina's hand to wake her up quickly; she didn't want to make their grandmother angry.

They walked hand in hand to the door. The house was hardly a house, but more of a detached flat with a common playground with an old swing and slide held together with two green pillars. Lupe looked around and saw a big sandbox where someone had left a red bucket and plastic shovel. She wondered if they would have a chance to go and play there today with their *primo*.

The building was brownish and looked like it had had its fair share of damage throughout the years. The day itself had remained grey since morning, and the only inviting light was feeding from the ground floor windows. Lupe wondered which one of them would belong to their *Tia* Carmen and *Primo* Christian. Luckily, she didn't have to wonder long because as soon as they reached the door, a woman with black curly hair opened it.

"*Buenos dias niñas*, we have been waiting for you!" the woman said in perfect Spanish and stepped aside to let them enter the house. "Come on you two, get inside, it's terribly cold weather and the gas and electricity are made of gold in this country!" she said and winked.

The woman reminded Lupe of an actress. She was wearing big golden hoops in her ears that made her ear lobes hang low and several different types and sizes of necklace around her neck. When she motioned the girls to enter the house, Lupe noticed that both her hands had rings on every finger with different colours of stone in them. They looked like diamonds, Lupe thought.

She was wearing a dark blue tunic, a grey fine-knitted vest and black leggings. Lupe could see she had a slightly lighter build than their mother and she was taller with her brown boots with gold details. Lupe looked at her face and could see heavy, dark make-up that reminded her of what their mother would wear when going out.

Reina thanked the woman and presented herself and Lupe. "Hello, my name is Reina and this is my little sister Lupe," she said coyly and looked down at the ground.

"It is very nice to meet you, Reina and Lupe. My name is Carmen, I'm your mum's sister."

A little boy appeared and tugged on the woman's tunic hem. "Oh, this is Christian," Carmen said and gently patted the little boy's cheek. "He is your cousin. I think he might be the same age as you Reina. Around four."

Reina hurried to correct her. "No, no, I'm already five. My sister Lupe is four, so he is the same age as her."

"Clever girl you are Reina. Now come in quickly, it's freezing outside."

*

They all entered the house. Lupe looked around curiously. It was the first time she had met any relatives and there were only a few occasions when their mother or Sam had taken them to meet their friends. When their mother had been alone, she would have usually asked *abuela* to watch them.

The house felt warm; much warmer than their house had been, but then again, that would be normal as they would be farther away from the ocean breeze she assumed practically. *Tia* Carmen was living alone with the boy she called their cousin. They had a much bigger house than they had had with their mother. From the entrance hall, Lupe could see an open door on the right leading to a small but smartly decorated kitchen. The dominating furniture was a four-seater kitchen table with a yellow and orange fabric tablecloth and a bowl of oranges and pears. The kitchen had a window that opened towards the street where they had left their *abuela's* car.

On the left side, there was another corridor leading to two separate rooms. *Tia* Carmen had told Christian to show Reina and Lupe his room and toys while she heated up lunch. At the end of the corridor, Lupe could see one door leading to a small living room with a beige set of sofas and a large bookshelf covering one whole wall of the room. She wasn't particularly interested in the books standing on the shelf but the small porcelain figures placed on the other side of the shelf caught her eye. She wondered if she would have an opportunity to go closer and touch any of them at some point.

"This room is mine and my mum's," Christian said proudly, stopping at the last remaining door and pushing it open. Both Reina and Lupe looked around curiously.

Although the room was shared with *Tia* Carmen, most of it was covered with children's toys. The main room area was clearly owned by Christian and on the left side of the room, there was a small recess fitting an adult bed and a white wooden side table. The bedding was dark green and covered by a large knitted yellow throw. The pillows were all different sizes and colours and seeing them made Lupe feel like jumping into them. On the side table, there was a lamp providing the only light in the entire room and some unfinished knitting work. *Tia* Carmen seemed to enjoy knitting, Lupe thought.

The rest of the room was Christian's. He had his own small bed on the other side of the room, with a tiny blue side table where he had placed his police car and ambulance. The side table had one drawer, which was left slightly open and Lupe could see several handmade drawings overflowing onto the floor. On the other side of the bed stood a modest white closet.

In the middle of the room was a blue, round rug and several colouring books and pens had been left open on it.

"If you want, we can do some colouring work," Christian said in perfect Spanish. Reina and Lupe nodded quickly and all of them sat on the carpet and Christian handed them a piece of paper to start their work. Lupe quickly picked the colour red. It was her favourite colour.

They coloured until *Tia* Carmen peeked from the door to let them know lunch was ready. She had prepared traditional Peruvian chicken soup and chopped bananas. There were two boiled eggs in the soup for protein which she said they would have to share as she didn't have any more. Lupe, Reina and Christian sat at the table. The food was a big change compared to the pasta and sausages they had been used to since living alone with Sam. It tasted like heaven. The warm soup heated up Lupe's dreamling body and made her shoulders relax. The soup was rich in flavour and *Tia* Carmen had used a lot of spices. Lupe could feel chilli burning her mouth which made her grab the water glass with two hands. *Tia* Carmen laughed heartily. "Easy there *cariño*, the soup is very hot; be careful not to burn your mouth."

Lupe nodded.

There was a contented silence; the only sound was clacking cutlery as each of them finished their meal.

It was *Doña* Margaret who interrupted the silence. "Have you booked the ticket yet?"

"No *ma*, I haven't."

Doña Margaret sighed in frustration. "Cristiano better send the money soon. The spineless coward, abandoning the family here in Germany. What a sight of a man."

Tia Carmen sighed. "No *ma*, he had to go as he didn't plan to stay here anyway. He was on duty when we met and unluckily his job here ended. He will send the money, you will see."

Doña Margaret eyed her suspiciously. "I hope so. I had children to take care of me when I'm old, not because I wanted to take care of my grandchildren because my daughters are not able to pick suitable men to marry" she said and spread her hands. "Look at your sister – she left her children behind because of *un marinero cabrón* , stupid sailor. If it wasn't for me, the children would be on their way to an orphanage!"

Lupe listened to the conversation curiously, as she always did when their mother was the topic. She had never really understood what had happened to her and always wondered when she would see her again.

Tia Carmen looked at her intently.

"*Ma*, don't speak like that in front of the children! I have already sent a message to Cristiano asking him to borrow money so we can take Altagracia's children with us. He will say yes, you will see."

*

It was the end of the week when *Tia* Carmen received a letter from Peru. Inside the letter was a pile of money; more money than Lupe had ever seen in her life. *Tia* Carmen was seemingly happy as she took Christian in her arms and danced around the house singing.

Lupe watched her mesmerised.

Tia Carmen soon noticed her intense stare and slowly put Christian down and, all of a sudden, grabbed Lupe in her arms, pressing her tightly against her chest and humming the song whilst dancing around the living room. Lupe got so excited she clapped her hands together and sang at the top of her lungs with her made-up words. The words were a mix of German and Spanish and sounded more like a wolf cub screech.

After a while, *Tia* Carmen put her down.

"Oh, *cariño*, did you wet your jeans?" she said and looked at the big wet stain on Lupe's jeans. She looked down and felt ashamed.

Christian stared at her. "Wet pants girl, wet pants girl!" he laughed and pointed at Lupe.

"Hush, Christian." *Tia* Carmen said as she took Lupe's trousers off. "It is OK *cariño*, we will wash these and put them on the heater to dry. They will be as good as new in no time." Lupe nodded and Christian handed her a knitted shawl to put around her.

"You can use this until the jeans are dry again. I'm sorry I laughed at you," he said and followed his mother to the kitchen to wash the jeans.

Lupe sat in front of the heater, enjoying the warmth. She would wait here until the jeans were dry again.

*

Two days later, their *abuela* rang the doorbell.

There had been a strange atmosphere in the house, and Lupe knew something was going on, as *Tia* Carmen kept cleaning and packing the house. Some of the drawings they had made during the week ended up in the rubbish and Lupe had been able to save only a couple of them which she had folded into tiny pieces and hidden in the pocket of her jeans. It looked like the world was ending.

"Carmen, are you ready?" *Doña* Margaret asked.

"Yes *ma,* I think I have everything," she said nervously.

"Good. The ship leaves at midday, so let's get going," she said and turned around without helping with any of the luggage.

Tia Carmen seemed to have very little luggage, Lupe thought. So far, she had only one suitcase and a handbag that she carried to their *abuela's* car and lifted into the trunk. Christian had his knitted backpack which he had filled with as many toys as possible. He followed his mother to the car. Lupe and Reina didn't have any luggage with them and instead stood at the entrance of the house. Reina was holding her doll.

Doña Margaret turned to look at them. "What are you still doing there girls? Move on will you, we are in a hurry," she said and rushed them both towards the car.

"*Abuela,* where are we going?" Reina asked, confused.

"You are going to Peru."

PART II

Chapter 9

Lupe and Reina arrived in Peru after seven long days at sea. It was night and they were woken by the whistle of the ship giving notice of arriving to the shore.

They had occupied a small cabin with their *Tia* Carmen and *Primo* Christian and a bunch of other people. *Tia* Carmen had ensured a small corner for them to sit, eat and sleep. The first night, she had drawn the yellow knitted throw from her luggage and covered all of them with it.

"Sleep close to each other to keep warm, it will be a cold night tonight," she said on their first night and Lupe had wrapped her hands tighter around Reina's waist. Reina fell asleep quickly, but Lupe stayed awake and listened to the whining of the wind and occasional shout from the sailors outside handling the ship. She was scared and cold. Her head ached from sleeping without a pillow and the heave of the sea made her nauseous.

She was studying *Tia* Carmen and her silhouette when she realised her aunt's eyes were open.

"*Tia* Carmen, why are you going to Peru?" she whispered in the air.

Tia Carmen slowly turned to face her. "Because Christian's father is waiting for us there."

Lupe weighed the answer a while. "Why is he there and not with you here?"

"*Cariño*, it's complicated. Adult stuff," *Tia* Carmen responded and looked at the ceiling.

Her eyes had been watery, and Lupe had been scared she had made her cry. She stayed silent for a while, but couldn't hold the burning question that she had wondered ever since their *abuela* had rushed them into the car. "Why are we going to Peru?"

Tia Carmen turned again to face her. "Because your mother is waiting for you there."

Lupe was taken by surprise. Not in a million years had she expected the answer *Tia* Carmen had given her. "My mother is waiting for us there?"

"Yes, *cariño*, that's why you are both travelling with me and Christian. Your mother will be waiting for you in Jaen."

A rush of joy filled Lupe and she couldn't wait to wake Reina to tell her the great news: their mother was waiting for them in Peru.

She turned to wake Reina, but changed her mind at the last minute. She wanted to enjoy the attention of her *Tia* Carmen a little bit longer. The news could wait until the morning. Instead, she turned back. "*Tia por favor*, please teach me everything you know about Peru. I want to know."

Tia Carmen smiled, took a better position and closed Lupe under her arms. Lupe pressed her head against her warm chest and listened to her strong heart beating. It was a totally new feeling for her, and she enjoyed it. She felt her muscles relaxing and she fell asleep hearing whispers of the great mountains of Peru, Amazonas, the eternal sun and the Incas. The stories became their pattern for the nights, which they didn't talk about during the day. It was their own ritual and after seven days at sea, Lupe was heartbroken to hear the whistle indicating that the ship was arriving at the shore. It was during those nights that Lupe formed a strong connection with a new adult in her life, who she now called *Tia* Carmen.

*

"Girls, we have arrived, wake up!" *Tia* Carmen said in a soft, sleepy voice and brushed her fingers through her black hair. They all woke up quickly and started to dress. Once they got to the outer wear, *Tia* Carmen stopped them. "I don't think we need jackets here, please tie them around your hips."

Reina and Lupe looked at each other but did as they were told. *Tia* Carmen promptly packed all their loose items, made sure Christian had his backpack on and started to rush them out of the ship.

All the people seemed to be in a hurry. Reina got hit by a pushy young man with his leather suitcase. She fell down and started crying. "Lupe, please help your sister up and remain close, it will be tight here."

Lupe took Reina's hand and pulled her up from the floor. She then grabbed the knitted backpack their *primo* was carrying and soon they were all walking in a queue. Magically, it worked, and they all got out in one piece.

Outside was bright and the sun was shining at its full force – so strong, they had to protect their eyes with one hand. Lupe looked around at the busy harbour. It looked like a busy market street during Christmas time in Kiel, she thought and looked closer. The market traders were selling mostly seafood and the buyers were discussing loudly, as if they were arguing.

Reina stepped closer to Lupe who turned to ask *Tia* Carmen where their mother was, but she didn't have chance before *Tia* Carmen's eyes locked with someone and she started waving her hands as a sign. A young gentleman with dark hair approached them and grabbed *Tia* Carmen in his arms. "*Amor*, finally you are here! Welcome to the port of Iquitos, *mi vida*."

Tia Carmen laughed and kissed him. They did quick introductions and Lupe learnt he was Christian's father.

"I hope you are enjoying our little port of Iquitos," he said and started walking. "Did you know it's the biggest port on the Amazon River in north-eastern Peru?"

Lupe and Reina felt shy replying and Christian seemed happy to take care of the talking with his father "Are you serious *papá*?" he asked, his eyes wide open.

Cristiano laughed and swung Christian in his arms. "Positive *hijo*. It is located about 3700 kilometres upstream from the Atlantic Ocean on the Amazon and 1030 kilometres northeast of the nation's capital, Lima. This port was a big deal in the late nineteenth century during the rubber boom."

Tia Carmen laughed. "*Amor*, I don't think Christian truly understands the geography lesson, he is only four years old."

Cristiano eyed his wife with warmth in his eyes. "You are right *mi vida*, the teaching jobs I'm now taking after long years at sea are taking the best of me."

Tia Carmen caressed his tattooed arm. "I wouldn't say that *mi amor*. I quite frankly enjoy it," she said and winked at him. The fire lit in his eyes and he had to look away.

She giggled and changed the subject. "Have you seen Altagracia?" *Tia* Carmen asked and looked around. "She should be here by now."

"*No amor*, I haven't but I sent the message to her letting her know when and where to arrive," he said. "She should be here somewhere."

Tia Carmen didn't seem to be convinced. "OK, that's fine. Let's go, the children need to eat – we didn't have a chance for breakfast this morning."

"Say no more," he said and tumbled Christian onto his shoulders and grabbed *Tia* Carmen's luggage to speed them up.

Christian screamed out in joy.

"If she is not here, we will stay at my uncle's place for tonight and wait for Altagracia to arrive," he said.

One night turned into three nights and several messages and phone calls. On the fourth day, the doorbell rang. Cristiano hurried to answer the door.

"Surprise!" Altagracia yelled and opened her arms as if she were the protagonist of a great show.

Lupe and Reina hurried to the door. Reina started crying and threw herself into their mother's arms. Lupe soon joined them and tried to wrap her arms around both of them but soon realised she was not able to reach even her mother's back and the distance seemed odd. Reina noticed it too and they both stood back, looking at their mother.

"Children, this is the second surprise for you today! Please say hello to your unborn brother," she said and tapped her enlarged belly.

Chapter 10

Jaen, Peru, eight years later…

"Go higher, *primo*! I can't see over the fence!" Lupe laughed while her cousin tried to push the old swing harder. It was a warm afternoon in Jaen and the *cantutas* flowers had just started to bloom again.

Lupe had always loved flowers and admired their beauty, especially *cantutas*. She knew *cantutas* were considered the sacred flower of the Incas and were the national flower of Peru, although people arriving from Cuzco often referred to them as *qantus* in Quechua. Internationally, the flower also carried the name Peruvian Magic Tree, even though Lupe had never witnessed any magic – unless their beauty was considered magical.

For a moment, she focused on admiring the tall flowering plant with its small leaves and cluster of brilliant pink narrow tubular flowers. They were at their best in early spring and would bloom if protected from direct sun and the temperature remained above 5°C. The beauty of the flower was not the only reason Lupe liked it – she also loved the Inca legend associated with the flower; the legend of two kings named Ilimani and Illampu and their sons.

According to the tale, both kings were powerful and wealthy rulers of a vast country in the old Qullasuyu region, and each had a beloved son whom the people held in great esteem. However, as the time passed, the two kings became irritated at each other's prosperity and eventually one of them attacked the other. During the battle, the kings mortally wounded each other and were carried away. Both of them, on their death beds, tormented by the anger, called their sons and had them vow to revenge their deaths. The sons had been opposed to the war in the first place but didn't want to break the pledge given to their dying fathers, so they prepared and led a second war, even though they held no grudges against each other. As history repeated itself, they fatally wounded each other but instead of anger and harsh words, the dying sons generously forgave each other, and asked their servants to place them side by side on the green grass of the battlefield. As they laid on the grass, Pachamama, the goddess of fertility, appeared. Just before they died, she told the young sons that they should not have suffered from their fathers' unjustified enmity. To punish their dead fathers, their stars fell from the sky and became the snow-covered mountains still named as Ilimani and Illampu. Today, the mountains belong inside Bolivian borders and are some of the highest peaks of the country.

Lupe had often heard village people, who were still very much connected to nature and still made their living harvesting, saying that the rivers from the mountains formed by the slowly melting snow were their tears of regret and had fertilising power on the ground in the valleys. The bloom of *cantutas* symbolises the people's unity and the plant carries the colours of the two kings' sons: red and yellow as well as green, standing for hope. Sometimes, Lupe would touch the flower and she would feel the shot of hope like an electric shock going through her body. Even though she didn't entirely buy the Peruvian Magic Tree status of the flower, maybe the feeling of hope could be considered magic after all.

*

Lupe and her cousin were playing in an abandoned courtyard that had once been an open-air bar overlooking the border of Amazonas. It was a breathtaking location and used to be one of the main *miradoras* in the city for the local people; local legend said that if you listened closely enough, you could still hear the desperate screams of the Inca king Kuayna Capac attempting to conquer the *bracamoros* before being defeated and fleeing. The legend had it that his restless soul never stopped haunting the wildlife of the area and never recovered from losing his beloved land. The legend was one of the only ones Lupe didn't like although she respected it anyway. For her, it sounded more like a horror movie and the idea of a tormented soul wandering with them made her feel uneasy. In the name of fair play, threats should be visible so that both parties were able to defend, she thought practically.

Despite the bloody legend, Lupe loved the courtyard.

She knew her parents had come to the original bar, until the owner had died and the son had decided to tear it all down and build a small commercial centre consisting of tiny cafes, restaurants and artisan shops. Naturally, the idea had been good and people had been waiting for it to happen, but as time went by, they realised that the son didn't share the same passion for the place as his father and soon the courtyard had been abandoned and filled with drug addicts and homeless people trying to find shelter from the changing weather conditions. The existing concrete fence of the *mirador,* dividing Jaen city and the border of Amazonas, had been built later by the government to prevent people falling to their death, which had worked to some extent, but now blocked the beautiful view. People had been furious and someone had even started collecting the names of people from the neighbourhood who wanted the fence removed; however, despite countless efforts, the government had not provided any response. The fence still stood in its place and the only noticeable change had been the crumbling of the concrete caused by the strong midday sun, which would eventually make the fence fall apart. In the next hundred years if the people were lucky enough.

After the organisational changes in the government, the new mayor had decided to clean up the area and build a playground with swings, a sandbox and even small modern carousels in an attempt to attract young families to the area. However, his attempts had been short lived as the massive reconstruction had driven the prices up and left young families to inhabit only the borders of the area.

Lupe had spent countless nights finding a shelter for herself in the courtyard on the many occasions she had escaped from the challenging home conditions. It was not too far from her home and during hot summer nights, it wasn't too bad to sleep under the open sky. Naturally, sleeping outside alone exposed a small twelve-year-old girl to great risk and for that reason, thanks to her short curly hair and strong masculine body, Lupe tended to go by the name Francisco on the streets. She was clever at an early age and understood the limitations of being a girl in the South American world.

*

"Can you see it now *prima*?" her cousin sighed, breathing heavily.

Lupe gave out a tingling laugh. "No *primo*, push harder, I can almost see it!"

She could hear the screws of the old rusty swing starting to give in, but she was determined to see at least the top of the trees above the crumbling fence that obstructed her vision. Anyway, the speed of the swing was too great even if she wanted to try and stop it.

It didn't even take one more full swing before the screws that were holding the whole metallic structure and the swing together gave in, detaching the whole swing and sending Lupe flying through the air. Her cousin immediately ran after her.

"*Prima* are you ok?" her cousin asked, helping her up from the dirty soil.

Lupe laughed loudly. "*Wow*, that was amazing wasn't it *primo*? Hell, I could almost hear the Inca King himself!" she said and seconds later her cousin joined in and soon they were laughing so hard they had to hold their stomachs.

When her cousin opened his eyes again and wiped the tears from the corner of his eye, he pointed down to her knees. "*Prima* look at your shorts, you tore them on the knee and now you are bleeding."

Lupe glanced down to her knees. "Oh, looks like it," she said, spitting on her hand and cleaning up the injured area of the knee.

"*Asqueroso,* that's gross *prima*!" her cousin sniffed.

Lupe shrugged her shoulders carelessly. "Well you have to clean it somehow to avoid infection right?" she said and carefully spread saliva all over the injured area. "Now, give me a *pañuelo,* will you *primo.*"

Her cousin turned his pockets inside out but could only find a piece of dirty napkin for her.

"Thanks *primo.*" Lupe took the napkin and started drying her knee.

Her cousin wandered closer to the stone fence.

"Oh, look *prima*! We can see the view from here!" he suddenly said and pointed to a small hole in the fence, which appeared to be missing a couple of stones.

"We can make this hole bigger then both of us can look!" he said and started digging with his bare hands.

Lupe ran over to him and started digging herself, helping her cousin with the work. She could feel the little stones scratching under her fingernails and carving small cuts into her sensitive fingertips, but she didn't care and soon, they had made two head-sized holes in the fence.

"Look *prima,* this is our way to the other side of the city, to feel the fresh air of our ancestors," he said and deeply inhaled the fresh air into his lungs.

Lupe nodded approvingly. "Let's not tell anyone else, yeah? We can use these two rocks here to fill it temporarily, then we only have to mark the area so that we will know where it is when we come back."

They both quietened to admire the breathtaking view of the *mirador* and later, filled the hole with two stones.

They were drying their dusty hands on their shorts when a friend of theirs from the neighbourhood ran towards them. She didn't bother to run the whole way and instead yelled from afar: "Lupe, your mum is back! *Mi papá* saw her walking on the main street heading towards home!" After delivering her message, she sprinted off as fast as she had come.

Lupe looked at her cousin with excitement. He smiled at her. "What are you waiting for *prima*? Let's run home to meet your *mamá*!"

They sprinted off.

Chapter 11

They were still breathing heavily when they reached home. Lupe looked at the front door of the house she had considered home for as long as she could remember.

The house was modest even for the area they lived in, and consisted of one room which acted as a bedroom for five children and two adults, plus a kitchen, living room and salon combination. At the end of the room, there was a fabric door leading through the backyard to a small shack with a waterproof tarpaulin on top and bare ground underneath. Inside, there was a wooden pole set horizontally from one side to another dug deeply into the ground and used as a toilet and hand shower with the tiniest hot water boiler one had ever seen. The hot water boiler was not connected to either electricity or gas, which meant that they were fully dependent on Mother Nature's mercy in terms of hot water. If the weather was hot all day, it would heat up the cold water in the boiler for the first users, which meant that three of them could have a quick hot shower, leaving the rest of the children showering under the cold water.

It wasn't too bad during the summer, when the cold water was very refreshing, giving small relief under the burning sun. However, in wintertime, with cold air pushing down from the Andes, the cold shower was real torture and for that reason, Lupe tended to avoid showering in winter like the plague.

One side of the wall inside the house was dominated by a kitchen cupboard which hid the kitchen dishes such as plates, glasses, forks and knives, one for each of them. Their father had bought a used single bed with a mattress and placed it in the farthest corner of the house, next to the doorway to the toilet; this was occupied by the three smallest siblings, leaving the older ones to sleep on the floor with blankets and hands under their heads as pillows.

They would wake up early each day when the rooster from the backyard started crowing, which would set the older siblings off like a fire, running outside and chasing eggs for breakfast. Normally, they would find up to three eggs, from which their father would prepare a Spanish omelette with rice and divide the meal between the seven of them.

Their father never shared the breakfast with them and always settled for a hot cup of coffee and a morning cigarette. For as long as Lupe could remember, she had never seen him touching food at home, which made her believe he lived on only coffee and cigarettes.

The front door was usually kept open as there was simply nothing to steal and to avoid anyone breaking and entering as fixing any damage in the house would be more costly than replacing anything stolen. The best way of protecting their family was a gun and luck. Luck you were born with or not, and a gun, their father carried with him everywhere he went and would place next to him when sleeping.

Lupe opened the door and quickly entered the house, finding her mother sitting on the ground, legs crossed, holding her smallest son in her arms and hugging him tightly. Lupe's other siblings, Reina, Celestina and Jose-Luis, had gathered around her and their father was standing a couple of feet away watching them.

"*Ma,* you're home!" she yelled and ran to her mother with open arms, crushing her smallest brother, Jorge, in between them.

Altagracia laughed and gently held her at arm's length. "Hold on *cariño*, you are going to crush your brother!"

"I don't care *ma*, I'm so happy to see you again! I hope you are well," she said and pushed tighter towards her, unable to hide her excitement at seeing her mother again. This was not the first time their mother had taken off looking for cigarettes and stayed away for days, sometimes even weeks, leaving their father and *abuela* responsible for the whole herd, but they were always happy to welcome her home again.

Altagracia smiled at her and petted her cheek. "I'm OK *cariño*, I'm home now. I had to go a long way to find the cigarettes I smoke, I had to go to another city to find them!" she said, moving her hands in the air and making big circles to demonstrate the long way she had taken whilst trying to find cigarettes. All of them were impressed at the trouble she had gone to and with wide eyes, they sat in silence around her to hear the whole story.

Lupe eyed their father who had turned to the kitchenette cabinet to make coffee. For some reason, she could feel the disappointment written on his back, which she didn't quite understand.

"But I have some nice surprises for everyone!" her mother said and clapped her hands together to get the full attention of everyone. As a result, all of them ran around her, screaming cheerfully and jumping in the air, waiting for their surprise to reveal itself. It did work well, and Lupe turned her head back to their mother. In no time, all of them had received something small: the boys received new colourful rubber wheels for a bike they shared, and the girls got traditional hair accessories and caramel apples, which would no doubt make them lose one of their teeth. The last gift was wrapped in transparent plastic when Altagracia handed it to Lupe. "This is for you *cariño.*"

Eyes glowing with excitement, she grabbed it from her mother's hands with poorly hidden excitement at being the only one receiving a gift with wrappings around. She hurried to unwrap the plastic to find a bright yellow dress.

The dress was knee length with big puffy short sleeves and a wide hem with white lace details. The waistline was an imitation corset and there were two white ribbons to fasten and tighten up the dress according to the wearer's size. The dress was beautiful and Reina and Celestina were terribly excited by it. They ripped the dress out of Lupe's hands and started planning who would wear it and when. Lupe quickly ran after them, not because of the dress, but to ask if her sisters wanted to give their caramel apples in exchange for the dress. She was secretly confused by how her mother could have forgotten that she didn't wear dresses and was always wearing basic shorts and t-shirts. Without hesitation, Reina and Celestina quickly agreed with her suggestion and handed over their red caramel apples.

Altagracia appeared behind them and grabbed the caramel apples from Lupe's hand. "Not so fast my *darlings*."

The girls grew silent and looked at each other.

"This is not how it works *niñas*. You can't change the gifts I have given to you," she said.

They looked at each other in disbelief, not understanding the problem. As the eldest, Reina spoke first. "*Ma*, it's not only us who want to change," she said and nodded towards her younger sister. "Lupe *can't* wear the dress, but she wants the apples, so naturally we can change with her because Celestina and I *want* to wear the dress."

Reina had always been the voice of reason in the family and Celestina and Jose-Luis nodded their heads approvingly. Feeling uncomfortable and circled in the room, and as if sensing what was about to happen, Lupe started walking towards the door.

Altagracia pulled her back by the hand. "Reina, would you explain to me why Lupe *can't* wear the dress? After all, she is a girl, isn't she?" she said and raised Lupe's hand high up in the air, exposing her lower stomach which hung out due to the one-size-too-small shorts and t-shirt she was wearing. "Even though a little chubby one," she said and laughed hard.

Reina looked first at their mother and then at Lupe, who was close to tears. Despite being the oldest of the five siblings, she couldn't rationalise what their mother was saying so she stayed quiet until Celestina stepped from behind her. "*Ma*, you know Lupe never wears dresses. She doesn't like them!" she said and opened her arms as if stating the obvious.

"Celestina, I'm so sorry, but now she has to because I bought it for her as a *gift* from my long trip," she said and took the dress from Reina's hands and pulled Lupe closer, starting to undress her.

Knowing what was about to happen, Lupe started screaming and flailing her hands in the air, trying to grab her mother's hair and filling the tiny house with sounds of desperation and fear. Jose-Luis quickly lifted Jorge from the floor and gracefully left the house.

Lupe kicked and spat at their mother; every time Altagracia managed to put one of Lupe's hands in a sleeve, she would tear the limb out of the dress as if it would burn her. They ended up wrestling on the floor, Lupe screaming at the top of her lungs and her mother on top of her, holding her body down with her knees on her upper back. Reina and Celestina escaped to the backyard and were watching through the fabric door. Celestina was silently crying behind Reina's back.

The show didn't impress their father who bawled, "For heaven's sake, Altagracia, leave her alone; she doesn't want to wear the dress, end of story."

Altagracia looked at her husband angrily. "Oh *really*, and how do you feel when our neighbours start talking about her looking like a boy and warning that she will end up liking girls and chasing them around, terrorising the whole neighbourhood, trying to touch them inappropriately and turning them into *lesbians*?" Altagracia screamed, her cheeks red from the physical struggle on the floor with her daughter. "Don't you see? We will be *marked* forever! It is a *fucking* disgusting idea. She is a girl and she will wear dresses just like everyone else!"

Altagracia's words only increased her anger towards her daughter who was trapped under her. She grabbed her hair, pulling her head up and stretching her neck as much as possible. "You understand this Lupe, I'm only doing this to *save* you. Your mind is sick and disgusting. You will wear this dress day and night, even if it is the last thing I do," she screamed and smacked Lupe's head hard on the dirty concrete floor.

The blow to her skull set Lupe's head spinning and made her feel nauseous. She could see small drops of blood coming down her nose and colouring the brown ground beneath her. She stayed silent and motionless while her mother finished dressing her and pulling the waistline as tight as she could, making triple knots instead of nice bows to make sure she wouldn't be able to unfasten the dress herself.

"Look how nice you look now *cariño*," she said and clapped her hands together as if the whole battle had never happened. Lupe looked at the ground, avoiding her mother's eyes. She had never felt more embarrassed in her entire life. She desperately looked for her plain t-shirt and shorts.

Her mother laughed at her. "You are looking for these, *cariño?*" she asked, holding Lupe's t-shirt and torn shorts in her hand and waving them in front of her face.

Lupe looked at her silently, searching for mercy, and shyly reached out her aching hand towards her old clothing.

"No, no *cariño*, these clothes belong to boys not you. You are a girl," she said, wagging her finger at her. "In fact, let me get rid of these, I don't think I want any of my boys even to wear these," she said, striking a match, but instead of lighting a cigarette, she set the shorts and t-shirt on fire.

"*Ma*, no!" Lupe screamed in terror, jumping towards her to try and save the remains of her clothes, but her mother stopped her by grabbing her hair. Lupe felt her scalp burning as strands of her hair came out one by one; she would rather have lost all her hair than watch helplessly as her clothing turned into ashes, but the fire reached the waist of the shorts quickly and burnt the whole fabric down.

The anger shook her entire body as she tried to fill her lungs, but the corset on the dress made her breathing difficult and she ended up vomiting on the floor.

"Look what you did, stupid *lesbian* idiot!" Altagracia yelled and grabbed both her hands, forcing them down on the ground and into the vomit. "How do you feel about cleaning your own mess up, *stupid girl?*" she said, holding Lupe's hand down in the vomit. "You won't be using the hot water boiler to wash your hands as this is your own fault and your own mess," she added.

Lupe was crying out loud; she could smell the warm vomit and feel the acid from it burning the little cuts she had got in her fingertips from digging the hole in the fence just half an hour earlier with her cousin. Her small twelve-year-old body was cramping again as a new wave of nausea ran through her, forcing anything left in her stomach out. Luckily, she didn't have anything left in her stomach and she ended up burping only air.

Her torture was interrupted by a noise coming from the open window, which caught her mother's attention; she left Lupe lying on the ground, tired and gasping for breath in her own vomit.

As soon as their mother left the room, Reina and Celestina opened the fabric door and entered the house again. They were too afraid to reach out to Lupe, scared of their mother's fury if they dared to help their sister.

Lupe slowly pushed herself up from the floor. Her whole body was tired and ached due to the battle she had gone through with her own mother. She felt a sharp pain in her upper back, right up to her neckline and couldn't move her head from side to side. Her nose was still bleeding and the cut on her knee from earlier in the day had started bleeding again. She wiped her nose on her arm, leaving long red marks which reminded her of a tiger's stripes. She could see the pity in her sisters' eyes and felt the unbearable embarrassment of the dress she was still wearing, which set her off running away from the house through the fabric door.

Lupe ran as fast as she could through the backyards of the houses to avoid anyone coming across her in this vulnerable state. She gasped for fresh air in her lungs, hoping if she could run fast enough, she would lose the smell of vomit on her hands. She didn't care about the long grass reaching almost to her chin, which locals would usually consider a dangerous and suicidal path where lurking wildlife such as crocodiles and pythons were waiting to claim their share. Lupe couldn't care less as she ran, finally reaching her grandmother's house.

She ran behind the house to the ladders leading to the roof and quickly climbed up. When she was up on the roof, she felt safe enough to start ripping off the yellow dress. She got rid of the sleeves and the hem and was soon wearing only the corset which she couldn't tear apart; on the contrary, the triple knots her mother had made seemed to be getting tighter the more she struggled. She was red in the face, and smelt of a mixture of sweat and vomit.

She started hysterically crying and screaming, trying desperately to pull off the remains of the dress.

In her desperate battle to escape from the dress that felt like it was burning her skin, she didn't hear someone approaching and climbing up the stairs to the roof and reaching out to her from behind with something sharp in their hands.

Lupe froze and stopped breathing. Next thing she knew, she heard a sharp snap and felt the corset loosening around her belly and dropping onto the roof before slowly sliding down the roof tiles until she couldn't see it anymore.

Lupe turned around and saw her cousin with scissors in his hand. They stared at each other for a moment and then without words, her cousin handed her a piece of soap and a bottle of water to clean up. It wasn't clean water from the boiler and looked and smelled more like water from the small green pond they used to go swimming in, but for Lupe, it looked like a lifesaver and she took the soap and water and started washing herself.

After she was done, her cousin handed her a t-shirt and shorts that still had a clothes peg attached, clearly snatched from someone's yard. Lupe quickly put on the t-shirt and new pair of shorts that fitted like a glove. In her new clothing, without saying a word, she turned to climb down from the roof before sprinting off, leaving her cousin to stare after her from the roof.

She didn't go home that night. Instead, she wandered back to the *mirador* they had played in earlier. She found a dry spot close to the hole they had made in the fence. She curled up, trembling slightly as the temperature went down as the night approached. She was tired and soon fell asleep only to dream about the terror of the little yellow dress.

Chapter 12

After the yellow dress incident, Lupe stayed away from the house for days, earning money by selling items, whatever she could get her hands on.

She used to wander around the white houses with beautifully maintained gardens and wait until the bright day turned to sunset before climbing over the fence to steal apples from the trees. She would then walk hours to the closest sugar farm and grab a bunch of sugar canes and make a small fire on the side of the road. Warming up in the glow of the fire, she would peel and melt the sugar off the cane and, with a circular motion, caramelise the stolen apples to sell for a couple of soles on the streets. At the end of the week, her fingers would be so burned from the melting sugar, she couldn't feel them anymore.

The sugar farms were owned by the government but left unmaintained most of the time, letting the sugar canes and grass reach almost the height of a small building, providing an easy hiding place for anyone wishing to steal a couple of strands. Even though the sun was at its best in Peru in January, and strong enough to burn the wooden roofs of the houses in many villages, the farms stayed alive and green due to the humidity caused by the monsoon rains typical of an area so close to the Amazon.

Sometimes she saw cars passing by and would hail a lift to reach the sugar farm before the night. The drivers didn't seem to mind giving a ride to a small boyish girl with a heavy sack of apples on her shoulders.

Lupe never really minded the lift either, even though she kept quiet during the drive, occasionally answering a question or two just to make sure she wasn't being impolite to someone offering her a lift. Female drivers with at least one child in the back seat were her preference as, despite her young age, she was not clueless of the things that happened to young girls travelling in strangers' cars: there was evidence of it around the city, with missing girl adverts printed on white paper.

The missing girls were not normally found alive; if the parents were lucky, the police would find the remains of the body, which the parents could then bury and establish a final resting place for their beloved daughters. Usually, the parents were not that lucky and were sentenced to spend the rest of their lives wondering about the unknown fate of their child. Mothers often refused to accept the assumed fate and kept imagining their children growing up in places such as the US and coming back one day. Lupe knew it was a lie.

Even the weather in Peru seemed to favour the mystery of a crime as the humidity and close proximity to the Amazon made sure any clues would be destroyed and disposed of by nature itself.

Unfortunately, cars were still considered more of a male hobby in Latin America and female drivers were not a common sight on the roads. Lupe would usually judge the drivers by the way they were driving, if they were alone and if they had pets with them. She really liked dogs, and many times the drivers would let her pet them. As she ran her fingers through the dog's fur and heard the soothing breath of the animal, only then would she feel safe.

Only once had she made the mistake of jumping into an older man's car. It had been a hot day and her feet had swollen and sweated, causing blisters so bad they had made her feet bleed and itch as a result of the fine sand inside her shoes rubbing against her sensitive skin. There had been no water point for a long time and she was feeling dizzy from walking in the direct sun. The air had been dry, and her shoes caused a small dust cloud with every step, making her sneeze and causing her lungs to burn. There had been no cars along the road for hours and she had started to feel extremely desperate, wondering if she would meet her end on the road right then and there, when a dark grey, battered car had approached her slowly. She had dragged herself from the side of the road to the main road and held one hand up in the air, balancing the apple sack with the other. The car had slowed down and the driver with a shabby cap on his head had opened the door for her.

"You looking to go somewhere?" he had asked, exposing his four missing front teeth. Lupe squinted her eyes into the sun, trying to see him better, but she was so badly dehydrated that once she had seen a freshly opened water bottle next to the driver's seat she hadn't thought twice and had hopped into the car.

"Yes, I'm trying to reach the sugar cane farm on the west side of Jaen before sunset," she said politely.

The driver nodded. "Fair enough, I'm going the same way," he said and engaged the gear to move the car. "I can drop you off at the next roundabout, from there, it isn't a long way to walk and the whole way is covered by *ceiba* trees, which should offer you cover from the heat."

Lupe nodded but didn't reply.

Inside the car, she could smell sweat and cigarettes mixed with the scent of the car air freshener that hung on the windshield. She saw numerous empty water and beer bottles, some of them used as ashtrays, lying on the front and back seats. The seat felt sticky from dirt and humidity, and the passenger seat Lupe was sitting on was covered in cigarette burns on the left side, as if the driver had tried to target the ashtrays while driving but missed them several times.

They had been driving only a couple of minutes when he had opened the water bottle with one hand and taken a long sip. Lupe couldn't help looking at the bottle with such a hunger that caught the driver's attention and slowly he offered the bottle to her. Lupe drunk greedily.

"It's dangerous to forget your water bottle in such hot weather, it can kill you," the driver said. Lupe hadn't been able to reply as she had been busy trying to finish the bottle as soon as possible before he could take it away from her.

He laughed. "Slow down will you, otherwise you will make us stop for a leak before we have even driven a couple of miles."

Lupe brushed her wet face on her arm. "Thank you for the water," she said politely and turned her head to look out of the window.

They drove a couple more miles along the road before the driver started chatting again. "Where is your mum *darling*? You know, such a little child like yourself shouldn't walk around alone. Who knows what might happen to you."

"My mum is waiting for me at home."

That had been a lie, and Lupe wasn't sure what had signalled to the driver that she was alone without responsible parents around, but soon she noticed that they had taken a wrong road, heading deeper into the Amazonas and the driver had added speed.

Her internal alarm system shot straight to red.

"*Señor*, I think you have taken a wrong turn," she said and tried to secretly open the car door only to notice that the driver had locked it. The driver turned to look at her again. "I think this is just the right way," he said, giving her a smile that turned into a grimace and started humming.

"Can you please leave me here, I will walk from here, my mum is waiting for me."

"I think we both know that's a lie. Pretty children like yourself shouldn't lie," the driver said and shook his head in disappointment but didn't slow the car down.

"*Señor*, I want you to stop this car right now," Lupe said with terror reaching her voice.

The driver laughed again. "And I want to take off your shorts and fuck you hard in your little asshole, but that will have to wait another five minutes," he said and reached out his hand to touch Lupe's thigh.

The panic made her react – she jumped onto the back seat, rolled one of the windows halfway down and started to climb out of the speeding car.

"Hey, what the hell do you think you're doing?" the driver yelled and stopped the car at the side of the road. But Lupe didn't wait. She jumped out of the car, rolled her body along the ground, clambered up onto her feet and as soon as she felt the solid ground under her feet she sprinted off to the forest as fast as her wobbly legs allowed her to.

Lupe saw the man getting out of the car with a gun in his hands and thanked God for the water she had drunk in the car which had allowed her body to hydrate and to function as normally as possible. She quickly lost track of how long she had been running for, but finally slowed down when she couldn't hear the yells of the driver anymore.

She hid in the bushes for a while to catch her breath and calm her beating heart. The incident in the car had caused her to lose all the apples she had carried with her and she had red bruises all over her legs and arms and an aching pain in the shoulder that had taken most of the impact of the fall. Her shoes were wet and dirty from running in the forest. She could no longer feel the blisters on her feet that had originally caused her to take the ride from the stranger.

Lupe stayed in her hiding place for a few more minutes before deciding to continue as she was still afraid of the driver looking for her in the forest. She stood up and waited a second to balance her blood pressure before continuing. By now, her blood sugar was dangerously low as she hadn't eaten since last night and she could feel the pain of her stomach acids burning her stomach.

She didn't know how long she had been walking but apparently, she had taken the right turn as she soon arrived at the familiar sugar cane farm. A smile of relief broke across her face as she quickly hid from the farm workers in the field. She had been lucky.

Chapter 13

As the days passed, Lupe missed home and only determination and the deep humiliation she had suffered kept her at bay. She also knew their father was a very proud man who had a steady hand and zero patience towards runners – there would be a birch waiting for her no matter how she saw it.

The birch was a wooden stick that their father used to manage horses and other wild animals, but occasionally, when his outfit didn't include a belt, he would use the birch to educate his children. Lupe preferred the birch any day over the belt, because the marks the birch would leave were less painful than the damage of a fine leather belt with a massive buckle. Their father also lacked a sense of time when he was in the mood for punishing his children. He could go on for hours and not even the loudest cries and deepest tears would stop him. Celestina was his pet, but only because she was scared to death of him. Frankly, their father took her behaviour as obedience, but in reality, she couldn't bear the thought of the punishments she had witnessed so many times before. Lupe had always had a soft spot for her little sister, and in fact, several times, had taken the blame and a beating for her. After all, she was her baby sister.

Eventually, the starvation and cold drove Lupe to return home. She missed her family dearly and life on the streets didn't do well for anyone. The winter season was approaching and after the sun had gone down, the cold air came down from the almighty Andes and caused Lupe's hands to become numb and her body to shake at night in her hiding place. Anywhere except outside would be better and at least she would see her sisters and brothers again.

*

She made her way back to the house where she saw Jose-Luis outside trying to ride a bicycle. He was seven years younger than Lupe, practically still a baby, but had been forced to grow up quickly in order to survive in the family. He had not picked up all of the skills that he should have by now and sometimes learning took him a lot of time as he would easily get distracted and frustrated over anything, riding a bicycle being one of them.

Lupe watched the small red bicycle with tassels on both sides of the colourful handlebar. She didn't recognise the bicycle and thought the girly tassels were a peculiar choice for Jose-Luis who was used to showing off his macho side at a very young age.

He had inherited the style from their father and many mornings he would sit next to him while he was shaving. Lupe was fascinated by the ritual and sometimes lurked by the windows to see them both in action. Their father would sit on the stone staircase at the back of the house with a red bucket of fresh cold water from the river and a big knife and piece of soap in his hand. He would wet the soap and his face in the bucket and apply soap all over his bearded face. He would then show the knife to Jose-Luis , who was sitting next to him quietly watching, make a couple of movements in the air showing off the sharp blade and then tighten his skin and slowly run the knife over his face, removing his facial hair. Jose-Luis would usually hold his breath and exhale only when his father washed the soap and facial hair off the knife in the bucket. Finally, their father would apply the scent of musk around his neck and roar out loud as the liquid touched the sensitive part of the freshly shaved skin, causing it to redden and itch. It would hurt for only a moment, he always said.

*

"What are you doing *hermano*?" Lupe walked over to him.

Jose-Luis lifted his head as if he had been caught doing something wrong.

Lupe stood in front of him, hands in her pockets. "I take it that's not yours?"

He waited for a moment before shaking his head. "I found it in the yard next to the park and brought it home."

"Mmmm," Lupe knew it was a lie but frankly, she wasn't interested in the detail. She had learnt from a young age not to ask too many questions as knowing the truth would always come back to haunt: the *messenger* would be punished as well.

Jose-Luis turned to face the bike again and tried to jump on it. It was an unsuccessful try, causing him to hit his crotch on the crossbar between the saddle and handlebar. The bike fell over with a loud ring of the bell.

"Ouch, ouch, ouch!" Jose-Luis yelled and jumped around holding his stomach. "Stupid bike, stupid bike!" He lost his temper and kicked the bike with his sandal. The bike jolted on the ground and the bell rang with every kick as if it was complaining about the bad treatment. Lupe wanted to avoid the scandal, so she pushed her brother onto the ground again.

"Stop that *estupido*, you want everyone to see you with your stolen girly bike?" She watched him freeze immediately.

"Now, I will help you to ride but I need you first to bring me something to eat from inside," she said and pointed to the entrance of the house. "But you can't tell anyone it is for me, got it?"

Jose-Luis nodded and sprinted on his way.

Lupe watched him go – he was so excited at someone giving him an important task to do and waiting to be taught how to ride a bike.

He sprinted into the house which was empty and quickly scooped his hand into a pot of leftover morning quinoa porridge and ran over to his sister again. He proudly showed his findings to his sister and offered his hand to her. Lupe looked at his hand, covered in mud and sand from falling over and over again with the bicycle, mixed with the sticky porridge. Jose-Luis was not the sharpest brain in the family, she thought, but her hunger made her close her eyes and scrape all of the porridge from her brother's hand and stuff it in her mouth as fast as she could.

The taste was not as bad as she expected. The mud had no taste at all and the sand cracked between her teeth which felt like eating tasteless candy. She quickly swallowed and stuffed the rest of the porridge in her mouth, quickly filling up her small stomach. She then walked to the side of the house where their mother would hold rainwater for washing. She washed her hands and mouth before making a little cup of her hands and drank.

"OK, now I'm done," she said and shook her hands and dried them on her t-shirt. "Let's make you ride the bike *hermano*!"

Jose-Luis's eyes lit up in excitement as Lupe took the bicycle from her brother's hands and started walking.

They walked side by side to a free zone area of the city where there wouldn't be a risk of someone coming to look for the stolen bike, or any other unnecessary distractions to her brother's overactive mind. The pavement was much flatter, which would hopefully help Jose-Luis to stay on the bike without falling, Lupe thought and glanced at her younger brother.

It took them half an hour to walk to the place Lupe had planned for the riding practice.

"OK *hermanito*, watch me first," she said and put one leg over the bike and sat on the saddle. "This way, you balance the bike but you have to kick off with your feet to get some speed before you can lift your feet up onto the pedals, otherwise you will fall," she instructed, making a kicking movement in the air to emphasise her words. Jose-Luis listened carefully.

Then she kicked herself off and rode a couple of metres before making a U-turn and stopping abruptly in front of her brother.

"See that *hermanito*, that's how you ride a bike," she said and winked.

Jose-Luis's eyes were glittering and his legs were drumming on the ground as he couldn't wait to take over the handlebars. Lupe stepped off the bike to help her brother. He hauled one leg over the bike to sit on the saddle, but he was too short to reach the saddle with his legs on the ground. It was obvious the bicycle was too big for him. He looked at Lupe with watery eyes.

"*No pasa nada hermanito*. It's OK." She hurried to console him and lifted his skinny body onto the saddle while balancing the bike.

"Now, put your hands on the handlebar and your feet on the pedals. I will run next to you and push to give you some speed so that you can ride," she said and started moving slowly forwards. The pedals under Jose-Luis's feet started turning themselves before he was able to catch the rhythm.

"Look at you, you are riding a bike!" Lupe said and grinned. Jose-Luis's face was full of joy. His face had always been very expressive no matter what he felt, Lupe thought.

They rode a couple of metres and Jose-Luis seemed to catch the idea and started pushing more speed through the pedals. Lupe had no choice but to increase her speed at his side.

"Careful *hermanito*, don't go too fast," she said breathing heavily, but Jose-Luis seemed to be too excited at his newly discovered skill and when they reached a small downhill, he let the pedals take over.

"Slow down, brake!" Lupe screamed as she felt herself losing her grip on the bike. She fell onto the ground on her stomach and watched her brother carry on with the bike. The flat pavement ended in the middle of the downhill and changed into a bumpy ride with muddy puddles. On the first bump, Jose-Luis lost control of his bike and fell into the muddy pool of water just before the road ended. Lupe ran to him.

"Are you OK *hermanito?*" she asked and grabbed him up by his armpits. His clothes and sandals were dripping dirty water and stained with mud. She was scared he had hurt himself.

"Wow, that was the most amazing thing ever *hermana*, let's do it again!" he said grinning. Lupe sighed with relief and gave him a gentle slap on his head. "Yes, we can do it again, but when I say brake, you brake – I have to bring you back home in one piece!" she said and eyed his dirty clothing again. Even with a muddy face and dirty clothes his grin shone out. Lupe smiled at her brother. "OK, let's do this again as many times as you like," she said and lifted the bike from the water.

*

It was already evening when they both walked home. They had hidden the bike in the free zone area along with some rubbish, hoping the local rubbish men would miss the spot as they seemingly had done for the past weeks. It would raise too many questions in the area if they left it in their yard as it was no secret to their neighbours the financial difficulties their father went through trying to feed five children. Lupe hoped the bike would still be there the next day.

By the time they arrived home, it was already dark and there was a pale light coming from the window. They must have eaten already, Lupe thought and put her hand on her brother's shoulder. She would be fine without dinner as her stomach had got used to not eating after spending several days on the streets, but she was worried for her brother who was so skinny his collarbones stuck out under his skin. He had lost weight in the weeks she had been gone.

They approached the door and heard someone hurrying over to it before they had a chance to knock. Celestina opened the door.

"Shhh, quiet, *ma* is already sleeping and *papi* is outside," she said and opened the door slightly to let them both in. The air in the house was humid and stank of old alcohol and sweat. Their mother was snoring heavily on the only bed in the room, an empty bottle of cheap rum next to her. Reina had curled up at the end of the bed with a bright red blanket their grandmother had knitted for them. She had always enjoyed knitting and kept telling them that it kept her mind fresh. Lupe had sometimes sold her knitting on the streets and had been rewarded with a meaty dinner in her grandmother's house. There was a dead silence in the room.

Celestina hurried to the kitchenette and tried to scrape off any leftovers from the dinner. She found a small piece of bread and brought them to Lupe and Jose-Luis. Lupe watched as Jose-Luis grabbed the piece of bread and ran it over the little plate to get at least the taste of dinner in his mouth. Lupe felt her stomach protest but ignored it and went to the bed and curled herself inside the blanket as well. In a second, Celestina and Jose-Luis followed and in no time, they were all curled up together, looking for comfort and warmth from each other. They fell asleep to the rhythmic snores of their drunken mother.

Chapter 14

It wasn't long after when a cholera epidemic hit the Peruvian coast and within a year, it had spread over the little village of Jaen. It had first spread to Ecuador and then Colombia and by 1993, all Latin American countries except Uruguay and the islands of the Caribbean had reported cholera cases. However, over 80% of the cases were concentrated in Peru. The epidemic spread rapidly between countries and lasted over three years before the governments were able to control it. As a result, Peru was isolated from other Latin American countries. Soldiers on the borders wore masks and were instructed to shoot people on sight, causing numerous unnecessary deaths; the bodies were left on the ground and family members were forced to collect their dead relatives. Sometimes the bodies stayed on the ground for days as the soldiers didn't have a clue of their identity and were too afraid to go near the body due to infection risk. The smell of rotting and burning flesh in the sun was unspeakable and not even the vultures would come and dine.

Sadly, not even rapid and intense surveillance stopped the disease spreading. People didn't understand that the most common routes of transmission were related to drinking water and general risk of disease. People were still highly unhygienic, consuming a great deal of unwashed fruits and vegetables and eating food from street vendors. Peru was also a big consumer of crabmeat, which was highly popular because of its cheap price, which eventually turned out to be the biggest cause of the disease spreading as contaminated crab meat travelled from family to family. Despite an extensive oral rehydration therapy program that the government had launched earlier in the year with the help of international aid programs in the areas, the lack of a clean water supply and inadequate sanitation facilities, where people still dug holes in the ground to use as toilets, caused a high death toll in small villages like Jaen. It was like a plague turning friends and neighbours against each other.

The first symptoms were not obvious. Lupe had been at home for seven days but she was still avoiding her mother and couldn't bear to look her in the eyes; in the small home they all shared, avoiding someone was easiest achieved outside, which meant she spent most of her days outside or at her grandmother's place, helping with little chores she gave her. In exchange, she was a welcome guest at her dinner table, and would close her eyes whenever Lupe's fingers disappeared first into the pod and then into her mouth while they cooked together.

She had always been her grandmother's favourite. She felt that they shared the same ideology in life, and she was very easy going. She accepted her the way she was although she wouldn't hesitate for a second to give her an earful for poor behaviour.

Her grandmother lived in a modest house of three rooms, which she had inherited from their grandfather when he had died. The house consisted of a bedroom, living room and large kitchen which contained a wooden table for six. The table was by the windows that brought all the daylight into the room, which made the kitchen the most popular room in the house as in any typical Latin family. There was no electricity in the house and the toilet facilities were outside, but the house was well kept and looked after. She was a real *ama de la casa*, and had always taken good care of her husband and children, which had caused the main friction between Lupe's mother and their grandmother. She had always been ready to stand up for her grandchildren and her son.

There were two doors in the kitchen, one of which led to the toilet facilities outside of the house and a little garden where their grandmother grew vegetables and farmed chickens. Since last year, there had also been a very mean donkey which she had found tied up on a leash in an abandoned house and rescued from starvation. The poor animal had been on his last legs, ready to give up and waiting for life to slowly escape as he breathed heavily in the direct sun. Lupe's grandmother had quickly cut the leash but the poor animal had been too defeated to even walk away, so she had gone inside the abandoned house and found a bucket of dirty water and thrown it over the donkey and fed it with the vegetables she had bought at the market. She had placed the scarf she carried with her to protect her shoulders from the sun on the back of the animal. The donkey had quickly recovered and been able to walk and she had walked it to her backyard. With time and love, the donkey had recovered fully with only ugly sunburnt skin on its right side as a reminder and the main reason why no one could put a saddle on the animal ever. In Lupe's father's eyes, the animal was completely useless, and he had threatened many times to make dinner out of it, but Lupe's grandmother had held her ground and now the ugly donkey was like family. Lupe was fascinated by the animal and dreamt of one day being able to touch and pet it, but under their grandmother's watchful eye, it wouldn't be possible so she was left no choice but to admire the animal from afar.

*

Next morning Lupe woke up feeling dizzy and nauseous but assumed it was due to the food she had eaten for dinner last night. They had been on a porridge diet for weeks now – meat was a rare luxury for adults only. It was the summer holiday from school which meant all teachers stayed at home with their families without pay for at least two months. Normally, the families would save for months to survive the summer holiday, but for Lupe's father, the spring had been hard and he had medicated himself alone in the local bar, spending all his pay on alcohol and leaving the family to fend for themselves. It was clear their parents were going through a hard time in their relationship as during those hot summer nights, Lupe often saw their mother going out, all dressed up with her make-up done, and not returning until the next day. She was tempted to follow her, but so far, she had fought the temptation. Her return would usually result in aggressive fights at home, leaving the youngest ones confused, scared and crying. Reina, Lupe and Celestina, the older ones, would pick up the younger ones and carry them outside and distract them with games and playing until the screams and sounds of breaking glass ended.

All of them were suffering from poor nutrition, especially the younger boys. Jose-Luis's skin had turned pale and waxy and under his t-shirt, his spine and ribs stuck out through the skin. He seemed to have started losing hair again due to lack of vitamin B, which he had done last summer as well. Her brother seemed weaker every day and the weaker he grew the angrier he got. Lupe had seen him starting fights with bigger boys in the playground and wondered if it was something she should intervene in, but she wasn't sure.

In the morning, she dressed in her old t-shirt and shorts and started to make her way to their grandmother's house, but halfway there she had to stop to catch her breath. After standing still for a couple of minutes with her heart pounding, she decided to sit down for a while in the shadowy staircase on the street. The cold staircase felt good under her lower back and bottom, but before long she started feeling extremely cold and began shivering uncontrollably. The shivers ravaged her small body and hurt her stomach and seconds later, she felt an uncontrollable need to use the toilet. She turned to run back home but as she stood up, she felt warm, brown liquid dripping down her thighs and onto her sandals. She looked down and felt extreme embarrassment. She started walking as fast as she could towards the house. She felt mortified and kept her eyes on the house and calculated the metres and seconds it would take to get home. She was at the door when the next involuntary muscular contraction came and this time it forced her onto her knees and again her body gave in and released another trail of brown liquid down from her shorts.

Jose-Luis was playing outside and saw the scene and ran home. He was too small to help but immediately understood something was terribly wrong.

"Reina, Celes! Lupe is not well! She is hurt *ven rapido*!" he kept yelling and waving his cap in the air like a flag.

Lupe looked at her baby brother and smiled. His ears were giant and looked two sizes too big for his small head. They all teased the boy about it and last time, he had got so mad he had pierced his ears to make them even more noticeable. Their mother had been horrified and their father had beaten him for hours for being "gay" at the age of four, but he had refused to take them off and now covered his head with a cap or hat inside the house. Only on rare occasions was he willing to take the hat off. Lupe was secretly happy that this was one of them.

Celestina opened the front door but stopped on her heels after seeing and smelling the scene.

"Oh my god, *Por Dios, que te pasa hermana?* What is wrong with you?" She wanted to help but the smell and the brown mess dripping from her sister onto the porch kept her in her place, waiting for their big sister to take charge.

"Reina, please hurry up, I think something is very wrong with Lupe!" she yelled and disappeared inside the house. Jose-Luis and Lupe waited in the front yard for what felt like ages to Lupe before Reina showed up at the door. She eyed the situation and quickly took charge. "Celes, get me a bucket of water from the backyard and Jose-Luis, help me to undress her," she said and rolled her sleeves up and tied their mother's cooking apron around her waist. Jose-Luis didn't seem to mind the mess or the smell and was eager to help.

They managed to undress her and splash some cold water to wash her before dragging her inside. They didn't dare use the only bed in the house, instead Reina wrapped all the blankets and sheets she could and made a small lying place for Lupe in the corner of the house where it would be the shortest way to the toilet. It was literally just a bunch of blankets thrown in the corner and looked more like a dog sleeper, but

Lupe was grateful for it anyway. Celestina had disappeared with her clothes and promised to wash them instead of throwing them away. Lupe laid down naked under the blankets but even if they had brought her all the blankets from the house, it didn't help the inner shivers that tormented her body.

It was cholera. Their father had arrived home and found them all around Lupe. By the night, she had started vomiting and couldn't hold water inside. He had called the doctor and without examination, the doctor diagnosed her with cholera. He pressed the cold stethoscope on her hot chest and listened carefully.

"I must warn you all, the cholera cases I have seen so far are not good. There is little chance, especially with children. If they can't hold food and water in, they will eventually drift away and die of starvation and dehydration." The room stayed quiet, waiting for the doctor to continue. He eyed his audience under his thick eyebrows and cleared his throat. "I'm sorry for bringing the bad news," he said finally and prescribed some natural remedies before leaving. Once the door shut, they all looked at each other silently. Even their mother, who had finally arrived home and been briefed of the situation, looked thoughtful as she sat at the kitchenette table smoking a third cigarette holding the smoke in her lungs before exhaling slowly.

The next days, Lupe's father stayed at home. He only left the house a couple of times and invited their grandmother to watch the children. Lupe's condition deteriorated from bad to worse. She lost half of her body weight and her skin developed deep lines around her mouth and eyes. The colour of her skin had first turned ash grey and now started taking bluish shades. During the first days, she had spent a lot of time in the toilet, but as her condition got worse, she couldn't make it to the toilet on time anymore. Reina was by her side, changing and washing the blankets and Celestina insisted on feeding her.

She cooked broth for her from any leftovers from breakfast, lunch and dinner and took the trouble of going to the local market early in the morning. She never had any money to spend and usually wandered on the edges of the market with her bucket where the local fishermen prepared their bait ready for sale. They would clean and wash the catch and normally there was a good chance of leftovers such as fish heads, bones and fins. Fish heads provided a great addition to broths and soups and were full of flavour and vitamins, but had nearly no sales value and usually were thrown away and left for rats and mice. Many times, she went unnoticed in the busy area as she picked the fish heads from the ground, but increasingly often, she would attract unwanted attention.

Celestina, the third of the siblings and born in Peru, was a beauty and well-developed for her age, a total contrast to Reina, who still looked like a child. Celestina's body had taken a womanly form at an early age and now, in her childish white linen dress which had once been totally suitable for a young girl but was now hugging her hips turning heads wherever she went. She had inherited the best features of both her parents: the clear white skin and raving dark hair from her mother that would fall freely down to her waist and the dark mystic eyes and full lips of her father that reminded of the heat and fire of the hot summer days.

She was their father's favourite and enjoyed a quiet life, staying inside the house under his controlling eye.

On the fourth day, she came back from the market and emptied the fish heads and intestines into a bucket of water to wash them, but the lack of movement in Lupe's corner bed alarmed her. She was afraid but approached the bed.

"Lupe, are you awake?" she tried. "Lupe, I brought more fish heads, I will make fresh broth today. You can eat very soon," she tried again and touched her forehead examining her face. Lupe's eyes were closed, and she was breathing sharply. Celestina caressed her sticky skin.

"Any good news, Celes?" the door opened and Reina entered the house. She had been washing the sheets and picking up the new ones.

"No, nothing Rei," she said and gave a quick look at her older sister. "She is not moving at all today and looks really bad."

Reina left the sheets on the bed and came closer. As she arrived and kneeled on their sister's bed, her body started shivering again and her mouth opened in her sleep as if desperately looking for something to eat. Her mouth was dried out due to dehydration and made clunking noises like a puppet when she opened and closed her mouth. They both looked at her.

"You know, she won't last much longer," Reina said quietly. "I think we should call the doctor and grandmother." Celestina nodded her head, holding back tears that had been on the way for days.

The doctor came early evening and all of them gathered around Lupe's bed waiting for a miracle to happen. Their mother had refused to be around the bed, claiming that she would be the first one to be infected with the disease and without her the whole family would be totally lost. Their grandmother, who had arrived to hear the news, looked at her daughter-in-law with disgust but remained silent.

The doctor performed a quick examination. "All the broth and salt you give her is good for dehydration, but her body is too weak to recover. I would give her no more than 36 hours," the doctor concluded and washed his hands in the bucket Celestina had given to him.

The whole family felt numb at the news and even their father ran his hand in his hair, pulling nervously. The doctor gave them a pitying look, collected his medical equipment and removed the facemask he had used for the examination. He was at the door when their grandmother asked: "Doctor, is there any hope left? Anything we could do or try at least?"

The doctor glanced back from the door. "She is not receiving the proper nutrients and probably lacks vitamins such as zinc," he said and turned back to the door.

"But doctor, which are the primary sources of zinc?"

The doctor looked back with pity written in his face. "The number one source of zinc is red meat," he said and gave a knowing look at the skinny bodies of Jose-Luis and Reina before closing the door behind himself.

The whole family stayed silent for a moment, mourning for what was to come. They all knew there was simply no money to spend on luxuries such as red meat, and even if there was, the impact on the whole family would be much greater than saving one life, if that would even help. There was no guarantee. Their father left the house in a fury and headed to the bar – he couldn't bear the thought of his daughter slowly drifting away on his watch, knowing that due to his incompetence in taking care of his family, one of his daughters was dying and there was very little he could do. So he drank, and didn't come back home.

Meanwhile, their grandmother had been left with her thoughts in the house. She had finally grown tired of her daughter-in-law's attitude and had sent her away from the house. She was thoughtful. Celestina approached her. "*Abuela*, what are you thinking?" she asked and put her hand on her arm.

"*Nada mi niña*, I'm just thinking," she said.

Celestina eyed her curiously. "Are you thinking about Lupe?"

Their grandmother didn't meet her eyes. "Yes *hija*, I'm thinking of any potential ways of saving her. There must be a way."

Celestina looked at her sister. "They say God has a plan for all of us; maybe it is His plan to take her. You know He only takes the best of us?" she said and approached Lupe's corner bed to adjust the blanket that had dropped from her shoulders after another spam.

Suddenly their grandmother stood up abruptly. "*Hija*, maybe you are right, but not today at least," she said and left the house, leaving Celestina watching after her.

The next day, their grandmother came back with the neighbour's boy carrying a giant bag on his shoulder. Jose-Luis, Reina and Celestina ran to meet her. "What is it, what is it?" Jose-Luis asked and jumped around their grandmother.

"It's food *hijo*, now get in and let's start cooking. *Rapido,* quickly."

They all went in and their grandmother opened the bag. They looked eagerly inside.

It was Celestina who freaked out first. "Oh, *abuela* it stinks!" she said and held her nose.

"*Claro mi hija*, it's raw meat. Freshly butchered last night," she said and looked around her. "Now all of you, help me here," she said and gave every one of them a chore to do to prepare the meat. They all worked in cooperation and silence like an oiled engine.

The children didn't quite understand the purpose of the effort, but they were happy to see proper food after several weeks of porridge and just to be around a caring adult. Their father had not returned from the bar last night and their mother had left on her own adventures once again.

"Jose-Luis, would you please check the taste of the soup?" their grandmother finally asked. He ran to pick up a chair and place it in front of the hot hob. "Hmmm, *abuela, que rico!*" he closed his eyes and smiled. It was truly a rare luxury for the whole family to eat meat.

They all sat around the table and said a prayer before eating. Their grandmother prepared a plate for Lupe and knelt next to her bed. She was sure the sweet meaty smell of the freshly cooked meal would wake her up and give her strength to eat, but she was too weak and couldn't even open her eyes. She stood up and looked around the room as if seeking advice on what to do next when Jose-Luis, who had already finished his plate and was hoping for more, caught her eye.

"Jose-Luis, *ven aqui hijo rapido*. Come quickly."

Jose-Luis, feeling the strength coming back to his four-year-old body after a proper meal, came jumping. "What is it *abuela*?"

"*Hijo*, I need you to do me a favour. Can you please chew the meat and put it in your sister's mouth?"

Jose-Luis eyed her suspiciously. "Why would I do that and not swallow myself?" he asked. "Because your sister is too weak to eat for herself, but we need to get food inside her now," she said, stressing her words on every syllable. "Tonight, she might already be gone."

Maybe it was the commanding tone of her voice or maybe it was that Jose-Luis finally understood the seriousness of his sister's condition but he nodded his head slowly and took the first spoonful of meat. He chewed it into small tender pieces and took the pieces from his mouth and placed them in Lupe's mouth. Their grandmother gently pressed her lower jaw to open her mouth more.

"Now what?" Jose-Luis asked.

"We wait," she said.

By this time, all of the children had finished their meals and gathered around Lupe's bed to wait. They didn't have to wait for long before they saw a slight movement in her jaw as she quickly swallowed without chewing.

"*Rapidito hijo*, give her more," their grandmother said.

*

From that day, all the children were offered freshly cooked meat for lunch and dinner and one of the siblings would chew some meat for Lupe. Their grandmother then instructed Celestina to spoon-feed the soup, meat and vegetables to her. Lupe was too weak to even open her eyes and most of the liquid dribbled down her chin, but they were persistent. On the first day, Lupe started releasing the food through diarrhoea, which had stayed away for days as her body had not had anything to release anymore, resulting in painful spams and muscle aches that made her face twist with pain. But as the days went by, the diarrhoea seemed to ease and there was less coming out, which made Jose-Luis worried. "*Abuela*, where is it all going??"

Their grandmother smiled and patted his skinny shoulders. "Don't worry *hijo*, you will see."

On the third day, Lupe started moving and opened her eyes. She started trying to feed herself, even though Celestina insisted on doing it for her. By the fifth day, she felt strong enough to go to the toilet herself. The doctor was invited to visit her and after a quick examination he congratulated them all and prescribed antibiotics for the inflammation in her body. They were all excited to see their sister getting better.

By the end of the month, Lupe had fully recovered and had started walking short distances to make her body used to physical activity once again.

One day she walked to their grandmother's house and sat at her kitchen table. "*Abuela*, only God knows what you have done for me. You saved my life. Thank you for it," she said. "Because of you, all my brothers and sisters have meat to eat until next year or so," she said and laughed. "I hope you didn't have to sell your soul for it," she said and laughed before running out of the door again.

Their grandmother walked to the door and saw her running after Jose-Luis who had followed her. He always did nowadays. She looked after her with sadness in her eyes. "No *hija*, me too," she said and couldn't bear to look out of the window to the backyard. There was an empty donkey leash hanging in the air.

Chapter 15

After Lupe recovered from cholera, life in the family continued like nothing had happened. Their mother's sister had arrived for the summer to the city after a new love affair with a Peruvian gentleman she had met in Spain. They had married quickly and soon enough, she was expecting her third child, the first for her new husband. She had arrived alone in Peru to pursue her new life, leaving two of her children with their fathers, the first one in Germany and the second one in Spain.

Her name was Esperanza. She was the third born of the four sisters and unlike her name presented, she wasn't much of a hope to the family. In fact, she wasn't much of a mother at all, but her beauty was extraordinary, especially in the community she lived in. She had a slender and delicate figure, with long legs, light brown hair, distinctive bright blue eyes and a pearly white set of teeth and when she laughed, it sounded like jingle bells at Christmas.

All the men who ever crossed her path couldn't resist her charm and she was greedy for attention, which usually resulted in promises of eternal love, a quick marriage and pregnancy before routine life revealed her true character. Unfortunately, her beauty was only external and deep inside she was a selfish person, without patience and completely lacking in empathy, which made her an unbearable partner and dangerous in many senses.

Every time she was mentioned in conversations between her mother and her two other sisters, Lupe could feel the temperature drop several degrees. They didn't really hate her, but they preferred to keep their distance because even the selfish nature of Lupe's mother couldn't compete with her sister's.

Therefore, it wasn't a surprise when she informed the family of her plans to arrive in Peru and Jaen with her new husband, which caused a great chaos in the minds of the three remaining sisters and drove Lupe's mother Altagracia to the point of insanity who had always been in constant competition with her sister.

Lupe didn't really understand the cause of the friction between the sisters, although she did know something was wrong. She would never imagine feeling the same enmity and hatred towards her siblings; on the contrary, she couldn't bear the thought of losing any of them. She adored them to the moon and back.

Esperanza arrived after the summer months in June. Lupe had recovered well and was playing outside with Jose-Luis when she arrived. She was wearing a bright blue linen dress that complemented her eyes and showed her small pregnancy bump, and had her hair tied up with a blue ribbon. Her walk was elegant even in her high-heeled sandals.

Next to her walked her new husband, holding her hand and monitoring her every step. He wasn't much of an eye-catcher with his sunburnt skin and dark straight hair that he had combed back with gel. He seemed to be well over fifty and was wearing an old grey suit and a shirt which was open enough to reveal a bronze cross around his neck.

Lupe had never met her aunt before and only recognised her from pictures, but they didn't do justice to her beauty in real life. In fact, Lupe couldn't stop staring at her. Jose-Luis followed her gaze. "Wow," he said.

"Wow indeed *hermano*," Lupe replied. "Wow indeed."

Esperanza smiled at them both and tenderly waved her hand in their direction before entering the house with her new husband. Jose-Luis and Lupe ran quickly to the window. Like the rest of the family, when there was a chance for gossip, they wanted to be the first to hear it.

They saw the newlyweds sitting at the table in the kitchenette with their mother and father. Celestina was serving coffee and biscuits as their mother seemed for once to be totally unable to let go of their father's arm, showing slight signs of jealousy which made Lupe's heart race with hope – maybe their parents' relationship wasn't so bad after all and this would be the beginning of a new happy year in their life, she thought.

Unfortunately, she couldn't have been more wrong.

*

"Altagracia, I'm telling you, trust me; it is a good deal. It is only for a couple of months and she can continue school after," Esperanza said and waved her manicured hand in the air carelessly. "I know the summer was really difficult for the whole family and you can't rely on the support of Jorge's mother anymore," she leaned closer to her sister. "She is becoming senile and will soon be gone anyway, and then who will be left to help look after the children?" She sat back in her seat with poorly hidden pity written in her face.

Altagracia listened carefully and urged her husband to silence when he tried to object to the suggestion.

"Well, if we do it, I would definitely send Lupe," she said thoughtfully. "After all, she is much bigger than Reina. We need Celestina in the house and the boys are far too young."

Esperanza nodded understandingly.

"Moreover, you might not know, but she brought cholera into the home earlier this year and risked the rest of the family as well," Altagracia lowered her voice. "I think you agree that she should definitely pay back for all the tender care and attention the family provided during that time."

Esperanza nodded. "I totally agree with you Altagracia, I think you are making a smart choice," she said and looked at her sister with a contented smile on her face.

After the coffee, they invited all the family inside and Esperanza gave small presents to the children.

"From Spain with love," she smiled.

Lupe felt special as she held the little giftbox in her hand. The wrapping paper was red with a shiny finish and was held together with a curled green ribbon. It was the first wrapped present she had received since the yellow dress incident and she almost felt like not opening it at all.

She opened it carefully by unfastening the ribbon and unfolding the wrapping paper, making sure she didn't cause one single tear in the paper. It was too valuable for her to lose and she wanted to savour the moment.

Inside the box, there was a stone necklace. Lupe lifted the necklace from the box to view it better. It was a simple necklace with a black choker and a rough grey stone attached with a metal fastener.

Her aunt's husband opened his mouth for the first time since they had arrived. "It is a piece of a Mayan stela," he said. "Researchers have discovered monuments that were fashioned by the Mayan civilisation. It represents the concept of divine kingship."

His words sank into her mind like a sponge as she caressed the rough surface of the stone. She quickly attached the necklace around her neck and hid the stone under her t-shirt.

The other siblings also opened their small presents. There wasn't much thought put into the presents and it was obvious that the newlywed husband had been in charge of the presents rather than their aunt. The girls received hair ribbons and the boys got necklaces just like Lupe. Celestina was extremely happy with her new hair ribbon and attached it immediately in her hair. Unfortunately for Reina, she didn't have enough hair to hold the ribbon still, resulting in it pulling at the little hair she had.

Reina was very skinny and her body was highly sensitive to any seasonal and dietary changes, resulting in her losing chunks of hair every year during the tough summer months, although this summer had been better for her due to the meat-rich diet thanks to Lupe's illness. Nonetheless, the endless optimism and happiness that was deeply embedded in her character saved her from many sad moments and she ended up making a joke of her own state by pulling the ribbon below her nose and onto her hairy legs. All the siblings laughed including Lupe.

Esperanza turned to face Lupe. "Lupe, I have talked to your mum today and we have agreed that you will start working for us."

The laughter stopped and the room grew quiet.

"But what about school?" Jose-Luis asked looking worriedly at everyone in the room. He was worried as Lupe usually walked him to school every morning to make sure no one had a chance to bully him on the way as everyone in his class was afraid of her due to her sturdy size and explosive character. She didn't hesitate to punch anyone who dared to disrespect her family.

"Don't worry about that, she will continue after a couple of months," Esperanza petted his head whilst focusing her attention on Lupe. "The job is very easy. You will work in the countryside helping an old couple to maintain *una hacienda*," she said. "Anyway, your school scores clearly tell that you have no chance of an academic career," she laughed. "You are not smart enough *cariño*."

Their mother joined with her laughter.

Lupe felt embarrassed and eyed her sandals. She didn't feel the subjects at school were particularly difficult, she just found it hard to focus as most days the teacher had trouble controlling the class, resulting in the noise increasing to unbearable levels and making it impossible for Lupe to focus and not get distracted.

"That's decided then," Esperanza said and clapped her hands. "I will pick up Lupe tomorrow and Fernando will drive her to the *hacienda* the next day."

They all stood up from the table and Celestina started collecting dishes. Esperanza and Fernando headed to the door, accompanied by the whole family. Lupe followed on behind.

Esperanza flicked her hair and looked over her shoulder. "It was good to see you all and hopefully we will see you more often now that I live only a couple of blocks away in a *good* area of the city," she said as she disappeared with her new husband. "Lupe, see you tomorrow."

They all remained at the door watching them go, each of them deeply in their own thoughts. Altagracia narrowed her eyes on the backs of her sister and her new husband. She wasn't sure how to translate the visit – as a sign of good luck or as a threat.

*

Esperanza and Fernando arrived in the morning as agreed with a small rusty truck with two seats in the cabin. Lupe would have to travel in the back of the truck Esperanza said. Lupe didn't have anything to pack and left the house without breakfast carrying only the clothes she was wearing and the new necklace that she had received the previous day. She had combed her hair back as she had seen Fernando do, resulting in her looking even more like a small boy making her mother to narrow her eyes at her and struggle to hold her tongue but she remained silent. All the siblings gathered outside to wish her good luck. They were not really happy to lose her but didn't dare show their sadness in front of their mother as they knew any sign of weakness would result in ridicule and possibly a punishment. Even Jose-Luis, who would be affected the most by her absence, was holding back the tears.

Lupe climbed into the back of the truck and they started their bumpy journey. Alone in the back of the truck, she finally let her tears come. It had been a tough year for her, but it didn't reduce the sadness and hopelessness she felt watching her home disappearing in the sand dust as they drove away.

*

In the end, the promised two months turned into the eight longest

114

months of Lupe' life.

On the way to the countryside, her aunt had treated her with candy and a full breakfast with pork liver cooked with onion, tomatoes and fresh bread followed by papaya and chilli apples, a typical Peruvian breakfast. Lupe was ecstatic as it was the first time in her life she had been treated like a princess.

"Careful *cariño,* you might split in half if you continue eating like this," Esperanza said and patted the palm of her hand. Lupe grinned but continued eating. Esperanza and Fernando quickly finished their coffees and Fernando went to the cashier. Esperanza touched Lupe's arm. "Remember *cariño,* these people are very important and you need to do anything they want," she said and looked back at the cash desk. Fernando was still paying for their meal. "You need to pay for what you put your family through this year and the only way you can do it is by working like a bull," she said quickly before welcoming Fernando back to the table with a smile.

"What are you girls talking about?" he asked whilst putting his thick wallet back in his jacket's inner pocket.

"Oh, don't you worry about it *amorcito*, just girl stuff," she giggled and patted his chest. They all left the table and moved back to the car to continue their journey.

The *hacienda* was on the border of Amazonas and consisted of three main buildings with a large well-maintained coffee field on one side of the main house and green overgrown corn field on the other side. Lupe eyed the area with interest. The buildings were built of stone to prevent them from turning into saunas during the summer months and were painted in light yellow shades with brown roofs. The main building had a big patio around the building and a table and chairs were set up on the front offering the best view across the *hacienda.* Lupe didn't see any workers out, but automatically assumed they had arrived during the *siesta* time which meant most of the workers would probably be napping in their houses or in the coffee fields.

Fernando stopped the car in front of the main building and killed the engine. Esperanza hurried Lupe down from the back of the truck.

"Remember, not a word inside and listen to every instruction," she whispered in her ear, before urging her to enter the house.

A busty lady with long black hair and the most visible lady moustache wobbled into the entrance. "No, no, leave the girl outside. I don't want any *piejos* or dirt inside the house!" she said, waving her chubby hands in the air to emphasise her instruction.

"Oh, no problem," Esperanza said and hustled Lupe outside, closing the door in front of her.

Lupe placed her ear against the door to see if she could hear what was said inside but she couldn't hear a dicky bird. She turned around to inspect her new surroundings. It was indeed a beautiful view from the patio, she thought.

*

On her first night at the *hacienda*, she was shown her room which was a basement area with ground flooring under the main building. She would need to enter through a small wooden door barely visible to anyone who didn't know it existed. The area was basically a room filled with hay for the animals of the *hacienda* and llama wool for making warm clothes or for selling. A foldable bed had been opened for her in front of the hay packs. She didn't have a pillow but someone had left a colourful blanket for her to use. There were no toilet facilities in the room, but an empty water bucket was forgotten in the corner of the room which she decided to use for washing purposes.

The facilities were modest, but she got used to this quickly and she was actually happy with the room, which offered her quick access around the *hacienda* without attracting any attention, especially from the owner who had a tendency to yell and hit her with a birch if she failed to follow any instructions.

The room offered a cool relief from the heat during the remaining summer months, but was a freezing place once the monsoon rains arrived from the mountains. The rain would ooze down to the basement room under the door, turning the floor into a muddy puddle. Lupe didn't have anything to protect her feet from the mud and cold which resulted in her suffering from flu and other infections for nearly the whole eight months of her sentence at the *hacienda*. During the coldest months, when she couldn't feel her feet anymore, she would grab a piece of llama wool and wrap it around her feet. Usually she would end up being punished for using the wool, but she felt that the punishment of bloody red marks on her back was better than losing her toes due to the cold.

She was working twelve hours per day at the coffee fields that were not really coffee fields as she quickly learnt. She arrived at the fields before sunrise to find other children already kneeling at the bushes of cocaine leaves. Most of the children didn't talk and had white powder on their hands which Lupe later learnt was to ease the burning sensation of the small cuts the leaves would cause. She didn't have the luxury of the white powder and none of the children ever brought it with them when they arrived. They seemed to arrive from nowhere and disappear back to nowhere at sunset, just like Lupe.

The picking and kneeling caused unbearable pain in Lupe's knees and joints, post-symptoms of cholera, that forced her to tears during the last hours of her work at the fields. She would crawl back to her room in the basement to find her only meal of the day that a black lady working in the kitchen of one of the main buildings provided her. Lupe had never seen a black person in her life, but she couldn't really reject the kind gesture of the woman, especially as it was her only meal of the day.

Besides, even if she felt she was treated badly at the *hacienda*, it was nothing compared to the screams of the old black lady that tormented her nights.

*

The weight Lupe had gained in the post-cholera period, she lost at the *hacienda*. The lack of food and extreme working conditions made her body fat-free and slender like a young boy's. Her head looked too big for her body as the humidity and heat made her curly hair look like an Afro. The nights were freezing after the sun had set and caused her limb and joint pain which made her drag one of her legs behind her due to the pain, so much so that the owner and the weekly visitors to the *hacienda* started referring to her as Quasimodo. She completely lost the nails on her fingers and the long hours in the fields made her fingers curl automatically in like an eagle's claw. She didn't have the luxury of the white powder the other children used in the fields to ease the pain of the work but she quickly learnt that urine would also release the pain and neutralise the acid released by the cocaine leaves during the picking stage. So on a morning, she would urinate in the bucket she used for washing, and then wash her hands and neck to keep the insects and pain away before going to work.

She continued working at the *hacienda* for eight months in total before one day, she arrived back from the field to find her only meal of the day missing. She ran to the back of the kitchen to see two men digging a deep hole in the ground. They had a colourful blanket rolled up next to them and when they lifted it, something fell down from the roll. It was a chubby black arm.

Lupe covered her mouth so as not to scream and backed away to the entrance of her room. On the same day, at that moment, she left the *hacienda* by foot without taking anything with her. She simply walked away.

*

She didn't have a direction nor destination in mind, but somehow she ended up at Chachapoyas, only eighty miles from Jaen. She hitchhiked her way back to Jaen and only three weeks later, she was looking again at the door of her old home. Even the hunger she felt in her stomach couldn't hinder the joy she felt to be back home and she eagerly opened the door. Celestina was washing dishes after breakfast and froze to see her.

Lupe entered the house. "Good morning *hermanita*, is this how you greet your older sister?" she said and looked around the house. It still looked exactly the same as on the day she had left.

Celestina gasped. "Lupe, is that you?"

Lupe smiled. "You should really check your eyesight! Of course it's me, I promised I would be back, didn't I?"

They eyed each other for a moment before Lupe opened her arms and Celestina ran to her, almost making them fall. "*Hermana*, you have no idea how happy I'm to see you again!" she said. "We have missed you."

Tears filled Lupe's eyes to hear and see her sister. Reina arrived soon at the house and by the end of the day, all her siblings had warmly welcomed her back home. Their relationship hadn't changed at all since she had left but they all looked older as if the time she had been gone had not been kind to them. The boys especially had grown, and Jose-Luis was nearly as tall as Celestina, who was the tallest of the sisters.

They were on the floor in a circle listening to her stories when their father arrived. Even he seemed to be happy to see her and came to give her a quick pat on her head before heading outside to the bar. Lupe asked about their mother but no one had seen her for days.

The first night at home, Lupe dreamt of the people at the *hacienda* and she woke up to her own screams. She was tormented by the sight on the last day, a story she had chosen not to share with her siblings. She was too scared to fall asleep again and decided to take a walk around the backyard. She opened the backdoor of the house and closed her eyes to breathe the fresh air and let the night sounds calm her mind when she heard muffled whining close to the toilet facilities. She walked down the steps to the grass and followed the sound behind the toilet, assuming it was an injured animal. She wasn't prepared for the sight she would witness as she walked to the corner of the toilet to see the naked back of her father and female legs crossed around his hips. Her father had his trousers down around his ankles and he was naked, leaning on the toilet wall lost in rhythmic movement. Lupe felt immediately embarrassed to be looking at the tender sexual moment and was about to sneak away when the female flicked her head and Lupe could see light brown hair running down from her father's back. It was not her mother – it was her aunt Esperanza.

*

Next day, Lupe learnt that Esperanza had divorced her husband Fernando right after the baby had been born and had started an affair with their father. In the chaotic months that followed, no one had remembered Lupe at the *hacienda*, a job that had been organised by Fernando, and she had been left there when Fernando had disappeared with his new-born child.

According to Reina, their mother had discovered her husband's love affair at an early stage and was now more explosive and unstable than ever. She didn't come home anymore and rather spent her days in the local bars and at friends' houses. The marriage was undoubtedly over and probably had been for many years before the affair started but they had still remained together until this point. Esperanza had started stopping by the house more often and one night, Reina had heard their father telling her that he would consider taking their mother to a doctor and hopefully having her locked up in a mental institution to guarantee them a peaceful life together with his children without a mentally unstable ex-wife. Esperanza had nodded sympathetically and placed a tender kiss on his lips. Reina had felt a chill go through her spine after the conversation and wanted to find their mother to warn her, but considering the state she was in most of the time, talking to her would just result in violent behaviour.

The week after Lupe came back, she returned to school. She was now thirteen years old and had been in and out of school for years, but this time she felt proud and motivated to be back. Due to her absence for the past full semester, she was still going to the same school as Jose-Luis and was able to escort him just like before.

Jose-Luis had grown a lot during her absence. He was now nearly as tall as Celestina and his hair had grown out and turned into dreadlocks. He didn't talk much and looked rough with a small scar above his right eyebrow that made his eyelid slightly drag on top of his eye. Lupe eyed her brother, she felt that he had closed down completely in just one year, leaving him operating like a robot most of the time.

Close to Christmas time the school always organised a play for the proud parents and relatives. Usually the play involved a religious theme and most years, the *nacimiento*, birth of Jesus Christ, was played over and over again with little twists dependent on the students.

On the day, Lupe had been in the right place at the right time and had been chosen to play the guard of an evil emperor. The theme for the year was to use modern clothing and she had taken the trouble to ask her cousin if she could borrow his father's military uniform. The uniform was too big for her but she had been ecstatic at borrowing something so powerful and spent hours at the school just looking at herself in the mirror. She felt empowered in her masculine attire and it felt good to her.

For as long as she could remember, she had preferred shorts over skirts and had kept her hair short without any girly ribbons or other accessories that her sisters were always fighting to get. She was not interested in make-up and had found herself drawn more to her masculine side, spending hours in the window watching her father shaving his beard and later combing her hair back, imitating the style of her father. The bullying didn't start until her early teens, when she noticed her preference for her masculine side didn't only include clothing, and she found herself being sexually drawn towards the female body; increasingly, she noticed her mind filling with erotic thoughts of relationships with women. The harassment and bullying on the street, when people sometimes threw a stone or two at her over her masculine appearance, didn't bother her too much as she was not ashamed of covering her boyish body with masculine clothing; on the contrary, she felt free being able to express herself on both ways.

Naturally, these were thoughts she kept strictly to herself; she knew

Reina had her doubts, although she never brought them up with her. The problem was, there was nothing Lupe could tell her as sexuality was till taboo in Latin America and strictly kept between a couple, which she was not. She didn't feel confused – rather, she felt free and more comfortable than she had ever been.

The last day of the school term was the grand opening of the play. All parents had been invited, including Lupe's parents. She had spent hours looking for her mother in every bar in Jaen and she had finally found her sitting on the lap of an older man she had never seen before.

Altagracia eyed her middle daughter through drunken eyes. "Oh *cariño*, is that you?" she slurred. "You have become bigger. Fatter," she said and opened her arms, waiting for a hug. She smelled of alcohol and cigarettes.

"*Ma*, good to see you. I have been looking all over for you," Lupe said.

"Oh *cariño*, why would you be looking for me?"

Lupe changed weight on her foot indecisively. "There is a play at school and all parents are invited." She hesitated for a moment. "I have a role in the play as well. I'm a guardian of an evil emperor who is trying to kill baby Jesus."

"I see," her mother replied and lit another cigarette.

Lupe felt uncomfortable for asking anything from their mother as she had always been a bully and never really appreciated her, but a child's unconditional love for a parent still burnt strong. "So, I was wondering if you could come," she said and looked at the man whose lap she was sitting on. "*Papá* promised to come too."

Something lit in the eyes of her mother again. "Well then, of course *cariño*, I will be there," she said and exhaled the remaining smoke out of her lungs before stubbing the empty filter on the ashtray on the table. It still had the red lipstick stain all over it. "What time is it?"

Lupe was surprised but hurried to give her the details. "The play starts at six p.m. today *ma*. I will reserve front row seats for you both," she said and sprinted off.

*

Lupe was excited. Not only had both of her parents promised to come but this could be the chance they needed to reconcile, Lupe thought and hummed all the way home.

At home, she took a cold shower and combed her curly hair back the same way she had seen Fernando do just before they had taken her to the *hacienda*. Ex-husband or not, he had good taste, Lupe thought.

"*Por Dios*, Lupe, you look so handsome!" Reina whooped.

"*Gracias hermana*," Lupe turned and grinned at her.

Reina had changed her white linen dress for one of their mother's dresses as her belly was growing nearly every day. Her skin was radiant, and she had grown a full head of hair. For the first time in her life, she looked stunning and she didn't have to make a joke of it.

Reina, who had matured more in the last year of her life than in the previous fourteen years combined, was now three months pregnant with a boyfriend she had met six months before. The boyfriend was her first and the pregnancy an accident by two young teenagers who really had no idea what they were doing. Even today, looking at her sister getting ready for the school play, she seemed to be totally oblivious that her life was about to change in six short months.

"Are you ready for your big show?" she asked, crossing her hands and looking at Lupe through the mirror.

"Yes Rei, but I'm nervous. What if I forget my lines?"

Reina looked at her. "Lupe you don't have any lines, your part is to stand next to the king who is trying to kill baby Jesus."

Lupe raised her hand and shook her head. "I know, I know, but still." She turned and adjusted the medals on her right chest pocket. She had a last look and put the military hat on.

The green of the military uniform suited her very well and complemented her hair colour, Reina thought while she massaged her stretching belly, but she didn't dare say it out loud as she watched her sister go.

Lupe walked to the school wearing the military uniform. She was attracting the attention of people who didn't dare yell or shout any bullying words, out of respect for her military uniform, which she was secretly happy about.

When she arrived, there was full-blown chaos backstage as the teachers were trying to organise the children into their correct places. Lupe looked at the scene with a smile. She couldn't wait for her parents to see her perform for the first time in her life.

Lupe stayed backstage and waited nervously until the end of the play when it was her turn to take to the stage. She marched proudly onto the stage only to see two empty chairs in the front row.

PART III

Chapter 16

Madrid, Spain, 2008

Lupe was running behind her own schedule.

Her long-term companion, Viviana had once again caused drama for no reason and Lupe hadn't been able to leave the house until she had calmed down. This was usually the case when she was drinking and my God, how the girl could drink, Lupe thought.

Viviana was the type of woman who could easily drink a bigger *marinero* under the table, which was usually something they would laugh about and which had, in fact, won them many free drunken nights in the past.

She was a tall and heavily built lady, which was an obvious sign she was able to handle large amounts of alcohol and men's egos wouldn't allow them to not accept a drinking bet from a woman, resulting in many free drinks over the years. It had been fun and all for the past ten years. However, Lupe was really getting bored with it now.

The fun and entertainment usually ended in the bar and was often followed by aggressive behaviour at home. Lupe tended to send Viviana home early and would make sure she herself would be back after she had fallen asleep. However, on some unfortunate occasions, Viviana would stay awake waiting for her, drunk as a skunk and ready for an argument which she was often not able to even explain through her drunkenness and would end up roaring on the floor until she fell asleep. Sometimes, she would wait for Lupe, sitting in the armchair in the entrance, partly awake, her long black hair falling into a full ashtray next to her. Lupe was surprised she had never burnt her hair and only ended up reeking of smoke like a chimney.

She was a big strong girl and even though Lupe didn't consider herself a fragile little lady, she got hurt most of the time. Obviously, this wasn't something she liked to advertise on the streets and it was starting to annoy her more and more.

Viviana would insult her first, followed by nasty name calling and saying things she couldn't take back. Not that she even *tried,* Lupe thought.

She would hit her with her fists and pull her hair so hard Lupe felt her scalp was about to peel off. It was unimaginable pain but also reminded her how her mother had mistreated her and her sisters when they had been young, breaking her childish heart again. When the words didn't have the desired outcome, Viviana would start throwing anything at hand, dishes and other small items. Luckily, the dishes were mostly commercial mugs and other cheap stuff as she wasn't much of an *ama de la casa*, Lupe snorted.

Lupe would try to calm her down and hold her hands to stop her scratching her face, which normally didn't help at all and in the end, she would be chased onto the street from her own house like a dog, resulting in her sleeping outside in a park as she was too embarrassed to call any of her friends.

She hated every moment of it.

Despite having been a heavy drinker herself for years, Lupe simply couldn't stand drunk women. Drunk women were highly unpredictable and she had had her fair share of experiences with those women.

The truth was, she was overly bored with Viviana and their life style. She had always felt she didn't have much to share with the group she was hanging out with, but life itself had forced her in their direction and there was no way of getting out of it now. Even with Viviana, there had been good times and for the sake of those good times, she was willing to overlook her shortcomings just a bit longer, she sighed as she made her way on the narrow streets of Madrid.

Chapter 17

The night was getting darker in Madrid as she walked down the street she knew so well by now. She had made sure to spend every single evening carefully watching the street for the past two weeks, not wandering around of course, but just to wait and watch the people who lived around the area, forming patterns of their daily lives.

She stopped under the metallic balcony of a red-tiled building and jumped lightly to catch and pull down the metallic ladder connected to the balcony just like in American TV programmes. The ladder gave out a long loud complaint as the rusty parts rubbed against each other as a result of the pulling. Lupe pulled harder to get the ladder to climbing height and then quickly stepped onto it and climbed to the first level and agilely swung herself onto the balcony. She looked around as she pulled the ladder back up to make sure she had not caught any unnecessary attention.

The street remained silent.

She sat down and pulled down the visor of her black Homer Simpson cap and snuggled deeper into her black bomber jacket. She loved the Simpsons characters, especially Homer. His innocence and carefree attitude towards life was catching, especially after all the hardship he went through in each episode; there was always a happy ending. Unfortunately in real life, there was no such luxury.

Lupe yawned and leaned on the building wall closing her eyes for a second. She hadn't been sleeping well for days. The red tile dust would probably colour her backside red but that would be easily brushed away as long as she did it before leaving the balcony. There was no chance to attract any attention like that, she knew it. She turned to face the building and ran her fingers over its rough surface. It was a majestic building that had once glowed gloriously in the sun but was now covered in brownish crumbling shades. Like many other buildings in the area, it had not been maintained for years, even though the surroundings of the building had been clean and tidy this morning, she thought.

Lately, the government had been busy trying to upgrade the reputation of the area to attract wealthy couples and families, but one could see that the area was still occupied by hundreds of people living off government benefit schemes.

Many of the windows were covered in black dusty sheets, although in some windows wet clothes were hung in a range of creative ways to dry in the sun to save on the electricity bill. Lupe looked at the colourful spectrum of clothes pegs that stopped the laundry from falling in the wind. She smiled – it reminded her of her home in Peru and her grandmother.

She looked down on the street and saw the green rubbish bins attached to the metal benches. The bins were tidy and freshly cleaned before five o'clock every morning. Lupe knew this as she had many friends working in the maintenance department for the city of Madrid. They were all hard-working people and the pay was also good. No wonder Madrid was still considered one of the cleanest capitals in the world, she thought.

The government's upgrading initiative for the area had been welcomed by the decision-makers of the city and they had eagerly started approaching people living in the flats, offering them more and more attractive re-housing options without any remarkable success. The people living in the buildings had simply refused to move out from their homes of many years.

The government still failed to realise it was not all about money, Lupe thought sceptically. Yes, money would ease their lives but adjusting to a totally new living environment, especially if you had children, like many of them did, wasn't easy. She sighed and focused her attention again on the street.

*

Her family had migrated to Spain shortly after Lupe had turned sixteen. They had been forced to move after their mother had been diagnosed with early stage breast cancer. The treatment would have cost a fortune in Peru, something they didn't have, so *Altagracia*, as Lupe referred to her by now, had made a choice to move back to Spain. After all, she was Spanish and had a chance to be treated for free by an excellent medical team with excellent odds for a full recovery.

Altagracia hadn't worried about leaving her husband, father of her children, behind. After all, he had had an affair with her sister and they hadn't had intimate relationships ever since. In fact, Lupe still remembered how she used to tell them she had seen it coming from the moment her sister had visited the house for the first time. She had been disgusted by it all and medicated herself in local bars with alcohol that had only fuelled her rage at his betrayal. Her anger had boiled under the surface and resulted in violent encounters with her husband of such intensity that she had nearly ended up in a mental institution which was what her dear traitor husband and sister had planned for her.

It would have been the end of her life, Lupe thought, as a mental institution referral was considered one of the worst kind of sentences in South America. The institutions were old, and the treatments provided were controversial and normally very far away from following any real medical science. The patients would usually get referred involuntarily for life and consisted of people with socially unacceptable sexual orientations, disabilities or elderly people who didn't have family to look after them. Very few of the patients would survive the hard treatment programme the institution had in place and if they did, they would be so badly damaged physically and mentally, they would never be able to live a normal life again.

"I'm not up for those kinds of games," Altagracia had said and left with her children. She had instructed them all to pack their bags and borrowed money from an acquaintance from a local bar. The man had been hopelessly in love with her and considered them practically a family, which had made it so easy to convince him to lend her the money.

She was planning to repay the man.

One day.

They had left one night. Their father had not even come home for the night which had made it almost too easy for them to leave for the airport.

Lupe could still remember the fear of the unknown and how they had grabbed each other's hands and prayed for God to lead them somewhere better. Especially Reina who had been almost nine months pregnant. Altagracia had talked to the local doctor and had him fake the due date to ensure she could fly with them.

Reina had been heartbroken to leave her boyfriend behind who knew nothing about her plan to leave the country with his baby in her belly. That night, she shed hot tears when she climbed up onto the truck full of people that took them to the Shumba Airport in Jaen to their new life.

They had arrived at Adolfo Suárez Madrid–Barajas Airport in Madrid and one of her mother's cousins had driven them to Coruña on the coast of Spain. The trip had taken nearly six hours and they had been overly exhausted when they had eventually arrived. The first stop had been a convent run by nuns where their mother had explained she needed to establish her life first in the country before she could even consider taking care of anyone else and for that reason she had left Celestina, Jose-Luis and Lupe behind. She had taken Reina, who was the most useful for her, pregnant or not, and their baby brother Jorge who had always been her favourite, before she had restarted the engine and driven away.

She had left them standing on one side of the road in front of the grey stone building that looked more like a prison to them. They had watched her go but none of them had cried.

Chapter 18

"Know your area" was the first step in every well-planned robbery. Nowadays, endless holiday pictures on social media, posted travel plans on Facebook and bragging about expensive items had made it so easy to rob a house in no time, Lupe thought and laughed silently from her hiding place in the blind spot corner across the street, where the streetlight had burnt out. People didn't realise that indications on social media of upcoming holidays and trips provided free information for burglars to target specific houses. Extravagant lifestyles imposed *envy* among people, Lupe knew it.

Cameras or motion detectors really didn't matter or deter anyone anymore as many burglars had quite advanced IT skills – they knew their *shit*, Lupe thought.

She concentrated her attention again on the house on the opposite side of the road.

They had picked that specific house based on the people who lived in it. The father was travelling most of the time for work and the wife was keeping herself busy with a lover on a private estate in Lake Como in Italy. Lupe had seen them yesterday morning leaving the house with suitcases, cuddling and kissing on the way to the taxi. They had two children, a girl and a boy, who were both studying abroad, which meant the house was often left unattended.

Lupe knew from her social media research that the daughter was in her early twenties and studying at the prestigious University of Bocconi in Milan, which was considered one of the top universities in Europe. Lupe never went to university herself, which was something she had always been quite bitter about. She knew that if she had only been given a chance, she would have had an amazing life ahead of her. She could have been a legitimate businesswoman running her own chain of Peruvian restaurants. She had had so much planned. The plan had ended up flying out of the window when Reina had needed Lupe's deposit to bail out her ex-husband from jail. Lupe would have left him to rot in there, but for the sake of her niece, she couldn't do it, so she had used her deposit to bail him out and lost her dream.

That's what families are for, she sighed and sat down, leaning back on the wall.

She would have also settled for a career as a police officer but during the physical tests she was told she was too short for a law enforcement career.

Once again, the cards she had been dealt in life had not been in her favour.

*

The house stood peacefully in its place. Lupe closed her eyes for a moment. She could sit like this for hours. She had spent three years in jail, sitting and counting the tiles on the walls, for a very poorly planned jewellery shop robbery. It had been a painful way of learning but consequently she felt so much stronger now.

Jose-Luis, her younger brother, had also been involved in the robbery and for his sake, during the three-month investigation process, Lupe had executed a plan to move him from Spain to the UK.

The 17-year-old boy in a man's body, without a word of English, had shed tears at the airport and begged her not to put him on the plane.

"*Hermana*, I don't know anyone there, I don't know the language, please let me stay here," he had cried and nervously wiped his eyes and nose on the grey hoodie Lupe had stolen from the souvenir shop in the airport. It said "I love Madrid", which she thought would have been a bittersweet memory but instead, Jose-Luis had thrown a vigorous punch at her, landing on her lower lip and making it bleed.

She was heavily built, and he was still a boy so the fight had quickly dried up as she had pushed him down on the ground and given him a couple of firm slaps on the face.

It was called respect in their family: you respect your elders and strength is everything. For some reason it didn't make her smile anymore as she looked at the face of her baby brother filled with sorrow.

She had patted his hair and noticed it was covered in *piejos*. Lice.

"*Mierda,*" she said and turned his head from one side to the other to inspect the damage further.

His head had bristled with the small insects and when he had shaken his head the lice eggs had fallen down like snowflakes on his shoulders. "What are you looking at?" he had asked and scratched his head.

"Nothing *hermano*," Lupe had said and taken her cap and put it on her brother's head. This will do, she had thought, hoping the flight attendants wouldn't notice anything before they had landed making a silent note to send him medicine for lice in London.

Sending her baby brother away was probably the hardest thing she had ever done in her life but deep down in her heart she knew it was the right thing to do. In Spain, he wouldn't stand a chance of changing his life. His friends wouldn't allow him to do it. He would be condemned to a rotten life of criminality and looking over his shoulder for the rest of his life. They said prison would make him or break him but Lupe wasn't worried about other prisoners breaking him. She was worried about the man they would make him.

She couldn't allow that to happen.

*

The lights were still on in the house.

The father usually left the lights or TV on when he left for short business trips to prevent anyone knowing the house was empty, which made Lupe almost laugh out loud.

People failed to realise that robbery was a result of carefully planned operations and every carefully planned operation started with *watching* the house for days.

Lights or loud TV on in a residential area two days in a row day and night wasn't really believable and usually there were two options: the house was left empty or someone inside had suffered a heart attack or equivalent accident. Either way, the house was an attractive target for a robbery.

Lupe had started her research with the basics: she had stalked the children on social media and gained information about the whole family's daily life from their Instagram and Facebook accounts.

Additionally, there was a bunch of good gentlemen driving taxis in Madrid who were in desperate need of quick cash and didn't mind sharing information about their passengers if rewarded well for it. Luckily, in this case, the family almost religiously used the same taxi company for their travels, so Lupe had been able to get her hands on their travel timetable for weeks which had made it even easier to plan the robbery. It had cost her only some hundreds of euros, but the return on the investment would be worth it, she thought.

Lupe wasn't particularly proud of her choice of living, but she was proud of how professionally she *handled* her business. After all, they were all honest, hard-working citizens trying to make a living which was not easy in an expensive city like Madrid.

True, honesty and integrity had to be *bent* from time to time, however, she tended to rather point the finger at the careless people who left their homes unsecured like this, almost as if *wanting* to challenge people like her to try their luck.

Plus, they usually had full insurance cover so they really didn't lose anything they wouldn't get back, she thought. Nevertheless, she had a rule never to touch or take any personal items such as photos or rings with someone's initial or a note engraved. It was *too personal*, she thought and touched the rough grey stone necklace around her neck that had become her talisman for luck over the years.

No, she only targeted the valuable items that were easy to sell and able to generate quick cash for her, and people's memories were worthless in that sense. She dug her mobile phone from her pocket to check the time then slowly stood up on the balcony and carefully, without a sound, slid down the ladder.

It was time.

*

She jogged to the end of the street, their agreed meeting place.

The others had arrived already and were waiting for her in a white van she had arranged for them earlier in the day.

She always made sure the van was equipped with a powerful engine, but was a basic model and colour that wouldn't attract any attention on the streets. White was good, as they were often used as courier vehicles. She knew this after spending years in the traffic as a courier. She still did it from time to time to keep one legal job and to enable her to explain her earnings and spending. A lesson she had learnt the hard way long ago.

*

She arrived silently and nodded her head to the team. They opened the back door and she jumped in.

She loved her team like a family: Nelson, her trusted driver, ex-courier as well, who reminded her of Jose-Luis, her dear baby brother, whom she had taught to dance salsa and then abandoned and sent to the UK.

For his own good though.

Lupe had never liked having him do these jobs with her, but before she had sent him away, he had suffered some major set-backs after dropping out from school and losing his job, so he really hadn't had many options considering how difficult it was to find a decent job in Madrid.

She also loved Marcos and Randolfo very dearly, the crazy brothers she had met in a bar fight years ago. It had been a nasty bar fight and they had lost not only their dignity, but also one dear common friend, which had only made them closer. True, the boys were not the sharpest pencils in a pencil case, but they meant well, and they were the muscle for these kind of projects.

All very loyal and long-time friends.

*

They drove slowly up the street and finally stopped the car in front of the garage connected to the house. Nelson killed the engine.

They waited a moment to see if they had woken up any neighbours, but the street remained peaceful. They opened the car doors when Marcos lost control of his door and it slammed shut. All of them jumped in the air.

"You stupid moron, why don't you call the police, the priest and your ex-wife, *joder*!" Lupe hissed as loud as she could, glaring at him. He made a peace sign in the air as an apology. Lupe rolled her eyes.

They switched on their flashlights and started walking towards the door. Earlier in the day, Randolfo had worked his magic and switched off the four closest streetlights, leaving only a dim light towards the side door they planned to use to enter the house.

He was often used as their electrician because he used to work as an electrician for a small company downtown of Madrid before they had sacked him for stealing supplies to refurbish his ex-wife's flat in the city centre in the hopes of gaining her back. It hadn't worked, and he had lost his job. Although the work he did for them wasn't anything Lupe couldn't have done herself, she thought proudly, remembering the countless lessons in maintenance work a gentle man called Sam had once given her.

All Randolfo had to do was cut the right wire to turn off the light so that the light bulb itself wouldn't explode and attract unnecessary attention. So far, he had done good work; the lights were unbroken but not lit.

Lupe could feel the familiar adrenaline rush going through her body like electric shocks as they proceeded to the door.

She knew the house had an alarm system, and a good one too. Luckily, they were blessed with a machine that, if connected right, would suppress the alarm system for the required period of time.

In practical terms, they would intercept the frequency signals sent between the motherboard and the sensors and take control of the alarm system and prevent it triggering the alarm.

Once they were out but within two miles distance, Lupe would turn off the machine and allow the signals to run freely again, without anyone noticing anything.

She had paid a lot of money for the machine, but it had definitely been worth every penny and had already paid itself off many times. More importantly, it provided some peace of mind to the team, which was one of the most important aspects of a robbery; one couldn't put a price on focus and concentration.

They had chosen the side door mainly as the doors on the main entrance were usually heavier built and the locks more difficult to pick. Besides, the main control was usually situated not at the front entrance, but at the most used door of the house: the side door leading to the garage.

They stopped in front of the door and Lupe quickly picked the lock and opened the door. Before the alarm went off, she connected the alarm silencer to the main control board. The alarm gave a sleepy sound before going silent again.

It was deactivated.

Lupe motioned the boys to get into the house behind her. They were smiling and entered the door leading to the kitchen.

They were all dressed in dark colours with caps and gloves, but Lupe was still worried about leaving evidence behind. "Don't touch anything you are not going to take and for Christ's sake, keep your caps on," she said and the boys nodded their heads and continued to the corridor.

Lupe followed but as she entered the house, a cold shiver ran through her body as if someone had walked over her grave.

She stopped for a second to let her racing heart calm down. After all, this was not the time to lose focus, which could end badly for all of them, she thought and waited, but the edge of panic never arrived.

On the contrary, she felt her luck was about to change.

Chapter 19

Ellen was tired.

She had arrived earlier at Gisela's family house in Madrid via Barcelona.

Many Iberian flights flew through Barcelona nowadays instead of direct flights from Italy, which made Ellen annoyed for wasting numerous hours at the airports for short distance flights.

This was definitely not the best use of her time, she thought and brushed her blonde hair from her sweaty forehead whilst wheeling her small cabin bag up the front stairs of the house. She opened the door and cool air welcomed her and she sighed for relief as she made her way upstairs to the guest room.

It was evening but the temperature remained high in the heart of the city without a breeze of fresh air, which made it feel like a hellhole for Ellen.

Truth being told, Lucas had offered her a priority ticket, which would have included full access to the golden priority lounge and a first-class ticket, but Ellen had declined his kind offer.

Now that she thought about it, she didn't exactly remember why she had said no to him, but the idea of starting her trip with something offered by him gave her stomach a twist. She felt the need to be *in control* of the situation. Gain her independence back, which she had lost completely after meeting Lucas. Rebel. Fight back.

His full name was Lucas Bernard. A complete gentleman from head to toe. Suited and booted with expensive Italian clothing covering his six foot figure.

He had grown up in a small village close to Naples in Southern Italy, and spent a good part of his teens in the countryside in Scotland and his university years in London. He had earned his full attorney licence at the age of 29 and moved back to London. He hadn't come back to Italy until seven years later with numerous victorious court cases up his sleeve and a fully shaped British accent to charm the ladies on the Milanese streets.

Ellen had met him in a small coffee shop close to the *Duomo* called Three Sisters. It had been a small family-owned coffee shop close to Ellen's university where she had studied at that time.

It had been a hot day and Ellen had opened the top button of her light blue dress shirt, rolled up her long sleeves above her elbows and clipped her long blonde locks up. The sweat had been running down her tights as a result of a tight pencil skirt she had worn, which had made her delicate and tanned legs glow in the sun. This had not been left unnoticed by the fellow commuters and every now and then Ellen could feel the intensive Italian stares on her body.

She had arrived at the coffee shop in rush hour and the place had been full of people casually enjoying their morning coffee and brioche at the counter. She had joined the queue and soon made her order. Whilst Ellen had been looking for coins from her handbag to pay for her café macchiato, a hand had appeared behind her and dropped some euro coins on the counter.

"It's on me," a masculine British accent behind her said.

Ellen had turned around and in seconds been face to face with a man wearing a new Armani suit.

There was nothing British about his tall dark figure and nearly black eyes. He stood straight and although he didn't exactly look athletic he was definitely someone who took care of himself. His straight hair was forced back with shiny gel and his smile offered her a full set of perfectly lined white teeth. He had been wearing a basic black Armani suit as Ellen had thought in the first place, and around his wrist had been a traditional Gucci watch with a red-green strap.

He had looked everything Ellen had hoped for on paper; hence she had made no objections when he offered to pay for her coffee and invited her to sit down with him.

She had been smitten immediately, so much that she had skipped her classes for the day.

Soon after, they agreed to go on a date, which had led to a second and third one and before she knew it, she had been in a fully committed relationship.

Ellen couldn't believe her luck.

They quickly formed a routine in their lives, spending most of the weekdays in Milan and on weekends they usually flew down to the south to his parents' estate.

The estate was a massive collection of well-planned buildings, sports courts and swimming pools. The tennis court was the biggest private court Ellen had ever seen, even though she had never seen anyone actually using it. Close to the swimming pool was a table and chairs set that could have seated twenty people, and behind the table was a fully established kitchen hub including a barbeque and pizza oven, custom made in Naples, an honorary gift for Lucas' father.

The estate was situated very close to the Amalfi Coast and during the early hours of the mornings, Ellen tended to sneak out alone and walk along the beach breathing the fresh air and digging her toes deep into the cool sand. It seemed to calm down her anxious mind and racing thoughts.

Ellen had always loved Southern Europe and Mediterranean culture. She was fascinated by a culture that allowed individuals to openly express their feelings, a culture where it was OK not to feel OK. It was completely opposite to the culture she had grown up with where she had been well-fed and educated but expressing one's feelings was often considered a sign of weakness. Her father had been the worst in the family and even the hottest tears of a young child couldn't soften him, and he had turned his back on it every time.

In theory, it was the most practical system to follow, but supressing one's feelings often resulted in mental illness, alcoholism and increased suicide rates; people simply didn't feel good. The suicide rates in the country and isolation of the individuals were sky high and during the long, dark winter months when the sun didn't rise at all, it was like a plague wiping out the weak across the country and only letting the strongest ones live, Ellen thought and closed her eyes letting the memories wash over her mind. Life was not about pleasure and enjoyment but hard work and suffering that wouldn't save anyone in the end. The American dream was taught to be a fantasy and finding a workplace and staying there until the bitter end was recommended. Ellen knew it, it was even said in the national anthem of the country.

The closed minds, poverty and the struggle to accept the mentality had driven her away from her beloved the country and made her vulnerable, desperately seeking her place in the world of happiness and sense of belongingness. She knew she was meant for something different.

Hence why Ellen had been ecstatic at having met Lucas who seemed to be everything she ever hoped for. However, as she spent more time with him, she started noticing that in his case, the stereotypes didn't seem to work in her favour at all.

Although Lucas was born to a Mediterranean culture, his character was a mixture of the bad qualities of the different cultures he had been exposed to ever since he was a little boy.

He had British calmness in his acts but remained totally under his parents' control without questioning them at all. He completely lacked a sense of humour or his own opinion and very soon Ellen had started to resent spending time alone with him.

When she had tried to confront him and raised her voice, he had locked her inside the tennis court garage. She had stayed in the garage for hours and when he had released her, Ellen had completely shut down and to her surprise, he seemed to have no problem with it. On the contrary, he seemed to be quite happy.

Whereas Lucas was completely oblivious of her needs, his mother had taken a firm role in educating her son's new foreign girlfriend.

She had instructed someone to follow her around and Ellen was almost completely sure someone was lurking around most of the time when they were together.

Just before Ellen had left to go to Madrid, Lucas had made a proposal that they would move permanently to his parents' estate and occupy part of the house his parents lived in.

"Ellen, I'm quite sure you realise that the rents in Milan are sky high and we spend all our weekends here anyway. I can do my work from here and fly to Milan a couple of times per week and you can finish your studies here," he had said to her.

Ellen had been stunned and didn't know what to say which he had taken as silent approval.

"And I can even contact your professors," he had continued. "Most of them are clients of the firm anyway. I'm sure they wouldn't mind your distance studies as you are so close to graduating," he had said, placing his hands on her shoulders.

Ellen had looked in his eyes and seen his open pride at coming up with a such great idea which was obviously initiated and fed by his mother.

She had said nothing and instead smiled politely, excused herself and walked to her room and made arrangements for her trip to Spain.

In the plane she had had time to think and reconsider their relationship. On paper, he was the perfect husband candidate for her but for some reason he left her completely cold in other aspects; the good points would not be enough to compensate for the dictator mother and the lack of connection and chemistry.

Ellen sighed and glanced quickly at the next seat.

The gentleman in 5C had tried to start a conversation with her since they took off from Malpensa Airport. He was a nice-looking Italian businessman wearing a designer suit, as they all did. Ellen hadn't responded to his eye contact attempts and admiring stares, but she was fully aware of them.

She wasn't trying to be cocky, but she knew she was beautiful and she had had her ways with men for as long as she could remember. She knew her neck arched beautifully, and her narrow ankles were made to wear a dress. At the end of the day, she knew she was not the most beautiful woman in the world, but what other women were still completely clueless about was that it was all about biology, science and manipulation.

Passion was a myth and there was no such thing as love, that couldn't have been measured by one's bank account balance and ability to provide. Ellen knew it and she never made the mistake of thinking otherwise.

In this case, however, the price of a comfortable life might be too high as she still hoped deep down for some sort of passion she admitted and sighed.

Luckily, there were plenty of fish in the sea and if the price to be with Lucas was too high, the man in seat 5C might just be the cure, she thought and locked her eyes with his.

He dropped his *Financial Times* immediately and ordered two glasses of champagne.

*

Ellen opened the bathroom door and hot steam escaped from the room like smoke. She felt her muscles tense again due to the drop in temperature and tied the bath towel tighter around her body.

She walked to the dressing stand and changed her bath towel for a lace dressing gown she had found in the guest room.

She was just about to finish applying lotion to herself when she heard the front door opening and closing.

At first, she thought her mind was playing tricks on her as she was quite sure Gisela hadn't mentioned any scheduled cleaning or handyman work for the weekend and had said her father would not be coming back before tomorrow. However, there was always a chance she had missed something, or the business requirements had changed, Ellen thought and quietly opened the bedroom door and tightened the dressing gown around her waist.

Truth being told, she really didn't want to end up alone with Gisela's father – she still remembered the lustful, wandering eyes she had witnessed the first time she had met him. She couldn't decide which would be the worst scenario: being robbed or spending time alone with her friend's father. After all, she knew how older Italian men were and their mentality of Eastern European women.

She kept moving towards the stairs and went down to the ground floor of the house where she heard quiet whispers and the sound of pulling and pushing of furniture followed by a string of Spanish swear words.

She froze and stood quietly.

She wasn't really up for chitchat with anyone, especially in her dressing gown, but she wanted to make her presence known as soon as possible. After all, it would only be common courtesy considering Gisela's family had allowed her to stay in their house for the weekend at very short notice; she also wanted to avoid anyone mistaking her for a burglar who had entered the house.

She passed the corridor to the kitchen and saw the alarm light off, but the door firmly closed. The alarm didn't really worry her yet as Gisela had mentioned occasional power cuts in the house that would come back eventually. She listened tentatively and followed the voices to the main living room and peeked inside from the corner of the entrance arch but wasn't prepared to witness the sight in front of her eyes.

It was like time stopped as she saw four black-dressed and hooded men holding a giant TV that Gisela's father had purchased last year before the school year had started, which had been ripped down from the wall.

The men froze immediately when they saw her peeking from the corridor like a rabbit caught in the headlights.

The shortest of the hooded men recovered from the shock first. "*Rubia*, please don't move, we are just about to leave," he said and held his hands up as a surrendering gesture.

"This is the last item we want," he said and waved at the MacBook Pro in his hands. "You never saw us, and we never saw you, *entiendes amor?*" he smiled behind his mask.

He had a very heavy accent and Ellen wasn't able to determine if he was local or foreign. She was in shock and couldn't move but just stared at the intruders. The seconds passed and finally the intruder lost his patience. "*Por favor* blondie *reactiona*! We don't have all night here!"

His rude and demanding voice was enough to break the spell and fuelled Ellen's body with adrenaline. So she turned around and ran.

"Lupe, go after her! The bitch is going to call the cops!" Nelson screamed with panic in his voice. Lupe let out nearly all the swear words she could think of and passed the MacBook Pro to him. He was so nervous he almost dropped it. "Careful with that *amigo,* if you break it, you buy it," she winked. "Don't worry, I'll deal with her," she said and jogged after the blonde girl.

Chapter 20

*D*amn, the blondie was a quick and very unfortunate addition to her perfectly planned project Lupe thought and eyed the stairway, which she was pretty sure the blondie had run up. She would have to tie her down in one of the rooms making sure she wasn't able to use the phone before they were done with their work. She might even cut the telephone lines in the house just to be sure.

Lupe sighed with frustration.

She didn't like it when her plans went wrong. In card games it felt like a joker was put on the table. Now, she was just forced to sort it out.

Risk mitigation, she called it.

Risk mitigation.

Lupe ran upstairs taking two steps at a time.

"Lupe, take care of *la gringa* will you? We will finish the job here and wait for you in the car!" Marcos yelled after her.

Lupe eyed the space with curiosity. The upstairs hallway was more of a large corridor with several closed doors. The walls were painted in light burgundy and decorated with rectangular mirrors with golden details to create a sense of space. At the beginning of the hallway there was a side table with golden framed family photos, matching with the rest of the décor. Designer made, Lupe assumed.

All the doors were closed.

It would take her forever to find the blondie who was probably already on the phone to the police.

"Lupe! Are you OK?" she heard again the nagging, high-pitched voice that belonged to Marcos.

Lupe frowned. "For goodness sake, stop calling me by my name, *cabrón*. Get in the car now!" she yelled back in frustration.

"Right…."

She heard a dragging sound as Marcos dragged his legs against the floor on the way to the car. A clear sign he was annoyed with her, but she just had to deal with his drama later. That would be after she had found *gringa linda, foreign girl,* as she had named her in her head.

She almost thought their exchange of words had ruined her attempt of finding the blondie, but the moment Marcos raised his voice again, Lupe heard a slight movement behind the third door on the right.

She smiled silently; she would need to thank Marcos later.

Lupe approached the door without making a sound. Silence was always an asset before attacking as it would offer her an element of surprise, she thought and almost chuckled. The blondie wouldn't see her coming and would probably panic and beg her not to kill her.

The thought of the blondie on her knees in front of her made butterflies run through her stomach but she ignored them. It was only adrenaline, she was sure.

Lupe reached the door that was still slightly ajar and pushed it more open to peek inside.

She scanned the whole room but couldn't see the blondie anywhere.

Like other parts of the house, the room was decorated with a good eye.

It was a clear bedroom and office combination. The room had two sets of massive windows with heavy curtains settling all the way down to the floor. One of the window sets was situated on the left side of the room and the other on the right side at the front and bringing light to a dark mahogany office table sitting in the corner with a small filing cabinet beside it.

The room was dominated by a massive bed in the middle with shiny burgundy bed covers including pillows and matching nightstands on each side of the bed. There was a paperback book on one of the nightstands on the left with coins on top and a vanilla lip balm. The corners of the book were twisted as if the blondie had read it many nights before going to sleep.

Lupe smiled softly.

She loved intellectual women and the thought of someone reading in bed before going to sleep reminded her of a stability she had never had in her life. She had always wondered how it would feel after a long hard day at work to see someone in bed concentrating on a book while waiting for her. Naturally, that someone would lift her head, smile and invite her to the bed before making love to her softly.

For some reason, a picture of the blondie rose in her mind.

She had never shared the thought with anyone, as most of her mates were more fascinated by hard core porn, but for her, that was porn to the fullest.

Lupe visually checked the windows, both tightly closed including the curtains.

The office table was matched with a leather chair and next to it, by the window, was a white door leading presumably to the bathroom. The door was closed, but one of the long window curtain corners was stuck between the door and the doorway as if someone had slammed the door closed in a hurry.

Lupe closed the bedroom door behind her and started slowly approaching the bathroom door.

"*Rubia mia*, I know you are in there," she sang. "Listen, I'm not going to hurt you, I just want to make sure you are not doing anything stupid, *corazon*," she said. "I know you don't live in this house, so there is literally nothing we are taking from you," she continued and quickly looked around to see if there were any valuables. "We are just a bunch of good guys trying to make a living in these difficult economic times, do you understand me?"

Lupe waited and listened.

She heard nothing and froze for a second.

OK, she wasn't going to play hide and seek with the blondie, Lupe thought. She literally didn't have time for it.

She hardened her voice. "*Rubia,* I know you are in there, answer me! It will be much easier if you cooperate!"

Lupe was convinced the blondie was hiding in the bathroom. That was the most obvious place where people hid, not realising that while the lock on the door might momentarily protect them from the intruder the room wouldn't offer any escape from the house itself. In the worst case, there was no phone connection or any other communication method to the outside world, which would leave the most persistent intruder in an advantageous position. She must be in the bathroom, she couldn't have gone farther, Lupe thought.

Suddenly she stopped on her heels.

What if she didn't speak English at all? Lupe wondered and quickly forced the image of the blondie in front of her eyes.

To be honest, she hadn't looked like a typical English girl as far as Lupe knew. She had looked different, but Lupe couldn't exactly determine how – Polish or Romanian perhaps?

Lupe reached the bathroom door and was ready to try the doorknob when she saw a sudden movement out of the corner of her right eye.

The blondie attacked her with a lamp she had presumably taken from the office table. No wonder the table had looked suspiciously empty, Lupe thought as she got ready to take the upcoming hit.

The lamp landed on her right arm and shoulder area and the lamp foot, made of glass, shattered on her, making small cuts on her tattooed arm.

"Aaah, *mierda*, stupid blonde bitch!" Lupe cried out loud, holding her arm.

She couldn't believe the blondie had used the element of surprise on her.

The blondie had attacked her from the right, injuring her stronger side, but luckily, years of experience in street fighting had taught her to withstand pain well and she turned around quickly to avoid a second hit.

There wasn't much left of the lamp anyway and when the next hit came, Lupe was able to grab the remains of it. "Careful with that *amor*, you wouldn't want to hurt me, would you? A prison is not really for your type of little ladies, trust me," she said and smiled. "You would need someone to protect you day and night *mamita* and I'm not sure that would even be enough to keep you safe." She said and looked into her eyes.

They looked *wild*.

The blondie didn't hit hard. Lupe could tell she didn't have a single violent gene in her tiny body. She was more *determined*. In survival mode. Desperate to save herself from the unknown.

Lupe had to admire her for that.

Before the blondie was able to land a third hit, Lupe grabbed the lamp and twisted the blondie's hands above her head.

Lupe noticed that she was a bit taller than her, and realised that raising her hands as high as possible would make her loosen her grip. She was right and a few seconds later she could feel the blondie's hands around the lamp loosen.

She was tired, consumed by all the adrenaline, *pobrecita*, Lupe smiled.

She shoved her hands forward over the blondie's head and pushed them both up against the office table to get her off balance. She gave out a protesting whine as Lupe leaned on top of her.

For the first time she was able to take a good look at the blonde mystery lady.

She wasn't as tiny as Lupe had thought in the first place and was more of a curvy type of a woman. She had a very feminine appearance with moderate sized perky breasts, a pair of slender legs, a small waist and rounded behind, all hidden under her black lace dressing gown and when Lupe looked down, she could see pink nail polish on her toenails. A bunch of her wavy, blonde hair had fallen out of the hair clip and was framing her heart-shaped face. She smelled divine, lilies or jasmine, Lupe couldn't decide.

She had clearly just strutted out from the shower, which was probably the reason why they hadn't heard her when they had arrived, Lupe thought and let her eyes travel from her body to her eyes.

Lupe gasped.

Her eyes were captivating.

Her blue eyes were like the raging Pacific Ocean during the worst storms off the coast of Peru which she had seen so many times before; waves hitting the shore aggressively and forming a greenish and bluish mixture of colours, offering a challenge to anyone who dared to disrespect them.

At first, Lupe thought she saw fear in them, but looking closer, she noticed that the blue eyes were full of anger. *Rage.*

The blondie was pissed off and mad as hell.

Lupe didn't know why, but she liked the observation as strong characters had always been very appealing to her.

It *fascinated* her.

The blondie broke the spell first.

She jerked her body forward trying to get out of her unfavourable position, but she didn't have the strength for it. Lupe tried to take the lamp out of her hands, but the blondie was like a pit-bull holding the lamp as if her life depended on it.

"OK *gringa linda*, it is a tie then?" Lupe said and moved her head closer to hers. Their lips were only a couple of inches apart and she could smell the sweet vanilla scent of the lip balm on her lips.

"How would you like to proceed? You are alone and I have my mates downstairs who are dying to come upstairs and see you. Do you really want that?" Encouraged by the slight hesitance Lupe could see in her eyes she continued. "I should also mention that they are all single, far from being gentlemen and have been without a woman for some time now. I highly doubt they would respect your virtue, you know *niña mia*?"

The blondie stayed silent, looking at her intently.

Lupe was stunned. She didn't want the blondie to panic but she would have expected a small reaction after her threats and in the situation itself. Normally, there would have already been a series of screams and begging of not wanting to get killed, but this woman was like a wall.

No, like an *ice castle*.

If she was a player, she would have done amazing in poker, Lupe thought.

Then she noticed something shifting in her eyes, fear or pain maybe. The blondie was seemingly feeling uncomfortable as she started shuffling under her.

Lupe looked around, trying to understand the source of her discomfort.

Her instincts had been on high alert when she had scanned the room in the first place but she ran her eyes around once more to ensure there was no danger before slowly moving her eyes back to the blondie and down to her body to find one of the perfect creamy breasts peeking out from the black lace dressing gown she was wearing.

The blondie was equipped with a perfect pair, Lupe thought as she admired the rounded, creamy breast with its pink hardened nipple.

The blondie looked at her with a frightened stare as a rabbit caught in the headlights.

For the first time since Lupe had seen her, she let the rush of desire wash over her. It felt like warm caramel and butterflies deep down in her stomach making her toes curl in her black shoes and sweat break under her mask. She didn't exactly plan her next move, just followed her instinct and lowered her head to take the nipple in her mouth.

The moment her lips touched the delicate skin, she felt like lightning had struck her and run an electrical current through her body.

It was chemistry. *Connection.*

She started sucking greedily and swirling her tongue around the hardened nipple.

Lupe felt the blondie tense under her body but then literally melt in her arms.

She closed her eyes and let a gasp of desire escape from her lips and whimpered.

Lupe gently let go of the blondie's hands to allow her other hand to cup her other breast, caressing it with slow round movements, taking her time. Her skin felt like silk and she smelled like lilies in the summer, like an ocean breeze.

She hesitated for a second and then felt the blondie's fingers on her head, running through her curls. She stopped for a moment to see if the blondie was going to try something, but her touch felt genuine.

The whisper that came from her soft lips sent Lupe out of the planet and the world she lived in.

"Oh, please don't stop."

At first, Lupe thought she had imagined the words coming out of her mouth as every single cell of her body was focused on sensing this amazing sexual desire she had felt since she had laid her eyes on the blondie in the living room entrance and run after her.

Her words were real and set her off like a storm.

Without a second thought, Lupe picked her up and lifted her on top of the table. She crushed her body against her chest and ripped her dressing gown off her shoulders.

The blondie was just as taken as she was, possessed. She held her small hands tightly on Lupe's head guiding her mouth deeper onto her breasts, giving a little tug on her hair. She threw her head from one side to another and bit her lip. She looked stunning, like a goddess.

Deeply entranced and lost within each other, they barely heard Marco's voice from downstairs. "Lupe, are you OK? Ten minutes and we are out *amiga*!"

They both froze and the blondie tensed under her before she started fighting against her like a wounded animal trying to wriggle her body free.

Lupe could tell some of her movements were taken from action movies, which worked great on TV but had no value in the real world.

She felt sorry for her. She didn't stand a chance.

Determined, Lupe pushed her all the way down on the table and trapped her hands above her head and forced her legs around both sides of her body. With curiosity, she slowly opened her dressing gown just to learn that the blondie had been fully naked all this time with a beautiful, well trained body and a belly button piercing.

"*Por Dios amor mio,*" Lupe gasped. "I knew there was something special about you, but my imagination didn't reach even close to the reality. You look like a porn star," she smiled. "I would buy all your movies from the market to ensure no one would see them but me, *corazon mio*, no doubt."

The blondie didn't respond immediately but was not fighting back as forcefully as before and allowed Lupe to run her hands against her naked body. "Naughty, very naughty girl you are *mi niña*, my girl, I can tell," she said and kissed her on her stomach right next to the belly button piercing she had been admiring.

The fight inside the blondie quickly died completely and with glazed eyes she let Lupe grab the rope from her pocket that she carried for emergencies.

Normally, the emergency would involve using the rope as a last resort for climbing out of a window, but this would do just fine, she thought and swirled the rope around the blondie's hands and leaned on top of her to thread it around the table before catching it with her knees on the other side. She picked up the rope from between her legs and tightened it up.

The blondie's hands jerked above, and she gave a loud cry.

Aroused by her cry and excited by freeing her hands, she greedily ran them over her body and touched her belly button piercing.

A blue diamond. Like her eyes, she thought and slid the rest of the dressing gown off from her legs to expose her body fully.

She wasn't prepared for the sight in front of her eyes. The blondie was beautiful in more than one way and when she touched the naked skin around her sex she could feel her fingers slide up and down in her wetness. She forced their bodies closer. "Oh, *niña mia*, you are so wet," she said and closed her eyes. "What are you doing to me?" she murmured and tried to slide two fingers inside her just to feel the heat of her body, but the blondie was so small and tight she hesitated. After all, her intention wasn't to hurt her, just to enjoy her for a moment.

The blondie moved under her.

"Shh, *con calma amor mio*, relax and let me enjoy you for a moment. God, you feel so good I can barely breath," Lupe said.

She knew she couldn't be a virgin but there was something innocent and *evil* about her at the same time, she couldn't entirely explain. Truth being told, the blondie didn't feel overly experienced, and her reactions felt very natural to her but still there was something she couldn't put her finger on, no matter how much she tried. She could hear her whispers and quiet moans that she so adorably tried to hide from her. "Oh, *corazon mio*, I can feel how your body trembles under my touch it is driving me crazy. Let me own you, take you to the moon and back until you forget your last name and have mine on your lips. Trust me."

If possible, encouraged by her words, the blondie got even wetter under her and Lupe could sense her body was trembling and waiting for fulfilment.

She was so close. Lupe could feel it.

She slid her finger out of her and knelt to kiss her between her inner thighs. She let her kisses wander to where her legs joined and let her tongue gently touch her sensitive area, gently teasing it, sucking it.

"Oh my God," the blonde tensed and a long moan escaped from her lips.

Her loud moans drove Lupe's determination of having her orgasm right there for her. To own her.

Her thoughts drove her to the edge of insanity and, just then and there, Lupe lost track of time and place and decided it wasn't going to be only *the blondie* who would enjoy this. She was scared of losing the memory of her and wanted to have some of it with her before she left the apartment tonight.

Un solo recuerdo. She didn't ask anything more.

The blondie protested loudly when Lupe quickly let go of her to undress herself, only undoing her belt and letting the black trousers fall down to her ankles. She couldn't risk letting her see her face and recognising her in the future, *judging* her for what she was about to do.

The black trousers fell easily, as she had lost a bit of weight lately.

She forced the blondie's legs more open and lifted her lower body up from her buttocks to bring her closer to her, adjusting her legs around her waist and gaining even better contact with her.

The blondie's eyes widened and were full of passion and excitement.

She felt magical in her arms.

Lupe touched her sex again and lubricated her all around to be ready for her and then connected her naked sex against hers.

She felt like she had arrived home.

She pushed her sex against hers as hard as she could and started rubbing her clitoris against hers. The blondie's upper body jolted up and she grabbed her around her neck. Lupe could tell she was very close to finishing, as was she. "Oh my God, I think I'm going to come," the blondie whispered.

She didn't have to say it out loud. Lupe knew it already.

She could *feel* the blondie tense first and then let herself go as the orgasm came and ravished her body.

Lupe watched the orgasm take over her body and held her tight until she could feel the last bits of it calm down. It had been too long if ever, since Lupe had experienced this level of passion and connection with anyone, so she threw her head back and came, loud and long.

After they climaxed, Lupe met her eyes again. She had definitely come, there was no question about it, and she had enjoyed it, big time.

They stared at each other for a moment and for the first time, the blondie let her lazy eyes wander down Lupe's half-naked body. Her eyes stopped in between her legs. She didn't say anything, just intently stared at her.

For the first time, Lupe felt body conscious and shy. *Embarrassed* even.

She quickly bent down to pull up her trousers and fastened the belt and took off like lions were after her, leaving the blondie still tied down on the table. She didn't want to hear whatever was on the blondie's mind.

Not that she would have cared anyway.

*

"Guess who is going to buy a new motorbike with this money!"

Nelson said and rubbed his hands together on the steering wheel. "It couldn't have gone better."

"Yeah, even though I was sure *la gringa* would have ruined the whole plan, but Lupe took care of it very well, didn't you *amiga?*" Marcos said and gave a look at the back seat expecting Lupe to react.

She sat quietly in the back of the van.

Even though she usually wanted to drive off the crime scene, this time she had granted the honour to Nelson for a reason.

The high-definition curved plasma TV was tightly attached to the van wall and a laptop and a bunch of jewels were placed in Ikea shopping bags and attached to the other corner of the van. They usually didn't focus on expensive artwork but rather went for cash and items they could quickly sell such as laptops, smartphones and jewels. Even a TV would be a risky item to take for two main reasons. Firstly, TVs these days were way too big for a quick in and out project and attracted too much attention on the street. Secondly, the resale value of TVs went down remarkably quickly. The beauty they had in the van now, they would have to sell on the black market before the new season hit the stores as this model would soon be old, losing at least thirty percent of its original value the minute the new models hit the stores. Even as much as fifty percent as they were going to sell it on the black market, Lupe thought.

"Of course, guys, would I ever disappoint you?" she said laughing and gave him a firm pat on the back from the back seat.

"Well, I know you wouldn't, but you understand *amiga,* we are still very interested to know how you did it. She was fast, looked like a fighter," Nelson said and looked to his right for support.

"Correction, a *stunning* fighter," Randolfo corrected from the back seat and smiled at her. Marcos eyed him annoyed but decided to let his rude interruption pass.

"It seems you came out of the fight without a scratch, so you need to reveal your secret with ladies to hopeless single lads like us, right Marcos?" Nelson continued laughing.

"*Por supuesto amigo*, but you know the drill, this money will give us a head start with the ladies, but you know they won't stay only for the money. Unless we are millionaires and that ain't happening with these jobs," Marcos laughed.

"Correction again, a good woman will stay with you without money if you treat her well." Randolfo pointed out.

"*Callate estúpido* with your stupid corrections and let me finish!" Marcos roared and turned to slap his brother's head.

The van lost stability for a moment.

"Guys, careful and stop fighting – the job is still not finished until we get the hell out of here!" Lupe ordered.

Both looked at each other but followed her orders and stayed silent.

Lupe looked away for a moment and didn't say anything.

Her mind shifted back to the blondie she had left upstairs just ten minutes ago. Her eyes had been huge like a pair of blue lagoons. They had been filled with tears as she watched her leave even though she had bravely tried to stop them falling down her cheeks.

Lupe had felt it even though she had kept her gaze down and walked towards the door.

She hadn't untied her she remembered suddenly.

The blondie's hands had still been firmly tied with a rope when she had walked away.

On her way out, Lupe had given a quick look around the room with new eyes. She had noticed the blondie had obviously just arrived herself, probably just a couple of minutes before they had as her unopened cabin bag had been placed behind the door.

Lupe hadn't seen it at all at first.

On the cabin bag, Lupe had noticed a flag with a white background and a blue cross in the middle. She hadn't dared ask the blondie which country the flag was from but the image was burnt behind her eyes, she would never forget it. Maybe she would even check online, she thought, just to calm her racing mind.

"Guys, do you know which country has a flag with a white background and a blue cross?" Lupe asked.

"Mmmm, I'm not sure Lupe, why you ask?" Nelson replied first and looked at her via the driver's mirror.

"Nah, I just noticed a flag in the living room and got interested since I haven't seen it before, that's all," Lupe said and focused her eyes on the road, preparing to hold onto the door handle as they moved on to an old road.

After each project, she preferred to use older roads with less traffic for obvious reasons. Less traffic, less *policía*. They were also driving slower for *la mercancía* as they didn't want to damage the goods before selling them. It would drive down the market price, leaving them with a smaller cut.

"What flag, I didn't see any in the living room," Marcos said and scratched his head.

"Well did you even look around *estúpido*?" Randolfo said and crossed his arms.

"No, unless there's a pair of boobs or money involved," Marcos said and showed his teeth to his brother. Nelson laughed and raised his hand for high fives.

"I just googled it Lupe," Randolfo said and continued, "and the only country that has a flag with a white background and kind of a fallen blue cross in the middle is Finland," he said and looked expectantly at her.

"Where the hell is Finland?" Marcos asked. "Isn't it in the North Pole or something, one of the coldest countries in the world?"

"Without lights at all!" Nelson continued and looked next to him with badly hidden horror on his face.

"Finland eh?" Lupe said and looked out of the window.

She could see the night turning into an early morning and the sky taking blueish shades.

Just like *her* eyes, she thought.

When she turned back she wondered if she would be able to keep her secret from her dear friends. Was there something different about her she wondered as she felt like a completely new woman.

Her silence made all of them turn their heads to face her. Randolfo raised his eyebrows knowingly and Marcos had a grin on his face.

Lupe eyed them. "Oh, come on all of you. Nothing happened. I ran after her, caught her, she was too frightened to move so I tied her down and then made sure she would stay quiet and left. That's all."

"Mmm, sounds almost believable but you forget one of the most important elements in this case," Randolfo said. "Time. You were upstairs at least 35 minutes and that's only the time I calculated in my head," he continued.

"Well, what do you want me to say? It took me time to find her first," Lupe said with rising irritation in her voice which alarmed them into shutting up.

"Oh, come on *amiga,* we were just joking, we –"

"Yeah, I know, just focus on the road now and get this piece of shit safely to the destination will you, we don't want to get stopped by la *policia* for unsafe driving," she said.

"In fact, my friend, you are very much right," Nelson stepped into the conversation and turned back to follow the traffic with Marcos who had stayed quiet after Lupe's emotional outburst. He was looking at her with a thoughtful face.

He didn't say anything.

"*Amiga,* I'm just glad you came out of the house in good shape, did you see her nails? Long ones, she could have scratched your face!"

Nelson said. "That would have been difficult to explain at home."

The others nodded their heads approvingly.

Lupe nodded too.

Too bad she couldn't shake the growing feeling of uncertainty inside her.

The blondie might have left her body without any visible marks, but she knew already that she had dug her nails deep under her skin in those short 35 minutes.

She wondered if she could ever forget her and heal the invisible marks she had made on her. She had always been afraid of dying but the thought of the blondie left her without breath, gasping for air as if drowning. Perhaps if heaven felt like this, if angels felt like her, maybe it wouldn't be so bad to die after all.

Chapter 21

"Miss, I understand the hardship you have gone through tonight and trust me, my team and myself, we are doing our best to track these villains, but in order to proceed with the investigation, we need to know everything you saw and heard tonight," the chief police officer said with a heavy Spanish accent.

He struggled to find words in English and normally Ellen would speak Spanish as she was fluent in both, but tonight she was too preoccupied.

"We need to act as quickly as possible in order to recover the stolen property," the chief police officer continued. "So, one last time Miss, can you please describe their appearance – what they were wearing, height, body build, smell or if they said anything to you?"

Ellen glanced at him.

He was a short man with greasy skin and a black moustache covering his top lip and when he talked, the overgrown moustache tended to tickle the sensitive area in his lip which made him unintentionally exhale slightly harder to keep it at bay, resulting in him being out of breath most of the time as if he had run a mile. He had his standard police uniform with a high-vis vest signalling he was at a crime scene, which was dangerously stretched over his swollen belly. He looked as if he would usually sit behind his desk filing reports and eating *churros,* delegating work to people instead of carrying out any tasks himself, Ellen thought. This must have been an extraordinary night for him, hence he seemed to be over excited.

In fact, the whole team had arrived just twenty minutes after she had recovered from the attack and called the police. They had arrived at the crime scene and started looking for evidence, which basically meant touching and moving items inside the house and leaving their own fingerprints everywhere and possibly destroying any existing evidence, assuming there was any. Ellen was amused.

"I'm really sorry officer but I didn't see or hear anything. I just heard noised downstairs and called the police."

The face of the chief police officer fell. "But you said there were many of them," he said and smiled. "I doubt you can say that without seeing them?"

Ellen sighed. "Look, I heard several steps as I said before and automatically assumed there would be many. It's simple common sense."

"Look Miss, if you are worried about these villains coming after you, I can reassure you there won't be any harm coming your way, I will personally make sure of that," he said and placed his hand on her shoulder. "Now, can you please tell me anything you know?"

Ellen turned to face the officer and changed into fluent Spanish. "Now, I'm flattered and frankly very interested to know how you are able to make this commitment and tell me you are going to *personally* make sure they won't come after me," Ellen said. "With all due respect, it sounds very unrealistic to me, if you don't mind me saying."

The chest of the chief grew as he failed to hear the irony in her voice. "Yes Miss, as a matter of fact I'm very proud of my team, in fact we are the most – "

Ellen cut him short. "Chief, I'm sorry, but I believe you missed my point. What I meant to say is that your promises are a piece of *mierda* for me," she smiled sweetly. "Is that more understandable for you?"

The face of the chief reddened as he realised the sarcasm in her voice. He closed his notebook loudly and turned around to walk back to his team, talking quickly and loudly in Spanish.

Ellen could tell he wasn't happy about her not being cooperative, but she didn't really care.

Once she saw the chief's full focus was directed somewhere else, she sighed with relief and turned her back to the police team and walked out of the room.

The sky was just getting prepared for sunrise with its first sweet clips of morning light.

The weather was bright but chilly and Ellen shivered in her dressing gown. She crossed her hands around her body and looked up to the sky. She didn't feel tired even though it was already 4 a.m. Her mind was still racing through the evening's events.

The thieves had taken almost all the valuable items that Gisela's father had had in the house including the TV, one laptop and Gisela's family jewellery. The laptop was basically worthless to the thieves as it belonged to the company, so even if they were able to break through the password and set the device to factory settings again, there was a very low chance they would be able to sell it on the black market as company devices usually had powerful data protection settings, which meant that for the next unfortunate user of the computer, there would always be "ghost" applications and notifications consuming the memory of the device, which the new user wouldn't be able delete no matter how hard they tried. However, the police had also said there was very little chance of recovering the TV or laptop as the selling platforms for these kind of stolen goods were endless, starting from flea markets to untraceable internet sites.

The police had said that the most valuable items they had taken were the family jewels. They had taken all the gold necklaces and Gisela's mum's white gold engagement and weddings rings, which the police had explained they would sell to gold shops to be melted down to unrecognisable liquid gold and then sold on. No identification or serial numbers, just liquid gold. Fast and easy.

The most difficult part was probably going to be the moment Gisela's mother had to explain to her husband why she had left on vacation without her wedding bands Ellen thought ironically.

She knew all about her affair with the young Australian golfer boy Bryan. Gisela's mum had met him at the country club last year and travelled frequently to his family estate ever since.

As far as Ellen was aware, Gisela's father didn't know anything about the affair and simply thought his wife was spending time bonding with the other housewives in the area. Most of them had affairs so they were more than happy to cover for each other if needed, at the right price of course. The price would have nothing to do with money, as each of them had more than they could spend in their lifetime no matter how hard they tried. The price would be measured in favours and balancing the power within the community and other charity events. Each family would have their moment to shine over another, which ultimately formed the game of thrones in the political circles.

Despite having a wandering eye, Gisela's father would be crushed to learn this new piece of information about his wife. Something Ellen wished not to be part of.

She felt bad for Gisela and her brother as she knew they were very close.

Ellen sat down on the entrance stairs and crossed her arms around her knees.

The thieves had carefully planned and had known when the house would be empty, Ellen thought, which explained their surprise to see her in the house as her visit was never planned and rather was a consequence of another fight with Lucas. She had talked on the phone with Gisela who had suggested she take the last flight to Madrid and relax there for the weekend rather than staying at home fighting.

Change the location, change the mind-set, she had told her.

Unfortunately, Gisela had informed her at the last minute when she was already boarding that she was unable to join her as she had received an emergency assignment for university that was due next Monday.

However, she had encouraged her to still embrace her short time in Madrid and get into trouble. Which she had done with success, Ellen thought ironically.

She closed her eyes and let the morning wind blow cool air on her face. Her mind shifted back to the evening's events.

She had lied to the police on purpose.

Contrary to the story she had told the police, she had seen every one of them in detail. She remembered every detail of them, height, weight, body build, even voice.

Especially *hers*.

Ellen wasn't ready yet to go down the memory lane or even share the events of the evening with anyone. It felt like a sweet dream she was unable to erase from her memory and instead it would haunt her peace of mind for the rest of her life.

The memory of her eyes burnt deeply into her soul and the scent of her skin itched the delicate skin around her neck as if she had received invisible burn marks caused by flames.

Chapter 22

Madrid, Spain, 2010

Lupe woke up sweating on the verge of a panic attack. She looked around disoriented for a moment gasping to get air into her lungs before realising she was at home in her bedroom. The old writing table was still there and the dark green velvet armchair by the window with the brown seen-better-days coffee table beside it that she liked to put her feet on when she was smoking.

She looked at the open window and yellow curtains full of dust and cigarette holes slowly playing in the wind. Now that she thought of it, she wasn't sure if the curtains had originally been yellow or if smoking inside the apartment had caused them to turn a yellowish shade.

I must quit smoking for good, she thought.

It was a hot, early Spanish morning. She could hear the emergency vehicles running down the street. She looked at her side and saw and *heard* Viviana snoring loudly.

She had been drinking heavily last night but for once, she had behaved well and controlled her drinking. They had gone early to bed and during the dark night hours they had had sex for the first time in a long time.

It had been good but not amazing which made her work her very best to finish as soon as possible. It would be expected after being together for years, Lupe thought.

Viviana had asked her to hold her until she fell asleep and as soon as she had started snoring, Lupe had rolled around on her side of the bed to face the ceiling, waiting for the night demons to take control of her dreams, which happened ever so often.

This night hadn't been any different.

Lupe threw the covers aside and stood up from the bed; dragging her way to the armchair beside the window she lit up a cigarette.

She inhaled deeply and let the cool morning wind caress her skin.

They had shared some thoughts about their future before going to sleep. Viviana still refused to divorce her ex-husband, but she was more open to making their relationship official, which made Lupe content, hoping this stable period would last. She had never had anything stable in her life, and the idea of establishing something official with someone felt right. They had been together on and off for years and despite her alcohol problem and short temper, she would be able to manage her. It wasn't love, as love didn't exist for her, but she had helped her to get on her feet when she had arrived in Madrid the first time and introduced her to her friends and acquaintances. Now, they shared the same circle of friends, so it felt only right to continue as it was. Why break it, if it was holding together on its own, Lupe thought.

So she was really upset and *angry* for the nightmare she had had yet again. She called them nightmares as she was always upset afterwards and needed a day or two to get back on track in her life again.

Until the nightmares would come back again to haunt her.

The nightmare always followed the same pattern around *her gringa linda* who she had had the pleasure to meet exactly two years ago.

Lupe looked outside at the empty street.

She had named her my *gringa linda*, her *foreign girl*, as she felt that considering the number of nightmares and the amount of distress she kept causing her after all these years, she was entitled to call her *mine*.

She liked the sound of it and the idea of even picturing her with someone else's arms around her made her want to smash her bare hand through the wall.

She had been the first truly blonde lady she had ever slept with. Despite all the ladies with dyed blonde locks and blue contact lenses she had been with, *gringa linda* had been authentic with her creamy pale skin, soft blonde locks and vicious blue eyes that could have turned any weaker person into ice.

La Reina, the Queen.

She had crushed all Lupe's stereotypes of European women. She hadn't had tons of make-up on, her bony body hadn't been covered in the cheapest piece of skirt she could find, and she hadn't been completely cold. On the contrary, the memory of her heated touch on her body still burnt her like fire and her passionate whispers in her ear didn't let her soul rest no matter what she did or how much she drank. The raging sea she had seen in her blue eyes just before she had come and the calm ocean breeze when the storm inside her had finally set. The memory of her seemed to live deep under her skin leaving her silently whispering her name in the air just before passing out. She had proved to be much more passionate than she could have ever imagined.

Considering the circumstances they had found themselves in, she wouldn't have expected the level of chemistry and connection they had found in that short half an hour they had spent together. She had been so open and *ready* for her. So *willing*.

Maybe that was the reason why she kept haunting her in her dreams, Lupe thought. Usually, she wouldn't let her mind wander back to that special moment, it was *forbidden* for her, but this time she decided to make an exception.

Live it once more and let it out of your system, she thought and took a better position on the chair.

She wondered where she was now and if she had told the police about their little *rendezvous* upstairs. More importantly, Lupe was dying to know if she had enjoyed it. She knew she hadn't hurt her physically and that she had found sweet release in her arms as the aftermath of an orgasm had made her tiny body tremble to her very core, but after the heat had died inside, she was worried she had found their encounter disgusting.

Rape even.

It was something that truly bothered her every time she thought about her. She couldn't stand the idea of their special moment being called something like that.

Technically, she hadn't violently penetrated her so there wouldn't be any sign of rape to investigate even if she had gone to the hospital to report her. The beauty of lesbian sex, she thought and smiled.

It had definitely been her first time with a woman. There was no question about it, Lupe thought possessively. The thought of it made her feel excited and proud knowing there was a blonde goddess walking on this earth whom she had put her mark on first.

She always knew her Latin blood was calling her, but since living a long time in Spain she thought she had buried all those feelings for good. Before *her*. She had never felt this much ownership and possession for another person as she did when she thought of her *gringa linda*. It was like a burning rash under her skin that she couldn't scratch.

She wasn't sure where all of sudden care and interest of a stranger was coming from as she knew just how dangerous it could be, but she couldn't help it as she felt her body warm up and her hands moving restlessly along the velvet handles of the armchair.

She lifted one foot onto the coffee table and opened her legs.

Her *gringa linda* would probably burn her delicate white skin in the Spanish sun and her hair would grow volume and waves in the salty ocean. She might even have freckles around her nose.

Lupe smiled at the thought.

She still remembered how she had felt under her body, her taste and scent. How she had trembled at her first touch when she had slid her finger in between her hot wet lips and how she had moved her hips in a common rhythm with her, rubbing her swollen sex against hers, looking desperately for the release that only she could have given to her. Lupe still remembered how she had pushed her swollen clitoris against hers and the immediate electric connection she had felt raising them towards the orgasm.

Lupe had been desperate to let the moment last forever, but she had been worried the other guys might have got curious of her whereabouts. Who knew what they could have done to her. The guys were loyal and great, but they wouldn't exactly win the boyfriend of the year award.

She had opened like a flower to her. If only she had had more time, she would have used all the time to worship her body and tease her, stopping just before she was about to orgasm and instead of touching her, blowing cool air onto her hotness and waiting until the sensation of hot and cold sent her off to orgasm. She would have then finally taken her in her mouth and sucked all the sweetness into her system. It would work as a cure, her sweetness would be the elixir of life, it would save her.

Be her salvation.

Lupe gasped and opened her eyes wide. She was quickly reaching her climax as she vigorously twirled her finger around her sex. Just an image of *her* made her breast heavy and her sex drawling down to the tights.

She normally wasn't very keen on masturbating as she had people to take care of that for her, but the idea of someone ruining the image of her *gringa linda* in her mind stopped her. For *her*, she wanted to do it herself. Or even better, have *her* do it.

She quickly reached her climax and bit her hand not to scream out loud with the intensity of the orgasm. It was something completely different from what she had had the night before. Her *gringa linda* had the power over her even in her wildest mind.

She lit another cigarette and exhaled deeply, closing her eyes again.

It was going to be another hot day in Madrid.

PART IV

Chapter 23

London, England, 2018

"Excuse me, is this my coffee? *Decaf-latte, extra-hot-with-one-shot-and-soy-milk*, yes?" Ellen asked and raised the cup to the man in front of the coffee machine.

"Yes madam, this is a decaf-latte, extra-hot-with-one-shot-and-*semi-skimmed milk*," the man behind the counter shot a look at the growing queue of angry morning customers waiting for their order. "Is that OK or would you like to change it?"

Ellen sighed. "Well, I asked for a soy latte didn't I? Look, it is even written on my receipt," Ellen said and showed the cashier her receipt with one hand whilst trying to balance her laptop, handbag and lunchbox in the other.

"OK madam, it will take ten minutes because we already have other customer orders in, is that OK?"

Ellen looked at her watch. "That doesn't make any sense, I was here first," she was already close to running late on her first day.

The man shrugged his shoulders.

"Actually, on second thoughts, this is just fine, thanks!" She took the coffee from the counter and hurried out of the coffee shop. She had a very important day ahead and she didn't want to miss it for such a silly reason as coffee.

It was a cold January morning.

Ellen had flown back to London two days before, after signing her permanent contract with the company.

She was excited.

Who knew after four months of a project that the London organisation would have been ready to offer her a permanent deal, especially while the Brexit rumours still circulated over the whole UK, she thought and pulled her handbag handle up onto her shoulder, spilling her morning latte all over her jacket sleeve. She cursed loudly.

It was a good deal she had made considering she had been relatively new in the Finnish organisation and a total newbie in London. They had made her an offer good enough that it had allowed her to find a place of her own instead of having to rent a share house somewhere outside of London.

House sharing would have been an option for her as she used to live with her Russian friends whilst staying in Italy, but with total strangers, she wasn't sure she would have been totally comfortable. She liked it on her own.

So, with a little bit of financial planning and sticking within her monthly budget, she was sure she would be able to make it.

She smiled and crossed the road to the hospital entrance.

She had also made sure she would have her first appraisal and salary negotiations within six months, and she was confident she would be able to perform well enough to earn her first salary increase in no time.

Chapter 24

Ellen was born into a typical Finnish family.

Her parents were still married with a perfect average of 2.6 children. All of them were born and raised in Finland and no more than three years apart by age.

They had lived in a wooden house close to the centre of a small town with only 80,000 people.

Their house had consisted of two floors, a wild garden for her mother with direct access to a no-man's land forest and a big garage for her father, as he had always been a big fan of cars and couldn't stand the thought of leaving his precious cars unattended on the streets during the night, even in a small town.

Both of her parents had grown up in the countryside in big houses with a garden and lots of animals around them.

Probably for this reason, they had always had pets running around since Ellen could remember. She was a huge animal lover herself from a young age and used to spend her major holidays from school volunteering at local animal rescue centres. One time she had found a wounded cat in the forest. The sad animal had its orange fur covered in fleas and its right front paw was trapped in a wire fence it couldn't get off. Ellen hadn't noticed at first but then heard its frantic whining as if the small animal had been using its last strength to cry for help. She had followed the noise and seen three young boys throwing stones at the small defenceless animal. The stones hadn't been big, and merely to scare the cat but seeing the injustice had made her see red and blackened her mind. She had attacked the biggest one of them, clearly the leader of the group, and had torn and mauled his face until she had seen blood. The other boys had tried to tear them apart, first by their clothes and then by pulling her braided hair, but she had been so consumed by the rage she hadn't even noticed the hood of her new red jacket tearing off. After seeing the damage done to her jacket and hearing the animal-like sounds she was making whilst attacking the boy, the others had backed off in fear and at the first chance they had got, they had pulled her off their friend and, before she had been able to attack again, they had run away as quickly as possible without looking back. Ellen had waited until she couldn't see them anymore and slowly approached the small animal. The tiny cat had been mesmerised by the show and hadn't made a sound when she approached and helped it detangle from the fence. She had carried it to her house and taken care of the small abrasion on its paw caused by the fence. She had then called the local animal centre and with the pocket money stolen from her porcelain piggy bank, ridden her bike to the centre and picked up flea shampoo and proper cat food. After proper food and a warm bath to get rid of the fleas, the animal had been more than content and curled up on her lap and purred all night long.

Unfortunately, her sister had been allergic to cats and her mother had been worried of the unsuitability of a cat in their family home, so she hadn't had a choice but to give the animal to her grandparents and only see it in the summer holidays. She had been crushed and had shed hot tears as she begged her parents to let her keep the cat, but they had not been able to handle the emotional outburst of their middle daughter and rather turned their back on her. The small animal had been on its way before the end of the week and left a cat-shaped hole in Ellen's heart. She had vowed that one day she would be in such a fortunate position to dedicate more time and money to helping animals like the tiny orange cat.

*

When Ellen had reached teenage years, she already looked like the typical "stereotype" of a Nordic girl.

She was bright and blonde as one would expect. She was just five foot two with long blonde hair, fair skin, a heart-shaped face with full lips and blue eyes with a hint of green in the irises that would make her eyes change shade depending on her make-up.

As she grew older, her beauty reached new heights. Her charm and beauty alone were enough to take people's breath away, but her intelligence was the final straw that impressed most people. Many people would have classified her as *intimidating* based on the way she commanded respect even from much older people.

She was a charming character with a wicked mind and a brain as sharp as a knife even to the point of obsession for anything and anyone who would dare to disrespect her.

It was her determination and passion for life that made her constantly chip away at the invisible chains to break free from the Finnish society where being average was not only the norm but recommended. She was determined to follow her own path in life and make a difference, have a purpose.

Be *different*.

When she had been just five years old her parents had attended a parents' evening at her school where the children had played a game: *"Who do you want to be when you grow up?"* Her classmates had been running around making sounds of fire trucks and some treating others like doctors, but for some reason, Ellen had stayed still in the corner looking at her classmates with boredom.

Her teacher had approached her. "Ellen, what are you doing here alone?" she had asked and tilted her head. "It's OK if you don't know yet what you want to become when you grow up, but you should definitely join your friends in the game," she had said and patted Ellen's shoulder before turning away.

"Rich."

The teacher had stopped and laughed awkwardly. "Ellen, I'm sure that's what everyone wishes for but you need to have a proper job too, having money is not a real job and may make you sound slightly arrogant," the teacher had educated her.

"Fine, filthy rich then."

The room had gone silent and the parents of her classmates had been glancing at her with disapproving stares as if trying to figure out what had gone so wrong in her upbringing that being average was not enough.

Her mother had been mortified and had gone quiet like everyone else, but her father had broken the ice and blurted, "Well, at least we will have one millionaire in the family!" He had laughed awkwardly with the rest of the room.

It had been the last parents' evening Ellen's parents had ever attended at her school.

However, there had been a seed of truth.

She had always been very clear about creating her own success in life which she expected to be measured in more traditional terms such as money and power. It didn't matter if her family and the local educational system tried to explain to her that being average and settling for a more humble life would be the most optimal outcome in life and even advisable to manage the envy, one of the greatest sins of life.

Ellen had always been popular in school and well advanced compared to her classmates, which had usually made her a leader of the group. She had always known very well how to use her assets and how to *manipulate* people to her side. It had come very naturally for her without any specific effort.

In her early university years, the teachers had even tried to calm her down with her ambitions as her extreme levels of determination and pushiness were not considered the best assets to have in a Nordic country in the late 1990s when teamwork was still the key word used in schools and business life. Entrepreneurship and standing out from the crowd had never been targets according to Finnish culture, where communism was still visible and deeply embedded in the mentality inherited from its history under the Soviet Union. Equality for the masses had been taken to extremes in this small country that had always been so proud of its independence. They had all been brought up to appreciate their independence and were taught to never forget how much sweat, blood and silent tears had been shed during those painful hunger years while the little country had been pushing herself out of the influence of Big Brother Russia.

However, this also meant that anyone whose dreams differed from the generally accepted mentality had usually been put down with a passive aggressive or even a negative response from their families.

It was called *realism* they had always said.

The arms of the mentality and cultural approach had reached out across the whole country even though mental health and wellbeing problems caused an overloading of the social security systems due to a culture where expressing feelings was considered a sign of weakness.

Since a young age, Ellen had felt that freedom of expression had been calling her and speaking her mind had been one of her necessities of life to prevent her suffocating or losing herself completely.

The Finnish approach was a brutal mindset and Ellen had seen some friends and family members break due to the death of a relative or even when they had been going through a divorce. Those individuals had simply disappeared from the friends and family list. They had simply stopped existing.

Ellen's parents were no different from the crowd.

They had always been emotionally strict and never shared physical or verbal affection with their children. Parental love for children was seen as a given and for this reason, there hadn't been any need to show it.

Even though Ellen loved her parents to death, she had always felt a void. This lack of *something* tormented her to her very core and not being able to determine the cause of the emptiness inside had driven her to the point of insanity. But after all, how would she have been able to identify something she had never had?

She had craved physical affection and acceptance from her parents for as long as she could remember, but in the end, they had always taken good care of their family in other aspects and left them all healthy and well educated. Outside, she was a perfect example of a modern society young woman.

However, deep inside, she felt the damage of the lifestyle and understood that her emotional struggle had been inherited from her past and her void was still acting as a constant reminder.

By the age of 27 she had already developed her own coping mechanisms, mainly filling her time with work and business. She had collected an army of business associates rather than friends and the contact list on her smartphone within just a couple of years would have made any businessperson green with envy.

Ellen had always been proud of her achievements in life but deep down, she was a scared young girl who was desperate for affection and acceptance in life and would have loved to have a group of friends to turn to for comfort. But after all, what value could she have offered to any friends if she was already dead inside?

Chapter 25

London, England, 2018

Ellen arrived at the hospital on time.

She had paid careful attention to her appearance that morning. She had chosen to wear a black silky shirt with ruffles at the front and a black curve-hugging pencil skirt with a visible golden zipper behind. She had left the zipper open from the hem just enough not to expose her 10-denier black lacey stay-up stockings but to allow her to walk in her black stiletto pumps.

She had finished her look with a combination of copper and brown eyeshadow brushed lightly on her eyelids, two coats of black mascara and her signature red lipstick. It enhanced the bright blue in her eyes, that's what she had been told so many times. She had decided to wear her hair down and straight this morning and before she had stormed out of the door, she had lightly touched her neck and wrists with Giorgio Armani Acqua di Gioia perfume, her signature.

The outfit was nothing extraordinary for her. Most of the clothing in her wardrobe was black and business-like with a feminine and sexy touch.

She liked it that way.

Imposing power and respect in her own feminine way was a valuable weapon in business life, a skill not many women had discovered yet, she thought and pictured the ugly masculine trouser suits she had seen women wear in most of the board meetings in the previous company she had worked for. They could have easily been mistaken for a man with their masculine trouser suit and short hair, something that Ellen respected but would never allow herself to become.

"Good morning *Madam*, how may I help you?" the receptionist greeted her with a wide smile.

"Good morning, I'm looking for the property management office, please," Ellen replied.

"Very well, *Madam*, it is actually just around the corner. Go to the end of the corridor, at the glass window, turn to your left and continue until you see the grey double doors. That's the place."

"Sounds easy, thank you so much," Ellen said and hurried down the corridor.

*

She arrived at the office during the morning hustle.

There were employees waiting to see their managers, managers printing daily reports and a helpdesk taking calls every 30 seconds. It was intense as she looked around at the people hurrying back and forth in the office.

"Hi *Miss*, are you OK?" an Indian man sitting in the helpdesk chair turned to her. Ellen winced but recovered quickly, "Oh, hi there, I'm terribly sorry to interrupt your work but I have a meeting with Evelyn Brown at 9 a.m. She is Divisional Dir-"

The man in the helpdesk chair interrupted her, "We all know who Evelyn is love, she should be here any minute; you can sit down and wait." He looked around. "If you can find a free chair," and winked.

Ellen looked around but there were only three blue chairs in the entrance and all of them were already taken by two black women and one Chinese woman waiting to be called to the Managers' Office. The two black women were arguing loudly about who would be called first to the office as apparently, they had arrived at the same time. They were pointing fingers and calling each other names in a language Ellen couldn't determine.

"Thank you but I'd rather stand," she said, keeping her head up.

She tried to act confidently, but she could feel her confidence going down the drain the longer she stayed standing in the entrance. What had she been thinking by accepting the job offer in the first place? she thought for a second. This was a whole other level compared to Finland and Norway where she had lived for a couple of months.

Right before she was about to turn away and call off the whole thing, a young man appeared from the side office. "Hi, good morning, my name is Jack Delfino. I'm Operations Manager for this site. May I ask you to join me in the office?" he asked politely and bowed his head slightly at her. "You can wait for Evelyn there. It will be more comfortable for you."

Ellen smiled in relief. "Oh, thank you Mr Delfino that's very nice of you," she said and followed him to his office.

"Grab a seat here, let me just move the reports away." he said and picked up a heavy pile of papers from the chair. "You know, it's amazing how I always ask the managers to leave their reports on the desk rather than on the chair and still, I always find them on the chair," he said smiling.

"You should consider printing the instructions on your door and sending via email to them. That way you would have proof that you have given the instructions to them," Ellen said. "Then you could do management performance for the individuals failing to follow their line manager's instructions. After three attempts you could let them go and find new ones without any legal consequences."

He turned to look at her. "Actually, that's not a bad idea at all."

Ellen smiled politely before taking a good look at the office.

It was small and plain. There were only two seats: one in front of his desk and one on the opposite side of the desk for guests. Behind the desk she could see filing cabinets and on top of them, various certificates and honorary plates with his name on them. On the other side of the desk there was a small coffee table with company coffee mugs and sweets for guests presumably. Behind her she could see yet another filing complex with a four-storey shelf with files named and set neatly after one another.

He seemed to be very organised and she could see that the office, no matter how tiny it was, was well organised and maintained.

"So, I assume Evelyn will take some time to arrive. She just phoned and let me know she is stuck in traffic. This is very typical in London I assure you," he said and hesitated for a second. "Ellen wasn't it? I'm sorry, I just saw your name in a couple of emails, so I assumed it must be you. Pretty name," he smiled.

Ellen studied him silently whilst he jumped up to prepare coffee for them and fill the silence between them. Ellen smiled, she never asked for a coffee but could see he was very nervous around her.

They always were, she thought examining him further.

He was average height, a young guy with hazel eyes and neatly cut short hair; he was wearing a plain black suit with a white dress shirt and around his neck, he wore a tie with smiley snowmen on a green background which was a playful addition to his formal attire. Based on his appearance, he couldn't be more than thirty years old, she thought.

"Thank you, Jack, yes it's been a couple of weeks now since I accepted this job offer so I would assume you have seen my name somewhere as I will be working with you and your team," she said and sat down on the offered chair now cleared of paperwork.

"Yes, I heard. You must be the new business analyst they were talking about, am I right?" he said and handed her a steaming mug.

Ellen reached out and carefully took it without burning herself.

"Yes, that's me. I will be working on this site but will also take over the other sites belonging to the same Trust." She shrugged her shoulders and continued. "That's the long-term plan at least but we start here and see where we go."

Jack hit his hands together a little bit too eagerly. "Sounds great! I assume you have lived in London before? Otherwise you probably wouldn't have made this big step for you and your family."

Ellen took a sip of her coffee before replying. "I have lived here since last year, but I was working in a different part of London," she said. "And no, I don't have family of my own. It's only me."

"Oh, I see," he said and looked at her with new interest in his eyes.

Ellen recognised the look and stayed silent. She crossed her legs slowly without taking her eyes off his. "Yes, only me."

There was a moment of awkward silence before he cleared his throat. "OK then, I will introduce you to the management team, I'm sure they are all dying to meet you too."

He stood up abruptly from his chair. "Let's see, I have altogether ten property managers on this site, three of them working on evening shifts so you probably won't see them too much, but the rest are working on day shifts. One of them is on sick leave at the moment. Lupe had a bad knee injury some time back, but she should be fully recovered in a couple of weeks' time," he said and left his untouched coffee on the table before heading towards the office door. "You will love all the team. They are a great mix of different cultures. Shall we?" He opened the office door and waited for her to stand up and follow him.

"I'm sure I will," Ellen said and followed him to another office.

Jack opened the door without knocking. "Team, this is Ellen, she is the new business analyst for the Southern London Trust covering all sites. She will be monitoring you guys and seeing how efficient you are and what we could potentially do to achieve even better results at the end of the year."

The team turned their heads and eyed her from head to toe. Some of them gave a small nod at her.

Ellen felt like she was on display which she was usually more than comfortable with, but this time she could feel something in the air, something she wasn't able to determine as she scanned through the office filled with nine managers.

Jack turned to look at Ellen again. "OK, I can see you have your laptop and lunchbox. Why don't you leave your lunch in the fridge at the entrance and take the desk next to Paolo?"

Ellen followed his gaze and saw a middle-aged Portuguese guy lifting his hand in the air and pointing at the empty chair next to him. "That's Lupe's desk but she's on leave so you can sit there until we sort out something else."

Ellen smiled. "Sounds great, thank you," she said and made her way to the empty seat in the tiny office space, carefully making sure not to bump into anyone on her way.

She placed her belongings on the desk and hurried to the entrance to put her lunch in the fridge. When she came back, she could see the not-so-well-hidden curious looks coming at her when she sat down and started working. She managed to open her laptop before she heard a voice behind her. "Hi there *Miss*. My name is property supervisor for this hospital."

Ellen looked behind her and lifted her eyebrow in amusement. "Excuse me, your name is…?"

The girl smiled apologetically. "Oh, I mean my name is Giuliana and I work as a property manager at this hospital. I mean property supervisor," she said nervously. "I used to work in an Italian restaurant when I came to London five years ago."

"I see," Ellen said and waited for her to continue.

The girl looked at her as if having so many things to say but failing to find the words. "So, it is nice to meet you. I didn't mention, I'm Italian, originally from Firenze. Very beautiful city actually, very popular with tourists," she nodded her head at herself as if trying to convince herself that what she said was true.

Ellen tried to keep herself from laughing out loud. The girl was clearly nervous, but her curiosity had beaten her common sense. She was brave as well for opening her mouth first and approaching her, more than anyone else in the office, she had to give her that.

"Nice to meet you Giuliana. Italy is a lovely country, Firenze especially," she said and gave her the sweetest smile she could, trying to calm her down and make her feel more comfortable. She liked her for some reason. "I should know, as I lived in Italy for over a year. I used to go to Firenze at least a couple of times per month for business but always made sure to have at least one additional day just to enjoy the city. It is one of my favourite cities in the country."

She had made a right move as she saw Giuliana break into a wide smile. "Oh, nice! If you have a minute, I can give you a very quick introduction to the managers working here. If you like?"

"Sure," Ellen said and turned around in her chair to have a better view of the team.

"So, Paolo you already saw; he is usually working on night shift but this week he does morning shift because we need to cover Lupe who is on leave." Ellen nodded lightly to him and saw him blush under his tan.

"Then we have Nicola, Pamela, Joseph, Mark, and Andy on day shift and then Jimmy and Peter working only at evening time," Giuliana said pointing to them one at a time.

They all waved their hands when Giuliana mentioned their names and Ellen greeted them with a small smile before turning back to her work again.

It was a hint directed at all of them to illustrate that she had come here to work and not to make friends and she was cool with that.

Always had been.

But for some reason Giuliana couldn't seem to read the hint as well as the others. "Well, I can see you are busy, so it was a nice chat. If you need my help with anything just shout," Giuliana babbled, stretching to see Ellen's laptop screen over her shoulder. Ellen's fingers paused from typing and she glanced at her again. Giuliana immediately backed off, nearly falling over a chair she had been swinging on its two feet. "I was thinking, if you like, we can have lunch or something in the restaurant downstairs today?"

"Thank you, Giuliana but I brought my own lunch today and I will be meeting Evelyn so I don't know what time I will be free," Ellen said and turned back to her work.

Her direct response killed the smile on Giuliana's face. "Oh, OK, that's fine then. I hope you have a great day," Giuliana said and soon Ellen could hear her walk away to her desktop station and sit down on her seat. Ellen felt like the biggest jerk in the world. *Crap.*

She hadn't meant to be mean to her, but it had been true what she had said about her lunch and meetings. She was busy.

Ellen glanced again behind her at the back of Giuliana. She seemed a sweet girl, she thought. Maybe even too sweet to handle being her friend. After all, she didn't know where to start even if she wanted.

The morning flew by and she didn't have to wait long before Evelyn arrived and took her to the board room where they spent all day drafting an action plan for the next few months. It was around 6 p.m. when she headed back to the office to collect her belongings.

Giuliana was still in the office with a dark-haired woman whose name Ellen couldn't remember, Nicola maybe.

"OK, bye guys, I'm done for today," she said and collected her coat from the chair she had left it on for the day.

"OK Ellen, it was lovely meeting you today. See you tomorrow!" Giuliana said and waved her hand at her. "Oh, you just missed Lupe, one of the evening managers, she just left. If you hurry, you can probably catch her. She is one of our property managers who is on leave. Knee injury at the age of 39, can you imagine? She came to visit us today as she was bored at home."

Ellen smiled and put her coat on. "No harm done; I'm sure I will have the pleasure of working with her in the near future once she is fully recovered," she said. She turned around to leave the office but suddenly felt a sense of deja-vu running through her and her heartbeat quickened. The scent in the air was familiar but she couldn't connect it to an actual memory.

She froze.

"Ellen, are you OK? If you feel dizzy, sit down, please." Giuliana stood up and hurried towards her.

Ellen raised her hand to stop her. "No, I'm OK, I'm just really sensitive to perfumes," she said and scratched her neck which had become itchy all of a sudden.

Giuliana looked confused before her face brightened again. "Oh, I know! Lupe wears perfume and she sat on your chair just before you came in. Chanel Blu I believe it is; we got it for her as a speedy recovery present," Giuliana said.

Ellen didn't respond, just smiled politely before grabbing her bag again and opening the office door.

Giuliana watched her go. "Ellen, do you already have a place to stay?" she asked before Ellen was able to close the office door.

She tried to hide the annoyance from her voice. "No Giuliana, I'm currently staying in a hotel. I will have to look into that once I have time," she said and massaged her neck again trying to ease the stiffness in her shoulders.

"OK Ellen, but let me tell you, living in London is extremely expensive and finding a nice flat is a pain. I think you should talk to Lupe, she knows a lot of good areas in London and can suggest which agencies to use."

Ellen sighed. "OK, thanks Giuliana, I will keep that in mind," she said and left the office.

She rushed towards the revolving doors at the entrance of the hospital without stopping.

She was tired. It had been a long first day for her.

The sky was black with some minor drizzle.

Ellen lifted the collar of her coat and snuggled deeper into her scarf. There was still a hint of Chanel Blu on it.

Chapter 26

L upe was waiting for the bus at the metro station.

It had taken her almost twenty minutes to move three hundred metres from the hospital office to the metro station with her injured leg and crutches. She looked down at her leg. The white sock covering the cast was soaking wet and dirty from the rain.

"*Mierda!*" she cried out loud and tried to lift her leg higher from the ground. She would need to change the sock as soon as she got home to prevent the humidity reaching the inner bandage of the cast and causing any further infection.

What a life, she thought and looked up to see how many minutes until the next bus was due to arrive. It wouldn't be long as the route was on the main road where the buses ran every three minutes. She would be home in no time, she thought and thanked the old lady at the bus stop who had kindly offered her a seat, but indicated that she would be more than fine standing on her one foot.

She didn't like being useless but that's how she felt not being able to ride her motorcycle, as she knew she couldn't drive with her injured knee yet, so she was forced to use public transport. Something she hated dearly.

She sighed and pulled the collar of her leather jacket up to protect her from the wind and rain.

The bus arrived and the people waiting at the bus stop cleared the street to allow the passengers to jump out of the bus first before entering. Lupe hopped in last, as she wanted to make sure no one would knock her down – the evening commuters could be compared to a pack of hungry wolves, dangerous and ready to kill anything on their way home. She snorted and entered the bus finding the last empty seat offered by the same old lady whose last offer she had declined at the bus stop. This time she didn't decline the kind offer and gratefully nodded her head before sitting down.

They were about to leave the bus stop when the driver braked unexpectedly.

Lupe's body jolted forwards and with the quick reflexes she had, she was able to grab the front seat before ending up on the floor. "*Fuck,* come on, I have an injured leg! Take it easy *cabrón*!!" she yelled and reached to caress her injured leg.

"Hi, good evening, I'm so sorry, thank you for waiting for me," a soft voice said as a woman entered the bus.

Lupe eyed the front with mild curiosity, but she couldn't see the woman's face properly without her glasses and the pain in her leg was killing her.

However, she was able to distinguish a blonde woman wearing a long black coat down to her knees and tightened with a thick belt which enhanced her small waist. She was wearing stilettos and her blonde hair was wet from the rain and dripping down her back to her waistline. Her coat curved slightly at the back hinting at a rounded peachy behind.

Great choice of clothing Lupe thought. No wonder the driver was ready to risk everyone's life just to let her on.

Puta, Lupe thought and closed her eyes.

She was tired from the painkillers.

As she fell asleep, her mind started drifting again.

She was dreaming of summer in Spain, at the seaside. Feeling the warmth of the sun on her skin and hearing the sound of waves hitting the shore.

She felt *happy*.

When she opened her eyes, she saw *her gringa linda* next to her wearing only a blue sarong on top of her bikini. She was smiling at her with her blue eyes sparkling. They spoke at the same time, but the wind caught her words as she bent down to kiss her. Lupe was stunned but kissed her back passionately.

She felt her hands around her neck and on her shoulders massaging gently, relieving the tension and deepening the kiss. Lupe could feel her tongue inside her mouth swirling around playfully fuelling her body with her sweet taste of honey and apples.

She inhaled her smell of ocean breeze and jasmine into her lungs and ran her hands down her chest, pinching her nipple.

"Oh…" she could hear her soft voice in her ear.

Lupe smiled and continued her journey down to her stomach where she could feel her belly button piercing, a blue diamond, just like her eyes. She ran her hands lazily around her navel and down to her moist entrance, gently running her fingers up and down before pushing one finger into her, waiting for her body to adjust and stretch around her finger.

She gave out a long moan and threw her head back exposing her long swan neck. Lupe could feel her juices dripping down her palm and up to her elbow as she started pumping her finger in and out. Suddenly, she felt an uncontrollable desire to lick it off, taste her.

Her heart was heavy and ached for her, her whole body did. It was like an infection burning her body and making her sex clench. She needed to have her again, just one more time. Otherwise she felt she would stop existing, drift away completely, she thought as she pulled her body on top of hers and started peeling off her sarong and bikini.

She wanted to see all of her like she once had, on that magical night in Madrid many years ago.

She untied her sarong and bikini top, letting her round breast fall freely into her hands, just as she remembered.

She smiled at her and laughed. Lupe smiled back and ran her hands down to her ankles expecting to feel her bare feet but when she reached her feet, they were not bare, she was wearing black stilettos.

*

Lupe snapped awake gasping for breath and looking around disorientated.

She was only one stop away from her destination and she quickly collected her belongings and stood up from her seat, making her way to the exit. Luckily, she hadn't missed her stop by daydreaming, she thought and glanced around to see if the blonde girl who had arrived on the bus late was still there.

As she stood up, she felt her underwear was soaking wet and her sex was still clenching, her body screaming fulfilment for the unfinished dream.

She would need to ask her doctor to prescribe new painkillers as these were giving her nightmares, she thought as she arrived at her stop and waited for the doors to be opened.

Unluckily for her, the bus stop had a deeper gap between the bus and the footpath and she needed some assistance from her fellow passengers to get off the bus. Once she was safely standing on both her feet, she turned to thank her helpers and her heart skipped a beat.

When the bus doors closed, she could feel a hint of ocean breeze and jasmine in her nose.

Chapter 27

The two weeks Lupe had left of her sick leave flew quickly by.

She was so ready to go back to work and couldn't stand the thought of staying alone in the house anymore. She had felt alone since her last relationship had broken down.

She had dated Monique, a 52-year-old mother of one, on and off for four years. They hadn't lived together officially but had spent most of their time in Lupe's house in North London but since they broke up Monique had left the flat.

Monique was a beautiful woman for her age. Long dark hair and big brown eyes with some minor wrinkles at the corners of her eyes when she laughed. Lupe had always preferred dating more mature women over young girls, mostly because of stability. She knew she wasn't a traditional beauty queen herself and was aware of some shortcomings of her own in respect to relationships, so she didn't ever expect to date a model. Normal, mature women were more her style. Moreover, they usually had children, and there was nothing in this life she loved more than children.

In fact, she had dreamt for a long time of having a child of her own, but due to the injuries from a motorcycle accident she had suffered in her last year before leaving Spain, the doctors didn't believe she could carry a child herself. The injuries had been treated well but left scarring in the inner layers of her uterus and the painkillers she was taking for the chronic pain would be risky for a baby. In the worst case scenario, even if she fell pregnant, there was a high chance the child would be born with a drug addiction or some serious defect due to her medication.

It was something Lupe didn't want to even think about going through and for this reason, she tried to enjoy the children of her partners.

Obviously, it was not the same as having her own family with someone and having her partner carry a child for her. That was the major shortcoming of mature partners, they were usually well beyond their fertile years and their children already had a father.

They were not looking for a second mother for their children.

Sometimes, she hoped she would find a younger partner who would be ready to create a family together with her.

Carry *their* child.

She would often wander in the maternity ward in the hospital and see couples coming and going for their regular check-ups or just after labour. The look in their eyes was something surreal to her.

Despite her broken past, she knew if she was only given a chance, she would be the best mother and she would never, for any reason, abandon her child. She would raise the child to have everything she never had and would avoid all the mistakes her mother had made with her. With her past, she would be aware of what not to do and that was a strength in her opinion.

Unfortunately, younger partners were often highly unstable, disloyal and unpredictable, and would change their minds in the blink of an eye, not to mention they liked to party and drink a lot.

Lupe had nothing against drinking or partying, in fact she enjoyed a crazy night out every now and then herself, but for her purposes, she now needed someone with a calm and healthy lifestyle.

She had had enough of infidelity and partners with drinking problems.

Those types of behaviour would only rip the relationship apart so she had made a conscious decision to focus on dating mature women and enjoying their family, where she could.

However, it wasn't easy, as she would never be truly part of the family as, in the end, she had no rights to their children nor a say in raising them. It was something that had been made very clear for her with all the partners she had been with. Even the unsuitable, abusive fathers had more rights than she did, which made Lupe gasp in anger.

Life was not fair in the end.

*

"Good morning Lupe, how is the knee?" Joseph asked from behind the reception desk when she arrived at the hospital.

"It's much better Joseph, thank you for asking. How is hospital life? What's new?" she asked and patted Joseph on his back.

"Oh, nothing new really, they have started to refurbish the West Wing and found out that the patient hotel is infested with rats. Can you imagine?" Joseph shook his head. "All this time, we have kept telling the residents to stop leaving food everywhere, *now* they come and complain about the rat issue," Joseph said and opened his arms in the air in frustration." God, I hope Jack tells them off or sells them a pest control package at a very high price, am I right or not?"

Lupe smiled, "Yeah Joseph, you are right. Is Jack in the office? I will have a quick catch up with him as I still need to be careful with my knee and probably will be on amended duties for the next couple of months."

Joseph nodded. "Sure thing Lupe, he arrived early today. He is going through some numbers with our new business analyst."

Lupe stopped and turned around. "Business analyst, what the hell is that?"

Joseph raised his eyes from the computer screen. "Oh yeah, you never met her because she started working only a couple of weeks back when you were still on sick leave," he said preoccupied. "I have no idea who she is or what she does. In fact, I haven't talked to her much. She seems intimidating and only works with Jack or Evelyn, so she must be someone important." He laughed and winked.

Lupe rolled her eyes. "*Vale,* Joseph, I will try not to disturb her either. Old hags like her probably have no life and live with a house full of cats. No wonder they need to be acting all important and intimidating just to validate their existence," she said and looked at her watch. "OK Joseph, I need to go or I will be late for clocking in. See you later *amigo*!"

Joseph looked at Lupe as she hurried down the corridor towards the office as fast as she could, slightly dragging her injured leg. On her way, she raised her hand several times to greet people who responded to her greeting with a smile. Joseph knew she had been working in the hospital for the past eight years and there weren't many people she didn't know by now.

However, she was probably going to have the heart attack of her life this time as she had yet to meet their new business analyst who wasn't an old hag at all.

In fact, he would dare to say she was quite *beautiful*.

*

"Good morning people!" Lupe said entering the management office and imitating Giuliana's Italian accent.

Giuliana was the first one to greet her. "Oh, Lupe! Good morning *cariño*! You are walking again!" she said and opened her arms to offer her a hug, "Welcome back! We have missed you so much."

"Thanks *biscocho mio*, I missed you too. *La luz de mi jardin* y *el amor de mi crappy vida*!"

Giuliana chuckled coyly. "No, Lupe, stop – you make me blush!"

"Ha ha, I bet you missed me," Lupe smiled and winked.

"Yes, we all did," she said and eyed her knee suspiciously. "Are you ready to pick up where you left off last time?" she asked with worry in her voice.

"Anything that doesn't kill me makes me stronger, right?" she said and took a series of salsa moves to demonstrate she was fully ready to start working.

"Ha ha, OK *cariño,* I believe you now," Giuliana said and turned around on the seat to pick up some notes from her desk.

"I'm afraid we need to start working immediately, Lupe. One of the evening managers is sick, so Paolo had to step in for him so now we are one manager short on the day shift," she said and made a cross over her chest. "Thank God you came in today otherwise we would be screwed."

"Right, let me open my laptop and then we can do a morning walk of all areas, *sí?* I'm sure you guys have messed up my portfolio and I will have to spend all of my first week picking up *your shit.*"

Giuliana seemed apologetic. "Well, we did what we could but you know how it is in here. Let's go then!"

Lupe turned to hang her leather jacket and backpack on the hooks on the wall.

"Yeah, give me a minute here, my legs are not as fast as they used to be. I had surgery just four weeks ago, so take it easy."

Giuliana went pale under her deep natural tan. "Oh *cariño* I'm so sorry! Please, take all the time you need, I'm in no rush," she said and sat down again. "Anyway, I want to do the walk around properly as I saw the new business analyst walking around in some of the areas belonging to your portfolio earlier this week making notes."

Lupe turned around to look Giuliana. "What does she have to do in my areas? I don't understand."

"Don't get annoyed Lupe, she did that to all of our areas. Apparently, Ellen is working on trying to make us work more efficiently," she said and rolled her eyes. "Whatever that means."

The annoyance in Lupe's voice increased. "Who the hell is Ellen?"

she asked.

"Oh, right, you never met her. She is the new business analyst for the Southern London Trust. But she is mostly based here with us. She is cool. Quiet but nice. I like her. Very business-like if you know what I mean."

"Yeah, I heard about her from Joseph," Lupe said and the tension in her voice disappeared. "Old hag with no life nor husband, pouring her bitterness on us and trying to make savings out of our asses, right?"

For a moment Giuliana looked confused. "Well, I wouldn't put it that way Lupe, she is really nice,!" Giuliana said and continued. "Look, she even brought some weird candies from Finland for all of us. Isn't that nice of her?"

Lupe's hands froze on the keyboard and she turned to her. "Giuliana, where did you say she was from again?"

She didn't sense the tension in the air and therefore didn't even turn around from her desktop screen to reply. "Apparently, she comes from Finland, but she lived in many countries before coming here, including Italy!" Giuliana said and swung around smiling. "I think we could become best friends."

Lupe frowned. "I thought I was your best friend."

Giuliana's eyes widened. "*Cariño*, of course you are, but she is nice too! I hope you will meet her soon. She's in Jack's office today. I'm sure we could go and say hi to her if you want."

"Well, fine with me, let's put a face to this old lady," Lupe said and stood up.

"Bring your notebook. First, we go to say hi to Jack and to this business analyst and then we go for our walk around, *entiendes*?"

Lupe was eager to shake the uncomfortable feeling off her shoulders. It was like someone had walked over her grave when she had heard where the new business analyst was from. It made her remember the white flag with a blue fallen cross sewn on the cabin bag of her *gringa linda* all those years ago.

"OK Lupe, let's see if we can catch her," Giuliana said and stood up from her chair and left the office, expecting Lupe to follow her. "By the way, I don't know how you got the impression she would be old. She is young, actually. I would say she isn't much older than 35 and she is stunning!"

The smile died on Lupe's face and she felt her heart start beating faster. These were two coincidences too close for one morning, she thought. It had been nearly a decade since she had seen *her gringa linda* despite her image torturing her during the nights.

Her dreams with *her* had been haunting her for years, ever since they had met in Madrid, but within recent weeks they had become more frequent. The nightmares were still there, but now she found herself not being able to even fall asleep without thinking about *her*.

She was *everywhere*.

To make matters worse, Lupe found herself constantly aroused in the mornings, rubbing herself vigorously chasing her in her dreams until she would wake up only to see her *gringa linda* was gone. Her body ached for the touch Lupe couldn't forget no matter how much she tried.

She had a list of women she had met over the years, both married and single, who were ready for a night or two of fun, no strings attached. It was easy because the husbands would never even in their wildest dreams suspect anything was going on – on the contrary, they would encourage the friendship, providing money to go to movies or restaurants. Naturally, they never ended up using the money and it would usually end up in Lupe's pockets as the women would be too afraid to show up at home with the money meant for entertainment.

Sadly, none of them were even a close image of *her*, but one of them would have to serve the purpose of satisfying her needs tonight, otherwise she would become insane, she thought.

If she closed her eyes, she could even pretend it was *her* who she was having sex with.

They walked to Jack's office and knocked on the door.

Lupe felt anxiety and she was nervous. Probably for no reason but something didn't feel right to her. There was something electric in the air.

"Giuliana, Lupe, come in please. I'm happy to see you on your feet again," Jack opened the door for them.

"Good morning Jack, we just wanted to come quickly to say hi to you and Ellen," Giuliana said and peaked curiously inside the office. "Lupe hasn't met her before because she was on sick leave, remember."

Jack snapped his fingers in acknowledgement. "Oh, you are right, but I'm sorry to disappoint you; she just left, and she won't be back this week because Michael needs her on another site," he said and smiled. "Don't worry, Lupe. I'll introduce her to you once she is back."

A wave of disappointment washed over her but she forced herself to reply. "OK Jack, very well then. In any case, I just wanted to let you know I'm back and ready to start working again. It has been real *shit* staying at home alone doing nothing all the time."

Jack smiled again and shook her hand. "Say no more, welcome back. We will catch up properly later but for now, go with Giuliana and do the walk around and report back if anything is wrong," he said before closing the door behind them.

"Sure thing, boss," Lupe said to the door and bowed deeply almost to the floor. Giuliana held her laughter until they got back to their office.

As they entered the office, Giuliana was babbling in her usual way, but Lupe couldn't enjoy the easy-going babble as she used to and instead, let the air out of her lungs and sighed for relief. She hadn't noticed she had been holding her hands in a fist all this time.

Chapter 28

It had been three weeks since Ellen had started her new position in London.

So far, she had enjoyed her work even though it had required extensive travelling around and long working hours. That's why she was so happy to see the familiar revolving doors to the St Thomas Hospital at the end of another long day. She had missed the place.

It wasn't only good to be back at her home base of work, but she was also now temporarily staying in hospital accommodation while she found something permanent to rent. It had been a suggestion made by the general manager of the hospital and Ellen had gratefully accepted it. It would give her more time to plan her next step in the London accommodation market, which was tough she had to admit.

She was humming when she entered the main entrance of the hospital and saw Nicola, one of the day managers, taking notes in front of the reception desk. She had made sure to learn at least their first names, so that no one would think her rude. "Good morning Nicola!" she said and waved her hand.

Nicola lifted her gaze from the paperwork, surprised. "Hi Miss, I haven't seen you here for a long time, have you been on holiday?"

Ellen shook her head. "No not at all, I have been visiting other sites for the past two weeks."

"That's great, hopefully we will see you more in this hospital too. How is the accommodation?"

"So far, so good." Ellen smiled. "Thank you again for organising everything so nicely for me."

"No problem *Miss*, that's our job," Nicola said and nodded her head slightly.

"Of course, in any case, thank you," Ellen said and hurried down the corridor towards the office.

She didn't get too far before she saw Giuliana, walking towards her. Once she recognised her, Giuliana broke into a wide smile and hurried her step towards her.

Ellen glanced at the rose gold watch around her wrist and sighed; it might take another fifteen minutes to start working.

By now, Ellen had fallen into a routine. She would arrive in the office slightly early to have her morning coffee in peace and to send the most important email correspondence before the morning managers started their shift. Once the other managers arrived, she could barely hear her own thoughts in the office but to make matters worse, Giuliana had decided to take her under her wing and make sure she would feel "welcomed" every day by sitting next to her and babbling all day long.

"Oh, Ellen it is nice to see you!" Giuliana said and enclosed her in a bear hug.

Ellen stiffened but softened her reaction by patting her hand clumsily on her back. "Likewise, Giuliana," she said and forced a smile onto her face.

"It is good to see you again in our hospital. I feel like we haven't seen you for ages," Giuliana said and grabbed her firmly by her shoulders.

Ellen laughed nervously. The physical affection between friends still made her feel uneasy and uncomfortable. "I haven't been gone that long and you could have called me," she said and tried passing her on one side, but Giuliana stood in the middle of the corridor.

Giuliana tilted her head. "I would have but I don't have your number."

Ellen blushed. "Oh, in that case I will need to give it to you at some point."

"I'd like that," Giuliana smiled. "Then I would be able to call you and ask you to go shopping at weekends with me."

Crap.

"Sounds great! Now, will you excuse me, I need to go and start the day," she said and forced her way past.

Giuliana stopped her. "Wait Ellen, I wanted to ask you how your life has been in London so far and if you managed to get to know the city at all?"

Ellen suppressed a sigh. "That's nice of you to ask, Giuliana, but unfortunately, no, I have been fully occupied with work to be honest. Catching up with things and so on," Ellen said and adjusted the files in her hands that she had brought from home. "Nevertheless, it's OK as this is not my first time in London. I used to do at least two trips per month here before the company offered me a permanent contract," Ellen said.

Giuliana nodded. "Oh, I see Ellen. Anyway, you should enjoy more of your time in London now that you are local," she said and patted her on the shoulder. "You know, go to places, meet new people and so on."

Ellen closed her eyes and breathed deeply in and out, counting to three before responding. This woman really had a tendency to push herself into other people's business.

She forced the smile back on her face. "You are quite right, but I'm good at multitasking my life. In fact, I will be meeting someone tonight, so if you will excuse me, I need to deliver these papers to the office and then I need to run," Ellen said and walked away before she had a chance to reply.

Giuliana watched her go. "Oh, that's an excellent start. I'm so happy for you!" she shouted to her back and waved her hand.

The people in the corridor raised their eyebrows curiously and Ellen couldn't help feeling slightly embarrassed. She wasn't used to sharing her personal life with anyone let alone with a colleague and a bunch of strangers in the corridor.

She raised her hand without turning around as a signal that she had heard what Giuliana had said and hoped it would be enough to shut her up for the day.

Ellen entered the office quickly and placed the heavy files on the closest available chair. She massaged the pain in her arm and looked around. The office was quiet and felt abandoned without its daily hustle. She imagined people had taken the opportunity to start their weekend early, she thought.

The filing cabinet key was left in place and Ellen decided to take the opportunity to not only return the files she had taken to their original place but also to empty her bag of unnecessary papers. It was not only pointless but also a confidentiality risk to carry them around.

*

Whilst she filed the papers and emptied her handbag she couldn't help but wonder if she had pushed it too far with Giuliana and even offended her. She didn't mean to but creating emotionally stable and satisfying friendships was still a mystery to her, especially between women. There always seemed to be a continuous competition between women and too high a risk of being backstabbed, whereas with men, the problem was they always expected the friendship to turn into something Ellen simply didn't have to offer. They would usually find it refreshing and challenging at first to meet a woman who had goals of her own which didn't include getting a ring on their finger. However, after several charming attempts, she would have to make it crystal clear to them that there was nothing more she could and was willing to offer, and they would usually disappear from her life or, even worse, make her life complicated.

It was *exhausting*.

But with Giuliana, the friendship felt different, she thought.

She had put up every barrier she could to the point of being so obviously rude that no one would mistake it for anything else, but she still deliberately sought her company and seemed to enjoy it. She was easy-going and kind, so obviously naive that sometimes Ellen had to pinch herself not to laugh at her, but in the end, she meant well and had a good heart. They didn't share any career goals or ambitions either, which felt odd but refreshing. Ellen almost felt she could be someone she could trust, which made her smile, just a little bit.

Suddenly the alarm went off on her phone, breaking her from her thoughts. She had set up the alarm so as not to forget her date in the evening. She had a quick look at her watch, locked the reports in the drawer and was on her way.

Luckily, she lived right next to the hospital otherwise commuting would be a pain, she thought and hurried out of the hospital entrance to get ready.

Chapter 29

Lupe was bored and tried to make herself look busy while reorganising the files in the back office. The files were dusty and it looked like no one had really paid any attention to them for ages. She didn't dare to look inside of the dates of last updates, she knew already the documents inside were all expired.

She was just about to finish her boring task when one of the evening managers entered the office.

"Guys, we have a problem," Brenda said.

She was a big middle-aged African woman who had worked for the company for more than a decade. She had long hair braided with teeny tiny beads as suitable for any respectable African woman and skin as black as the night sky. Not many of the managers knew Brenda's age but she was well past fifty and already had one grandchild, whose picture she eagerly showed around to anyone who was willing to look. She reminded Lupe of the black African lady she had met at the *hacienda* a long time ago in her childhood – a memory she refused to dwell on and that still gave her chills despite the more than a decade that had passed.

Even though she looked all soft and easy-going, Brenda was clever and had more character than many of the younger managers, something that made her opinion very well respected inside the hospital community.

Giuliana hurried to greet her first. "Brenda, what is the problem? Please share quickly."

"Oh, Giuliana, one of the domestics from the hospital hotel has called in sick for this evening and we have no one to cover her," Brenda panted as if she had been running.

"No way, again? Can one of the on-call domestics cover her? I think anyone else who might be suitable is on holiday. I don't think we can get anyone to travel in from home for only a couple of hours," Giuliana said and looked back to Lupe worriedly. "You know most of our staff don't even live in central London." Brenda nodded at her approvingly.

Even though Giuliana had been in the position only a short period of time, she was learning quickly and always had everyone's best interests at heart. She was a very intuitive person and that often helped her to get out of difficult situations when she didn't have the necessary experience.

"True Giuliana, you are right. Do we have someone already in the hospital we could use and who could work independently in the area?" Brenda asked and flicked two of her braids over her shoulder. "I don't want to get a new complaint from that area. God forbid, the doctors are filthy as pigs but they surely don't hold their tongue when leaving a nasty complaint" She raised her finger to make her point.

"No one comes to my mind now," Giuliana said and nervously massaged her forehead. "What are we going to do now?" she asked, slight panic in her voice.

They both stayed quiet for a while, deep in their thoughts, before Brenda spoke again. "Lupe, do I remember correctly that you used to be the team leader of the hospital accommodation area?" Brenda asked and looked tentatively over Giuliana's shoulder.

Giuliana turned to look at her with hope written on her face.

Lupe's hands froze from going through the reports on her desk. "Well once upon a time, yes," she said. "But I'm not staying late tonight ladies, I have a social life to take care of outside of this hospital."

Giuliana knelt dramatically in front of her. "Lupe, please it's only until 9 p.m. and you have plenty of time to enjoy your social life after that," she said with her best puppy dog face.

Lupe smiled sweetly and patted her head before standing up and picking up her jacket. "The answer is still no."

Giuliana watched her before a light bulb lit up in her head. "Lupe wait, isn't it you who is here tomorrow morning?" she asked raising her eyebrows knowingly. "You would be the first person to receive any complaints since I'm off tomorrow."

Lupe stopped and looked at her. "What's your point?"

She grinned. "Think about it, do you really want to start your day listening to criticism of a poorly made decision when you could have done the job yourself in a couple of hours?"

Lupe raised her eyebrows. She was making a valid point. The only problem was that the older lady she was meeting tonight had a husband and they were having too many troubles as it was to sneak out together for their secret meet-ups. The lady wasn't going to be able to make it after 9 p.m., Lupe was sure of it. But on the other hand, she didn't want to start her day tomorrow with Jack breathing down her neck either.

She sighed. "OK, I'll do it but as soon as I'm done, I'm out of the door and I will not be running the machine. I will only do the essentials. Do we have a deal?"

Giuliana ran and crushed her in her arms. "Lupe, you are a lifesaver!" she said and squeezed both her cheeks.

Even Brenda, who usually didn't care for physical affection, approached her and patted her on the shoulder. "Lupe, thank you so much; this really is the teamwork Jack has been talking about all along."

When the crisis had been solved, they all turned back to their duties for another half an hour before Giuliana yawned loudly. "I think I'm off now, I still want to go to the gym and I'm starving."

Lupe looked at her in surprise. "You are not going to stay behind with me?"

Giuliana looked at her apologetically. "No Lupe, I don't know the area at all, so I don't think I would be of any assistance to you, plus I promised my friend I'd meet her right after work, so I'm already running late." She pulled on her furry jacket. "But I'm sure you are able to manage it, and as soon as you are done, just leave and go home. Easy-peasy!" she said winking her eye at her before leaving the office.

Lupe looked at the closed door. *Great*, she thought. Well, at least she would make a couple of extra pounds from working overtime, she thought and prepared to head to the hospital accommodation, but first, she would need to get changed.

Chapter 30

Ellen was preparing herself for dinner.

She had picked an emerald green silk blouse and a black leather pencil skirt to go with it. The leather skirt had an opening side zip that ran across her right thigh which she had opened just enough for a casual look. She loved the skirt mainly for its versatility. With the zip closed, the skirt was work appropriate and with it open, it was casual enough for dinner dates.

Ellen had always appreciated versatile clothing, but even more so for the past three years after moving back and forth within several countries inside the Baltics and Europe where she had to rely on clothing that would serve multiple purposes and that would be easy to maintain.

She stretched her leg to slide up black hold-ups and paired her outfit with black stilettos. She didn't wear tights at all, mostly due to the uncomfortable feeling around the waist but to also feel sexier with herself. She knew *feeling* confident and sexy was the main component of *looking* sexy. It was something she could have proven just by looking at different women on the streets of London. How they walked on the street and interacted with other people.

The black stilettos were almost a year old and would require a trip to the cobblers soon but they would do for now. She had a good dozen pairs of shoes but she had a special love affair with this particular pair. Not only because of the designer labelling, she had paid a lot of money for the pair in Corte Ingles on her last business trip to Barcelona, but also because, despite having a four inch heel, the shoes were extremely comfortable and again versatile enough to wear either at work or during free time.

Women would always look their best in heels, she thought. It was something about building the posture and confidence and adding a feminine touch to every outfit.

High heels presented power to her, a *can-do* attitude.

She smiled at her thoughts, taking a last look at her reflection in the mirror and leaning forward to finish her look with red lipstick.

The matt deep red had been her signature look as long as she could remember. She wasn't a big fan of heavy eye make-up, even though she did try once in a while or for a special occasion; but normally the red lips, her glowing, flawless fresh-looking skin, defined eyebrows and two layers of mascara would do the trick for her.

She used her ring finger to apply some shiny lip balm to the centre of her lower lip and Cupid's bow to enhance the arch of her lip and slipped her lipstick, handkerchief, perfume and credit card into her Louis Vuitton mini pochette.

So far, she never had to pay for anything on dates – that was the man's job, but she wanted to be prepared for anything. Her phone wouldn't fit inside the pochette so she would have to carry it in her hand or use the pockets of her jacket, which would be fine. She liked to play safe and stay in control, even though she wouldn't say it out loud.

She put on her jacket and took a last look at her room in the hospital accommodation. She had to admit the room was not exactly spacious and had come with furniture that looked old and tired. The decoration of the room had been very simple from the start but Ellen had tried to make it as cosy as possible, not only for her own sanity but also to avoid making a poor renting decision just to move out of the hospital.

She had bought a new duvet and pillows and covered her single bed with expensive Egyptian cotton sheets. She had bought a roster tea kettle and set it up on the writing table in the only corner of the room with a power socket and had shopped in Primark for some sparkling, colourful toiletries bags to place on the side of her individual sink in front of the only mirror she had in the room. Now she had sparking pink, silver and blue bags holding all her make-up, toiletries and some small items she didn't want to lose but didn't want to hold openly on the writing table for the cleaner to see. Furthermore, she didn't like clutter at all. Clean and airy surfaces made her soul rest.

The walls had once been all white but when they were last painted, the colour had transformed into a dusty looking cream. The floor was covered with green carpet and the room had a view to the main street, which allowed some natural light to come in.

Ellen had also visited Harrods to buy some stylish closet scent for her wardrobe, which had probably been an unnecessary splurge at the end of the day, but she had to admit she took quite a lot of personal pleasure in having her clean clothes hanging in a nicely scented wardrobe. It added cosiness to the tiny room and made it feel more like home.

She turned to pick up her keys as she had almost forgotten them and checked the time on the clock on the wall. It was almost 8 p.m. – she should head downstairs soon, she thought and picked up her tea mug to wash in the kitchenette, which was part of the communal areas, in case she wanted to have a cup of tea later. She didn't plan to stay out late anyway and tomorrow she would have to work again.

The communal areas included a small kitchenette, bathroom and living room, which were shared with the other residents who consisted more or less of visiting surgeons or nurses and other lecturers. She didn't mind having them around every now and then, as long as she was able to quickly move to her own room if needed and didn't have to fight for bathing time in the evenings or mornings. Luckily, the other guests were quite self-sufficient themselves, so it had been quite painless living so far, she had to admit.

She washed her mug and placed it to dry on the counter.

When she had arrived in London, she had received a set of basic dishes by a famous Finnish designer from her colleagues as a goodbye present: a mug, three different-sized plates and one tiny cereal bowl. They looked very different from the plain dish sets the hospital had provided, so hopefully no one would feel the need to steal them, she thought and threw her lightly curled hair back.

Her hair had already developed a wavy look due to the humidity instead of the voluminous curls she had planned for the night. Thank god her date had said he would pick her up in his car, she thought and looked out of the small kitchenette window, as it looked like it would start raining soon.

Chapter 31

Lupe opened the domestic's cupboard only to find a dirty cleaning trolley with most of the necessary items for the shift missing. She looked at the trolley in annoyance. How come, even though they were reminded millions of times, the domestics still managed to forget their final task of the day: clean and restock the bloody trolley.

It wasn't only for themselves but also to make sure the evening staff would have a nice start to their shift too. She could already imagine the number of arguments this dirty trolley would have caused for the manager responsible for the area. Most probably the evening domestic would have left the shift early due to a lack of suitable equipment. And they wouldn't have been completely wrong to do so, Lupe had to admit it, as providing the employees with the necessary equipment to perform their work was indeed the manager's responsibility. For this reason, even if the domestic would have left as a result of lack of equipment, the manager wouldn't have been able to give her a notice or warning.

Lupe sighed. They knew their rights too well.

She only wished the staff would show as much dedication to their work as they did to fighting for their rights, but that was never the case. The work they did simply wasn't motivating or rewarding enough.

Lupe looked at the dirty mop bucket and grinned – they were not completely wrong, there was nothing glamorous about it. The money was crappy and there wasn't really a reward system or any benefits for the staff, unfortunately.

She bent down to check if she had enough toilet rolls only to discover that she had only two left for the whole building.

Great, she thought, a trip to the main storage would take her an additional fifteen minutes, which meant the shift would take her longer than she had anticipated.

This wasn't really her day, Lupe thought and stood up and took a blue cloth and the detergent to mix with some water in the sink in the small room.

She finished cleaning and preparing the trolley in no time. After all, she had done it millions of times before, when she had arrived in the country many years ago without knowing a word of English.

She had arrived in England committed to changing the course of her life after serving prison time in Spain. She wanted to get clean and out of all trouble. She wanted to stop looking over her shoulder all the time and to enjoy life for a change. Naturally, that had meant first learning the language and starting from the bottom as she didn't have much to mention on her CV.

However, she was very proud of herself and what she had achieved since then. As soon as she had been able to communicate the basics in English, she had enrolled in catering school and gained her first official degree in food and hospitality. In other words, in addition to her current position, she was also a fully qualified chef.

Despite her qualification, she had never worked as a chef for more than a couple of months since she really only enjoyed spending time in the kitchen cooking for friends and the family she had in the country. Hence, why she had stayed working in the hospital, and slowly but steadily, got promoted to a team leader and later a management position.

The journey hadn't been easy, but she had definitely earned every single step of it thanks to her hard work and dedication.

Which meant, after all this, whilst cleaning the trolley, she really did wonder how the hell she still kept doing these favours for people.

What an irony, she thought and decided to start her job from the fifth floor as the floor belonged to visiting doctors, nurses and lecturers, which meant it was most probably empty, if she was lucky.

She started to make her way upstairs.

Chapter 32

Ellen had just locked the door behind her when all of a sudden, she heard the main door opening. She winced lightly and turned to greet the visitor at the door just as the lights turned off in the corridor.

She reached for the light switch closest to her door, but nothing happened.

Crap, Ellen thought and leaned on the wall to find another switch without a luck. The corridor stayed dark.

A sudden breeze of cool air ran past her giving her goosebumps and she shivered.

Someone was in the corridor with her.

"Hello?" Ellen whispered in the darkness and waited for a response, but the corridor stayed silent.

She cleared her throat and raised her voice. "Hello, is anyone there?"

When there was still no response, she frowned in the darkness. Logically, whoever had entered the corridor when the lights went off couldn't have left, she would have noticed it she thought. Besides, she could *feel* someone's presence in the same space.

Ellen touched the door handle behind her.

It would only take her a couple of seconds to unlock the door and escape inside her room, but she wasn't sure how close the person was in the corridor. More importantly, she couldn't guarantee she would be able to get the key in the lock fast enough without lights, and she could end up locked in the room with a stranger.

At least in the corridor, there was a marginal chance someone on the lower floors would hear her screams and come running if necessary she thought and tried to calm her rising heartbeat.

"Hello?" a breaking voice responded from the darkness.

Ellen stiffened. There was a slight accent in the responding voice, but Ellen couldn't determine the origin, Spanish maybe.

For some reason, the voice sounded oddly familiar to her and made sweat break out on her forehead. She could sense a familiar combination of musk and citrus in the air filling her nostrils. It made the adrenaline speed up in her body and set her brain spinning into the back of her mind trying to connect the scent and voice with a memory.

"Wh-who is this?" Ellen responded tentatively in the darkness. "I'm sorry I didn't see you before the lights went off. I tried to turn them on again, but it didn't work." She turned her head towards the light switch and pointed at it before realising the stranger couldn't see her.

"It's OK, I didn't see you properly either," the stranger's voice said, now closer to her.

Ellen took a step back and felt a hint of panic run through her body as she could feel the physical presence of the stranger getting closer.

"It must be the fuse again," the stranger said. "We have recently had quite a lot of trouble with the electricity on this floor, that's why the hospital prefers to fill the rooms on the first and fourth floors before assigning anyone here."

Double crap, that's why there were so many vacant rooms on the floor and the hospital had offered it at a discounted price, Ellen thought and rolled her eyes in the darkness.

"Great, just great," Ellen thought out loud and crossed her arms on her chest.

Soft laughter filled the corridor. "Sarcasm eh?"

Ellen winced but then felt her mouth curve into a small smile. The laughter was captivating.

"Well, better sarcasm than hysterical tears no?" she responded.

"Couldn't agree more," the stranger said. "Actually, I'm quite surprised to see anyone here to be honest. All the lecturing doctors and nurses are accommodated on the lower floors."

"I guess it is different for the regular staff of the hospital then," she said and glanced at her wrist. She didn't need to see her watch to know she was late. Her date probably wouldn't even wait for her, after all, she had never met him before and he would probably think she was a ghost, a stood up, a person who would set up a date and then not arrive at all.

She couldn't blame him, even though she didn't like it one bit.

Punctuality had always been one of her virtues.

"No, I'm not a nurse or a doctor for that matter," she said and cleared her throat. "I'm actually working for the property management department in this hospital on a consulting basis. I get paid for looking for efficiencies and financial savings," she said but when the stranger didn't reply, she hurried to explain herself more. "Property management is like FM which stands for…"

"I know what FM stands for, *darling*," the stranger interrupted, leaving a silence hanging in the air before continuing. "You must have something to do with the hospital's new business analyst then?"

Ellen raised her eyebrows in surprise. "Actually, I'm the new business analyst for the hospital," she said. "Or hospitals, I go around to the different Trusts and help them to…"

"Yeah, I know already, efficiencies and so on, my colleagues told me," the stranger interrupted her. "So, you basically do nothing and get paid very well for it?"

Ellen broke into laughter. It wasn't the first time someone had criticised her qualification or work. In fact, working in a man's world had always made her feel unappreciated every now and then.

"Well, we are all entitled to our own opinions, aren't we," she said diplomatically and continued. "Now, do you know what we should do? Where is this fuse and can we change it? I'm really late for my date."

"Calm down, *darling,*" the stranger said. "The fuse is usually located in the kitchenette of every floor. Right above the fridge in the grey box on the wall. You might have seen it before. There is always a spare fuse just in case."

"OK, great, so can I help you somehow? Or is it better if I just go?" Ellen asked, expecting the stranger to politely decline her offer of help, but before she could take the first step to leave, the stranger replied. "Actually, you might as well give me a hand here, I would like to finish my duties as soon as possible so that I can also enjoy my night or at least what is left of it anyway," the stranger said and moved. Ellen heard the dragging steps approaching her before she felt a light touch on her waist.

She flinched. "Wow, what you are doing there, *friend?*"

"Relax *gringuita*, I'm just trying to get past you to the kitchenette. You know you are standing right in front of the entrance, right?"

Ellen felt immediately embarrassed by her reaction and her cheeks turned red. "Oh of course, I'm sorry, I'm a little bit nervous, I don't like dark and small places."

"*Tranquila,* I don't think anyone does," the stranger said and patted her hip. "I'm just making sure we don't smash our heads together."

Ellen nodded her head even though she knew the stranger couldn't see her. The stranger's touch didn't make her feel as uncomfortable as she thought it would, as the familiarity of the moment filled her again, but she shook it off quickly.

"Oh, OK then," she said. "Now that we are properly introduced, can you please show me the way and what you want me to do."

"Certainly," the stranger said and grabbed her hand. "Let me lead the way."

Chapter 33

Lupe struggled to fit in the tiny kitchenette. Especially when she had the woman without a name in there with her.

She really didn't need her help. And based on her voice and the information she had shared with her about her job, Lupe knew she wasn't going to be much use to her anyway.

Still, she preferred her to stay with her.

It wasn't common knowledge, but Lupe had always been terrified of the dark and the woman's presence created a peace and calmness around her. Plus, she smelled divine, Lupe thought and inhaled the scented air around her.

There was something familiar in her scent and voice that Lupe couldn't exactly define. She hadn't touched her on purpose but somehow her hands had found their way to her waistline and later grabbed her hand. It felt like her body was silently *summoning* hers.

"OK *gringuita*, do you have your phone to hand? We are going to need light if we want to change the fuse and get electricity to this floor," she said.

A rustling noise filled the air. "Oh, I think I should have it in my handbag."

But after a few seconds, when there was still no light, Lupe grew impatient. "What is taking so long?"

"I'm trying to find it, but I don't know where I put it as my handbag is very small and it's not in there."

Lupe sighed. Unfortunately for this *gringa pendeja*, patience wasn't one of her virtues, she thought and ran her hands across the woman's hip and around her waistline again.

She felt her body tense again under her touch.

"What the hell…" she gasped angrily and pushed her hands away.

"Jesus Christ *princesa*, relax will you, there is your phone," she said and pushed the phone towards her until it touched lightly on her chest.

The woman hesitated when she took the phone. "How did you…"

"Easy, people normally put their phones in their pockets if they don't have room anywhere else," Lupe said and shrugged her shoulders remembering how easy it had been years ago to steal money from people's pockets with her siblings. All though for them it hadn't been a game at that time, it had been a *necessity* if they had wanted to eat.

"Oh, of course," the woman said.

Lupe could hear slight embarrassment in her voice and smiled but didn't say anything. It was cute, she thought and was immediately taken by surprise by her own thoughts.

"Why don't you just get a bigger handbag so you can fit all your nonsense in your handbag instead of your pockets," Lupe asked chattily and turned around to feel for the furniture in the small kitchenette to help her find her way to the fuse control panel.

The woman knocked her on the shoulder. "Well, not that it's any of your business, but I don't have anything bigger as I just moved here. My luggage will be arriving once I have found a permanent residence."

Lupe felt a moment of compassion as she would for anyone new in the country but brushed it off quickly. She knew how difficult and confusing the housing market was for newcomers, but the idea of this strange woman leaving the hospital accommodation annoyed her.

"Well good luck to you *gringuita*, it is quite a task to find a flat here in London, the whole housing system is messed up and pricing is entirely driven by market demand and not reflecting the conditions of the flat at all. You might need someone local to help you out."

Lupe played with the idea of offering to help but stayed silent. The first step in learning how to say no to people, she thought and grinned to herself.

"Thank you for your concern, but it is not necessary. I will have someone to assist me at work."

A shot of jealousy stabbed through Lupe's skin and she was taken aback. It was a completely disproportionate reaction considering she hadn't even seen the woman's face.

"I'm glad, hopefully this person knows at least something about the housing market in London. I would hate to see you lose the beautiful shirt from your shoulders trying to cover the housing cost."

"Don't you worry about my shirt, I'm fine," the woman mumbled and turned to switch on her phone when Lupe heard loud bang on the floor.

"Oops…"

"What now?" Lupe asked annoyed.

"I'm sorry, the phone slipped from my hand because I just put on hand cream before leaving the room," the woman said, turning around and bending down to look for the phone.

"*Dios Mio*, could this be any more difficult…" Lupe's words were left in her throat when she felt something soft pushing her against the kitchen counter. Instinctively, she grabbed whatever was in front of her to keep her balance. She heard the woman's long nails scratching the floor.

"Crap, I'm sorry, I'm just trying to find the phone on the floor" the woman said and panted. "I'll try not to squash you to death."

For the first time in her life, Lupe was left without words.

The sensation of the woman's soft behind pressing against her navel just above her pubic bone set her gut on fire and the rhythmic rubs caused by the woman moving on the floor woke up her clitoral area, filling her with hot desire. She had to fight back the urge to move her hips and to rub her back.

Her hands on her lower waistline just above her soft buttocks burnt like a flame as she took a firmer grip on her. The familiar scent made her head spin.

The woman felt amazing and her height was just about right for her.

She was smaller than Lupe had originally thought but definitely curvy based on the width of her hips and the softness of her buttocks. She had a tight little body and she couldn't be over five feet tall without her high heels, Lupe thought. She had heard the echo when the woman had walked after her to the kitchenette. The carpet that would have softened her steps had been taken up on the fifth floor a couple of weeks back due to complaints about mold, Lupe remembered.

"Finally found it!" the woman said suddenly and straightened her body up. Lupe instantly let go of her hips as if they would have burnt her hands.

The woman turned around abruptly to hand over the phone, but the tiny kitchenette didn't leave much room for social distancing. She was standing very close to her now and Lupe could feel her menthol breath tickling her chin and her soft chest pressing against her body. There couldn't be more than inches between their lips.

"Can you change the fuse now?" the woman whispered, breaking the silence.

"Yes of course, in a second. I think we have a stool in every kitchenette," Lupe said and blindly started searching around the small kitchenette. It didn't take long for her hands to find the only item in the kitchenette.

"There we go, found it!" she said and took a firm grip of the back of the stool.

"Now we need to find the fridge as the fuse box is usually located above it," Lupe said and started touching around in order to understand the structure of the kitchenette and find the fridge.

"I'm quite sure the fridge is over here," a small voice responded as the woman tapped the fridge door with her long nail.

"Great, *gringuita,* sounds good, I can finally see you have made yourself useful to me," Lupe said sarcastically. "Except, I have no idea where you are pointing as I can't see anything in this *shit hole.*"

"Oh, that's true, sorry," the woman said and grabbed Lupe's hand to lead her towards the fridge.

Lupe took a small surprised step forward in the small kitchenette.

The woman's hand was warm and silky soft and smelt like vanilla and the caress of her long nails on the sensitive part of Lupe's wrist gave her goosebumps. It was like an electric shock making her wrist itch and the scent of her hand cream sent alarm to her brain and her heart skipped a beat. She panted as if she had run a mile.

For a moment, she was sure the woman was playing with her on purpose and would let her feel something other than the fridge.

"It's here, can you feel it now?" the woman asked tentatively.

Lupe cleared her throat loudly. "Yes, I can feel it just fine, thank you," she said and ripped her hand off hers, placing the small stool in front of the fridge. She heard the woman taking a step back to allow her more space.

"Now *gringuita,* I'm going to stand up on the stool and change the fuse, but meanwhile, could you kindly turn on the torch on the phone so that I can see something in this hell hole."

"Sure, no problem," the woman said and soon Lupe could hear her tapping the phone with her nails.

She hadn't seen the colour of her nails, but they would probably be devilish red, Lupe thought and for a second she pictured those nails running up and down her naked back leaving red marks on it. She sighed silently and felt the burning moistness growing between her legs.

It made her want to rub herself against the woman again. Hard, even *violently*.

She probably wouldn't last long, it would be very quick, Lupe thought and chuckled.

The woman couldn't possibly be oblivious of her impact on her, or on *anyone* for that matter, Lupe thought. The voice, the scent, the small curvy body, all of it was made for seduction. For a moment, Lupe played with the idea of asking her out. First as a friend of course and then see if there could be anything more.

Otherwise, she could just seduce her for one night to rub the itch and get it over with, she thought and smiled. It wouldn't be the first time she had seduced a first timer, she grinned.

Lupe completely lacked experience of women outside of the Latin community, which left her only guessing where the mysterious woman could be from as she wasn't English for sure based on the accent that kept flashing out every now and then. Who knew, she might be Eastern European, she smiled. In those countries, women were usually considered promiscuous and willing to try new things, Lupe weighed silently. Even to offer a little bit of money would be worth it, she thought.

Suddenly, the face of *her gringa linda* appeared in her mind.

Lupe hadn't even realised it was the first time she had used the pet name *gringuita* on anyone else except *her*.

Her face softened for a moment at the longing thought of her *gringa linda,* her *foreign girl.* Maybe this was finally the moment when she was ready to let go of the ghost that had haunted her for years and start her life again free from the influence of *her*. It would be painful and require time but based on her bodily reaction to the woman trapped in the small kitchenette with her, she couldn't be far away, she thought.

"Oh, I found the torch, look," the woman said suddenly. "Here we go, let there be light!" she said and the small kitchenette filled with light.

"Ah, finally!" Lupe said and rubbed her eyes without turning to face her, focusing instead on the fuse box in front of her. She couldn't bring herself to look at the woman as deep down, under all the layers of false confidence, she was a shy woman who had faced constant rejection her whole life. She didn't have to look at the woman to know she must be gorgeous and so far out of her league not even a spaceship would bring them together, she thought sadly.

The faster she fixed the fuse, the faster she was able to continue her night and get rid of the mystery lady in the kitchenette. They would go their separate ways, there was no doubt about it, and that was OK. She was content with it.

Anyway, she was sure being trapped in a dark confined place with someone had sharpened her other senses to cover the lack of eyesight. Some people would even start hearing or *feeling* things that didn't exist, she thought and sighed with relief as she found the spare fuse and quickly changed it.

The fridge started its loud generating noise again as Lupe wiped her dusty hands on the blue cloth she had put in her back pocket.

Maybe that would explain the moment of insanity in the tiny kitchenette with a strange woman, she thought and laughed inside. It had definitely been too long since she had got properly laid. It was something she was going to take care of tonight even if she had to use someone else from her back list she decided and closed the control panel.

"There you go *gringuita*, at your service!" Lupe said smiling and turned around to face the strange woman for the first time since they had been trapped in the corridor together.

The air left her lungs. It couldn't be. It was simply impossible.

Her eyes locked with the same blue eyes with a hint of green that had been haunting her for years. The heart-shaped mouth with devilish red lipstick framed by long blonde hair. The familiar scent circulated in the air as she recognised the source of it.

She looked exactly the same as on the first night they had met.

Lupe felt physically sick. Air was trapped in her lungs, unable to find its way out as if her body had gone into shock. The tingling feeling in her fingertips got stronger and her tongue swelled up inside her mouth. Cold sweat broke out on her forehead and she felt like she was having a heart attack. Suddenly, the whole room started spinning around in front of her as she closed her eyes and fell.

Chapter 34

Ellen saw the stranger's eyes rolling back as she started falling down from the stool. She knew she wouldn't be strong enough to hold her whole body weight, but her natural instinct was to protect the stranger from hurting herself.

Ellen opened her arms to catch her and when she tumbled against her in the tiny kitchenette, Ellen hit her back on the wall trying to balance them both.

The stranger was heavy, like a rag doll. Her dark curly hair tickled Ellen's nose and her strong body pressed tightly against her own body. Her hair smelled like fresh shampoo.

"Are you OK?" Ellen said and looked for a hint of reaction from her face without a luck.

My god, could the night be any worse? Ellen thought and leaned deeper against the wall, closing her eyes. It was going to take a while before the stranger woke up.

*

When she had dropped the phone on the floor, Ellen had bent down immediately to look for it. She had turned and bent so suddenly she must have taken the stranger by surprise as she had been forced to grab her hips to try and keep her balance.

The kitchenette was tiny and in order to bend all the way down to the floor to reach the phone, she had needed to stretch her buttocks as far back as she had been able. She hadn't intended to push forcefully, but lack of space had left her no choice but to rub her buttocks against the stranger's crotch.

When Ellen had felt the stranger's hands on her hips, she could have sworn she felt her pushing tighter against her.

Ellen had felt aroused. It had brought up the memory of an incident that had happened a long time ago in Spain.

The incident had haunted her for years, yet she hadn't shared it with anyone. It was the secret moment that came back to her mind every now and then and she still had mixed feelings about the whole event.

Truth being told, someone could have classified the events of that night as rape as Ellen hadn't been in the position of agreeing to any of it, but for some reason she couldn't bring herself to see it that way; in fact, she had been rather *intrigued* by the events of that night and how she had responded freely to the stranger's touch. The memory of it still made her hot and heavy in her gut and made her clit twist with desire.

Soon enough, she had found her phone and straightened her body quickly. As she had turned around to switch on the torch on her phone, the stranger had been standing very close to her. She could have sworn her lips had been only inches away from her chin. She had smelled a masculine perfume mixed with a hint of feminine scent, which most probably was her own body scent.

They had stood there for a moment before the stranger had moved to fix the fuse. It had taken only minutes and the room had filled with light and Ellen had seen the stranger for the first time.

She was a *handsome* woman. She had fair and flawless skin with barely noticeable freckles framing her tiny nose. Her dark, curly hair almost reached her strong shoulders which led to fully tattooed arms. She was wearing a white dress shirt and dark trousers with a black belt and when she had turned around and looked at her, Ellen had felt like a prisoner of her stare being stripped naked in front of her eyes.

Her eyes were a captivating brown, like dark chocolate, and full of shock and fear though Ellen didn't understand why.

They had been staring at each other without words but with such an intensity that Ellen could have sworn she felt a magnetic field around them before the stranger had rolled her eyes back and unconsciousness had swallowed her. She had fainted before Ellen could even ask her name.

The sudden movements of the stranger's limbs brought Ellen back to reality.

She smiled and gently touched the stranger's cheek and brushed a lonely curl from her face before realising the intimacy of her gesture and quickly putting her hands down and waiting for the stranger to open her eyes.

Chapter 35

Lupe opened her eyes slowly.

First, she gently moved her limbs; both of her legs and arms were moving normally without pain, which was good she thought. Her legs were slightly unsteady, and she realised she was almost on her knees, leaning on something soft in front of her. She was almost ready to close her eyes again when the reality hit her and she pushed herself up.

"Ouch! Slowly if I may ask," the woman said and massaged her arms where Lupe had pushed herself up.

Lupe stared at the sight in front of her. What she saw sent a sensation like icy water over her body, causing her to suck in her breath.

It was *her. Her gringa linda.*

The girl she had met all those years ago in Spain. The incident she had never told anyone about, yet it had haunted her day and night, taking her close to insanity. It had made her other relationships feel secondary and her one-night stands more and more passionless. She had been the main reason she had eventually left Viviana and walked away from the house they had shared. Viviana had cried, fought back, broken every single item in the house into small pieces and cut up all her clothing, leaving Lupe to walk away taking only what she had been wearing at that moment.

Since then, Lupe had tried to form new relationships, but she had always compared them to *her*. None of the other women could have hold the candle to her *gringa linda*.

They had stayed with her for a while, first complaining that something was missing and eventually finding someone else to satisfy their needs and desire for connection and care. How could she have opened up to anyone and explained that her affection and care had been stolen by a mystery woman she had found during a robbery, made love to while wearing a mask and left tied up waiting for the police to find her.

Lupe had hated her for a long time, blamed her for what she had done to her, but deep down she had known she had prompted the events of the night herself, taken a bite of the forbidden fruit and was now a slave to it for good.

One would have thought the time would have made the memory of her fade away, but on the contrary, time had only made the image clearer in her mind.

The sad truth was Lupe had *lived* for those nights with her in her dreams and all those dark hours before dawn when she had closed her eyes and almost felt her soft hands reaching out for her, caressing her cheeks with a butterfly touch.

She had been content with her life but felt something vital was missing, like sun after a long winter.

She had spent countless hours thinking about her and where she could be, yet she was in front of her now, eight long empty years later.

It felt surreal.

Lupe couldn't help letting her eyes wander from her face down to her body. She was even more beautiful than she remembered.

She looked more mature now, which made sense after eight years. Her voice was slightly lower, and her body definitely had more curves. Lupe could clearly see her well-defined tiny waist and soft deliciously round buttocks, which had rubbed against her just minutes ago.

She felt dizzy again.

The woman was wearing an emerald green silky blouse that complemented the green in her eyes and had felt heavenly in her hands when she had touched her. Her lower body was covered in a tight leather skirt, which made her waist look even tinier. The outfit was finished with black stiletto pumps and her wavy blonde hair framed her beautiful face.

Her gringa linda looked devilish, even *dangerous*.

"Mm, are you OK? How do you feel?" The woman eyed her worriedly. "Let me get you some water," she said and turned to open the kitchenette cupboards to find a glass and fill it with cold water from the tap. Lupe didn't respond but reached for the glass of water and took a long sip before swallowing loudly.

The woman looked at her thoughtfully.

"Looks like you went down there pretty hard. I hope you didn't hurt yourself," she said. "You do look quite pale. Should we get you to A&E?" she asked but Lupe shook her head.

"Are you sure?" she insisted.

Lupe nodded and finished her glass of water with one last sip before turning and placing the empty glass in the sink.

Her eyes followed her every movement tentatively as she waited for her to answer. Lupe couldn't take her eyes off her.

They stared at each other curiously in the small kitchenette before her *gringa linda* turned her gaze down and cleared her throat.

"OK then, great. Mmm is there anything else I can do for you now?" she asked.

Lupe looked for the words in her head as she slowly recovered from the shock of seeing her again but couldn't bring herself to speak.

Minutes passed without words, seemingly making *gringa linda* uncomfortable.

"OK, well I think I'm going to take off since you don't need medical attention, but just in case, please take my number. If you feel like you can't get home alone, I shouldn't be far away from the area anyway," she said and quickly scribbled her number on a dirty napkin she found on the kitchen counter before handing it to Lupe.

She had turned away to leave before Lupe opened her mouth for the first time since she had seen her. "I'm fine thank you. I have low blood pressure you see. And I'm afraid of heights," she added, immediately regretting her irrational answer.

It was only partially untrue as she did suffer from low blood pressure from time to time, but she wasn't afraid of heights. She had just made it up to explain her reaction.

She smiled and it took Lupe's breath away; her smile was *mesmerising*.

"OK then," she said and turned to pick up her small handbag that had fallen down when she had caught Lupe in her arms.

"I guess I'll leave you to it then, but give me a shout if your condition worsens tonight. I think you should finish for today and check at least your blood pressure with the doctor at your practice tomorrow. I'm sure your manager will understand," she said.

Lupe listened in silence and nodded her head as she watched her go, her hands burning under the napkin where her *gringa linda* had voluntarily written her phone number.

She had been right, her buttocks had the shape of a fresh peach and her hips moved alluringly from side to side as she walked away.

Lupe had to pinch herself to be sure she wasn't dreaming. It felt surreal to her, how they could meet after so many years in such a coincidental way. Someone had a sick idea of playing with destiny, she thought and quickly glanced up before realisation hit her like a slap in the face. Her *gringa linda* didn't recognise her because she had *never seen* her face on that night.

Lupe was a complete stranger to her.

*

Panic rose in her as she looked at the phone number. *Shit, was that a four or a seven?* She couldn't tell.

"*Princesa!*" she yelled which made the woman freeze and turn on her heels.

"What did you call me?"

Double shit, Lupe hadn't meant it but somehow the pet name she had used for her years ago escaped from her lips. "I mean *Miss*, is the final number in your telephone number a four or a seven?"

"It's a seven," *gringa linda* said, smiling softly and winking before she disappeared towards the elevator.

My lucky number, Lupe thought and caressed the dirty napkin in her hand before realising she had written something else at the top.

Ellen.

Her name was Ellen. Her *gringa linda* finally had a name, she thought and carefully folded and and placed the napkin in her pocket as if it was the most precious piece of paper she had ever owned.

After all these years, she finally had a name for the face. It was a pretty name she thought. It suited her well.

Sexy even.

The sudden ping of the elevator door put movement in her body and she hurried to the entrance window just in time to see Ellen approach a waiting car.

She didn't *want* to let her go. Who knew when she would see her again? A sudden feeling of loneliness hit her and she felt like crying to see her go.

There was a man in a suit waiting for her in a red Mini Cooper.

Lupe watched as she shook his hand and let him open the car door for her.

The man held the door open for her and placed his hand on her back as if to assist her into the car.

Piece of shit, Lupe thought and felt her nails crawling inside her fist.

She noticed Ellen taking a quick look back at the building before disappearing inside the car.

Looking for me? Lupe thought and her heart skipped another beat.

The man closed the door, walked back to the driver's side and drove away.

Lupe stayed in the window for some time before she remembered the original reason why she had been in the building.

She felt her phone vibrating. For a brief moment she pictured Ellen's name on her phone screen and how it would feel to see it.

She laughed out loud at her silly thoughts and fished her phone from her pocket.

It was her older lady friend calling her. Lupe had sent her a text cancelling their night together or postponing it to later in the evening due to work. She had texted back saying she couldn't make it out later so Lupe had ended up cancelling the whole meet up.

She looked at the ringing phone, but she couldn't bring herself to answer. The phone went silent again and within seconds she received a WhatsApp message from her saying she had managed to get out. Lupe read the message but didn't respond and instead went back to her work.

She finished the work in world record speed but decided to stay.

She wanted to wait for Ellen to come back.

Chapter 36

Ellen had had a nice evening.

Her date had taken her to a fancy hotel lounge bar in Chelsea Harbour, which was famous for its cocktails. She had to admit the cocktails had been almost a work of art and she had felt bad for even touching them let alone drinking them. She hadn't seen the bill but judging by the environment, the drinks had been expensive.

Not that she had ever seen a bill from her dates before, after all she was a real lady who expected her date to pay for her drinks if they wanted to take her out. There was nothing wrong with it, she thought. It was old-fashioned, but then Ellen had always considered herself old-fashioned. She also didn't mind taking care of the domestic chores around the house and putting her partner's wellbeing ahead of her own priorities.

It was boring but love for her.

Trading and exchanging skills benefitted both parties and the relationship had a better chance of surviving. It was called *complementing* each other.

The practicality of it was something most people were unable to understand, so she always made sure she dated someone intellectual enough and who was on the same page as her. They were usually lawyers, bankers, successful entrepreneurs or the equivalent and all had one thing in common: they all were filthy rich and powerful.

Ellen smiled and waved to the departing car before turning to walk back to her accommodation. It hadn't been long ago when she had also provided professional services for money as she called it.

When she had arrived in the country for the first time, she had bought a new cooker for her rented apartment, but due to lack of finances, she had ended up asking her new neighbour to install it instead of paying a professional. Unfortunately, the cooker hadn't been installed correctly and it had released more gas into the air than it should have and had ended up setting off the alarms in the whole building. Considering the severity of the situation, the fire brigade had been forced to break the door in to her flat to close the gas pipe. Ellen had been happy no one had got hurt, but as the insurance claim was put forward she had learnt that as the installation had not been carried out by a professional, she was unable to claim back the damage from her insurance company. In the end, Ellen had been personally responsible for all costs relating to the incident.

Replacing the door hadn't cost much but resetting the alarm system and providing additional gas leak inspections to all the other flats in the building had ended up being more costly to her wallet.

She had ended up using her credit cards to pay all of the costs before she had realised the interest rate for the cards had gone up dramatically. To avoid all the added costs from the interest she had ended up desperately scrolling through different websites for additional income before she had found a site linking attractive young women with busy businessmen.

The official mission of the website had been to link young and ambitious women with lonely or busy businessmen who would rather have a smart and fun relationship built on mutual interest and rules than a complicated relationship with a woman who would always want more than they could offer.

No strings attached and no mixed messages.

The website had never mentioned sex being part of any deals and described the service more as socialising and offering support or company, but Ellen hadn't been naïve in that sense.

In order to *gain*, one needed to be willing to *give*.

The idea didn't particularly please her as she had never been promiscuous and always chose carefully who she had sexual relations with. However, after years of trying, she had learnt that she was only able to fully relax and reach orgasm with herself alone and, therefore, all her sexual relationships had been a series of disappointing events for her. She had enjoyed her part without a doubt, but it had felt like just another chore for the day without sparkle or fireworks.

She understood that sex was a natural part of a relationship and, in the beginning, she had been very upset at her shortcomings in the field but after discovering she was still able to be her own master, it had changed her life. And as she didn't need to find her own satisfaction, she was able to give her full attention to the task at hand, which was pleasing the other person with her, and after years of practising and reading about the subject, she had become *good*. Master of the game.

Ellen had been sceptical when she signed up on the website, but after meeting a couple of gentlemen for dinner, she had been convinced it had been the right option for her as her job already included quite a lot of socialising with strangers on different corporate levels. She was smooth in small talk and keeping up light, flirtatious conversations. Some of them had asked for more than just hand holding, which she had not refused as long as there had been a mutual amicable connection and the person had held a high position in business life as she had still been eager to take every opportunity to learn new business skills that might help her in the future.

Continuous learning in life was the key to success.

On her second date with a successful businessman from Dubai she had mentioned her financial hardship at the dinner table.

He had invited her to a lovely restaurant called Sexy Fish in the heart of London with a view and white table linen and silver crockery. Quiet violin music had filled the restaurant and the food had been to die for.

She had quietly explained her situation to him and shed a tear in front of him while asking for advice. It had taken only a couple of minutes for him to fish out his wallet and hit the table with exactly £5000 in cash.

Of course, Ellen had at first refused the money, it was part of the game, but when he had been very adamant and pushed the money towards her, she had smiled coyly and put the money in her bag without counting it so as not to look too eager or to show her excitement about how easy it had been for her to gain the money back that she had lost.

After he had paid for the dinner, he had taken her home.

Even though there had been no physical attraction whatsoever from Ellen's side, she had let him kiss her on the doorstep.

It had affected him like a storm, and he had ended up crushing her against the door. Ellen had forced a little whimper from her lips.

"I have never met anyone like you, Ellen," he had muffled in between kisses. "Your eyes are full of passion and desire. I can feel it from your body."

Ellen had smiled back before she had coyly wished him goodnight and turned around to enter her house, blowing air kisses at him as he had walked back to his expensive car.

Ellen had stared out of the window until the rear lights of the classic red Ferrari disappeared as he turned onto the route to Central London.

He hadn't been wrong about what he had seen in her eyes when he had looked at her, she thought. Too bad he didn't know it had been the £5000 she had seen in front of her eyes all along.

Chapter 37

Lupe was napping in the domestic's cupboard on the fifth floor when she heard the elevator ping. She quickly turned off the lights and parted the door to see who was coming up. She smelled her before the elevator doors opened and she saw her walk out of the elevator alone.

Lupe exhaled silently without realising she had been holding her breath.

Ellen opened her coat and walked directly without looking around to the door leading to the on-call room she was staying in.

At the door, she suddenly stopped and lifted her head, looking around as if she could feel someone watching her.

Lupe stopped breathing and placed her hand over her mouth.

Ellen looked around the corridor before taking her keys out of her pocket and opening the door.

Lupe waited five minutes before opening the domestic's cupboard door fully. She looked at her watch. It was only 10 p.m.

Either her date had been really bad or it had been a business appointment, no one comes home this early from a good date, she thought, smiling to herself.

She inhaled the air in the corridor and closed her eyes. She couldn't get enough of her scent.

She smelled more woman now, familiar but definitely more woman she thought and opened the door to the fire exit stairs. She didn't want to take the lift; she didn't want to risk Ellen hearing her leave.

Chapter 38

The week passed by without Lupe seeing Ellen at all.

She was told the business analyst was on the road visiting other hospitals. No one seemed to know when she would return, which only made Lupe angrier. She was full of energy each morning and arrived at work early only to see her desk still empty. As the days passed, she was reaching her limit and couldn't stop dark jealousy creeping into her heart, which was ridiculous as she knew nothing about her.

Who knew, she might be married now with kids, she thought.

For a second, Lupe saw an image of a little boy with dark curly hair and sky-blue eyes in front of her, but she quickly shook the image of her.

Lupe had tried to discreetly ask her age from her co-workers, but no one seemed to know anything about her, which surprised Lupe because she knew she was quite talkative with the team. In fact, she had heard them talking about Ellen many times before.

Lupe had even gone so far as walking by the hospital accommodation she lived in and waiting for some time just to see her coming home. She had never showed up.

Fuelled by anger and dark jealousy, she had used her janitor's key to enter the building and walked up the stairs to the fifth floor. She had knocked on the entrance door before using the key to enter the corridor.

The memory of their first encounter had greeted her sweetly and made her stand at the entrance before entering the area. The *second encounter*, she reminded herself.

She quickly walked to the last door which Ellen had come out of on that night and leaned her ear on the door without hearing a thing.

Lupe weighed up for a moment whether she should open the door and just enter her room without permission, but she was too eager to get to know her and couldn't resist.

Technically, she didn't exactly ease the process by being away so much, so it was almost her responsibility to enter the room, she thought and unlocked the door.

The room was small, as all the on-call rooms on the floor. They had given her the only room without a view of the street and instead, rewarded her with a rooftop window which made the room look ever sadder.

Lupe scanned her surroundings quickly. The space was terribly small but somehow, Ellen had been able to keep it nicely organised. The room consisted of an old and tired wardrobe and writing desk standing on the left side of the room, a single bed and a lonely sink with two storage shelves and a mirror. The walls used to be white but had turned a dirty cream shade over the years. The dark brown furniture had definitely been a bargain buy from a second-hand shop and didn't do much to enhance the small space. The humidity entered the room via the rooftop window that was constantly wet and clearly lacked packing. The room reminded Lupe of a prison without bars.

She looked around curiously. Ellen was a neat person, which made Lupe glad as she hated clutter herself. She clearly had a soft spot for expensive linen, Lupe thought, as she touched the fluffy pillow and Egyptian duvet cover on the single bed. On the writing desk, she had a couple of books and a black kettle with peppermint teabags next to it.

She also liked mint tea, Lupe smiled, and touched the two pink polka dot mugs on the desk. The books were merely about business which didn't raise any interest in her, but then she noticed a small paperback book stuffed under the open business book. She carefully took it in her hand. *Her Salvation* she read on the cover which showed a beautiful blonde woman with a ripped white dress exposing her delicate neck and slender legs. The cover was shot in a jungle and behind the bushes there was a handsome man in an explorer outfit carrying a gun and staring passionately at the girl. It was clearly a romance novel and apparently Ellen had read the book many times judging by the worn book corners. Lupe opened the book in the middle and started reading random lines. Soon the lines turned into a full-blown erotic scene that made her blush and slam the book closed in embarrassment. She was about to stuff the book back where she had found it when a devilish smile sparked on her face and she opened the book again at the erotic scene and placed it carefully under the business book.

At least she would know what kind of dirt Ellen would be reading tonight, she thought and smiled.

Lupe turned around to the other side of the tiny room and looked at the sink area.

Ellen clearly liked the colour pink, she thought as she eyed the pink, blue and silver toiletries bags on the cabinet. One of the bags was overly full and couldn't close properly.

Lupe looked closer.

She could see a tube of lipstick sneaking out of the small bag. *Scarlett Red* 77 *by Dior*, she read on the tube and raised her eyebrows before putting the lipstick in her pocket.

She didn't have much time and was constantly worried that she could hear someone walking along the corridor but she couldn't help opening the wardrobe.

Where Ellen clearly loved pink in some items, it didn't match in her clothing: the closet was full of black clothing. Lupe touched a fur vest and leather skirt in the neatly organised closet.

She likes to dress sexy and dangerous, she thought and nodded approvingly. I will need to buy her something red, she smiled and closed the closet carefully, checking she had not changed the position of anything else except the scene in the dirty book Ellen had been reading. It brought the smile back to Lupe's face as she closed and locked the door to the room.

The corridor was still empty and she hurried towards the staircase without seeing anyone.

*

On the final day of the second week without seeing her, Lupe's patience was finally rewarded when she saw her handbag on a chair in the office. Her mood lifted instantly, and she entered the back office smiling and whistling.

"Wow, what's up with you Lupita? After wandering around with half a face for weeks, you are finally smiling again. Dare I ask what her name is?" Giuliana asked and winked at her.

"Nothing *cariño*, I'm just happy, it's nice weather outside and birds are singing, all that crap, you know."

Giuliana looked at her suspiciously. "Mmm, *cariño*, have you actually looked outside for the past hour? It is raining cats and dogs."

Lupe frowned.

Had she really been that oblivious of her surroundings, she thought.

Giuliana started laughing. "Got ya, *cariño*," she said. "I have no idea how the weather is outside but indeed, you are thinking about someone, I can see it from your face."

Lupe couldn't help but join in her fun and soon they were both laughing with happy tears in their eye corners.

They worked silently for a while with no sign of Ellen before Lupe gathered her courage and asked: "Giuliana, did you see Ellen when she arrived in the office today? I saw her bag, but I haven't seen her."

Giuliana didn't raise her gaze from the computer screen. "I'm not sure *cariño*, but she is definitely in. We are planning to have burgers and ice creams at Kings Street Byron. You know the place?"

Lupe's heart skipped a beat in excitement, but she didn't dare to look at her.

"Yeah, I know it. Do you know if she is coming?" Lupe asked casually.

Giuliana squinted her eyes at the computer screen and typed on the keyboard before responding. "I'm not sure *cariño*, but I will ask once she finishes the meeting with the site management team."

Lupe didn't have time to respond before she heard a familiar voice behind her.

"Someone mentioned my name?"

Lupe felt her heart burst with joy, but she couldn't turn around to face her.

Giuliana spoke first. "Ellen, sorry, I just mentioned your name because Lupe was asking if we were going for dinner today at Byron." She nodded towards Lupe, trying to make her turn around and greet Ellen, but she stayed focused on her desk, staring at the screen without saying a word and forcing Ellen to approach her. Lupe counted five before she could see Ellen's shadow above her and feel the familiar scent sweetly embracing her.

"Lupe?" Ellen said tentatively. "I didn't know we worked for the same company, it is nice to see you again," she said and placed her hand on her shoulder.

The touch affected Lupe like a fire, burning her skin through her shirt.

She jumped up to shake her hand off from her shoulder but before she knew it, she had turned around and placed a kiss on each of her cheeks.

Ellen looked stunned but answered both of the kisses. "Two kisses, eh? Am I lucky or what?" She smiled and lightly brushed her fingertips on Lupe's cheek.

The gesture looked innocent but Lupe could see a teasing look in her eyes, or was it just her imagination? She wasn't sure anymore.

"Wow, I didn't realise you two knew each other," Giuliana said and eyed them both curiously.

"We met some weeks back in the patient hotel when the fuse went off on my floor," Ellen said and broke the eye contact with Lupe. "Luckily for me, Lupe was there to change the fuse, I wouldn't have known what to do myself," she laughed.

"Really?" Giuliana raised her eyebrows to Lupe as if expecting her to make a joke. Lupe recovered quickly. "Well, I wouldn't want to leave a pretty lady in distress, would I? My mother raised me to know better," she said and winked.

Ellen looked at her with thoughtful eyes. "Right, well anyway, thanks for your help once again," she said and turned around to place the computer she was still holding into her bag.

Lupe's heart sank. It looked like she was leaving.

"Any luck with the house hunting?" she asked quickly.

Ellen turned back to face her. "Not really, I haven't had time to look," she said and continued packing.

Giuliana raised her head. "Oh I know, maybe Lupe can help you find a flat Ellen?" she said and nodded towards Lupe. "I told you before, she knows all kinds of people around the city and usually gets good deals."

Lupe could have kissed her for the comment, but instead shrugged her shoulders casually. "I might be able to help. If you just tell me your requirements, I can give you a call if I find something decent?"

"I think it's an excellent idea, I wish I had someone helping me when I arrived," Giuliana said, adding pressure for Ellen to reply.

Lupe smiled inside when she saw Ellen changing the weight between her legs hesitantly. Even if she hadn't seen her face on the night in Spain, she must *feel* the magical air between them. Even Giuliana had turned around fully to watch them.

"Appreciate it," Ellen said finally and turned to leave as Giuliana spoke again. "Wait Ellen, what about dinner at Byron tonight?" she said tentatively.

"I'm sorry Giuliana, I can't make it tonight, we will have to rearrange," she said apologetically before leaving the office.

"OK Ellen, don't worry I will ask if Lupe can do –" She didn't manage to finish her sentence before a hand was on her mouth cutting off her words.

She eyed Lupe angrily and shook her hand off. "What are you doing? I just wanted to reschedule the dinner with her."

"Yeah, I know but I don't want her to know I'm coming as well," Lupe said. Giuliana looked at her suspiciously. "Why does it matter if you are coming or not?"

Lupe didn't know if it was the electricity between them or the hesitancy in her voice that gave her away but she watched as realisation hit Giuliana's face and she gasped: "Oh my God, you like her don't you!" she said and pointed her finger at Lupe.

She shrugged her shoulders casually. "I might, she is beautiful and sexy, she might be entertaining company for a night or two."

"Are you sure? She doesn't look like any of the women you usually go out with," Giuliana said and looked at the door Ellen had disappeared through a couple of minutes before. "I don't know, she seems so much as a woman. You might get burnt along the way," she said and looked sadly at Lupe. "Who knows, she might not even like women."

Lupe didn't have time to answer before Jack entered the back office to invite them to a staff meeting. They both left the office, but the image of eight years back burnt Lupe's mind. Giuliana would be surprised if she only knew, she thought and touched the napkin in her pocket where Ellen had written her phone number some weeks back. She had sent her a WhatsApp message on the night to let her know she had been OK and so she could see whenever she was online on WhatsApp. The information itself didn't help her now but it could turn out to be important in the future, she had thought as she had heard her phone alerting her of an incoming message. She had quickly checked the screen and her face had softened as she had seen the sender's familiar face and read the message on her mobile phone screen: "I'm glad."

She had screenshotted the profile picture and looked at it closer. The picture had been taken abroad somewhere in front of an idyllic water fountain. Ellen had been wearing a white Bardot-style white crop top with long puff sleeves and classic high-waisted jeans with nude high-heel pumps. One hand had been in her pocket and the other was casually brushing her wavy hair out of her face. She didn't look at the camera but had a wide smile on her face and a hint of smudged red lipstick on her lips.

That night, Lupe had smashed her tea mug against the wall, letting the ugly brown liquid run down the white walls as she jealously imagined the face of the person who had caused the smile on her face and the lipstick smudge on her lips.

Chapter 39

Ellen was just about to enter her room after taking a hot steamy shower. She was freezing now in her towel and quickly reached for her dressing gown and slippers before she heard an incoming message on her phone.

Buenas noches muñequita, would you be interested in a flat near Paddington station?

Ellen eyed the unknown phone number before recalling that she had agreed to Lupe helping her find a flat.

She felt instant butterflies in her stomach.

I might be. What you got? She sent the reply.

She didn't manage to put the phone down before it received another text.

Studio flat, nice view and good shopping street. Free now if you can make the decision instantly.

Ellen rolled her eyes.

Studio flat with a view sounds nice if the price is affordable. Shopping street I really don't care, I'm not much of a shopper. Not sure if I can make a decision this fast. she wrote and hit reply again.

Really? You have surprised me. You look like a million dollars always, princesa.

Ellen frowned as something dark and familiar crossed her mind again and made her feel uneasy. She rubbed her neck before replying.

Thank you for the compliment. I try my best every day. she wrote and hesitated before continuing. *btw, don't call me princesa, please.* She hit the send button, placed the phone on the writing desk and got ready for bed.

Her intention was to leave the phone and enjoy reading before going to sleep but the vibration of incoming texts didn't leave her alone.

I'm sorry gringa linda, I will never make that mistake again. Besides, I'm sure your good style is more than skin deep and reaches under your plain work suit as well...

She was flirting with her, Ellen knew it but didn't know how to react to it. She was used to these messages and usually knew exactly what to say and how to react, but Lupe's messages made her feel something else, something *dark.*

She felt her body heat up under the duvet and her fingers quickly typed the only response she could think of.

Well, I have always enjoyed sexy lingerie and never wore tights in my entire life.

She waited for a couple of minutes before she saw an incoming text again. It was exactly the one she was expecting.

The ones you wore today with your black skirt were not tights? Entonces, what were they?

Ellen looked at the screen and searched for the picture she had taken earlier in the day of her legs with the black satin stay-up stockings and her black stiletto heels and sent it to her. She smiled devilishly and placed the phone carefully on the desk. The picture was taken at the perfect angle, elongating her legs and focusing on her delicate ankles.

It wouldn't take more than a couple of minutes for the next text to come she thought, and she was right.

Mi gringa linda... you will give me a heart attack one day...

Ellen smiled.

Happy we speak the same language, she wrote and was opening the book she had hidden under the business book when the final text came in.

We definitely do. Enjoy your book tonight.

Chapter 40

The next weeks were filled with teasing texts.

Lupe felt ecstatic and couldn't wait to go to work and, more importantly, to come back so that she could start texting with her.

The tone of their texts was light and fuelled with sexual chemistry. It was clear they had good chemistry, Lupe was sure of it but didn't really know how to make the next move with her. After all, they already knew each other physically, Ellen just didn't know it yet.

Lupe had played with the idea of them in bed together and the realisation on her face when she would remember her touch. The idea scared her.

What would she think of her then?

To make matters worse, she was tormented by the thought of her spending time with anyone else, especially after learning she had caught the eye of Jack, the Operations Manager on site who was now constantly after her.

She had barely been able to hold her tongue when Jack had invited her to the weekly management meeting and gently guided her to the meeting room by touching her back. It had made her fists heavy and it had taken all her self-control not to punch the pretty face of her boss.

She hated him.

Jack was a handsome Brazilian guy with a wife and a small child at home but that didn't seem to stop him from flirting with Ellen constantly. Lupe was sure he knew exactly how she felt about Ellen – she could see it in his eyes; the competition.

It killed her slowly inside and even Jose-Luis, her baby brother, had looked at Ellen's profile picture on her phone and told Lupe it would never happen for her. Lupe had felt crushed and only the burning memory of their hot bodies joining together, pleasing each other, driving them to the point of insanity and over the edge where there was nothing else but them, kept her soul alive and mind focused.

Lupe was focused on finding a flat for Ellen; good enough so that she would accept it but close enough so that she could keep an eye on her.

One Friday proved to be her lucky day, when her sister called about an available flat close to UpBridge Road in Shepherd's Bush.

Hola mi gringa linda. New flat available in Shepherd's Bush, can you make it to the viewing by 3 p.m. today?

Even though she knew Ellen was in a management meeting, she didn't have to wait for long.

Sure thing. Do you have pictures I can have a look at?

Lupe exhaled and sent a couple of pictures her sister had sent her earlier. She had scanned them quickly and added some lighting and filtering to ensure they would look appealing enough for Ellen to decide it would be worth the trip. She was too nervous to wait for her response.

I will pick you up from the hospital on my motorcycle. she wrote and waited until she could see two blue ticks on the message showing it had arrived.

Then she turned off her phone as she didn't want to give Ellen an opportunity to say no.

Shortly before 3 p.m. she left the hospital, rode her motorcycle to the hospital accommodation and killed the engine. It was a clear day and Ellen was standing in front of the reception looking at the main road.

She hadn't noticed her yet which gave Lupe some time to breathe in the image of her. She looked as beautiful as always wearing jeans and a leather jacket with a sky-blue scarf around her neck. She had her hair combed back and held in place by two sets of transparent pins and a small black handbag crossed over her body. She had clearly prepared herself for a ride on a motorcycle, Lupe thought and whistled to her.

Ellen raised her head instantly as if she knew the call was for her.

Connection, Lupe thought and waved her hand at her.

She put her hands in her pockets and started walking towards her. Lupe had never seen her wearing jeans before and she took a moment to appreciate her finely defined legs and round hips moving side to side alluringly.

If she looked this good with clothes on, she could only imagine how well the years had treated her under the clothing, Lupe shook her head.

"I don't know if I'm properly dressed for a motorcycle ride," Ellen said and stopped in front of her. "I have never been on one before."

"Well, it is my pleasure to teach you something you have never done before *mi gringa linda*," Lupe said and winked at her. "Hop behind me and whatever you do, don't take your hands off me," she said and handed her the additional helmet before starting the engine.

Ellen took the helmet and placed it on her head. She struggled with the fastener and Lupe stretched out her hands to help her. The fastener gave a loud click. "There you go *mi gringa linda*. Are you ready to hop on?" Lupe asked and ran her finger down her neck. "You better attach the scarf well unless you want to lose it."

Ellen added an extra knot in her scarf and hopped behind her, leaning as close as possible. Lupe could feel her breasts on her back, making her stomach twist.

"OK, let's go and rent you a flat then," Lupe said and stepped on the accelerator.

The drive was peaceful and they both enjoyed it greatly. Ellen was scared at first but soon enough Lupe felt her muscles relaxing around her body. It seemed she trusted her way of handling the vehicle instantly.

They arrived at the flat and parked at the back of the house. Lupe helped Ellen off the motorcycle and secured the vehicle with a big chain and a lock. They walked together to the door and Lupe fished out the keys of the flat from her pocket.

"I thought we would have an agent showing us around?" Ellen asked surprised.

Lupe shook her head. "The agent is a friend of mine and had to go home early today so you have to settle for my company," she said with an apologetic smile on her face. "But don't worry, if there is anything I can't answer, I can call him immediately."

Ellen nodded and waited for her to open the building door. They walked together to the lift and rode in silence to the third floor of the building and entered a large studio flat.

The flat had a rectangular kitchen, a bathroom and a large living area with a green carpet. The furniture was old but in good condition, consisting of a double bed, a shelving system, two armchairs and a wooden table with two matching chairs. All the rooms had a lot of natural light thanks to large double-glazed windows.

It was definitely an upgrade to what Ellen currently had at the hospital, Lupe thought and also it would be just around the corner from her, which Ellen had no idea about of course.

"Do you like it?" Lupe asked, searching for approval or rejection in her face.

Ellen hesitated for a moment. "Well, it is definitely better than what I have now and I like the area, very close to the hospital."

Lupe nodded. "I know, I have many friends living in the area, and they have always liked it," Lupe said and walked to the window to admire the view.

Ellen followed her. "Do you live close by yourself?" she asked.

"Quite close," she replied vaguely.

Ellen nodded but stayed silent, looking outside.

"Do you live alone?"

Her question surprised Lupe and she turned to look at her. "Yes, I live alone," she said and examined her face. "Why do you want to know?"

Ellen looked at her hands. "I don't know, I guess I was just curious."

Lupe took an unnoticeable step closer to her. "I see," she said and brushed a stray hair off her face that had escaped from her pin when she had taken the helmet off.

"Is there anything else you might be curious about?" she whispered and studied the expression on her face. She looked bare, confused and vulnerable.

Ellen turned to face her. "I don't know, is there anything you might want to show me?"

Lupe smiled. "Plenty," and leaned her head closer to hers, leaving only a couple of inches between their lips.

She could smell the Scarlett Red 77 By Dior on her lips. She knew the scent by now – she had carried the tube from her room in her pocket ever since.

The first touch was feather light when their lips met.

The lonely stubborn strand of her curly hair had fallen down her face and tickled the sensitive skin on Ellen's cheek. She had closed her eyes and leaned towards to answer the kiss.

Encouraged by her response, Lupe let her hands touch her hips and pull her closer to her body to deepen the kiss. Their bodies touched.

She guided her mouth open and feverishly searched for her tongue with hers.

Ellen gave out a little whine and replied by lifting her hands to her shoulders.

The touch of their tongues connecting sent electric shocks through

Lupe's body and burnt like a flame she couldn't resist.

It was like gasoline thrown on a fire and soon, they were both caught in the moment with each other, tearing their clothing off and trying desperately to find a skin-to-skin connection.

Lupe picked her up and pushed her violently up against the wall, like she had imagined so many times over the years.

Ellen responded feverishly, wrapping her legs around her waist and clawing inside her t-shirt with her nails, leaving red marks on her back. Lupe hoped they would last long enough so that she could go home and stare at herself in the mirror to make sure she wasn't dreaming.

Ellen bit her lower lip until Lupe tasted the salty blood on her lips which only seemed to drive her insane and before she knew it, she had pulled Ellen's shirt collar down nearly exposing her breasts. Lupe cupped her breasts and sank her face in between her soft chest, inhaling the sweet vanilla scent of the body cream she had used eight years ago. When she felt Ellen tightening her legs around her waist, she almost came at that moment.

A crash outside the flat woke them up from their trance.

"Oh, I'm sorry – you left the door open," a young man said and eyed the scene curiously before realisation hit his face and his mouth curled into a smile. "But if that's an invitation, maybe you could make me a sandwich or something," he said and winked tentatively.

Lupe reacted first. "*Vete a la mierda*, fuck off!" she yelled putting Ellen down and storming to close the door in front of his nose. As she closed the door, a heavy silence landed in the room.

Lupe broke the silence first. "Are you OK?" She looked at Ellen.

Ellen didn't look at her. "Yeah I'm OK," she said finally.

Lupe didn't know what to do; she wanted to comfort her, but she was still aroused and full of rage towards the poor young man who had ruined the moment for them both. She wanted to approach her somehow but before she could do anything, Ellen's phone received a text.

"Oh, it is Omar. I have a date with him tonight," she said and quickly hid the phone in her bag.

The blood in Lupe's veins turned into ice as she looked at the phone disappearing into her handbag. She didn't dare talk.

"Can I use the toilet quickly before we go?" Ellen asked.

Lupe's face was red with poorly hidden rage but she stepped aside. "By all means, toilet to the right."

Ellen hurried past her. "Thank you," she said and disappeared to the toilet.

Lupe waited for her at the entrance of the flat. "At least you can tell me if you want the flat or not," she said when Ellen emerged from the toilet.

She had cooled her face down and reorganised her hair after their passionate moment of insanity, which made Lupe crave to dig her fingers deep into her scalp and release the hair from the pins again.

"Yes, sure, I want to take it," Ellen said distractedly.

"Good, I will let the agent know. Your moving in day is next Monday. I can come and help you with moving if you want?" she said.

Ellen winced. "Oh, I don't think it's necessary. I will ask one of my guy friends to help me out, but thank you anyway," she said and ran out of the flat.

The moment Lupe heard the building door shut she smashed her fist into the mirror on the wall. It broke into thousands of pieces and made small cuts on Lupe' fist.

In your dreams *mi gringa linda,* she thought as she looked at the blood emerging from the cuts on her hand.

You belong to me now.

Chapter 41

Ellen didn't wait for Lupe to take her home. Instead she jumped on the first available bus on the street.

She exhaled deeply when the bus doors closed. She felt safe again and sat deeper into her seat and let the rhythmic ride sooth her racing thoughts. She hadn't meant to get physical with Lupe, but there had been something from the beginning that had been boiling under the surface. Electricity, desire, a void she couldn't fill no matter how hard she tried. She felt intrigued, fascinated yet somehow familiar around her. Her scent, the way she moved and her eyes following her around – it was as if she had seen it all before but she couldn't tell when and where.

Ellen massaged the sides of her forehead and changed position on the seat. Her panties still had the evidence of the moment and the moist fabric between her legs made **her uncomfortably conscious of her body**, touching her, *teasing* her and for the first time in her life, her body gave a knowing twist in her private area. Ellen sighed; she could only imagine what her touch might do to her, after the kiss that had taken her breath away and introduced her to the hell she had never known before.

Chapter 42

The next week, Ellen was packing her belongings when she heard a light knock on the door.

"Come in," she called softly.

She hadn't invited anyone to help her move so she was more than surprised to see Jack, the operations manager, at the door.

"Jack, what are you doing here?" she asked surprised. "I thought I had asked for two days off for moving."

"Yes, you have Ellen, don't worry. I just wanted to see how everything is going," he said and curiously eyed the items in one of the open cardboard boxes. "You seem to have very little with you, are you expecting a shipment anytime soon for the rest of your things?" he asked expectantly and picked up a book from one of the boxes.

Ellen walked over to him, took the book and placed it back in the cardboard box. "I travel light," she said and picked up the whole box and placed it on top of another.

She didn't like people touching her personal belongings.

"Ah, clever woman you are Ellen. It's refreshing to see a woman who has been blessed with not only beauty but brains too," he said and winked at her.

Ellen didn't have to wait long before he continued. "Anyway, I was just thinking, could I invite you for a welfare dinner today before you leave?"

Ellen smiled sweetly. No matter how handsome he was, he left her completely cold. "No thanks, Jack, I'm super busy," she said, but after seeing his defeated face she softened the rejection, "but I would love to another time."

The smile returned instantly to his boyish face. "Sounds great! I will try to plan something very soon," he said.

"OK, great!" Ellen smiled.

Purposefully, she let the silence hang between them until he cleared his throat. "So, I think I will just go now but good luck with the new flat," he said and offered her a hug.

"Thanks Jack, appreciate it," Ellen said and hugged him back before opening the door for him.

It wasn't long after he had gone before a new visitor stormed into the tiny room without knocking.

"Why Jack was here?" Lupe asked before Ellen even had a chance to greet her.

"Well, good afternoon to you too," she said and crossed her arms on her chest.

"Don't do that sarcastic *mierda* with me *muñequita mia*, why was he here?"

Ellen stared at her. "He came to ask if I needed help with moving," she said, and turned to put another sweater in one of the open boxes. Lupe approached her quickly and ripped the sweater out of her hands. "Help with moving?" she said, raising her eyebrows. "I thought I offered my help, that's not good enough?" she said and cornered her against the wall.

Ellen nervously brushed a fallen hair from her forehead. "I didn't invite him to come, he just popped up from downstairs. It was nice of him to ask."

Lupe's face turned red. "Nice?" she said and smashed her tattooed arms hard on the wall on either side of her.

Ellen covered her ears and backed off as much as she could. She was scared of her, but the fear drowned quickly under the excitement of feeling her close again.

She lowered her hands to her sides and stared into her eyes. "Yes, nice of him. No one else showed up. Even though I don't *need* his help, I think it was nice," Ellen said and pouted.

Lupe leaned closer to her and suddenly lifted her hand to touch her hair, laughing arrogantly. For a second, Ellen was sure she was about to slap her.

"Oh *munequita mia*, you can't be that blind – the guy clearly wants to sleep with you and have another notch on his bedpost in addition to many others," she said. "Let me remind you that he has a wife and a small child at home, so you're probably better off not messing around with him."

"Oh yeah, that's what you say," Ellen said angrily and tried to push her off, but her body was like a rock and didn't move an inch. "The funny thing is, isn't that exactly what you want from me?"

Lupe grabbed a chunk of her golden hair in her fist and pulled to bring her face closer. "That's different *mi gringa linda*."

Ellen licked her lower lip nervously. "Oh yeah, and why would that be?"

Lupe smiled softly. "Because you belong to me."

Ellen's hysterical laugh was cut short when she felt her lips crushing against hers.

The kiss was aggressive and would leave a bruise no doubt. It was a combination of desire and ownership as if she wanted to punish her, leave a mark on her.

Lupe could feel Ellen trying to pull her face back and to the side to reject her kiss and it would probably have been better to have stayed still and to have let the heated situation cool off but for some reason she found her lifting her hands to hold Ellen's head still and forcing apart her lips and opening her mouth.

Ellen gave out a muffled cry but once their tongues touched, Lupe felt her body starting to relax again as she slowly slid her hands up her tattooed arms before reaching her curly hair. Ellen gave a strong tug on her hair.

Lupe growled with pleasure as she felt the tingling of her fingertips massaging her scalp and slid her tongue deeper inside her mouth.

She tasted of sweet vanilla and her scent of jasmine and ocean breeze surrounded her as she had imagined so many times. It was like magic – intense, unstoppable.

Their heavy breath mixed together in the tiny room as Lupe picked Ellen up and laid her on the single bed.

It was now or never, she thought and pulled off the grey sweatshirt Ellen was wearing for moving day. Under the grey sweatshirt she was wearing a lacy burgundy push-up bra and Lupe took a moment to appreciate the sight in front of her.

She looked slightly confused but her eyes were filled with a naked desire that Lupe had never seen before. It took her by the storm as she leaned down to kiss her again.

Her strong body pressed Ellen's delicate body against the cheap mattress as it gave in and sank them both deeper into the bed covers. For a second, Lupe felt an extreme urge to hide her away from the outside world, to lock her up in a tower and be the only one to hold the key. She knew her thoughts were possessive and insane but with Ellen, she couldn't help it.

"Please don't."

Lupe's hands stopped on the fastener of her bra. "I can't stop now *mi cielo, entiendeme*, this is meant to happen," she said.

Ellen looked sad for a moment. "I don't want to be another notch on your bedpost either," she said quietly. "I'm not a competition."

Lupe smiled at her softly. "I would never consider you as another notch on my bedpost, *mi gringa linda*. You are something so much more," she said and slowly teased the waistband of her leggings before sliding them down and gently pushing her legs apart.

She took a long breath to inhale the sweet scent into her lungs. She already felt the healing effect of her, as her memory took her back eight years, but this was so much better.

Lupe quickly pushed herself up from the bed and removed her t-shirt to reveal her black sports bra.

She felt Ellen's stare at her inked body she had original tattooed to hide the painful scars that reminded her of her past.

Ellen didn't ask any questions, instead she reached her arm to touch the damaged skin. She ran her soft fingers across her arms, ending up at the chest area.

Lupe held her breath – this would be breaking point as she would need to accept the fact that she was about to sleep with a woman, not a man. *For the second time in her life*, she thought, although she didn't know it and the first time had been rather quick without identity. This time there were no masks to protect anyone. It was just them, bare skin to bare skin.

Ellen grabbed her sports bra and with one easy flick, freed her breasts in front of her.

Slowly and curiously, Ellen reached out to her heavy swollen breasts and brushed her hard nipples with her finger.

Lupe gave a satisfied growl.

She was not prepared for what she did next – she opened her mouth and took her nipple into it.

Lupe's body jolted as the sensation of the intimate touch sent vibration through her body like never before sending lethal fire down in between her legs.

It scared her to her core but when she felt tiny sucks on her nipple and saw Ellen's closed eyes enjoying what she was doing to her, she relaxed and embraced her in her arms for a long moment.

Lupe couldn't stop the tears building up in her eyes as she felt the orgasm rising up inside her. She held her close to her body and, when the orgasm came, it ripped her into so many pieces inside, taking her to the moon and back. She let out a long pained animal cry before she sank on top of her again.

When she opened her eyes slowly, she saw Ellen watching her. She had the most beautiful eyes Lupe had ever seen.

Lupe supported her upper body to bring herself so she could lose the jeans she was wearing and then slid next to her on the tiny single bed. Their hot bodies connected, and Lupe couldn't help but watch their bodies, so similar but so different at the same time. She brushed her nipples with her breasts and kissed her deeply before guiding her hand down to her navel and all the way to her hot sex, sliding her finger in between the moist folds.

She rubbed the soft knot rhythmically as she felt Ellen's body stiffen first and then melt under her touch Small whispering moans escaped her lips as she wriggled under her, panting heavily as a sign that her orgasm was reaching the surface; just before she came, Lupe climbed on top of her and parted her legs before settling in between them and connecting them together.

When their swollen sexes touched, she could feel Ellen's long exhale of pleasure tickling her ear as she started moving with a rhythmic speed, rubbing them together, teasing her and when they both came, she violently grabbed her hair in her fists and the loud cry of her second orgasm blended with the feminine scream that escaped from Ellen's lungs and, just like that, she felt she was finally ready to let go of the eight years of torment this woman had caused her.

Chapter 43

L upe woke up to a small breeze blowing on her face.

She opened her eyes and saw a pair of blue eyes staring at her curiously.

"Hi," Ellen smiled.

"Hey you." Lupe hadn't realised she had fallen asleep after the groundbreaking orgasms she had experienced and had no idea how long she had slept.

She quickly checked the small rooftop window; it was dark already, but then again, she couldn't remember if it had been dark when she had arrived.

She hadn't meant to come up, but on her regular check-up around her building she had noticed Jack entering the building and her mind had blacked out with jealousy. She had followed him and accidentally heard the exchange of words and invitation for dinner. When she had heard Ellen first decline but then say yes, she had barely been able to control her impulsive thoughts and had hidden inside the cleaners' cupboard waiting for him to go before storming in.

As she looked at her now, lying here next to her, she had millions of questions in her head but for some reason she felt too shy to even ask one. She was terrified of her response.

Lupe shivered and Ellen pulled the duvet up to cover her torso.

"Are you cold?" she asked and caressed her arm.

Lupe shook her head but pulled the duvet closer to her chin.

Ellen laughed slightly and brushed her fingertips across her face.

The sweetness of her gesture surprised Lupe as she realised that once again, she had absolutely no idea if she had enjoyed herself properly during their hurried session of madness. Lupe's cheeks blushed with embarrassment, she was usually more considerate, but nothing with this woman made sense – it was like she was possessed around her.

"How do you feel?" she finally asked and forced her fingers to massage her shoulder. Now that the heat had died, she was shy and even scared to touch her. Fear of rejection boiled strong under the surface.

Ellen's shoulder was cold. "Are you cold *mi vida*?" she asked and opened the duvet to fit her in as well. She snuggled in immediately and placed her head in her sensitive neckline. "A little," she said.

They lay down, eyes closed, both lost in their own thoughts that the other had no idea of before Ellen whispered. "Are you ready to go again?"

Lupe raised her eyebrows at her before her mouth curved into a teasing smile. "Whatever you ask *mi cielo*, I'm all yours," she said and cupped her breast in her hand.

They were creamy white and soft with pink nipples; she hadn't had time to appreciate them on the first round she thought and brought one of the hardened nipples to her mouth.

Ellen gave out a muffled moan and leaned back onto the mattress exposing all her body to her.

Lupe looked at her body with desire – she was like a goddess. The years had treated her well she thought, as she ran her eyes down her body.

"Kiss me," she begged and Lupe couldn't resist her soft but

demanding voice that would lose its accent when she was aroused.

She kissed her and let her wandering hand continue its journey down to her navel area to touch her swollen sex. It was still wet from their first round, but quickly produced more moisture, dripping down her inner tights.

Ellen jumped a little when her finger reached her soft spot but Lupe pushed her down.

"Shhh, *mi vida*, it's ok, I will be gentle this time," she said and gently rubbed her ring finger around the soft area of her sex.

Ellen moaned and reached out to touch her breasts again. Her breath got heavier as she approached her climax, giving out a disapproving whimper when Lupe slid her finger out and pushed her way down the bed.

"You are not going to leave now are you?" Ellen panted, her eyes glistening.

Lupe winced in surprise. "*Mi vida*, I would never leave you," she said and caressed the sensitive skin around her tights before opening her legs as wide as she could and placing her head in between them.

Her sex was as beautiful as she was, delicate, light pink, swollen like a flower pumping its nectar out.

Before Ellen had a chance to speak, Lupe couldn't help but to take a long taste of her juices moving her tongue as deep in her as she could.

Ellen felt her body tense as she moaned loudly and gasped.

Her eyes opened wide and their eyes met.

Lupe was glad, she wanted her to see who was doing this to her, so that there wouldn't be the slightest chance she would imagine anyone else in her place.

She worked her tongue faster, swirling around her sensitive folds as she felt her come close to her climax again and just then and there, she came, loudly, on her face. Her body trembled at the intensity of the orgasm, but Lupe forced her body down and didn't let her tongue leave her inner folds until she couldn't feel her tremble anymore.

*

They both woke up in the middle of the night with hungry stomachs.

Lupe parted her eyes lazily when she couldn't feel the warmth of Ellen next to her. The shadow of loneliness started to crawl back to her. She opened her eyes.

Ellen was putting on her dressing gown.

"*Mi vida* where are you going?" she asked, wide awake now.

Ellen turned around and placed a finger on top of her mouth signalling her to be quiet.

"I'm just going to the kitchen to get something to eat. I think I should have fruit in the fridge," she whispered.

Lupe lifted herself from the bed to accompany her but Ellen pushed her back to the bed by her shoulders. "I don't think so, *tiger*," she said and eyed her naked body with a smile. "I think this dressing gown wouldn't be your style," she said and winked before slightly opening the door and disappearing to the kitchen.

Lupe smiled and stretched her relaxed body.

For the first time in a long time, she felt completely relaxed and at peace. It had been better than she had ever hoped for in her wildest dreams. She was not only beautiful on the outside but a sweet person on the inside as well. Lupe felt complete trust and totally at ease around her, naked or dressed. It was very natural, just like the first time, she thought.

She didn't feel body conscious at all even though their bodies were very different. Whereas Ellen was soft and delicate, Lupe was bulky with wide shoulders and ink covering her back, arms and lower legs. She would need to ink her onto her skin once this was all over, she thought before realising she didn't *want* it to be over, ever.

She hadn't imagined the chemistry the first time, it had been there all along, despite the unusual circumstances in which they had met, she thought and turned around to admire the red passion marks Ellen had left on her back. She was pretty sure she had left her mark around Ellen's neck as well.

Lupe grinned devilishly, she would need to wear a scarf for the next week or so to cover the marks. At least for next week, there wouldn't be competition. She had won the first round and the evidence was written all around her neck.

Ellen came back with a bowl of strawberries and some Parma ham and fresh bread.

"Sorry *amorcito*, I couldn't find anything else in the fridge, I hope these are OK," she said and placed the food on the writing desk and turned on the kettle.

Lupe looked at her. "What did you call me again?"

Ellen looked confused. "I said *tiger*."

Lupe shook her head. "No no, after that, just now."

"*Amorcito?*" Ellen asked and raised her eyebrows.

Lupe looked suspiciously at her. "*Hablas español?* Do you speak Spanish?" she asked in disbelief.

"I speak some, but I'm not very good anymore," Ellen replied calmly in Spanish.

She had a heavy foreign accent, which was totally normal for a non-native speaker, but Lupe was surprised how different it sounded compared to all the other *gringos* she had ever heard trying to speak Spanish. She had strong pronunciation without an English accent at all.

"Where did you learn Spanish?" she asked curiously and fished a strawberry from the bowl.

Ellen waited for the kettle to whistle and poured water into both pink polka dot mugs on the desk. "I studied Spanish at university mainly because I'm a huge fan of all Latin soap operas, which are usually played without subtitles," she said and eyed Lupe who was smiling. "Or with very crappy ones at least."

Lupe eyed her. "You are telling me you learnt a whole new language just for television shows?"

Ellen took a sip of her tea and shook her head. "I have always been fascinated by the language and the countries in South America," she said. "I always pictured myself as a famous writer or explorer visiting all those places in the world."

Lupe watched her talking, her eyes sparkling. "You know, you could still do it."

Their eyes locked.

"I know, one day," Ellen said.

A brief silence hung between them as they stared at each other. The silence was not shadowed by anything uncomfortable. It was more of a calm, easy environment.

Ellen cleared her throat. "I don't know about you, but for some reason I feel like I have known you forever," she said turning her eyes to the ground.

Lupe leaned from the bed and touched her chin gently to bring her gaze up again.

Her heart missed a beat. "I feel the same *mi vida*. It feels amazing," she said.

Ellen smiled and reached for another strawberry and offered it to her. "Do you want to go again?" she smiled and let the dressing gown drop to the floor, exposing her naked body in all its glory.

Lupe felt her stomach twist with desire and opened the duvet. "Hop in *mi vida*."

Chapter 44

The next day, Lupe woke up relaxed and happy for the first time in a long time.

She had held Ellen in her arms for the whole night, letting the warmth of her body act as a cure for the emptiness and sadness she had carried inside for so long. And during the night, when she had woken up scared of the darkness, Ellen had turned around and embraced her, scaring away the demons of the night that had haunted Lupe all her life.

She helped her pack the rest of her belongings in the cardboard boxes and ordered her an Uber to move the luggage to the new flat. Ellen looked peaceful as well, although she was suspiciously quiet which made Lupe feel slightly anxious.

"You are ready to go?" she asked, breaking the silence between them.

Ellen jumped slightly as if she had been deep in her own thoughts and smiled. "Yes, ready to leave this place."

Lupe smiled at her. "OK then," she said and opened the door to the Uber.

"Wait, don't you have to go to work yourself?" Ellen asked suprised when Lupe sat next to her in the car.

"It's fine *mi vida*, I already called in sick."

Ellen raised her eyebrows. "Oh, you shouldn't have done that for me," she said guilt written on her face.

Lupe gently touched her cheek. "It's OK *mi cielo*, I'm not even lying, I'm sick with the feelings for you," she said and smiled.

Ellen smiled back.

The ride to the new house was relatively short without traffic. Lupe helped Ellen to unpack the car and carry everything to the front door and then they returned downstairs to wait for the agent to bring the keys to the flat. They both sat on the doorsteps next to each other.

After half an hour, Ellen started to look nervously around, touching her hair.

"Are you sure the agent has the correct address? He should be here by now."

Lupe frowned and fished her phone from her pocket. "He should know the area better than anyone, he sent me the details of the house in the first place," she said and dialled the familiar number.

*

The agent answered on the eighth ring and Lupe burst into quick Spanish patter. "*Hermano, que pasa*, we are here outside the flat, waiting to move in."

She had barely finished the sentence before Ellen heard his fast flood of Spanish words. She eyed Lupe expectantly.

"You have got to be kidding me *hermano*! This cannot be," Lupe said and stood up from the doorstep.

Ellen raised her eyebrows and grabbed Lupe by her arm. "What is it?" she asked.

Lupe hung up the phone and stayed silent, trying to gather her thoughts before she spoke. "Ellen, it looks like there has been some confusion with the flat," she said.

Ellen raised her eyebrows, waiting for her to continue. "So, it looks like no one confirmed the flat yesterday and another girl showed up for a viewing and decided to take the flat immediately," Lupe said and let the information sink in.

Ellen stared at her. "What does that mean?"

Lupe looked at her. "It means that she paid the full deposit yesterday and the flat is hers. You can't move in here anymore."

"What?" Ellen's eyes grew wild and her lower lip started shaking when the news sank in. She buried her face in her hands and sat down again on the front doorsteps.

Lupe felt sorry for her and clumsily put her hand on her back to console her. She hadn't mentioned that the person who had forgot to confirm the flat was her. She couldn't bring herself to tell her. The agent had tried to call her yesterday, but she had been so furious at Jack for coming to Ellen's room and then with all that had followed soon after, she had simply forgotten to even look at her phone.

Ellen could never know. She would be devastated and might regret their night together or decide not to see her ever again. She had to think fast.

"Ellen, please don't cry," she said and dried the tears on her cheeks.

"How can this happen?" Ellen whispered. "You don't understand. I have no other place to go. I have all my belongings here on the street," she said and pointed at the cardboard boxes. "What am I supposed to do now?"

Lupe's response was drowned out by the noise of thunder. She looked at the sky. It would rain soon.

"Ok *mi vida*, stand up. I'm going to order another Uber for us."

Ellen raised her swollen eyes to her. "Where are we going?" she asked in surprise. Lupe confirmed the Uber order and raised a smile on her face. "Prepare yourself *munequita mia*, you are moving in with me."

Ellen gasped. "Absolutely not," she said and shook her head. "I'm more than happy to go to a hotel or even back to the hospital to ask for my old room back until I find something more permanent," she said and raised her chin proudly. "You have helped me more than enough. I can take care of myself from here."

Lupe didn't have time to answer before the first heavy drops fell from the sky followed by dull rumpling. "It looks to me like you don't have much of a choice for now, *gringa linda*," she said and eyed the sky. "You had better hop into the car now unless you want your precious belongings to get wet," she said and opened the arriving Uber's door.

Ellen stood still for a moment, but when lightening tore the sky and rain came with its full force, she didn't have a choice but to grab her belongings and get inside the car.

*

The ride to Lupe's place took less than five minutes and she was nervous that Ellen would ask questions about the suspiciously short drive between the flats, but after eyeing her surreptitiously during the car ride, she realised she was too worn out from the change of events to notice anything.

The Uber pulled up outside her building and they both got out quickly and placed the boxes under the roof covering the entrance.

"Are you ready to try again?" Lupe asked and shook the raindrops off her jacket.

"Yes, I guess," Ellen said and eyed the door curiously.

Lupe clapped her hands together loudly. "OK then, grab the bags, I will bring the boxes, and I'll show you your new place."

Ellen did as told and carried two IKEA bags of her belongings to the lift.

"Good morning Lupita!" the concierge greeted her with a wide smile.

"Good morning James, how are you this morning?" Lupe replied to the young man behind the reception desk.

"I'm very well as always. I see you are moving a lot of stuff, would you like me to help you?"

Lupe eyed Ellen. She smiled but held on to her bags as if her life depended on it. Lupe smiled. "That's OK James, we've got it," she said. "I see you got a new haircut?"

"Oh yes, I tried something different this time. I hope it doesn't look too wild!" he said and carefully touched his sleek hair.

It was a wild haircut: short on the sides and purposefully too long in the middle so that he was able to tie it in a ponytail. He had dyed the middle blond, but it had become a dirty yellow after several washes and the sides were grass green. It was something very trendy these days but reminded Lupe of a pineapple. He had also let his beard grow, so he was a funny combination of a boyish haircut and an old man's beard. Very unusual for the concierge job he was in, Lupe thought, but she had seen it so many times before, it was nothing new to her.

"Looking dashing James. Carry on," she said and passed the concierge desk with Ellen.

They entered the lift and when the doors closed, and they felt they were on the move, they both burst into laughter. "Omg, that was the wildest haircut I have ever seen on a receptionist!" Ellen said and wiped happy tears from the corner of her eye.

"I know, can you imagine? He is a good kid and probably this is his first job. I can imagine he wasn't exactly the first choice of candidate for the job."

Ellen laughed again. "I know, but he seemed nice," she said.

"I know, he is," Lupe said and looked at Ellen.

The silence descended between them as they both grew quiet just staring at one another until the lift gave a loud ping to inform them they had arrived at the seventh floor.

Before Ellen had chance to turn around to exit the lift, Lupe hit the red stop button, preventing the doors sliding open.

She cornered her from behind against the wall.

"Lupe, what are you doing?" she whispered.

Lupe stared into her eyes and sighed, shaking her head. "I don't know but there is something about you that makes me go insane – your look, your laughter, it's like it's summoning me, *mi vida*. I can't control it," she said with sadness in her voice as if she wanted to apologise to her.

Ellen caressed the sensitive skin on her wrists and ran her fingernails along her arms. Her touch gave her goosebumps and she gave out a long groan and closed her eyes.

"What if you don't try to control it?" Ellen whispered and leaned closer to her ear. What if you just let it go?" she said and took her head gently in between her hands and kissed her, letting her tongue purposefully search for its counterpart.

The kiss was passionate and full of lust and promises, which took Lupe by surprise but soon she answered the kiss and grabbed her hips on both sides lifting her slightly from the ground onto her toes to access the kiss better. She pushed her body into hers and forced her mouth to open more and for a brief moment, the air in the small lift was filled by their sweet desire as the mirror on the wall lost its reflection under the steam created by their heavy gasps.

Lupe couldn't help lowering her hand, grabbing the waistband of Ellen's leggings and pushing her fingers deep into her panties. As she reached the moist folds again, she sighed – she was hot and wet again, for *her.*

Ellen moaned loudly but Lupe covered her mouth with a kiss to silence her.

She would have probably taken her then and there against the elevator wall, if the doors hadn't opened unexpectedly.

They both teared off each other as if the touch would have burnt and eyed the corridor like deer in the spotlight.

The corridor remained silent.

"I think someone just called the lift downstairs," Lupe said.

Ellen nodded her head without a word, still trying to catch her breath.

Lupe picked up the boxes again and turned left into the corridor.

Ellen followed her.

They stopped in front of flat 33 and Lupe opened the door. "Welcome to your new home *munequita mia*. Please make yourself comfortable," she said and stepped aside to let Ellen into the flat.

Lupe was slightly nervous as she allowed Ellen to pass her and enter the flat. For the first time, she looked at her tiny one-bedroom flat with critical eyes. It was clean and tidy, however she had never actually focused on making the house *feel* like home. She had purchased only the essentials: the bed, sofa, wardrobe and a giant TV on the wall. The rest, like the glass living room table and the small shelving unit under the TV, were gifted by her sister who had a serious interior design addiction, which was noticeable as those two pieces of furniture were the only ones in the entire flat that matched each other, Lupe thought and grinned.

Ellen observed her surroundings silently.

"It looks nice," she said finally and Lupe exhaled deeply.

"Where do you want me to sleep until I find something else?" she asked, eyeing the tiny place suspiciously.

Lupe marched across the room and opened the sliding doors into the small bedroom, which contained a double bed with deep blue covers pushed against the white clean wall and a white nightstand with a reading light. There were a pair of blue slippers in front of the bed. "You can sleep here, and I will sleep on the sofa," she said.

Ellen shook her head. "Oh, I can't ask you to do that," she said. "I can sleep on the sofa for now and then when I'm ready to go you will have your sofa back."

Lupe approached and took both of her hands into hers. "*Muñeca mia*, can you please stop saying for now all the time. This is your home now and you can stay as long as you want," she said and took her in her arms and kissed her.

The kiss was sweet and romantic, very different from the one they had shared in the lift, which still made Lupe feel weak in her knees. This was something darker and even more dangerous, Lupe thought as she tore herself away from the kiss.

"Stay as long as you need. The bedroom is yours, I sleep lightly anyway," she said and turned away to pick up an additional towel for her to use.

She wasn't lying when she had told Ellen to stay as long as she wanted, Lupe thought as she watched her moving from room to room to check out her new surroundings.

The idea of having Ellen under her constant watch in her house made Lupe feel ecstatic. She didn't ever want to consider the idea of her looking for anything else.

She wanted her to *stay* with her.

The realisation took her by surprise, and she paused at the kitchen entrance.

"Is everything OK?" Ellen asked softy and placed her hand on her shoulder.

"Yeah, everything is perfect," Lupe said and shook her hand off her shoulder. "I'll be out for a while, just make yourself at home," she said and stormed out of the flat.

*

It was late in the evening when she dragged her tired legs back to the flat.

She had spent all day downstairs playing billiards, first with her brother and then with her brother's friends who had joined them later. They had had a good time and Lupe felt the beer relaxing the pressure on both sides of her head. She couldn't bring herself to tell her brother she had invited Ellen to stay with her; he would find out about it later anyway, she thought as she opened the front door.

When she entered the flat she was greeted by the fresh scent of flowers. Lupe eyed the flat curiously and closed the door.

Ellen had clearly spent the rest of the day unpacking and making her tiny room more to her style. She had changed the bed linen and been down to the local shop to purchase fresh flowers.

"These are for you," Ellen said shyly and handed her a bouquet of yellow roses with red on the petals. "I think they would look nice on the living room table," she said and pointed across the room.

It was the first time Lupe had received flowers from anyone and she didn't know how to act. She felt feminine and spoiled, which was a new feeling for her. "Yeah, thanks. They will look great there," she said and handed the flowers back to her and let her eyes look at the rest of the flat.

She had not only organised the small bedroom but had also moved around the rest of the items in the small flat.

Lupe smiled – she had to admit it look better than ever.

"You hungry?" she asked and hung her leather jacket in the entrance.

Ellen smiled. "Starving."

"Great, let me prepare something for us to eat while you finish your unpacking," she said and made her way to the kitchen.

Even though she had her chef degree, she decided to make something cosy without trying to impress Ellen too much as she didn't want to rock the boat now that everything was settling into place. It felt like a second chance in life, that destiny had given them, she thought as she opened the kitchen cupboards to gather the ingredients she would need to prepare the meal. She didn't exactly know what type of food Ellen fancied but decided to take her chances and prepared a big pot of beans with pork and rice, a delicacy of Peru.

The aromas soon led Ellen to find her way to the kitchen. She touched both sides of her hips and peeked behind her. "What do we have for dinner?" she asked and smiled.

Lupe looked over her shoulder. "I hope you like beans and rice, it's a speciality of my country."

Ellen breathed the aroma into her lungs and purred. "Smells divine. Can I help you to set the table?" she asked and turned around in the small kitchen to look for the table.

"It's OK *mi vida*, I will do it, the table is behind the door," she said and pointed to the foldable brown table she had found at a bargain sale before she had hurt her knee. For a second, she felt embarrassed at not being able to offer her a bigger flat with a full-size kitchen table, but Ellen didn't seem to mind at all. She shrugged her shoulders and returned to the living room.

That evening they enjoyed their dinner together just like any other couple. Lupe was especially chatty and shared stories of her childhood and early days in Spain and England.

Ellen listened attentively and made short comments or asked clarifying questions now and then. Her eyes were alert and Lupe felt she was really interested in hearing her story, which she had never really shared with anyone else. She didn't feel under a spotlight, more of a connection with her, which was strange and a feeling she wasn't used to at all.

When the night came, she waited in the living room watching television and let Ellen do her normal evening routine tasks and change into her pyjamas.

When she disappeared into her bedroom and closed the sliding doors after her, Lupe stayed awake on her sofa for a long time and couldn't sleep. She almost smell the scent of her shampoo and shower gel from the bedroom and couldn't decide if she should enter the bedroom or not.

With thoughts of her in her mind, she finally fell into a restless sleep and in the early morning hours when the nightmares came, Ellen heard her screaming her name in her sleep alarming her to the living room.

"Lupe, are you OK?" she asked and gently brushed a disobedient stray curl from her forehead with eyes full of worry.

Lupe opened her tearful eyes and scanned her surroundings for danger.

"Lupe, it's me, Ellen. It's OK, it was just a bad dream," she said and petted her hair.

Lupe nodded and tried to hold her tears in but one lonely, stubborn tear fell down her cheek onto her pillow.

Ellen studied her scared face silently. "Right, well, if you don't mind, I think I will stay here with you and guard your dreams until the morning. I'm not tired anyway," she said and prompted Lupe to lift her upper body to give her room to sit. She then cupped her head and placed it on her thighs and lifted her legs up onto the coffee table. "There you go, sweetheart, sweet dreams, don't let the bed bugs bite," she said and closed her eyes.

Lupe felt stiff for the first moment as she watched Ellen's peaceful face until the relaxation in her body lulled her to a restful sleep until the morning.

There was nothing sexual in the moment; Ellen had acted more out of maternal instinct and had made Lupe feel more loved and secure than she could remember her own mother ever had. It was a dangerous feeling and the realisation that Ellen was starting to influence her life in more than one aspect made her stomach twist at the idea of losing her.

She could not afford it. *Ever.*

Chapter 45

They had lived together for a few months and life had been good. Their routines at home were amazingly complementary and Ellen acted as a true hostess of her house.

Lupe had even allowed Ellen to rescue a black cat she had seen wandering around on her way to work, dragging its front paw and meowing. Ellen had taken the small animal in her arms and called Lupe to pick them up from the local veterinary clinic. Lupe had been surprised to arrive at a veterinary clinic for the first time in her life to find Ellen sitting in the waiting area with a black cat with a cast on its front paw.

"I found it on the side of a road," Ellen explained. "It looks like a car hit him and broke his paw. Can I please keep him in your flat for now?" she asked.

Lupe eyed Ellen and then the small animal that had curled into a ball and was purring happily on Ellen's lap. She didn't have the strength to say no, even though she wasn't particularly fond of cats. She preferred big dogs.

"Sure, why not?" she said finally and pointed to the motorcycle outside on the street. "Let's go."

*

They lived like any other couple.

The only thing that bothered Lupe was that the sexual part of their relationship still remained undiscussed. After the encounter in the lift on the first day, she hadn't touched Ellen apart from affectionate touches here and there.

The sexual tension was still there, bubbling under the surface, and Lupe felt her limit approaching every time she saw Ellen arriving back from her routine evening walk before having dinner with her.

They didn't spend much time together and Lupe still didn't know Ellen's thoughts about their relationship and she was tormented by the idea that Ellen might be seeing someone else. On the other hand, she couldn't really stop it as she hadn't come forward with her own feelings either, she was too shy to do it.

A couple of times she had caught Ellen's eyes watching her after her shower when she had dropped her towel and changed into her pyjama t-shirt and shorts, but she had quickly forced her eyes the other way before Lupe had been able to claim them.

The first day of May, the office decided to organise an office party in one of the local pubs. It had been four months since they had moved in together although no one really knew about it.

Ellen still received her personal mail at the office. Lupe knew it as she checked her part of the post shelving every morning when she arrived at work. There wasn't much to check – so far, she had seen her right to vote letter, the termination of her rental agreement at the hospital and a couple of local shop and restaurant coupons.

They didn't behave like strangers in the office, but Lupe could feel Ellen tried to keep her distance. She didn't like it but respected it in the work environment.

It was frustrating to her, especially since she could see Jack was doing everything he could to catch her attention: leaving coffee on her desk in the morning and inviting her out to lunch.

Sometimes, Lupe got so angry she poured the full sugar packets into the coffee Jack brought and waited for her to taste it. She knew by now that Ellen couldn't stand sugar in her coffee and it gave her personal satisfaction when Jack appeared to chat with her only to find an empty desk and a full Costa Coffee cup in the rubbish bin.

One time he even asked: "Lupe, did you throw away the coffee I bought for Ellen?" and pointed at the full coffee cup in the rubbish bin.

Lupe looked at him innocently. "I have no idea what you're talking about but while you're buying coffee for her, why don't you buy for all of us?" she said and raised her voice just enough to allow the rest of the team members to hear her. As if instructed, they all turned around and started moaning until Jack raised both hands in the air as a sign of defeat. "OK, OK, you guys win, tomorrow coffee is on me," he said and rushed out of the office.

At 4 o'clock, Lupe wanted to close her computer, but she was worried as she hadn't seen Ellen all day. She had managed to send herself an invite to access Ellen's diary earlier in the week while Ellen was away from her laptop, allowing her to keep track of her whereabouts and to know the details of her meetings and appointments. So she knew she had a long meeting with the senior clinical team upstairs, which should have ended only a couple of minutes before. She expected Ellen to arrive in the office soon and wanted to wait for her.

She waited for a good half an hour before sending her a text message asking her where she was. The message didn't go through immediately which meant she was still in the hospital in area without reception.

She was just about to take another quick walk around to find her when she heard her voice in the corridor.

She was laughing at something.

Jealousy pierced her heart like a knife when she heard her soft enticing laughter.

"Thank you for your support on this Jack, I really appreciate it. You have been a great help with organising the teams in the Critical Care section, we all really appreciate your assistance and expertise," Ellen said and opened the office door, letting him enter first.

"Don't worry Ellen, the pleasure is all mine," he said and walked along with her to the end of the office. "By the way, are you coming today to the office party by any chance?" he asked casually before sitting down behind his desk.

Ellen raised her eyebrows questioningly. "I wasn't aware there was an office party," she said and smiled.

"It's OK, the secretary probably forgot to include you on the distribution list as you are still the newest addition to the management team," he said and smiled back. "Anyway, King's Arms, opposite the hospital, tables received including the cheapest bar snacks," he winked.

Ellen laughed again. "No problem, if I stay hungry, I will pop into Tesco for a £3 meal deal, I know how you English people love it," she said and winked back at him before closing his office door.

The rest of the team had already left, and they had turned off the light in the management office where Ellen had left her briefcase and jacket. She turned on the lights again and leaned over to pick up her jacket and briefcase.

It was a beautiful briefcase; a souvenir from her time in Italy, an expensive gift to herself made of finest Italian leather. She caressed the smooth leather with her hand. She had fallen in love with the briefcase the first moment she had seen it and despite it being small and only able to fit a couple of essentials in addition to her laptop, she had decided to splurge and buy it. It had been the right choice and she had used it ever since. It reminded her of the good times in Italy: her studies, the study trips and road trips they had taken across Italy and all the way to Southern France in the tiniest car they had been able to rent on a student budget.

She was still smiling at her thoughts as she closed the briefcase, threw her jacket on her shoulders and turned around to leave the office only to find herself caught face to face with Lupe.

"Jeez, Lupe, you almost scared the life out of me," Ellen said and took hold of her shoulder to keep her balance. Lupe moved instantly forward to keep her from falling.

"What are you still doing in the office?" Ellen asked. "I thought everyone already left for the office party in the King's Arms."

Lupe's face stayed neutral. "Oh, were you hoping to have a chance with Jack alone without anyone else being in the office?"

Ellen flicked her head up to face her. She looked at her to understand if she was being serious. Her eyes were fuming like a burning carbon.

"Lupe, I hope you are joking right now. Please tell me you are joking," she said and crossed her hands across her chest.

"What, I can't ask a simple question? Furthermore, I should probably be aware of these things since you live under my roof."

She knew it was wrong of her to take up the house as leverage in the discussion, but she couldn't help the jealousy – envy and doubt fill her heart.

Ellen studied her face in silence. "Well then, it is probably better that I should move out, isn't it?" she said, barely able to face her. "Anyway, I have taken advantage of your hospitality too long, it is about time I stood again on my own feet," she turned to leave but Lupe grabbed her arm.

"So, it is true then, you are interested in him?"

Ellen watched her. She could hear the hurt animal in her voice and any other day, she would have used her common sense to convince her, but for some reason, the accusations pierced something inside of her.

"No, I didn't mean that," she finally said and sighed. "I'm not interested in Jack and to be honest, I don't think he has any other interest in me except a professional one. He has always been a gentleman."

Lupe looked at her and laughed. "Are you kidding me? He can't wait to swim in your pants. It is called hunting baby and you are the newest addition to the team."

"Oh, is that so?" Ellen said and turned around completely to face her. "First of all, I think the tall Russian lady is now the newest addition to the team and secondly, isn't that what you are wanting as well?" Ellen said and shook her hand from Lupe's touch before turning around and leaving the office.

"Well I've already been in those pants and trust me, it wasn't too hard to get in them, so no wonder I'm worried about my safety in my own house!" she yelled and waited for the office door to close but she didn't hear it.

Instead she saw Ellen walking back to give her a firm slap across her face. She managed to recover before the second one reached her other cheek. Lupe grabbed Ellen's arm forcefully. "Careful *munequita mia*, the first one is free, the second is going to cost you," she murmured and ran her fingers through her blonde hair.

Ellen struggled to get away from her and ran from the office. She had tears in her eyes.

Lupe waited until she could no longer hear the echo of her heels in the empty hospital corridor.

She sat down and buried her face in her hands. Lupe knew she had gone too far and had let the green monster speak, but she couldn't believe Ellen was so blind and naive about her effect on men. In the worst case, it could actually end up being dangerous for her, she thought before packing her bag, collecting her motorbike helmet and turning the lights off in the office.

Lupe rode home hoping to find Ellen there, but there was only the sad sound of Ellen's cat greeting her at the door. She picked up the sad animal from the floor. "Your *mami* hasn't been here yet eh?" she asked and petted his furry back. The cat looked at her with his big bedroom eyes and started purring.

Lupe smiled and hugged the cat tightly.

She had had her reservations about the animal at first and had regretted allowing Ellen to keep him, but his character had finally won her heart over and now she couldn't imagine a day without the little creature in her life. He brought calmness into her head and soothed her chaotic mind. His fur was dark black and smooth like a peach while his ears were big and tentative like a fox. He still had the cast on his front paw and therefore, Ellen carried the animal around the flat every time it meowed.

"Lucky bastard," Lupe said out loud and placed the animal carefully on the floor.

Ellen had an endless amount of patience; in fact, Lupe was mesmerised and lost her track of thoughts every time watching her whispering encouraging words into the little animal's ear.

That's why she was terrified of losing her, she thought and recalled the nasty conversation they had had in the office before she had run away.

Lupe shook her head and took off her jacket to take a quick shower before changing. She would give a quick call to Giuliana. The girl was one of her best friends in the office and had a mouth bigger than a Sky news reporter, but in this case it would be useful, she thought.

Giuliana picked up on the third ring. "Giuliana, *cariño,* where are you? Are you already in the King's Arms?"

"Oh, *cariño,* we miss you so much here, please come quickly!" Giuliana babbled.

Lupe smiled, she could hear she had been drinking already.

"Don't worry *love,* I will be on my way soon. I just had to finish some work," she said and continued. "How is everything there, everyone arrived already?"

"I think everyone is here who is planning to come," Giuliana said and took a sip of beer before continuing. "By the way, you might want to hurry as we are already betting on when Ellen will reach her limit with Jack."

Lupe's blood went cold.

"Oh really? *Ha ha*, what is the slimy bastard up to now?" she asked casually but inside she felt the rage boiling up to the surface.

"Well, just following her around and offering her strong drinks, asking to teach her how to dance salsa."

Lupe closed her eyes and tightened her grip around the phone; she didn't want to ask the next question. "And is she willing? Are they dancing or kissing already?"

"No, they are not, in fact I think she looks bored with him. She's trying to give him hints to back off which he seems to be completely clueless about," Giuliana said. As if understanding the mindset of Lupe, she continued: "Anyway, I will go now and try and get a chance to talk or dance with her. I will see you shortly I assume?"

"You bet," Lupe said and hung up the phone before she had a chance to say goodbye to her.

Lupe arrived at the pub to see the pure glory of her work colleagues getting smashed on free beer and other drinks. She had always been fascinated by how alcohol seems to release tension within individuals and bring out whatever was boiling under the neat surface, but this time she wasn't too keen on getting involved in any of it as her eyes were already searching for the familiar face in the crowd.

It wasn't hard to locate her – she was the most exotic, beautiful woman in the room by far. Even the group of pretty Portuguese nurses she used to enjoy flirting with paled in front of her. She made them look cheap like a group of colourful chickens on the perch and it was something they realised as well, judging by the cold looks they shot at her from the bar.

Lupe approached the table of her colleagues.

Some lonely outsiders were trying to engage in the conversation but the group was too tight and only interested in discussing work-related topics.

And there was Ellen. Lupe smiled and stood still to admire her from afar.

She hadn't gone back home to change after their fight, she had simply taken off her blazer, rolled up the sleeves of her silky white dress shift and opened a couple of golden buttons at the top. She had pulled her hair up into a messy quick hair-do with a couple of strays hair falling smoothly down her cheeks.

The kind of hair-do one would usually only see in quality porn movies, Lupe thought and felt a twist of desire in her stomach.

There were no free chairs in the pub and Lupe watched Ellen moving her balance from one leg to another as she still couldn't give up the gorgeous black leather stilettos she loved to pair with her black lacey hold-ups. Lupe knew this after seeing her wash her underwear in the house countless of times or get ready for work in her room.

In her wildest fantasies she would be waiting for her in the house wearing nothing but hold-ups and heels. That day, she would ask her to marry her. No, *make* her marry her, Lupe thought.

Giuliana saw her first. "*Cariño*, what took you so long?" she said and pouted her lip.

Lupe gave her a quick bear-like hug. "I'm sorry *cariño*, I had to take care of some things before coming, such as feeding my cat," she said loudly, directing her words to the whole group.

The words hit the goal instantly and Ellen froze and turned to face her.

Lupe knew it was a low blow, but in love and war, all weapons were allowed weren't they, she thought and smiled back.

She knew Ellen could barely hold her tongue and couldn't wait to get her alone for a moment to ask her how her beloved companion was. Seeing worry fill her eyes, Lupe wanted to comfort her and tell her everything was fine, but she needed to play her cards right.

"Lupe, I didn't know you had a cat," one of her colleagues turned around.

"Well, you know me, always bringing stray bitches home to shelter," she said and everyone laughed including Ellen, but soon she realised her rough joke might have been inappropriate and went to stand next to her.

"So, what are we drinking today?" she asked and placed her hand discreetly on her back to calm her down. She didn't push her away, which was a good sign.

Giuliana hurried to reply. "Well, all beer orders are free and a couple of cocktails, but they are very sweet, so we are staying with beer for now. Also, Mark is paying for a bottle of Jack Daniel's in case you want to have whiskey and coca-cola," Giuliana pointed to the half-drunk bottle in the middle of the wooden table.

"Sounds great, let's start with the Jack then," Lupe said and turned around to pick up one of the clean glasses placed on the table next to the napkins and cutlery.

Ellen turned to reach the bottle of coke for her but Lupe grabbed her wrist before the dark liquid reached the glass.

"Didn't you know you should never spoil a good-quality drink with something as cheap as coke, *munequita mia*?" Ellen stared in her eyes and Lupe leaned over to whisper her ear, "As in every aspect in life," she said and abruptly let go of her wrist and turned to laugh at a joke one of her colleagues at the table had just told.

She hadn't got a clue what the joke was, but she didn't want Ellen to get all her attention immediately, she first needed to cool off her raging heart and burning jealousy.

She didn't have more than ten minutes to enjoy her time before she heard a familiar voice behind her.

"Are we ready to party?" Jack said and put his hand on Ellen's and Lupe's shoulders, placing his beer-smelling face close to Ellen's.

Lupe wanted to stand up, grab the man by his collar, drag him outside and beat the living shit out of him just as her years on the streets had taught her. But she couldn't, not her boss.

"All good Jack, thanks," Ellen said but didn't make an effort to move away from him.

"Good, *Ellenita,* I'm happy to hear you are enjoying your first after-work drinks with your colleagues," he said and exposed his perfectly white set of teeth. He had surely paid for those, Lupe thought as she discreetly listened to the conversation.

"Yes, it was nice of you to invite me, it feels great to meet up outside of the hospital," she smiled.

"Indeed," he said and glanced around as if looking for someone before slightly grabbing her arm. "Ellen, there is someone I would like to introduce you to. You see the short bald man in a grey suit and poorly tied tie?" he asked and pointed at the bar. "That's the divisional director for the Trust. I'm sure you would benefit from meeting him, I know he has been asking about your work," he added.

Lupe closed her eyes. Knowing Ellen, she knew he had hit the jackpot.

"Is that so?" Ellen asked as the interest in her eyes grew.

Jack smiled. "Of course, shall we?" he asked and offered his arm to her.

She didn't take his arm but collected her drink from the table and excused herself.

Lupe was fuming as she watched them go but she couldn't do much before someone on the table made another joke. She had to satisfy herself with carefully watching them from afar.

It didn't take long before all the drinks and beer had passed through her and she needed to go to the toilet.

She loudly excused herself from the table and walked downstairs to the toilet area. She knew Ellen wouldn't miss the opportunity to talk to her and waited for her outside the toilet in the darkest corner.

Ellen didn't disappoint her and she heard the familiar sound of her heels approaching on the wooden floor after a couple of seconds.

Lupe followed her from the darkness and touched her hand lightly before she was able to open the toilet door.

"Jeez, you scared me," Ellen winced and placed her hand on her heart.

"Twice in the same day, am I talented or what?" Lupe said and spread her arms.

Ellen watched her. "That's not funny what happened today in the office."

Lupe closed her arms. "Damn right it's not, you should know better and stop flirting with everyone like a *puta*," she said and looked her in her eyes.

Ellen gasped at being called a *bitch* but remained calm. "Anyway, how is my baby? I feel awful I didn't come and feed him myself today." The affection she felt for her little companion overpowered her in the moment and she grabbed Lupe's wrists.

Lupe winced – since their passionate night together, Ellen had not touched her once and even though the touch was initiated by an innocent cause, it flipped Lupe's world upside down.

"Your cat is fine *munequita mia*, don't worry," she said and pushed her hands from her arms. "Now, if you will excuse me, I need to get back to my original reason for being here, which is going to the toilet," she said and passed her to the toilet, locking the toilet door in front of her nose without looking back.

She waited a strategic couple of minutes to hear Ellen leaving the corridor and returning upstairs.

It wasn't a lot she had gained, but at least she had her undivided attention, she thought and hummed lightly whilst washing her hands and correcting the half ponytail of her curls before following her back upstairs.

Most of her colleagues had moved to the end of the bar and were occupying the tables around the small dance floor. Lupe saw Jack already showing off his ridiculous dance moves to the ladies including Ellen.

Lupe shook her head at the sight. He didn't dance well, it was mainly a mixture of basic salsa steps and modern English moves that he was desperately trying to put together.

Lupe rubbed her hands together; this would be her scene. This time she would send a clear message, she thought and approached the crowd.

On her way to the group, she stopped at the DJ desk for a song request. The DJ searched for a while but finally found the song and Lupe sighed with relief.

"Maestro, can you play it as the third song from now?" she asked.

"Certainly, not a problem," he said and gave her a thumbs up in case the loud music prevented her hearing him. Lupe winked at him and returned to the table.

She sat down and ordered a beer while observing Ellen and her other female colleagues around Jack.

She didn't seem overly impressed by him but stayed in the group. Lupe couldn't help noticing her eyes wandering towards her every now and then when she thought she wasn't looking. Lupe heard the familiar melody and knew it was her time.

She walked over to the group and stretched out her hand. "Ellen, would you like to dance real salsa?"

Ellen turned around as did her other colleagues. "You know how to dance?" she asked, raising her eyebrow.

"Of course, *munequita*, it is in my blood," she said and held her breath for a second before leaning over. "The real salsa, not the *mierda* he is trying to demonstrate to you."

She saw her eyes light up as she accepted the invitation. "Sure, why not? I have been taking a couple of salsa lessons myself, so don't try to fool me," she said and offered her hand to Lupe.

Lupe laughed. "Trust me *cielo mio*, this is something you won't learn in the classroom," she said.

The floor was crowded, which was even better than Lupe could have hoped for as she had a perfect reason to hold her close to her body and shield her from their nosy co-workers who had been overly curious at the change of scene.

Lupe grabbed Ellen from the hips and with a smooth gesture, moved her close to her body and took her hand into hers. Ellen gasped but moved.

"Now, close your eyes *munequita mia*, and let the music talk to you," she said and leaned closer. "Let me lead the way."

Ellen closed her eyes and the minute she did, Lupe could feel her tense body soften in her hands.

Lupe smiled and moved Ellen's hips with her hands for the first beats. She followed immediately.

Lupe had picked something old, easy to dance with easy rhythm but a clear message – Grupo 5's *Propriedad privada* couldn't have been clearer to anyone, she thought while she relaxed and took control of the dance.

Ellen danced well and had a good sense of rhythm. She was definitely a follower when it came to dancing or maybe it was just because *she* was leading her, Lupe thought and pressed their bodies closer to each other.

They were complementary in so many different ways that Lupe had lost count, she thought again as she led her through a more complex sequence of steps and twists.

It was hot and steamy on the dance floor and Ellen's skin was glowing in the spotlight. Lupe was desperate to taste her skin but didn't have the courage to do so and instead leaned her face closer to her collarbone and tightened her grip on her body.

She could feel her heartbeat against her chest and her soft breasts pressing against her. Her delicate body moved in her hands like a fine-tuned guitar responding to her touch.

She caressed the falling hair from her neck and placed a soft, unnoticeable kiss on her. She smelled divine, of ocean and jasmine; Lupe smiled as the familiar scent surrounded them.

She wasn't sure if it was a perfume, washing detergent or her personal smell, but she couldn't believe she still had the same scent as eight years ago, she thought and stepped back and motioned her for a quick twirl.

Ellen seemed surprised but followed without a doubt.

As she was returning to her arms from the twirl, Lupe turned her around abruptly and guided her from behind, letting her soft buttocks press against her crotch and allowing her to breathe her scent into the top of her lungs. She moved her hands on top of hers and placed all four of them intimately on her stomach.

Ellen turned her head to face her for a moment.

She had sweat dripping from her neck inside her blouse, her cheeks were flushed and her hair was messy after the twirls and from keeping up with the tempo of the music.

The free-falling strands of her hair were glued to her cheeks and it reminded her of their first night in London, so much so that Lupe could feel the exigency growing between her legs.

This is what she had always been waiting for she suddenly realised as she heard the last melodies play in the background.

She twirled her round to face her again and before the song ended, she arched her down until the tip of her hair touched the ground and stole a look in her eyes.

It was naked pleasure.

Lupe hadn't noticed but as they had danced, the crowd had slowly moved from the dance floor, either to give them room or to admire the chemistry between them.

She felt a moment of embarrassment but recovered quickly.

"Until next time *munequita mia.*" she whispered before their other colleagues surrounded her asking her to dance with them as well.

The rest of the evening passed with her teaching her other colleagues to dance, but she couldn't stop her eyes searching for Ellen.

Ellen hadn't approached her after their dance, not even once, and Lupe started feeling paranoid that maybe the dance hadn't been enough of an apology for the incident earlier in the office.

Technically, she had only spoken her mind, so she shouldn't even need to apologise, she thought. It wasn't her fault she had felt insulted. Everyone should always be free to express their minds.

Although she did feel bad at how the message had come out initially. It had been slightly rougher than she had intended in the first place, she thought.

Maluma's last song was about to end and the bartender had started to close the bar up when Lupe realised she had lost sight of Ellen.

A panic grew in her heart as she excused herself from the nurse from CCU she had taught how to dance. The nurse pouted as Lupe quickly murmured a thank you and left to search for Ellen. She couldn't care less as her only intention had been to make Ellen jealous, but the priorities had changed and at that moment her only priority was to find her.

She looked inside and outside, in front of the bar, in the smoking area and even went to the men's toilets but she couldn't see even a sign of strands of her blonde hair.

Mierda.

For a moment she wondered if she had caught an Uber home, but it didn't remove the nibbling feeling of paranoia in her head and reassure her. She was on her way downstairs to the female toilet again when she saw the back of Jack covering Ellen who was sitting on a bench in front of the ladies' toilets.

Lupe quickly hid in the corner.

"Come on Ellen, come home with me," Jack wheedled while rubbing Ellen's shoulder.

She smiled but gently pushed his hand away. "No seriously Jack, let it go, you are married, and I don't feel any sexual chemistry between us, I'm sorry," Ellen said, holding her head. "Besides, I have an awful headache, and I haven't been home since this morning."

"Ellen, I have mentioned to you previously that my marriage is over, it was a mistake all along, I was just trying to please my parents," he said.

Ellen looked at his boyish face with pity. "I'm sorry to hear that Jack, but there is nothing I can do for you at this stage," she said as politely as she could. "What can I say? I'm not interested in you in that way."

She watched his face turn red as he took a slight step back to look at her. "Oh, I see, you are waiting for good old Lupita to work her magic on you first, is that it?" he asked abruptly. "What is it with you ladies? You want to try it once and tick it off your bucket list is that it?" he said laughing and moved his hand onto her upper hip. "It's OK Ellen, I can wait until you get it out of your system, and then we can start off."

Ellen looked at him and jerked his hand off. "Sorry Jack, but what I do with my life is not your business and you can save your immature comments for someone who wants to hear them, for me, I'm done listening," she said and made an effort to stand up and leave but Jack caught her hand. "Ellen, I'm sorry, please don't go without giving me at least a goodnight kiss," he said and leaned over her face.

"Not in a million years, get off me!" she hissed and turned her head away before Jack nailed her against the wall and covered her mouth with his hand.

"Shhh, *Ellenita*, don't ruin the first moment we have together but rather enjoy it," he said and smiled, approaching her face with his lips curled into a kiss.

Ellen felt panic rising in her as she smelled the sweat on his t-shirt and his breath filled with alcohol. She tried to thrash around from his grip to freedom, but he was too heavy and drunk for her tired limbs.

She knew the bar was about to close and wasn't sure if she had seen the bartender already checking the toilets. She couldn't stop the fear creeping into her mind.

She knew he would play the *I don't-remember-anything* card at work and she was terrified of the humiliation to follow.

The cold sweat surfaced on her temples and a familiar acid taste came into her mouth which made her feel sick to her stomach. Jack was placing wet kisses on her lips and the bare shoulders he had exposed by ripping her lacy blouse down her arms. The button had given in, exposing her lacy bra and Ellen saw raw lust in his eyes. She cried out loud.

With her last strength, she tried to push him away before she heard the sound of a familiar voice. "Jack, let her go."

Jack turned his head in surprise. "Well, well, well, if it isn't the poodle who has followed Ellen around all evening. Why am I not surprised to see you here?" he said but didn't let go of her.

"Jack, I will ask once more before I shove my fist so hard into your pretty mouth that you will not be able to open it for the next decade, I swear," Lupe said and clicked her knuckles threateningly.

Jack stood back and eyed her clenched fists. "You can't do that, I'm your boss!"

Lupe shook her head. "I don't care, we are not at work and you are sexually assaulting Ellen, so I ask you once more, *let her go.*"

Maybe it was the alcohol or maybe it was the Latin macho culture running in his veins that made Jack step forward. "Try me –"

He didn't manage to finish his sentence before Lupe landed a full-blown punch on his right cheek. Ellen cried out and looked horrified when he stepped back holding the right side of his face which started turning black in front of her eyes.

He seemed to be surprised as he stumbled back, but recovered quickly, raising his fists and aggressively trying to land one on her, missing her head by half a metre and ending up blundering onto the floor.

She was half a head shorter than he was, but built with muscle and knowledge one could only learn on the street.

Jack didn't stand a chance.

Lupe followed and grabbed his t-shirt collar and landed another blow and a well-aimed kick to his side. He threw up on the floor, filling the air with the smell of acid.

It wasn't until Ellen screamed that Lupe woke up from her trance and realised what she was doing.

"Please Lupe, stop," Ellen whispered in a soft voice and touched her shoulder.

Lupe turned around aggressively to face her.

Ellen let go immediately and crossed her arms on her chest as if trying to protect herself. She looked scared and her lower lip was shaking.

"You OK?" asked Lupe.

Ellen nodded.

"Good, then let's get out of here," she said and pulled Ellen towards the stairs.

"Wait, what about him?" Ellen pointed at Jack who was still lying in his own vomit and apparently crying.

"I will sort it out, don't worry," Lupe said and on their way up she stopped the bartender briefly. "*Yo, amigo*, one of the guys apparently fell and vomited on the floor in the ladies' toilet, better check him out and send him home."

Lupe didn't bother to wait for the surprised bartender to answer before dragging Ellen out of the bar.

Ellen breathed the fresh air. "Jeez, how nice is the fresh air?"

Lupe nodded and handed her a helmet.

Ellen looked at her with wide eyes. "Lupe, I don't think you should drive. I have seen you drinking all night."

Lupe burst into angry laughter. "*Muñeca*, I have ridden more drunk than this all of my life. I'm a very safe rider I can assure you. You will be fine," she said and urged her to put the helmet on.

Ellen sighed but put on the helmet. Lupe handed her a jacket from the motorcycle's storage box.

Ellen eyed the jacket suspiciously. "How did you know I would come home with you?" she asked in disbelief.

"Blame the lucky stars," Lupe growled and helped her to close the jacket.

In that moment, something shifted in the air between them both and replaced the air with electricity. They both grew quiet and serious, eyes locked, only a breeze of air filling the small gap between them. Ellen shivered.

"Let's get home, fast," Lupe said and patted the back of the seat.

*

The ride was refreshing after the long night in the bar and Lupe was happy to have Ellen behind her grabbing her hands around her waist. Riding calmed her mind and gave her peace of mind as they travelled the empty streets of London before the sunrise.

They got home in less than twenty minutes and Lupe parked the motorcycle in front of the building and took off her black helmet before turning to help Ellen off the bike.

She grabbed her shoulders so as not to lose her balance and slid right into her arms.

Lupe reached out to open her helmet and a cascade of golden locks fell down. They still smelled like jasmine.

The sight made the air leave her body as if she had been kicked in the stomach. "Are you OK?" Lupe whispered to fill in the silence between them.

"Yes, I'm OK. Thank you for helping me out there," Ellen said and brushed her cheek with her fingertip.

The touch was soft and her hands still had the slight scent of vanilla hand cream that Lupe had seen on her nightstand numerous times. The bottle never seemed to move, so she hadn't been sure if she was even using it or only set it there as a decoration along with a fancy tissue holder. Now she knew.

With only one touch, Lupe felt the murderous rage she had felt inside after seeing Jack trying to kiss her starting to slowly die.

"Anytime, *pricesa mia,*" she said and turned around.

This time, Ellen remained quiet and let her use the pet name she didn't like.

Lupe sighed. The rage inside her was lethal and so real it scared even herself. She was not afraid of her own reaction, as she was ready to kill for her without hesitation. *Anyone* who would even try to touch Ellen didn't deserve to live and she would happily spend the rest of her life keeping her safe.

The rest of their lives, she thought as she entered the building reception area.

Ellen followed and grabbed her hand.

Lupe was taken by surprise and froze for a moment.

"Relax, it's OK," Ellen whispered and let her hand caress the back of her palm.

They entered the building and took the elevator to their floor.

The sad meow welcomed them at the door and without hesitation, Ellen bent down to enclose the small animal in her arms whilst Lupe turned on the light in the living room.

"*Mierda.*"

"What is it?" Ellen asked tentatively.

"The electricity is finished," Lupe sighed. "I'll be right back," she grabbed the motorcycle keys before Ellen stopped her. "It's OK, *amore*, we have candles don't we?" she asked and Lupe nodded confused.

"Sit down and make yourself comfortable," she said and disappeared into the kitchen.

A few seconds later, she came back with a pile of candles and started placing them around the flat.

The small house immediately lit up with a gorgeous glow and Lupe could feel the warmth of the wax and fire relaxing her tense muscles. She rubbed her knuckles.

"Are you hurt?" Ellen asked for the first time since the incident in the bar.

Lupe shook her head. "Nah, just bruises, I'll live," she said.

Ellen approached and sat next to her on the sofa, taking her hand in hers. "Let me check quickly," she said and examined her hand carefully.

Lupe held her breath and observed her face.

"Why are you doing this to me?" The question she was terrified to ask escaped from her lips, freezing Ellen's fingers running over her palm.

"What do you mean?"

"Why are you tormenting me like this?" she cried quietly and pulled her injured hand back.

"Isn't it enough that you are everywhere in my head and mind all the time? I can't sleep, work, eat without you being present in my thoughts," she said and buried her face in her hands. "It makes me act like an idiot, lose control."

Ellen sat quietly for a while before slowly lifting her head to face her.

"What if I say you are doing the same to me?"

Lupe's glossy eyes grew wide and a reply burnt her lips but Ellen raised her hand to stop her.

"Let me talk please. I don't know what this is, but I feel a very strong connection with you, and it is something I have never felt before," she said and continued. "I feel like I have known you for a long time."

She looked so adorable and lost at the same time in the candle light, as if she was trying to figure out something her body had recognised on their first night together, but her mind hadn't really caught up yet.

Why would it, Lupe thought, after all, she had never shown her face on that night.

In that moment, Lupe almost told her, *almost*.

Instead she turned fully to face her and brushed a stray hair from her forehead. "What if we both enjoy something we have been wanting to do for so long?" she said and examined her face closely.

"And what would that be?" Ellen whispered.

Lupe didn't respond but instead ran her finger along her lower lip line and leaned towards her, leaving only centimetres between their lips until the air between them disappeared.

Ellen closed her eyes when their lips met.

The kiss was intense but sweet and Lupe felt herself melting against her lips as she let all the weeks and months of frustration speak for themselves. She tasted the mixture of salty and sweet, a hint of alcohol as well, and for a second, Lupe was worried Ellen might be under the influence of alcohol, but the thought was quickly washed away when she tipped her tongue out, exploring inside her mouth and looking for her response.

Lupe felt the warmth of her inner thighs after the motorcycle ride as she ran her hands up, stopping to caress her breasts and swollen nipples.

Ellen was wearing a light blue transparent lace bra with white details which didn't leave too much to the imagination, Lupe observed as she unbuttoned her white silk blouse.

She had seen her underwear before, numerous times, when Ellen was handwashing her delicates in the sink and leaving them to dry on top of the shower curtain rail. The clothing would usually be gone before the morning and so Lupe had taken habit to wandering into the bathroom before going to sleep to see the delicate pastel colours and inhale the sweet mixture of fresh linen and the particular scent of Ellen that she couldn't really name yet.

She looked at her face as she caressed the delicate skin. Her skin was golden fair and felt like a peach under her touch. A tiny sigh escaped from her lips.

"Can I take your shift off?" Ellen asked hesitantly.

Lupe nodded, she couldn't say it out loud, and tensed when Ellen lifted her shirt off, leaving her in front of her wearing only her nude t-shirt bra.

The bra was Victoria's Secret and the only feminine luxury Lupe had spoiled herself with over the years. It was from the sports section and was the most basic style they had, yet the material felt like a hint of luxury.

She felt naked in front of her and sudden panic she didn't remember from before. The macho alfa slowly died in her and she felt like covering herself under Ellen's thoughtful gaze.

Ellen leaned over to open her bra. Her hands were still cold from the brief ride and it made goosebumps appear on her skin.

Lupe quickly leaned over to open Ellen's lacy bra.

They struggled for a brief moment to undo each other's bras before they ended up on the floor along with the shirts, Ellen's skirt and Lupe's trousers.

They both looked at each other with pleasure and Lupe could see Ellen's nipples turning from blush pink to burgundy red.

She had medium-sized, perky breasts and a beautiful curvy but athletic body, which clearly showed she was into a healthy lifestyle but didn't watch her calories too much.

It made Lupe feel very self-conscious of her own body. Her breasts were bigger than hers and her nipples larger, a shade of red and brown. Lupe had always secretly been proud of her own breasts but she wished they had been smaller as they had made her feel less of the macho alfa, a role she had been forced to take as long as she could remember.

Her back, which she didn't know if Ellen had seen yet, was covered in childhood scars and her arms were heavily tattooed. Her stomach had once been flat and tight but years of battling with weight and depression had left signs of stretchmarks along the way. Her skin was a light olive shade that had turned into a sun-kissed tanned colour in the candlelight and her legs were covered in soft black hairs that she never remembered to shave.

Mi pequeño osito, like her aunt used to call her, a memory that briefly washed over her mind before Ellen stood up in front of her and slid down her matching lace panties.

Lupe hurried to do the same.

Ellen gently pushed her by her shoulders back onto the sofa and sat down on the glass coffee table in front of her, opening her legs on both sides of Lupe to give her a full view of her naked body.

Lupe had seen it all before in all forms and shapes, but she had to stop and admire the full frontal of her; Ellen's sex had turned pink and swollen, her entrance folds drooling down her nectar.

It was like an orchid, a beautiful but rare flower waiting for a bee to fertilise it.

The inner folds had grown and were sleek with all the juices her body had produced.

What *she* had made her body produce, Lupe thought proudly.

Ellen sat quietly, letting her take her time to examine her body, and

Lupe looked.

She gently caressed and drew circles on the sensitive skin on her inner thigh and blew air to cool her steaming sex. Ellen sighed with pleasure and arched her neck back, exposing the lines of her collarbone and her swan neck.

Lupe couldn't stop admiring her; if she had been brave enough, she would have asked permission to take pictures of her just like that, but she couldn't bring herself to ask. *Another time*, she thought and continued her adventure over her skin and let her fingertips brush over her sex.

She heard Ellen gasp for air and saw her open her eyes. She smiled at her.

"Don't tease me, please," Ellen whispered.

"Why not, *mi gringa linda*?" she asked and moved her hands to stroke her bum. Ellen held her breath. "I can't wait much longer."

Lupe watched her beautiful glowing face. Her pupils were enormous, and her lips were swollen from their previous intense kiss.

"Listen *munequita mia*, I'm here to establish the rules," she said and turned her eyes back to her body. "I have been waiting for you for *too long*."

Ellen waited for her to continue. "And I saved you from from *ese estúpido* situation which you got yourself into by disobeying me," she squeezed her bum hard.

Ellen cried out.

"So technically, I should be the one making the rules, am I right?"

She wasn't sure if she had gone too far, and felt a slight panic when Ellen silently stood up and turned around, exposing her back to her. She was still wearing her heels and her round bum was now deliciously in front of Lupe's face. She knelt slightly in front of her, arching her peachy buttocks and exposing her sex to her from behind.

"Lead the way, *tiger*."

Lupe was shocked for a few seconds; she had never seen anything like this before, without paying for it of course.

She leaned over to caress the cold bum cheeks before giving her a tentative smack on her right bum cheek. Ellen didn't say a word.

She gave another one, harder.

She felt Ellen's body jerk forward but didn't hear a sound coming out of her mouth.

It made her angry – she wanted to get a reaction out of her and see her hand leaving a red mark on her pale skin.

She felt the dark forces in her mind filling the air as she prepared to give it to her harder. Suddenly a picture of Jack kissing Ellen rose to her mind and the hurt animal escaped its cage, roaring, as she swung her hand, giving her two hard smacks on both bum cheeks without holding back.

The force of the smacks and the adrenaline in her blood made her breath faster and jerked Ellen's body forward. The last one made her cry out loud like an animal.

Lupe closed her eyes and felt her sex convulse with desire; it was the sweetest sound she had heard in her life, it was like a trapped animal hoping for salvation, which was not coming.

At least not yet.

She stood up and went to stand in front of her, pushing the glass coffee table forward to allow them more space in the small living room.

Ellen panted at the pain and slowly tipped her face to look at her. Her cheeks were red, but her eyes were clear and observant.

Neither of them spoke, until Lupe urged her up from her knees and moved her back onto the sofa before sitting on the glass coffee table in front of her and spreading her legs wide open, giving the full front of *her* for a change. Something she had only done in her wildest fantasies.

"Now it's your turn."

Ellen's eyes widened as she looked down on her.

Lupe knew it was probably the first time she had been so exposed with another woman and the idea of it sent her obsessive mind for a spin. She knew she was clean and only allowed her pubic air to grow to a certain length, leaving only a fine line to trace back to her navel hairs, to show who wore the pants in the relationship, which was very typical in a relationship between two people like them: the *beauty* and the *beast*.

She had heard rumours of couples like them and none of them had ended well for her friends, but she would have never in her wildest dreams have thought of being in a situation like this. She always thought she would have settled for someone older and only attractive enough to awaken her desire but never to make her a slave to another person. It was a dangerous place to be, Lupe knew it.

"I don't know how," a small whisper brought Lupe back to reality.

She smiled and caressed her hair. "You will know *amor mio*, trust me," she said and urged her face closer between her legs.

Ellen resisted only for a second before grabbing her thighs with her hands. Lupe held her breath as she felt her hot breath close to her entrance. She had never let anyone do such an intimate thing to her, never allowed someone so close to her, not to mention let anyone caress her in that way as she had always felt uncomfortable with the thought, yet she couldn't wait to have Ellen *do it* to her.

The first kiss she felt on her entrance gave her the shock of her life and the first tentative lick to open her entrance left her lungs without air, so much so that she had to lean back and balance her strong body with her hands.

She looked down and saw Ellen watching her. "Keep going *princesa mia*, you are doing just fine," she said and pressed her full face against her sex.

Ellen wasn't shy at all – on the contrary, she closed her eyes devotionally and opened her mouth fully to please her.

She twirled her adventurous tongue up and down between her entrance folds until she found her clitoris and gently nudged the sensitive spot, giving small tentative sucks in between.

She was a natural pleaser, Lupe thought, and a sudden spike of jealousy pierced her heart at the thought that maybe she had lied to her and she had been with women before her.

She pressed Ellen's face deeper onto her, moving her hips, rubbing her face against her sex as she felt her end starting to build up quickly, and so did Ellen, knowingly increasing the pace of her touch, milking her towards an orgasm.

It was something Lupe had never felt before, and for that reason she wasn't prepared when the orgasm came stronger than ever, and made her sex convulse and squirt warm liquid around Ellen's face and breasts. For a brief moment she felt embarrassment at her bodily reaction to her, but seeing Ellen covered in her juices made her feel like a true macho who had marked her in all possible ways.

"You OK?" Ellen asked after a silence.

Lupe opened her eyes to look at her. "Yeah, I'm OK."

Ellen wiped the warm liquid off her chest and cheeks. "Did I do it right?"

Lupe laughed. "You, *amor mio,* did it like a veteran," she said and pushed herself up in front of her.

"Actually, so natural, I started wondering if you had been completely honest with me when you said you haven't been with a woman before," Lupe said and ran a lock of her golden hair around her finger before tugging a fistful and jerking her head close to hers. "Because if I find out you lied to me, and trust me I will, it will be your worst nightmare."

Ellen didn't have time to respond before Lupe clasped her hands around her legs and pushed her towards the sofa, following on top of her.

"Now, where were we?" Lupe said and opened her legs. "If you thought I would leave you without a prime ending, you are deadly wrong my *darling*. I have better manners than that," she said and kissed her on the lips whilst her finger searched for her sex and then brutally pressed deep down into her.

Ellen gasped but Lupe silenced her with her mouth, exhaling cool air into her mouth and allowing her to breathe it in.

She pressed harder before she found the hard spot inside on the wall of her sex and drew small circles before giving full focus to her clitoris, so hard she heard Ellen whimpering in pain.

Her plan wasn't to please her, but to punish her and claim her again for the lie she had seen in her eyes when she had asked her.

Now the only thing she was interested in was pumping the information out of her; whoever it was who had been there before her, she would find her and make sure she wouldn't live another day knowing she had touched the only thing she had wanted pure and innocent.

Tormented by her thoughts and the image of Ellen's body responding to anyone else's touch, she didn't notice Ellen gasping for breath and looking for a place to balance her hands while the forced orgasm ripped her body to pieces.

"Stop please, enough!" she yelled before gulping fresh air into her lungs and trying to escape from her lap.

Lupe grabbed her by her throat and continued to rub her clitoris until she could feel her body convulse for the second time. "Now *muñeca mia*, I know you lied to me, I can see it miles away, so you better start talking. Who was there before me?"

Ellen gasped and dropped to the floor on all fours, her body still convulsing from the second orgasm.

She was gasping for air. "I don't know what you are talking about."

Lupe followed her, pushing her down onto the floor with her body and blocking her airways with her hands. "Now I would imagine you want to rephrase that, *puta*. Otherwise this might be the last thing you do, if you don't start talking, now."

Ellen couldn't talk as her lips started turning blue and her oxygen level dropped dangerously. Her hands clawed Lupe's arms as her lungs burnt desperately in the need for air.

She would talk, Lupe knew it, she wouldn't want to die for someone who wasn't in the picture anymore. Or maybe she still was, she thought as she jerked her head aggressively against the floor.

"For the last time, talk!" Who was she?" she said and released the pressure around her neck to allow her to respond.

"I don't know, it was eight years ago, and I never saw her face!" Ellen whispered with her last breath before losing consciousness.

Her head dropped to the floor, making a loud echo in the empty flat as Lupe tore her hands off her neck as it would have burnt her.

Chapter 46

Ellen woke up to the smell of freshly squeezed orange juice and bread.

She turned around in her bed and frowned in confusion.

She glanced at the wrinkled bed sheets, which still had a dent in the pillow and warmth from last night indicating someone had carried her to the bed, dressed her in her pyjamas and then slept next to her as she didn't remember going to the bed on her own.

She stood up from the bed feeling lightheaded and sore in places she didn't even know she had. Slightly clinging she entered the kitchen.

"Good morning *princesa mia*," Lupe said and offered her a glass of orange juice with a kiss. "Did you sleep well?"

Ellen nodded, even her throat felt sore, she thought and touched her neck thoughtfully.

"Are you thinking of last night?"

Ellen glanced at her before the memory of last night returned to her mind. The glass with freshly squeezed orange juice fell to the floor, breaking into small pieces.

"Oh, look what you did *amor, cuidado*, there is glass everywhere!" Lupe said and motioned Ellen to sit down on the stool in the kitchen before grabbing a yellow cloth and kneeling to wipe the juice and glass off the floor. Ellen stayed frozen, looking past her as if trying to put a name to what had happened last night.

"Now, I think I might have overreacted slightly last night." Lupe broke the silence without looking at her.

Ellen eyed her ironically. "You think?"

"Don't take that tone with me *munequita*, you were there too, as excited as me," she said, shooting a quick glance at her before scanning the floor again for glass. "I think I got all the glass from the floor, but you should be careful and don't let the cat enter the kitchen before I have vacuumed, we wouldn't want him to hurt his paws on the glass now would we," she said and smiled at her.

"How could you do what you did last night?" Ellen asked quietly. "Didn't you see I couldn't breathe?"

Lupe examined the floor. "Finished, see, no more glass anywhere and luckily, I have more orange juice for you *amor*, but you better stay sitting and drink it slowly. You look a little bit pale," she said and poured another glass of orange juice into a plastic cup this time.

"I don't want more juice. I want answers, or I'm going to pack my stuff and leave!" Ellen huffed and pushed the juice cup away.

Her words stopped Lupe. "I don't think those drastic measures are necessary *munequita mia*," she said, lowering her voice. "We will have a safe word for you next time, so it won't happen again."

"That's not what I mean!" she cried in frustration and jumped off the stool to leave the kitchen. Lupe grabbed her wrist. "I know you didn't mean that and I'm sorry, I got too excited yesterday," she sighed. "Too jealous."

Ellen stopped. "But why?"

"Because I felt you were lying to me and I wanted to know why."

Ellen raised her eyebrows confused.

Lupe caressed the sensitive skin around her wrist but didn't let her go. "I knew you lied to me about not having been with another woman before," she said. "You were so natural and seemed to enjoy the things you did to me so much. I figured there couldn't have been another explanation, and in the end I was right."

Ellen looked at her with sadness in her eyes, "That's not exactly true," she said quietly, looking at the ground.

Lupe watched the expression shift on her face. The memory of the night eight years ago still haunted them both and now it was her golden opportunity to hear what had happened on that night according to Ellen. She couldn't wait to ask the question, but at the same time she was terrified of hearing the answer. Whilst carrying her to the bed, changing her into her pyjamas and spooning her cold body last night, she knew she had almost gone too far and lost the most beautiful thing in her life. This knowledge pushed her towards the next question.

"Do you want to talk about it?" Lupe asked and motioned them both to the living room. She had cleaned and ventilated the room in the morning removing all evidence of last night. She wasn't consumed by jealousy and obsession anymore. How could she be, since the person she had been tormented by was looking at her every time she looked in the mirror.

Ellen winced. "Well, there is nothing really to tell, it all happened very fast," she said and continued. "Actually, I haven't told anyone before, ever."

Lupe watched her thoughtfully and placed her hand on her shoulder protectively. "It's OK *princesa mia*, it's about time you shared it with someone, and I would be honoured."

When Ellen shook her head, Lupe pressed her finger on her lips to stop her from talking. "It's OK, I have all the time in the world," she said and sat them both on the sofa.

*

Ellen gave her a small smile before looking out of the living room window. "I don't remember much and sometimes I even think it might all have been a dream."

Lupe nodded her head. "It's OK, just tell me whatever you can remember," she said reassuringly.

Ellen didn't speak up immediately as if she was gathering her thoughts, but Lupe didn't want to rush her. In fact, she felt nearly as nervous as she was, after all, she was about to hear the answer to the million-dollar question she had tormented herself with for almost a decade.

Ellen cleared her throat. "Before I even start, I want to make sure you understand I wasn't lying to you before," she said but when Lupe frowned she hurried to continued. "Once you hear the story you will hopefully understand why I said it."

"OK," Lupe nodded.

"I was in Spain for a weekend," Ellen started. "It was early summer and just after the last week of university. At that time, I studied in Bocconi University in Milan, Italy. Economics, just like my parents always wanted me to do," she said and glanced quickly at Lupe.

She nodded, waiting for her to continue.

Ellen sighed. "I flew to Madrid to see a friend of mine. She studied on some of the same courses as me. Her name is Gisela, a Spanish girl."

"Do you still stay in touch with her?" Lupe asked curiously.

"No, not anymore," Ellen said and quickly looked at her before continuing the story.

"I flew to see her but as it turned out, she wasn't able to join me on that weekend but she didn't want me to cancel my trip as she knew I was short of money anyway; we all were at that time, except her," Ellen said and smirked ironically.

Lupe smiled.

"Anyhow, her father was at home but due to travel on business and her mum was out of the country, at Lake Como, I think it was," Ellen said. "She had a long-time lover as they were going through a nasty divorce but both of them were too stubborn to share their wealth and businesses and in the end, they were forced to stay legally together because of it," Ellen took a strategic pause as if the memory was still painful to her. "They were sort of in a limbo before her father suffered a heart attack and died some years later. I attended the funeral with Gisela."

Lupe nodded, she had read about it in the local newspaper exactly three years after they had robbed the house and she had met Ellen. She didn't know anyone who would have attended the funeral but if she had known, she would have maybe found Ellen before, she thought.

"They said he died of a heart ache after finding out about his wife's affair but he was quite a ladies' man himself as well, so I wouldn't blame it solely on Gisela's mum," Ellen said defensively.

"Don't worry, I don't imagine anyone really did," Lupe said and patted Ellen's palm to prompt her to continue.

It was a lie of course, the whole of Madrid had talked about Gisela's mum having done it on purpose to get the family fortune and live a long and happy life with her lover, but now that she thought about, she hadn't heard anything of the family since the father had died. She just assumed she had left the country and was having the time of her life in the French Riviera or somewhere.

Almost as though guessing her thoughts Ellen replied, "She never recovered from losing the love of her life. She retired and still lives in the same house in Madrid; she refuses to sell or leave it for the memory of her beloved husband." Ellen smiled. "Ironic, isn't it?"

Lupe smiled and nodded.

"So anyway, I was supposed to be alone in the house for the weekend. Just to get my mind away from studies and other things," she continued and stroked her hair. "I was in the shower that night and I heard some strange noises coming from downstairs. First, I thought I had forgotten to turn off the TV or it had somehow turned itself on, so I wanted to check it. It really creeped me out, you know?"

"I can imagine, *baby*," Lupe said understandingly as her mind raced through the events of the night. So far, their stories didn't differ much.

"So, I decided to go and check, but when I went downstairs, I saw four guys dressed in black suits and masks carrying the TV and other items in their hands."

Lupe kept her face neutral even though she could feel her heart racing.

Ellen turned to face her. "They were burglars, Lupe, robbing the house while I was in it!"

Lupe reacted the only way she knew how: "Oh my god, *baby*, I'm so sorry to hear – how terrifying!"

Ellen nodded her head. "I know, you would think someone would first find out if a house is empty before robbing it," Ellen laughed.

Lupe bit her tongue so hard not to answer her. They had in fact thought the house was empty and Ellen's trip was completely unplanned as she had said, Lupe thought, trying to recover from Ellen's comment that hit deeply to her professional pride.

"Anyway, what happened next? Did they do something to you?" she pushed her to continue, wanting to hear the end of the story.

Ellen licked her lip nervously. "Three of the men were carrying the heavy TV, so I knew they wouldn't come after me, but there was a fourth man, who didn't have anything heavy in his hands."

"And?"

"So, I ran back upstairs. I wanted to close myself in one of the rooms and hoped they would leave me alone, after all I didn't even see their faces so I couldn't have described them to the police even if I wanted to."

Lupe closed her eyes: it was what they should have done, especially since they had cut the network in the house as well. She couldn't have called the police anyway and she looked so foreign, by the time she had explained herself to the police they would have been long gone. *Coulda, woulda, shoulda.*

"She ran after me."

Lupe looked at her again, giving her full attention to the story.

"I was panicking and hid in the room I was occupying for the night. Probably not the wisest choice but I was in shock by that time and didn't think straight," Ellen grinned.

"She came after me and started calling to me in English." Ellen looked thoughtful before she continued. "I don't exactly know how she knew I wasn't Spanish given that I hadn't said anything at any point."

Lupe felt like laughing, with her *gringa linda*, she had noticed it millions of miles away.

"I hid behind the mahogany workstation Gisela's dad usually used as a home office when he was around, but since I knew he was travelling, I didn't hesitate to stay in the room." Ellen paused and closed her eyes as the memories of the night flooded back to her mind. "My purpose wasn't to confront her at all. I intended to stay hidden until her friends called her or she got bored of looking for me as the house was enormous."

Lupe nodded and realised it would have been more logical for herself as well, yet nothing had been normal on that night.

"But she didn't leave and when I realised that she wouldn't leave without finding me, I wanted to knock her out with something heavy so I could escape."

Lupe burst into laughter. "You would have run onto the streets in a dressing gown screaming for help? I would have liked to see that!"

Ellen froze. "How do you know what I was wearing?"

Mierda.

"I just assumed *amor mio* as you always wear a dressing gown at home. Now tell me what happened next?" she urged before Ellen could join the clues together, but she was too far down memory lane and let the matter slide.

"She was much stronger than me. I hit her with the closest object I could find, which was an expensive lamp from the workstation."

"Brave girl," Lupe nodded.

Ellen smiled.

"I got one good hit, but she was really fast and tried to grab the lamp from me. During the fight my dressing gown opened, and I was fully naked as I had showered just before," Ellen said and smirked. "You were right, I was wearing my dressing gown."

Lupe smiled back, at least it seemed the memory wasn't too painful for her.

"When she saw one of my exposed breasts she stopped, actually both of us stopped. But then she leaned down and started sucking my nipple," Ellen said and covered her face with her hands, sobbing as the memory returned to her mind.

Lupe felt her heart shattering. "I'm so sorry *baby girl*. I had no idea. It must have been a terrible experience," she said, her heart squeezing into a lump.

All the years she had cherished the memory of that magical night and all along she had been *the worst nightmare* of Ellen's life. She felt as though she was the lowest life on earth, almost signing the walk free from jail card for Ellen to leave her.

She would have done it if she didn't desperately need her to survive, to *live*.

Ellen shook her head. "I'm not crying because it was an awful experience."

Lupe's heart missed a beat. She felt hope arising in her heart. "What do you mean?"

Ellen took a deep breath. "I mean, it was a scary situation and I was scared for my life but what she did felt *good*," she said and hid her gaze on the ground. "In fact, it made me aroused to my core so much I could have screamed. I couldn't have waited for more."

Lupe was speechless.

"She then threw me on the workstation and dropped her trousers and opened my dressing gown fully."

"And did you know before then that she was a woman or was it a surprise to you?" Lupe held her breath, waiting for Ellen to answer.

Ellen turned to face her again. "Yes, I kind of sensed it from the beginning but I got my confirmation when our bodies touched." She winked at her, and it was Lupe's turn to blush. "She had a mixed scent of masculine and feminine and a soft body, if you know what I mean."

"What did she do next?" Lupe asked.

Ellen looked her in the eyes. "She climbed on top of me and made love to me."

Chapter 47

The next morning, Lupe woke up in the bed next to Ellen. Her soft, tiny body was wrapped around her waist and her head rested on the same pillow. If she would just move her head a tiny bit, she would be able to kiss her lips, Lupe thought but restrained herself as she still felt shy with that kind of intimacy.

After Ellen had told her what had happened eight years ago in Spain, they had stayed up until dawn, talking and laughing and sharing stories of their life. Ellen was a very good listener and had gasped several times when she had shared some painful memories of her past. She had placed her hand on top of hers and told her, "Lupe, I'm so sorry for everything you have gone through. God only knows, he gives the toughest battles to his bravest soldiers." She had paused for a second before she had said, "You are not alone anymore. I'm here now, and I will take care of you."

Her attention and kind words had melted her heart and for the first time in her entire life, she had felt safe enough to cry out loud from the bottom of her heart. In the end, her nose had bled, her eyes had been red, and her voice had turned hoarse as she had sobbed in Ellen's embrace where the demons from her past were not able to reach her.

At dawn, when they had both barely been able to keep their eyes open, they had walked hand in hand to the bedroom and gone to sleep.

It was the first night in a long time that Lupe had slept the whole night through without waking up or feeling a need to keep her guards up.

The last time had been in Ellen's tiny room in the hospital she realised and tightened her hold around Ellen.

Her hold seemed to disturb Ellen's sleep and she opened her eyes. "Good morning *amore.*"

Hearing her soft voice still husky from sleep made Lupe's heart skip a beat. "Good morning *princesa mia*. How do you feel this morning?"

Ellen rubbed her eyes for a second before a smile crossed her beautiful face. "I feel amazing," she said and leaned to kiss her.

Lupe gave her a quick kiss on the lips. "Oh really? You want me to make it even more amazing?" she asked and winked.

Ellen smiled and for the next couple of hours, silent sighs filled the room with thick air.

*

They stayed in the house for the whole weekend and only went outside to go for dinner.

Lupe chose a small Spanish restaurant near Notting Hill station called Pulpo as she knew Ellen loved seafood.

The whole restaurant had only six tables and was well known for its romantic atmosphere. The prices were relatively cheap considering the location of the restaurant and Lupe thought it was somewhere yet to be discovered by English people.

In general, Spanish food was not in fashion and couldn't compete with French or Italian in England, she wasn't sure why. She watched Ellen carefully deciding what to order from the menu.

She smiled, she already knew what she would order but waited patiently for her to go through the menu before setting it on the corner of the table as a sign she had made up her mind.

"Penny for your thoughts."

"What?" Lupe looked at Ellen in confusion.

Ellen smiled. "Penny for your thoughts – it means what are you thinking about right now?"

"Oh, that," Lupe said and relaxed again. "I was just wondering why you go to all the trouble of going through the whole menu when you know perfectly well what you going to order anyway."

Ellen raised her eyebrows. "Oh, you think?" she said and tapped the front of the closed menu on the table when the waiter arrived to take their order. When he turned to her, Ellen stopped him. "Hold on a second, it seems that my better half will do the ordering for me today," she said and lay back in her chair.

Lupe smiled. "Fair enough," she said and opened the menu.

"For mi *gringa linda*, I would like to have *patatas bravas*, *pimientos de padron* and *pulpo de gallega*. Easy with the ketchup, she prefers the *patatas bravas* sauce," Lupe said and closed the menu. "Oh, and for me, can I have *croquettas* and *conejo al ajillo*."

"That's an excellent choice, Madam," the waiter said and leaned to take the menus from the table. "Any drinks?"

"Just tap water for me with lemon and a small Peroni beer for her," Ellen said and sent the waiter away.

Lupe opened her hands. "Well, what do you think about my order?"

"Quite specific indeed, *partner*," Ellen said and took a small sip of her water.

"How did I do?"

"You did just fine. I hope I'm not becoming too boring for you," Ellen said and smiled.

"Never *mi vida*. Never," Lupe said and touched Ellen's hand. It was cold.

"Are you cold *mi vida*?" she asked and hurried to take off her jersey and put it on top of her shoulders before Ellen had chance to decline.

She curled deep into the jersey and took a long breath and inhaled the familiar scent on the fabric.

It was the most intimate thing Lupe had ever seen and she felt happy tears building in her eyes.

"Thank you *amore*, I'm OK now," Ellen smiled.

The food arrived quickly and they ate in the peaceful environment, listening to the melodies of live music in the restaurant. At the end of the performance, the singer approached Ellen and laid a red rose on the table.

"It's a rare occasion to see such a connection between partners," he said with a heavy French accent and made a heart shape in the air. "*Viva la vie!*"

Ellen smiled as they watched the man head to the next table.

Lupe felt there were so many things she wanted to share with her that a lifetime itself wouldn't be enough. Even just the thought of losing her made her stomach twist and acid build in her mouth. She could never allow it to happen, *never*.

They stayed in the restaurant until the lights were turned off and the staff started collecting the foldable tables and chairs from outside.

"*Amore*, shall we go home?" Ellen asked and wrapped her white cotton scarf around her neck.

Lupe looked at the hand Ellen offered her. "Yes, *mi vida*, let's go home."

*

The next week was full of work but Lupe tried to make sure she was home before five each day to have dinner with Ellen who had reduced her travelling significantly which had made Lupe very happy.

They were just like any other couple trying to maximise their time together. Her steps felt lighter every day and the sun felt warmer and brighter in the mornings. Life felt *normal*, Lupe thought as she slipped her shoes on in the morning to go to work.

Early on, Lupe had decided to present Ellen to her friends and therefore she had scheduled a late Saturday night dinner for all of them in the famous Buddha Bar in Central London she had heard Ellen mentioning a few times.

It had cost her an extra £20 to reserve a table for the night due to late notice, but it was all worth it if Ellen was happy, she thought as they dressed up for the evening. She had invited her closest friends and her brother to join them.

Her brother wasn't doing great with his wife and was feeling low, so a night out in a controlled environment could do the trick, Lupe thought when they arrived at the restaurant.

He had also been one of the greatest supporters of their relationship and he seemed to like hanging around with her and Ellen. In fact, on numerous occasions Lupe had arrived home from work to see her brother sitting comfortably on the sofa watching Ellen cooking in the kitchen. His gaze had been blank, but Lupe had a suspicion that he might have developed a crush on her. She couldn't feel jealous of her little brother but had decided to keep an eye on it, just in case. Anyway, it kept her brother out of trouble which was important for her.

"Madam, no trainers," the security guard said as he stopped her.

"Excuse me?" said Lupe.

"No trainers in the restaurant," the guard repeated.

Lupe looked back nervously at the queue of impatient customers and lowered her voice.

"Could you make an exception this time, mate? I promise we will just eat quickly and disappear."

"Sorry, we have a rule, no trainers in the bar. Period. Madam," the security guard said again and crossed his arms across his chest.

The security guard was bald, black and bulky, clearly from steroids rather than a healthy lifestyle. He had obviously failed to be accepted into the police academy once upon a time, hence why he wanted to exercise his absolute power on the door of a famous restaurant. Too bad she had Ellen with her otherwise she would have just lost it completely.

"I'm sorry. Can't you make an exception just this once?" she snarled between her teeth while trying to smile charmingly.

"Absolutely not, rules are rules. Now get out of the queue if you have nothing else to say," the security guard said and urged her to leave the queue.

Lupe was mortified. Her feet didn't seem to want to move as she tried to think her way out of this without losing her dignity completely. If only she had met him in a dark alley, she would have shown him the law of the streets and what happens to guys who try to act street smart without ever having been on the street. His bulky steroid-filled body wouldn't stand a chance with the rats like herself who had once lived on the streets, she thought.

"Excuse me, sir. I hate to interrupt but we are late, and I promised Mrs Ling I would stop by for a quick bite whilst checking that everything is fine with the shift." Ellen appeared behind Lupe and shook hands with the security guard. He looked bored but his face curled into a polite smile.

"Yo, what's up kitten? I'm sorry but she still can't enter with her trainers on."

Ellen tilted her head coyly, exposing her full swan neck. "That's totally understandable, and I agree with the restaurant policy, it should be followed at all times. However, Mrs Ling asked me to visit the restaurant at the last minute today and we didn't have time to change. I would hate to have to call her in Tokyo to sort this silly thing out," she said and continued. "I told her we wouldn't be appropriately dressed and she assured me it would be fine. She even promised we could use her table in the far right corner."

"Who the hell is this Mrs Ling you keep referring to?" the security guard snapped.

Ellen glanced at him knowingly and let an awkward silence fall between them.

The security guard tried to play it cool but the changing of his weight between his legs and the hand caressing his forehead told a different story. He seemed to be increasingly nervous and didn't know what to say.

Ellen placed her hand dramatically on her heart. "You are kidding me, right?" she said. She held a dramatic pause but not long enough to allow the security guard to reply. "Mrs Ling is the owner of this place, and not very well known for her patience for that matter, that's why the employee turnover is so high here because she doesn't approve of idiots who treat her friends rudely," Ellen said and closed her eyes as if trying to calm herself down before pointing her finger at him. "Now, she has kindly arranged a table for us at the last minute in return for my favour to her, so can you please show us the table and get this queue moving? Or do you also want to be responsible for declining sales for this evening?"

When the security guard didn't make any effort to let them pass, Ellen grabbed her phone from her bag. "For goodness sake, I will give her a call now so she can tell you herself."

Lupe watched her, waiting for whoever she was calling to answer. Someone picked up on the third ring and she started talking rapidly in a foreign language – it sounded like she was wishing someone into the lowest hell possible.

Lupe examined the face of the security guard, which remained unchanged but he was actively observing the situation as if weighing which solution would bring him least harm: letting one girl in with trainers or not letting one of the owner's acquaintances in and potentially risking his whole employment for bad customer service.

Soon, Ellen was finished with the phone call and handed the phone to him. "Now she wants to talk you, I bet you can guess what it is about," she said and smiled sweetly.

The security guard hesitated for a second before he made his choice and opened the door for them. "That's not necessary. Get in," he said and nodded towards the entrance.

"Thank you ever so much," Ellen smiled and said something on the phone before entering with Lupe.

Lupe held her breath until they were out of ear shot. "What the hell was that? Who did you call?" she asked.

Ellen shrugged her shoulders. "Chop chop," she said and walked into the bar, before stopping in front of a mirror to touch up her lipstick.

Lupe followed and looked at her in the mirror, letting other people pass them to get to the toilet.

"What the hell is chop chop? I heard someone talking on the other end of the phone," she insisted.

"Oh yes, that's right. I called the Chinese restaurant downstairs in our building and tried to order my favourite seafood dish but it seemed they were either out of fish or simply didn't understand the Chinese I learnt in University."

Lupe stood still. "What?"

Ellen looked at her and smiled. "Yes, although I hope they didn't recognise my voice, otherwise we might have some very questionable dishes left on our doorstep tonight!"

"So you don't know the owner?"

Ellen burst into laughter. "God no, I just know her name is Mrs Ling because I read it in *Metro* magazine on my way to work the other day. They are a mean elderly couple who just opened their third restaurant in their home country of Japan."

Lupe raised her eyebrows. "So it was a bluff?"

"Of course it was *amore*, I didn't want to waste time going home to change your shoes, especially since no one will even see them under the table," Ellen said and brushed her cheek lightly. "Shall we? Your friends are probably waiting for us," she said and prompted Lupe to enter the heavy mahogany double doors to the restaurant area.

The restaurant was an interesting combination of Asian fusion including Korean and Japanese food. The drink list didn't only include the most typical international cocktails but also offered a wide range of healthier cocktails containing vegetable options that made Lupe think of a salad. The interior was a replica of a temple with a mixture of Buddhism and Egyptian gold. All the tables were medium size and there was not a single chair in the restaurant as the guests were expected to sit on the comfortable pillows in Japanese style. The music was quiet and reminded Lupe of the book *One Thousand and One Nights*.

Ellen would look great in a belly dancing outfit, she thought briefly and made a mental note to order one for her from Amazon.

They sat down and before she knew it all her friends had arrived, along with her brother. The night was a success and Lupe was incredibly proud of how Ellen behaved in front of her friends, treating her as if she were the finest gold in the world.

She was slow answering in Spanish but didn't for a second assume her friends would speak English to her. Even though some of them had been in UK for the past 20 years. They had managed to survive in the country without speaking English by liaising only with people within the Latin community. Any official matters they paid someone else to do for them. It was a good business in some parts of the city, and Lupe knew people who earned £50 for translating a simple generic letter or making a phone call on behalf of someone in English. Something she had done for free for her closest friends every now and then.

She tried to help Ellen every now and then when she noticed she was struggling for a word. Ellen looked at her gratefully before continuing her story.

They were checking out the dessert menu when a dark figure approached and patted Ellen's shoulder.

"Elena?" he asked.

At first, Lupe wasn't sure if the man had addressed the question to Ellen but when she saw recognition in Ellen's eyes, she knew it had to be her.

"Omar, how lovely to see you here. How are you? I hope your wife is good."

Lupe observed her. Her voice was different, the tone was icy cold and so fake Lupe was amazed the gentleman didn't catch it.

He touched Ellen's hand and brought it to his lips. "I'm very well my dear, although I have been missing you a lot. My wife is great," he said and exposed a line of pearly white teeth so bright Lupe thought she would need sunglasses to protect her eyes if he didn't close his mouth.

Lupe didn't feel he was a threat to her, however the sight of his expensive black suit and gold custom-made Rolex watch which she could only dream of owning made the dark jealousy raise its ugly head.

Ellen giggled. "Oh, don't flirt with me, I know very well you got married this year and spent a considerable fortune on the wedding as well. Your wife is a lucky lady," she said.

"Well, I did what I had to do for the family, but you know my heart and soul always belong to you Elena," he said and moved his eyes around the table before he continued. "I'm terribly sorry, I didn't want to disturb your dinner with your friends. Can I offer you something now and maybe later we can have a late night drink together?" he asked with a wink.

Lupe saw a dark cloud brushing through Ellen's face before she replied. "Unfortunately, I'm fully booked tonight but maybe some other time."

The gentleman nodded. "OK, I respect your time but make sure you schedule me in as soon as possible. I miss you," he said.

Although Lupe didn't think he had ever missed anything in his entire life.

"Sure, thank you so much Omar and it was good seeing you."

"Always my pleasure," he said and brought her hand to his lips again before signalling the waiter. "Put the bill of this table on my tab and make sure to bring a glass of Dom Perignon to the lovely lady."

"Stingy, eh?" Ellen raised her eyebrow.

Omar laughed. "Never with you, my dear," and leaned closer. "So what do you want then?"

Ellen smiled devilishly. "I want the whole bottle."

He leaned lower to face her and for a second Lupe was sure he was going to kiss her before he shook his head. "Don't forget to call me, Elena," the man said and walked away without waiting for her response.

Ellen turned back to the table.

An uncomfortable silence fell over the table as the waiter hurried to bring tall champagne glasses and a bottle of their finest Dom Perignon.

"Well, if this is not a good way of getting your bills paid for you then I don't know what is!" Lupe said and gave out a goofy smile.

Immediately the atmosphere relaxed, and they continued to order more drinks and desserts for the table.

Lupe tried to observe Ellen's mood, but she kept the fake smile on for the rest of the dinner and Lupe was unable to read her completely.

They finished the dinner eventually and ordered Ubers for everyone. Lupe and Ellen decided to ride home with Marinela, one of her friends who lived in the same direction.

Ellen sat voluntarily in the front seat, which annoyed Lupe as she clearly wanted to put more space between them.

"Stop looking at her like you want to kill her," whispered Marinela.

Lupe shot a look to her side "What?"

"You heard me, stop looking at her like you want to kill her. It was an amazing night and the *cabrón* who came to the table clearly didn't know you two were together. Stop making it a big deal."

Lupe looked at her innocently. "I wasn't making it a big deal, in fact I had already forgotten about it."

Marinela rolled her eyes. "Stop bullshitting me *amiga*, I know you very well. You want to rip out the poor girl's heart and feed it to her, but you need to calm down a little bit, it was not her fault he saw her and came to talk."

"OK, but what about her behaviour and giggles? It was disrespectful to me."

Marinela sighed. "OK, that you can mention to her, but honestly I think she was only playing a role there. Even an idiot can see she truly likes you, otherwise she wouldn't have gone through all this with your crazy friends."

Lupe looked thoughtful. "You might be right *amiga*, but I need to understand fully what the hell is going on here and if this will be a normal occurrence with her."

"Stop it already, everyone has a past, you too *amiga*, a lot of it!" she said and opened her arms. "Hers just happens to wear a £40,000 watch on his bloody wrist."

"Right, this is exactly what I wanted to hear," Lupe said and leaned towards the cold window to cool her racing brain. She felt she was quickly losing control.

"Nonsense *amiga*, she is not with him or with anyone else but you – that means something." Marinela left a strategic pause. "Especially since you are not the easiest person in the world."

Lupe smiled. "Thanks *amiga*, I appreciate your honesty."

"With all the love in the world," she said and hopped out of the Uber, which had parked in front of her house.

She gave Lupe a kiss on both of her cheeks and leaned in through the front window to hug Ellen. "It was nice to meet you Ellen, I hope we meet again," she said.

Ellen patted her hand and smiled to her. "Same here."

*

They drove for another five minutes before the Uber reached its final destination.

Ellen was hesitant to leave the car, Lupe could tell.

They walked together to the lift and rode to the seventh floor in silence. Ellen had closed her eyes for the ride, she was clearly tired, but the discussion they were about to have couldn't wait, Lupe decided, otherwise she wouldn't be able to sleep all night thinking about it.

She felt she had started slipping away from her the moment the strange man had greeted her in the restaurant and she had seen a side of her she didn't particularly like. It made her scared – she was afraid of losing control again.

Nevertheless, she tried to give her the benefit of the doubt.

Ellen was a beautiful and intelligent woman, the biggest dream of any man or woman living on this earth, she thought. It wasn't just her killer looks, but she was an asset and a complementary part of any couple. Lupe felt inferior next to her and it troubled her as she felt she could easily get bored with her and leave her at any time – she didn't actually *need* her. On the contrary, what would happen when she realised Lupe needed *her* to live?

Therefore, she didn't really know how to react and to control the disproportionate boiling rage inside her. She was deadly scared to release the feeling, but if she didn't, she was afraid it would consume her for life.

"Is Ellen even your real name?" she asked once the door was closed behind her. Lupe locked it and slipped the key in her pocket sending a silent thank you prayer for old doors which still needed to be locked inside and out.

Ellen turned around to face her. "Of course it is."

Lupe slowly approached her like a preying tiger. "Funnily enough, the idiot in the bar seemed to think otherwise."

345

Ellen couldn't meet her eyes. "I know."

Lupe waited for her to continue but she stayed quiet. "Now why would that be the case?"

Ellen weighed up her response before opening her mouth. "Because that is the name, I gave him when we met."

Lupe could already see the reason in front of her eyes, yet she had to ask anyway. "Why?"

Ellen laughed ironically. "I'm actually not sure why, to protect my identity I guess. I didn't want him to find me if I didn't want to be found. It always felt safer that way," she said and looked at Lupe. "I guess I don't need to spell it out for you?"

Lupe shook her head. "No that's fine, I seem to understand the picture, but I just don't understand why. A girl like you with education and everything, why would you need it?"

Ellen stayed silent, weighing up the options in her head. "Well, I think I got hooked on the power I had over someone," she said and turned to remove some non-existent dust from the sofa next to her before she continued. "I was never rich but I always liked the treatment and the power of hanging out with these people and how it made me feel. And before you even ask, no, I don't have any sad story to justify my actions; I always had enough money to survive, food on my table and a roof over my head, so that's not part of my excuses," she said. "I was greedy, I wanted to achieve as much as I could and learning from these people, the connections it would offer, seemed to be the easiest and fastest way for it."

Lupe considered what she had heard before asking her next question; she didn't *want* to know the answer but she *needed* to know. "Did you enjoy it? I mean the physical part?"

Ellen looked straight in her eyes. "If you are trying to get a rape out of it, you are on the wrong path my friend, I always offered myself voluntarily. However, it was always work for me, I never enjoyed it the way I would enjoy it with someone I'm attracted to. Does that answer your question?"

"I guess so," Lupe said and shrugged her shoulders.

"Good," Ellen said and let the silence fall between them.

The silence grew thicker and they both seemed to be feeling extremely uncomfortable before Ellen couldn't take it anymore. "Look, I totally understand if this is something you can't live with, so instead of awkwardness and silent treatment, I will quickly pack my things and be out of your hair in no time," she said and turned to walk into the bedroom.

Lupe followed her and watched her fish her small suitcase out from under the bed. "You want to leave me?"

Ellen turned to face her angrily. "No I don't, but I can't live with having to look at the judgement in your eyes every day. Yes, I love you and for that reason I would be willing to let you go. I don't want you to hate me."

Lupe's heart skipped a beat. "What did you say?"

At first, Ellen looked confused. "I said I love you."

"You have never said that before."

Ellen smiled shyly. "I know, I have been thinking about it a lot and wanted to tell you in a very special way," she looked at her shoes which she still had on even though they had arrived home a while ago. "Needless to say, this was not part of the plan."

Lupe walked over to Ellen and took her in her arms. "I love you too."

"Oh yeah? Then let me spend a couple of nights somewhere else and give you some time, OK? I know this was not part of the plan for anyone," she said and turned to place another pair of high-heeled shoes in the suitcase.

Lupe watched her. "No."

An image of the handsome stranger with his golden Rolex waiting downstairs lurched into her mind.

"No?" Ellen asked tentatively.

"Give me your phone," Lupe said and held out her hand.

"My phone?" Ellen asked confused.

"Look, I don't have time for you to repeat everything I say. You are a smart girl, now hand the phone to me, NOW!" she raised her voice.

Ellen jumped slightly and hurried to fish out her mobile phone from her handbag.

With one firm movement, Lupe smashed Ellen's phone on the floor with such strength it sent pieces of transparent screen everywhere.

Ellen screamed and the cat hid under the bed.

"Now *princesa mia*, get changed and go to bed. *Descansa.* I need to deal with something before I join you," she said and headed quickly to the door.

Ellen didn't move from her spot, she felt paralysed by the unforeseen events. Lupe opened the front door and looked over her shoulder.

"Do you need me to help you with that?" she asked and pointed at the pieces of glass on the floor.

Ellen cleared her throat. "No it's OK," she said and walked over to clean up the sharp pieces from the floor.

"Good, be careful with your feet," she said and stepped out of the door. "In the meantime, do not touch the phone."

Ellen heard the key turning in the lock and the door handle going down as Lupe ensured the door was locked.

Ellen waited until she heard the elevator ping before hurrying to the wardrobe, grabbing everything she could and ramming the items into the small suitcase and closing it. She headed quickly to the door and listened silently, ensuring no one was outside the door before trying the door handle. It was locked.

She had seen Lupe lock it but hadn't actually expected to be trapped inside in the flat on the seventh floor.

"Shit," she cried and leaned against the cold door, letting her tears of frustration and fear come.

Lupe returned a couple of hours later and Ellen pretended to be asleep.

She had taken a quick shower to calm her nerves and felt surprisingly tired afterwards.

She had not dared touch the phone, and it would not have made any difference anyway as she could see that it was in millions of pieces and the screen was covered in a purple liquid clearly indicating it had been the last trip for the poor phone.

That night, they didn't make love, they were both exhausted by the events of night and, strangely enough, Ellen didn't try to seduce her like she used to, Lupe thought and turned to look at her back.

Little did she know, it kept her awake all night thinking. Her brain was burning with all the new information she had gained today about Ellen. True, she wasn't as innocent as she had thought at first, which she should have figured out for herself with her background but she had been too obsessed with having to safeguard all the potential external threats coming from all different directions, such as Jack at work or any other guy who would lay eyes on her in the supermarket or pub or wherever they went. However, she would have never thought the threat would come from inside.

She felt ridiculous for not having thought about that possibility before and her brain was burning to find a way of securing her life with Ellen for good, without any external or internal threats at all.

Lupe leaned closer to touch her shoulder lovingly. No, even with this new information she would never even consider letting her go and leaving her. True, today she had shown a small chink in her shiny armour but frankly, it only made her sexier in her eyes. Hell, maybe she even felt more courage to approach her in a less lady-like manner and let her dark desires speak out for themselves for once, Lupe thought and spooned her from behind. In a different world, she would actually have paid for her services and then locked her up in her house, never letting anyone else have a chance with her.

Unluckily for her, those days were long gone. Lupe smiled and closed her eyes again.

*

The next day, for once Lupe woke up before Ellen.

She had already prepared breakfast and poured orange juice and coffee when Ellen arrived in the kitchen.

She was wearing a pale pink lace nightdress and white slippers from the Ann Summers collection. Her blonde hair stood up at the back and her lips were swollen and glossy from the Ted Baker lip treatment she used at night. Lupe wasn't fond of the sticky lip balm on her lips and usually wiped it off before giving her the last goodnight kiss before going to bed. Ellen would laugh and add an additional layer afterwards from the tube she kept under her pillow, which Lupe thought was strange in a funny loving way. It was their night-time routine game and she loved every moment of it.

"Good morning *amor mio*."

Ellen stretched her body. "Good morning *amore*. Did you sleep well?"

"Like a truck in a garage," Lupe smiled.

Ellen laughed. "Or parked outside and waiting for a shout out."

"Oh, I'm sorry *amor*, did I snore a lot?"

Ellen took a sip of freshly squeezed orange juice and shook her head. "Not at all, anyhow I wouldn't know, I always sleep so tight I wouldn't even hear a fire alarm."

Lupe laughed. "Touché *mi amor*," she said and leaned to kiss her on the lips.

Ellen smiled and pulled the chair out. "So, should we talk?"

Lupe changed the weight between her legs; she was desperate to talk about anything else except what had happened last night. Luckily her prayers were answered when Ellen saw a package on the kitchen table.

"What is this?" she asked and pointed at the small carboard box.

"Oh, that's a new phone for you *amor*, I'm really sorry I broke yours last night."

Ellen eyed her suspiciously which made Lupe laugh out loud. "Oh, stop being so dramatic *amor mio*, here look, I already installed it for you and everything, you should be good to go now," she said and handed her the shiny black Samsung phone.

Ellen eyed the phone curiously but didn't take it from her hand.

"Take it *princesa mia*, you need to stay in touch with your family and I need to know where you are as well," she said and urged Ellen to pick up the phone.

She jerked her head up. "Is that so?" she said and raised her eyebrow challengingly.

Lupe took a step closer. "Yes *gringa mia*, in fact it is. Any problem with that?" she asked and stared her in the eye.

Ellen held her breath. "And what if I don't want my location to be... found?"

Lupe smiled. "Then I would be obliged to let you know that you don't have a choice," she said and pressed the phone into Ellen's hand.

Chapter 48

"Are you sure you want to do this *hermana*?" Jose-Luis asked but didn't turn his head to face her.

Lupe hesitated for a second and leaned towards the dirty concrete wall behind her. "Yes Jose-Luis, I need to do it."

He turned his head to face his big sister and brushed a strand of hair out of his eyes which were like a mirror reflection of her eyes. "I don't get it, you said everything was going so well and you love her, so why won't you trust her?"

Lupe gave him an angry look that didn't leave much room to argue. She didn't like her judgement to be questioned, especially by her little brother who she had helped so many times, and who hadn't had much success in his love life, no matter how handsome he was.

"I'm sorry, *hermanito*, but I don't see you happily married, trusting your heart and soul into your wife's hands," she said. "I don't think you are in a position to judge me."

"Touché," he said and gave a small ironic smile towards his big sister.

There was nothing really he could have said differently. He was married but not happy. Since he had come to the UK, he had married the first girl who had shown interest in him and who had not worked on the streets close to Paddington station at nights.

It was nothing personal, but he simply couldn't stand women selling their bodies for a quick buck in a land of opportunities. He felt it was an action fuelled by laziness – they couldn't be bothered trying to build something sustainable in their lives in a country that offered so many different paths and opportunities in the form of education or entrepreneurship, and the society silently approved it.

He hadn't always been against the world's oldest profession, but he had seen the sad stories of women who simply didn't have another choice, battling through their life against abuse, drug addiction and physical violence so cruel it had left even the bodies of the strongest ones lifeless on the streets waiting for the grim reaper to collect his share.

It was not only the principle that disgusted him. The thought of touching a body that went through several bodies every night or kissing lips that still had a hint of minty breath from a previous client made his boner die quicker than a bullet would kill. He would prefer to masturbate the rest of his life if no decent female came by; like many other men, he hated other men's leftovers.

Even if he was very selective about who he would sleep with, he had always enjoyed the game of seduction and taking home young girls from clubs and bars on weekend nights out. It had been like a hobby for him.

Obviously, they were always the good-girl type of Latin women, whose fathers had had high discipline and decency at home to make sure their beloved daughters weren't fooling around with anyone before marriage.

Jose-Luis knew he was playing double standards, but it had been the only way he had been able to truly enjoy the physical part of his late weekend night *rendezvous* without the worry of catching a deadly disease. He had been content and enjoyed his single life with his young conquests, but still felt there was much more to discover. Although his good-girl young women ticked the health criteria, his filthy mind craved something more.

They both saw Ellen coming out of the entrance of the hospital, waving goodbye to the girl behind the reception desk.

They dug down behind the 770L waste containers and reversed deeper behind the grey concrete wall.

Ellen looked left, right, left, had a quick look at her watch and crossed the busy street.

Lupe knew she would look left first instead of right. It didn't matter how many times she had told her to look right first, due to the left-hand side traffic in the UK, she seemed never to get it right. The thought raised a smile on her face as she watched her disappearing around the corner.

She didn't have to run after her to ask where she was going. She had already set a GPS tracker on her new phone to check her whereabouts whenever she needed to have reassurance she was telling her the truth.

It wasn't entirely true what Jose-Luis had said about her not trusting her. She *did* trust her. She just wanted to seek reassurance every now and then should she need. There was nothing bad about that, she thought.

Lupe lifted her gaze abruptly from the street just in time to see poorly hidden desire on her brother's face.

Jose-Luis quickly turned his face away and swallowed.

"You like her, don't you?" Lupe sighed and examined his face.

Jose-Luis stayed silent for a second weighing his answer before he cleared his throat. "You would be a fool not to, she is stunning," he said.

Lupe eyed her brother thoughtfully. She couldn't disagree with the obvious. "Jose-Luis, I don't want you to be there tonight," she said using his first name indicating she was serous this time. "Can I trust you on this?" she asked, raising her voice when he didn't reply. "Jose-Luis?"

"Yeah, I won't be there tonight." he mumbled. "I will call later to check that everything went as planned though," he said and looked down at his shoes. "At least to make sure she is brought to hospital."

Lupe saw the concern filling his face and almost felt sorry for her baby brother who, despite being just over 30 with his full life ahead of him, was already trapped in a prison he had created for himself. He could have waited like she had done, instead of binding himself to a marriage he no longer wanted to be part of.

Unfortunately, all of them had made their own decisions in life and finding her *gringa linda* again had been her salvation; she was not willing to risk it for anything.

"Jose-Luis, it's my job to look after her, not yours. You need to go back home and look after your family."

He grinned, exposing his white teeth. "I know *hermana*, I know."

*

Jose-Luis had met his wife for the first time while walking home from Sunday church.

He had worked as a postman at the time and had been in charge of delivering free marketing leaflets in a western London borough with his red, two-wheeled trolley and smart uniform consisting of blue shorts, red t-shirt and a blue cap with the Royal Mail logo on the front. He had nearly been turned down for the job, mainly because he had spoken no English whatsoever and had not had any education after secondary school, but due to his eagerness and the shortage of staff, they had offered him the job anyway.

He had always been bright and received decent grades in school, but his mother had never given him the recognition and instead, directed all her efforts towards his younger brother, who was the baby prince in the family. Before he had been born, Jose-Luis had held the post of baby brother in the family and had received the unlimited affection of his mother, but as the years passed and his brother was born, her affection had died slowly.

In his last school year, before he had dropped out, the teacher had discovered he was dyslexic and stammered slightly when he was nervous, which had made him even more shy about engaging with people on an academic level, and slowly but steadily he had found his new corners in Madrid, which had led him to get in trouble with the authorities. He had been angry at the world in general.

His breakthrough wasn't until his big sister had forced him to flee Spain and sent him to England to live with their distant relatives. This had turned out to be the best choice for him and for that he held a great gratitude towards his big sister. When he had arrived at the age of sixteen, the damage had already been done and he had barely been able to open his mouth publicly, observing his new surroundings curiously.

It had opened up another world to him. A world where he couldn't prove himself with fists and muscle anymore and rather had to use his secret chest of words and brain to fight his corners. He had quickly discovered that if he wanted to succeed in the country, he needed to pick up the language as quickly as possible, which he had done, slowly but steadily.

He had worked first as a cleaner, then when the small cleaning company had gone down, he had moved on to work in a small bakery shop close to the Chiswick area. Despite the daily alarm at four o'clock and the dark, cold English mornings, he had truly enjoyed his job in the bakery as the owner had been a very nice French lady who had adored him. The lady had spoken English but only to her customers and for anyone working with her, she communicated in French, which had forced Jose-Luis to pick up French as an additional language and he had been fluent ever since.

*

It hadn't taken much for him to notice her walking on the street.

She had worn a long white t-shirt dress and black leggings with black kitten-heel pumps with golden details. Her face had been free from make-up and her long black hair had been loose, pinned at the sides with pearl clips.

She hadn't noticed him as she had been busy talking to her mother at the moment they had passed him, so he had had all the time in the world to examine her.

They had been loud and Jose-Luis had been able to distinguish a hint of the familiar Colombian accent even though by the sound of it, he was convinced she had probably been born and raised in the UK based on the way she included English words with a perfect British accent in the middle of the Spanish conversation.

He had been intrigued and interested, for the first time not so much for weekend fun but he felt he had actually found a girl to marry and a mother for his children.

Since the first day he had seen her walking down the street, he had made sure to be in the same spot every single Sunday to deliver the leaflets. Some weekends, when there had been no need for an extra pair of hands at work, he had found himself wandering around the streets looking for her.

Close to the end of summer, when the leaves on the trees had started to take yellowish shades, he had seen her approach him. "Hello there," she had said in perfect English.

For a second he thought he had been mistaken in thinking she was Colombian, but he had quickly recovered and said with his broken English, "Hello Miss. How are you?"

She had looked at him for a second and then changed to fluent Spanish. "*Disculpame*, I wasn't sure if you were Spanish or not, I'm sorry," she had said and tilted her head flirtatiously. "I'm good, just about to go home for a late brunch. How are you?"

Jose-Luis hadn't been able to say or do anything but look at her beautiful face. He had been mesmerised.

They had stood there staring at each other for a while before her mother had wobbled over to greet them. "Maribel, what are you still doing here?" she had asked her.

The girl, now identified as Maribel, had turned to face her mother. "I'm sorry *mamá*, I didn't want to worry you. You see this boy here. He is new in the country and from Spain," she had pointed at him and tentatively searched his face to correct her if she had been mistaken.

She hadn't been, so Jose-Luis had just nodded his head in agreement.

"Marvellous," her mother had said and clapped her hands together. "Then you must come with us for a late brunch, I make a mean *arepas* for breakfast, no one is able to resist," she said proudly and looked at them both.

Jose-Luis hadn't been able to believe his luck and had automatically said yes to the friendly invitation. Even Maribel had looked content and given him a reassuring smile.

They had started dating casually but it hadn't taken long until they had noticed they were spending every single waking moment together.

Jose-Luis had quickly learnt that she was a virgin and innocent in so many ways, he couldn't believe his luck. It had taken all his willpower to stay indifferent to her charm and treat her respectfully under the watchful eyes of her parents.

She wasn't the type of girl he could have pulled by the hair and made her swallow his cock down her throat, not to say he wouldn't have enjoyed it, he thought.

After a couple of months of playing cat and mouse, he had noticed himself changing his route home to see engagement and wedding rings.

What could be so bad in marrying the girl of his dreams, he had thought. She was a decent girl with a good reputation and family, and he would be honoured if her parents would allow him to be part of their family, a family he never had. The thought had made him proud and with the newly gained courage he had marched into a jewellery shop and bought the biggest engagement ring he had been able to afford with his earnings.

That night he had decorated his room in the house he had shared with three other young men with rose petals and candles, prepared sangria with tapas and waited for her to arrive as planned.

It was already dark when she had entered the tiny room and she jumped when she heard him closing the door behind her and lighting every single candle in the room. She had crossed her fingers as if praying and waited patiently as the candlelight had lit up the room only to discover she was standing on red rose petals and he was on one knee in front of her. He had looked deep into her eyes, fished the newly bought ring from his pocket with shaky hands and asked her to marry him. She had been shocked at first, as any decent good girl would have been, but she had recovered in seconds and said yes to him.

Hearing her response had made him feel so high he had wanted to do something extreme for her, so after placing the too-big ring on her left ring finger, he had fished the army knife he carried with him everywhere from his belt and scarred her name in big block letters across his right arm. He hadn't bled much as the knife had merely cut the surface of the skin, however it had made her gasp and run downstairs to the kitchen to get the first aid kit.

He had smiled as he had watched her go as the feeling of having someone taking care of him was new to him and he didn't exactly know how to react to it.

It would have been perfect if he hadn't get too excited on the night of his proposal, but they had both been head-over-heels in love and had ended up losing control and making love all night.

It had been the first time for her, so he had been extra gentle for her sake even though it had taken all his efforts not to lose control and manhandle her properly. It had got better after the first time and he had taught her different ways to love a man. She had been eager to learn but had set clear boundaries and limits she would not cross, stating that some of his wishes were disrespectful to God and that she wanted to be treated like a lady in bed at all times.

He had been devastated at first, but quickly recovered. After all, she had been a good girl and would be the perfect mother for his children. Whatever more he wanted in bed, he could find a way to get it outside of the home, never disrespecting his wife-to-be of course, he had thought.

Unfortunately, or luckily, nature had taken its own course after their first and only night of passion and had blessed them both with a baby boy. First, he had been excited at the news, knowing he would soon have a family of his own to take care of, a family he had never had before. However, she had been shocked and terrified as if the possible consequences of the night hadn't even crossed her mind. The day they had found out, she had run off to her parents' house and confessed everything. They had been furious, claiming that he had seduced her to sin on purpose. It hadn't been enough that he had showed them the ring and tried to explain they were in love and wanted it this way; it had only made the situation worse, resulting in him wrestling on the floor with her father who had been visiting from Colombia. He had taken the punches gracefully, as he knew he would have been able to beat the life out of the old man, but for her sake he hadn't done it. In the aftermath, her parents had made sure they had got married immediately.

No friends, no family, not even a wedding cake. They had rented a black suit for him and an expensive white dress for her only for the pictures. The wedding day had been awful, and she had blamed him the entire time for seducing her to sin, making her betray her parents' trust and making her look fat in her own wedding dress.

First, she had even refused to wear white, but her mother had convinced her, as she would have not tolerated seeing her only daughter's wedding pictures without a white dress.

She had reluctantly agreed with her.

Jose-Luis had been helpless to know what to do and sought guidance from his sisters. They had been supportive and made him feel good about himself again, and slowly, after they had moved in together in her parents' house and the baby had been born the situation had resolved itself.

It had seemed as if all the anger and resentment had been forgotten; her parents had adored their first granddaughter and she had been a terrific mother from the start. Her father had eventually returned to Colombia once the baby had been born, leaving behind his wife ensuring she would be on top of the childcare whenever it was needed.

Despite the difficult start, Jose-Luis had been over the moon at having found the right girl to take care of his child, but eventually she had changed and become bitter and spoiled, only looking for approval from her parents, completely disregarding that she was a wife and a mother as well. She forgot all her wifely duties and spent most of her days on her studies leaving their only child to be raised by her grandmother, which she had done with pleasure. But it had also meant that Jose-Luis was forgotten in the picture and his responsibility as a father had been stripped to its very core and now they only lived together for their child's sake.

Jose-Luis had been crushed but had refused to move out as he couldn't bear the thought of breaking the illusion of family they had created for their only son. After all, he meant the world to him.

*

"Jose Luis, just remember, I want to see it on her left cheek. Don't disappoint me."

Jose-Luis rolled his eyes. "Jeez, *hermana,* you are insane."

She stared at him with empty eyes. "Yes *hermano,* trust me when I say I'm willing to do anything for this one; *anything.*"

Jose-Luis stayed silent for a second before lifting his head and looked at the point where the woman his sister was obsessed with had disappeared.

He nodded his head silently and started emptying his backpack of the items he might need in the next couple of hours. "I still don't understand what makes her so different. After all, she is a *gringa,* cold and empty inside like all Europeans."

Lupe stayed quiet for a moment. "Honestly, I don't know. Maybe it's just the way I feel when she looks at me. She makes me feel things I have never felt before. She makes me feel proud of *myself*."

Jose-Luis eyed the items in his hand trying to hide his smile. "And are you?"

Lupe landed her right hand on his side. "*Callate estúpido!*"

He ducked and laughed, raising his hands up as a sign of surrender. "OK, don't shoot me *hermana*, just one question."

"*Dime.*"

"Why do you want to mark her left cheek?"

Lupe weighed her words as if trying to decide whether to reveal it all to her baby brother. "Because I want to put my mark on her. I want her to remember she belongs to me every time she looks at herself in the mirror," she said and sighed. "Even if I'm gone, I don't want her to forget me. Forget *us*."

He shook his head. "Jeez, OK Romeo. Wouldn't it be easier to ask for matching tattoos or something?"

Lupe shot him a look that made him take one step back. "OK, got it. I'm out of here. See you later, *sis*."

Lupe watched her baby brother lifting the faux-fur collar of his giant jacket and hiding his hands deep in his pockets before striding from the corner they had been hiding in, looking both ways before sliding within the crowd of afternoon people on the street.

It had been chilly but sunny all day, but now it seemed dark clouds had started gathering in the sky. It seemed they were expecting stormy weather for tonight, which would be perfect: no clear vision, no public, *no witnesses*.

Chapter 49

Ellen had finished the day early. She had been asked to stay late but she had decided to say no for a change. The familiar excitement made butterflies dance in her stomach every time she made her way to her new home, to her new life and lover.

They had lived together for six months now, since the unfortunate incident with the rental property, which she had lost due to miscommunication. She had been devastated and had told herself the arrangement with Lupe was only temporary, but the first kiss at the flat had made her fall down the rabbit hole so fast she didn't know what had hit her.

She should have known it after the night in her tiny room in the hospital, but it felt like life had taken its own course and she was merely watching the events go by, helplessly unable to change any of it, and after the first night, she didn't even know if she wanted to.

When she was with her, it felt like the puzzle was complete without any missing pieces. She didn't know if it was only the consuming physical chemistry that had taken over her mind or the hurt animal inside her looking for someone to save her which made her forget everything and crawl back to her over and over again, unable to leave her. After all, she *wanted* to save her. She *understood* the hurt animal in her, and felt familiarity with her. Even though their backgrounds had been different, they shared so many elements of it, in their own way. Whereas, Lupe had suffered a lack of family and affection in a raw and more obvious way, Ellen had battled against the demons in her head craving for affection and appreciation from her cold family, desperately trying to fit in a world where suppressing any feelings was a norm and until she had felt she had not been left any other option but to run and create a life of her own.

She had never thought her questions would be answered in the form of the curly haired devil in female form that had crossed her path and Ellen was amazed they had even made it so far.

Traditionally, her relationships tended to die quickly after the honeymoon phase was over. They simply didn't speak the same love language or maybe it was her who didn't speak their language at all. They would become distant as Ellen would initiate the mental process of a break-up and slowly part ways with her partner.

They never saw it coming, which surprised Ellen every time. They would scream, beg, threaten, but in the end, it would never make a difference for her; when her feelings died, they were dead and buried once and for all. She couldn't take the blame for it, after trying so hard to hint, guide and convince; they would just never learn until it was too late.

This time, however, with Lupe, it all felt so different. She couldn't explain exactly why – the relationship had literally just happened as the flames around her had lit the sleeping blue heart of a fire Ellen had, and together they formed an ever-resisting fire that consumed and burnt down everything that dared to cross its way. *Including themselves.*

It was everything Ellen had ever hoped for in a romantic relationship: love, tenderness and consuming passion she had never felt before that drove them both towards insanity and burnt their souls so much it made them say and do things they later regretted.

Ellen smiled. Lupe was more erratic and incapable of apologising and every time Ellen was convinced she should flee like lions were after her, Lupe would force her back into the flames where she didn't stand a chance of escaping. The raging fire needed its blue heart, without it, it simply didn't survive, and vice versa, the blue heart of fire needed its raging fire flames around it to flourish in its full glory.

But none of it really mattered when they were together. The connection was undeniable, stronger than anything she had ever felt before, as if they had known each other from somewhere before, in a different life.

It was true their relationship was only at the beginning and she was her first girlfriend, but it felt already so natural and pure that Ellen had to pinch herself every now and then to make sure she wasn't dreaming. Despite all of it, she felt safe around her and a peace she hadn't felt in over eight years.

*

Deeply buried in her thoughts, she smiled at the receptionist on her way out, giving a quick look both ways before crossing the street.

Her legs ached from the heels she had worn all day, but she had not bothered to change to practical ballerinas before leaving. Heels made her feel sexy, desirable and in control. She had adopted the habit of wearing heels everywhere she went from her Russian friend in St Petersburg where she had studied for a short period of time. Still now she could recall the horror on her friend's face when she had put on brand-new Nike sneakers for a shopping trip. Her friend had given her the look of a lifetime and had lectured her about sloppiness and the inability of finding a husband without a clear sense of dress codes, which included being sexy and desirable at all times.

"Ellen, you have charm and looks any girl would gladly pay for, but you need to remember good looks and charm won't last forever, therefore you need to *enhance* and *embrace* the beauty you have been given and use it," she had said and pointed towards a set of black kitten heels and a mermaid hem skirt in her wardrobe. "Wear these sweetheart. Luckily we have such different taste in men, there won't be any competition," she had said and eyed her sneakers. "Not that there would be any anyway."

Ellen had laughed but changed her shoes to the kitten heels she had offered her. Interestingly enough, her friend had not been mistaken, as Ellen had felt an instant change in the air and she had suddenly become irresistible to any human being around her. She had always had beautiful, feminine legs that were made for wearing dresses and heels, which with some practise she could do but she wasn't prepared to walk outside and find the appreciative looks not only from men that made her feel uneasy but on her last day at the university she had found herself attracted to a handsome South African girl who had been shooting looks at her since the start of the semester.

Ellen had found the girl's boyfriend-style ripped jeans, white converse shoes and plain white t-shirt casually covered with an open dress shirt irresistible. She had been smitten and had giggled when she had touched her hair in an empty corridor after classes and inhaled the male musky scent mixed with a female scent, which had made butterflies grow in her stomach. The girl had taken her flirting as a sign of interest, and Ellen still didn't know if she had been too naïve or if she actually had meant it that way, when she had pulled her inside a cleaners' closet and placed a wet kiss on her lips.

Ellen had been shocked but had allowed herself to enjoy the kiss for a second before she had fled from the cleaners' cupboard, leaving the girl behind her without looking back.

The next day, the term had ended and she hadn't seen the girl ever again.

Knowing she had played with fire, as same-sex relationships were strictly forbidden in Russia and still considered a felony, she hadn't told anyone about the incident.

Smiling at the innocent memory, Ellen chose her normal route towards Earl's Court station to catch the bus home. It was a cold but humid day and the wind was blowing crossways so hard she had to dig into her black blazer and scarf she had luckily brought with her.

She had just crossed the main road when she saw the bus arriving at the bus stop and hurried towards it. Breathing heavily after the short run, she stepped in and found the last empty seat at the back of the double decker bus.

She looked outside as the bus started its long journey to the western borough of London when, all of a sudden, the bus driver hit the emergency brake so hard Ellen crashed into the seat in front of her.

She tried to look at the front of the bus to identify the cause of the sudden interruption of the journey.

A tall man, in his around 30s, entered the bus. He didn't smile and Ellen could hardly see his face because of the fake fur lining around the hood of the jacket he was wearing. He quickly entered the bus, looking for a seat and totally ignoring the noisy complaints from the other passengers. Unfortunately, the rush hour in London provided no mercy to tired travellers, and there were no empty seats available, so he gracefully stood in the centre aisle and turned his back towards the back-seat passengers.

Ellen couldn't stop looking at him. He didn't stand out from the other passengers in any particular way in his black winter jacket and ripped jeans, but there was something oddly familiar about him that wouldn't leave Ellen alone. The oversized clothes didn't do any justice to his boyish figure and as a result the jeans were hanging from his hips, barely staying up, and when he stretched his back, the jersey under his jacket rose up, revealing a tight stomach and navel hair following under the Calvin Klein boxers he wore under his jeans. The hood and green scarf around his face made it impossible to see his face, but the small tattoos of Roman numerals on each finger caught her attention before he slipped his hands into his pockets again. There was a black gym bag next to him, which seemed to hold nearly nothing as it kept moving around with the bus like it was filled with air.

As if feeling her stare, the man quickly turned around to face the passengers at the back and caught her staring.

Their eyes locked for a moment.

Blushing, Ellen turned quickly away to look out of the window but out of the corner of her eye she could see he hadn't been affected by her stare at all judging by his lazy way of moving his eyes from one passenger to another before fishing his phone out of his pocket and turning his back to her again. Ellen rolled her eyes and fished her own phone out of her bag and started reading the news, but for some reason, the uncomfortable feeling didn't leave her and she could feel a pair of eyes following her every move.

*

"Next stop, West End."

Ellen gasped and opened her eyes. She had been exhausted lately from the increased workload and the intensity of her newly found relationship – she could fall asleep anywhere with proper heating and an available seat. Sometimes even a seat wasn't needed and she would just lean on a wall or a pole in the bus and let herself drift off to sleep.

Quickly dropping her phone into her handbag and tightening the scarf around her neck, she stood up and made her way towards the open doors. The bus was almost empty by now and it had turned off its engine as this was the final stop before the driver either called it a day or started the journey back again. This time, the driver had collected his bag and was already waiting outside the bus to make sure all the passengers had left. Ellen quickly made her way to the doors, giving a final look at her seat to make sure she hadn't left anything behind.

The sky had turned dark blue as the sun had set and the buildings around the area created dark shadows on the dirty concrete walls. The wind screeched loudly in the corners as she hurried in between the concrete labyrinth. She had never been afraid of the dark, but it made her feel increasingly alert of her surroundings as she sped up to reach home quickly.

One thing in London Ellen had never really understood were all the oversized corners and holes left in buildings as if they had been built in a hurry and the construction team had put them together with unmatching pieces of a puzzle. It made the efficiency of the building very low and the utility cost sky high including all seasonal change challenges and pest control issues as it allowed mould to build up in the houses and pest infestations to occupy the dirty holes and additional corners everywhere.

Ellen wrapped her black blazer tighter around her and held her nose while passing the huge recycling hub of rubbish, where bins had been left open allowing pigeons to mess up the whole area. Next would be rats to join the dinner party, she thought as she made her way past the area.

Ellen was just about to pass the green recycling bin hub when she heard a slight whining behind the general waste bins. She stopped for a moment to locate the source of the sound but couldn't see anything. It sounded like a small animal, high-pitched, but she couldn't really tell as the wind screeching in the corners made the small sound vanish in the air.

She took two tentative steps before the whining started again. "Hello? Is someone there?" she shouted and looked around for additional support, but it was too dark to see anything.

Ellen felt indecisive about whether to stay to find out the cause of the voice, but her intuition told her to run as fast as she could.

She didn't run.

"Hello, is someone there? Do you need me to call an ambulance or something" she offered without approaching the bins.

The whining had stopped as she turned to fish her phone from her bag to turn on the torch. It was lousy weather for this this type of adventure and strangely the whole block of streetlights was dark, she thought and frowned.

She directed the torch light in between the general waste bins as an extraordinary silence surrounded her as if the whole world had just frozen. It made the hairs on the back of her neck stand up and she was turning to leave when she heard a clear voice.

"Stay."

Ellen broke into a run.

The adrenaline rushed through her body and made her feel like running a hundred miles per hour as she tried to reach the first streetlights on the main road and hopefully people, but just before reaching the main road corner she was pulled back into the darkness.

The grip was firm and she felt like her wrist was about to fall apart as she tried to struggle away from the unknown. The captor tightened his grip on her wrist and twisted, which made her fall to her knees due to the pain as he pulled her closer and wrapped his hands around her waist as soon as she was at arm's length. Ellen felt the rock-hard body up against her soft figure and she could feel the captor now breathing on her neck and breaking into a sweat as a result of the fight. The smell of sweat and the fight brought stomach acid into her throat as the flashbacks to the similar incident eight years ago returned to her mind but for some reason this time it was different.

She tried to yell but the rough hands around her neck didn't allow a single whisper to escape as he continued to squeeze her air pipe. She felt the air slowly leaving her body and her fingertips starting to tingle making her tongue swell in her mouth.

The loss was inevitable as her body started giving in and she only hoped it would be fast whatever was yet to come. As her legs started feeling too weak to carry her body weight, she felt the captor lifting her up in the air and for a second she hoped she would be able to see Lupe's face for one last time. She turned to face the captor's hooded face and for a second before the unconsciousness swallowed her into its merciful arms, she thought she was looking into Lupe's eyes and smiled.

Chapter 50

The phone rang around eleven at night.

Lupe had stayed awake waiting for the call but for some reason she jumped when she heard the familiar melody of her ringtone.

She glanced at the screen and saw an unknown number. "Hello, *digame?*"

"She is in A&E at St Thomas's Hospital." A familiar voice said before hanging up.

Lupe ended the call and erased it from the phone history before grabbing her leather bomber jacket and heading out of the door. The protesting meow stopped her on her heels at the door, as if asking her to leave the lights on. She smiled and turned them on again, she wouldn't be long anyway.

The ride to the hospital was quick as the traffic usually died down after eight in the evenings, Lupe thought as she veered into the parking lot of the hospital. She parked the motorbike in the dedicated area and headed to the revolving doors signalling A&E in red capital letters.

"I'm looking for Ellen, a blond girl around 5'2 tall, she was brought in some time ago, a possible attack?"

The black nurse with braided hair and a white uniform eyed her below her reading glasses. "And you are?"

Lupe quickly removed her helmet and scarf. "Sorry, I'm her roommate, I was called. I'm her 'in case of emergency' on her phone."

It was a lie and a truth at the same time as she was indeed the 'in case of emergency' person on her phone, but the hospital had not called her. They couldn't even get to her phone and past the security code even if they wanted to, she wondered but luckily, the detail went unnoticed.

"Oh, I'm sorry, looks like nobody has recorded it here as always," the nurse said as she went through the files on the reception table. "Are you able to give us the contact details of her family so that we can inform them as well?"

For a second, the blood went cold in Lupe's veins and she gasped loudly. "Is she that bad?"

The nurse waved her hand. "Oh, not at all, sorry, I didn't mean to scare you. It's just normal protocol for the hospital to contact the family."

Lupe relaxed and smiled apologetically. "I'm sorry, I don't know them at all."

It wasn't a lie, Lupe suddenly realised. They had never talked about her family, as their relationship had mostly focused on the physical part, which genuinely surprised Lupe and she made a mental note to connect with her mentally as well.

"Right OK, then we just need to reach them some other way, maybe through HR at her workplace?"

Lupe quickly gave her workplace contact details to the nurse before asking impatiently, "When can I see her?"

The nurse worked in slow motion, making Lupe impatiently change the weight between her leg as she watched her typing the notes on the computer screen. Probably due to working double shifts, she thought and sighed, the same story in all London hospitals.

Suddenly the nurse lifted her face from the computer screen as if surprised Lupe was still standing in front of her. "Go through the white doors, turn right at the first cubicle, she is in cubicle seven."

Lupe smiled and slammed her fist on the reception desk. "My lucky number."

The nurse didn't bother with another look. "Like for all of us."

*

Lupe sprinted towards the doors that led to the treatment area. The pungent odour of chlorine greeted her at the entrance. Luckily, at least she knew the area was cleaned properly she thought as she kept looking for cubicle seven. It didn't take her long to see a familiar pair of black stiletto heels peeping out of the last cubicle. She quickly checked the number before pulling the curtains aside.

For a second she felt surprised at the sight in front her. Ellen was asleep, laid on top of the bedding on the white bed. She had a pillow under her head, but she was shivering from the cold air entering the cubicle from the constantly opening entrance doors.

Lupe quickly stole a white blanket from the opposite cubicle and covered her up and pulled a chair to one side of the bed, brushing her hair from her face. As a result of her touch, Ellen winced and pulled her head away, giving a short whimpering sound.

"Shhh, *mi vida soy yo*. It's me. You are OK, don't worry."

Soothed by her voice, her head fell back onto the pillow and she was asleep again. It gave Lupe time to examine her; she still had her shoes on and excluding some holes in her stay-ups, she looked quite well. Her face had probably taken the most damage, Lupe thought as she slightly pulled down the scarf around her neck, revealing black marks around her neck as if someone had been squeezing hard. There was slight hematoma coming up under her left eye and dried blood on her lip leading towards her lower neckline where the clinical staff had placed a white patch.

"Are you a relative?"

Lupe jumped as a young doctor entered the cubicle.

"No, I'm just her roommate. Her 'In case of emergency' person."

The doctor ticked something on the file he held in his hand. "Right, good, vitals are fine, no loss of blood, minor concussion, some bruises, but she should be fine with some painkillers."

Lupe watched the doctor finishing the report. "Now we usually recommend testing for STDs just in case but there is nothing hinting at sexual assault only robbery, so we didn't. Do you want me to authorise it as well?"

The thought of the young doctor opening her legs and looking inside made Lupe recoil on her seat. "No, that's not necessary," she said quickly. "When can I take her home?"

"Alright then, you can take her home as soon as she opens her eyes. Just don't forget to file a crime record at the local police station OK? We have done it as well, but the victim should do it too, just in case," the doctor said and handed the report to her. "Sign here please, it's the discharge paperwork. You can use the information to file the crime record."

Lupe nodded her head and quickly signed the papers and waited for the doctor to leave the cubicle.

"*Amor*, are you awake *mi vida*?" she asked and gently held her hand. It was ice cold. "*Mi vida*, please wake up, let's go home."

Ellen parted her better eye. "Lupe, is it you?"

Lupe smiled. "Yes *mi vida*, it's me. How are you feeling?"

Ellen pushed herself slowly up from the bed. "Confused, I'm not sure what happened. I hopped off at my stop and then…"

The tears rose to her eyes when the horror of the events returned to her mind and she started to sob.

"Shh, *mi vida,* it's over, nothing bad is going to happen to you anymore, I'm here." Ellen grabbed her clothes as if her life depended on them and for some reason Lupe believed her. It made her feel warm inside, more at peace.

"Don't let go, please." Ellen whispered.

"Never, *mi vida*, I wouldn't even dream of it."

They stayed in the embrace for a moment until Lupe pulled out. "Listen *mi vida*, let's get you home now and in your pyjamas, would you like that?" She wiped the tears from her red eye and nodded silently.

"OK then, I will order a taxi for you and I will ride the motorcycle just behind you."

"No, don't leave me!" she cried out and buried her face in her neck again.

"*Mi vida*, I won't let the taxi from my sight, it's just going to be a short trip."

Ellen swallowed her sobs before lifting her gaze to her. "Please don't leave me now, ride with me," she said.

It only took a moment for Lupe to make a decision. "OK, I will ride with you, *mi vida*."

Ellen slowly collected her belongings from the white table that was left in the cubicle while Lupe arranged a taxi to come and pick them up and a local mechanic, who was also a friend, to pick up the motorcycle from the hospital car park. There weren't many things to collect anyway, the handbag she had carried had been stolen including everything in it.

Apparently, they had not bothered to look inside the fabric tote she had carried her work laptop and notes in, she thought and peeked inside to find her wallet untouched.

"Look *cielo*, my wallet is here. How strange is that?" she said and collected the wallet from the tote to show her.

Lupe turned her head from her phone. "*Por dios santo*, that's good news isn't it?" she said and turned her focus back to her phone.

"I guess," Ellen said, preoccupied.

She wasn't exactly sure how the thieves could have missed one of the most valuable items whilst conducting a robbery – the coin purse in her handbag merely contained her three pound meal deals per month. How come they had not checked the bag with the computer and wallet in it, she wondered.

"Ready to go *cariño?*" Lupe asked from behind while massaging her shoulders.

Ellen glanced around the cubicle one more time. "Yes I guess," she said as they turned around and left the hospital behind.

Chapter 51

The night was dark and the sky was almost black without clouds. The cold rain hit hard on the windows creating a rhythmic sound.

The sound of rain was one of the most relaxing things Lupe could think of as it reminded her of the small piece of childhood she had experienced in her grandma's house in Peru. She had felt totally safe and at peace in between those protective walls, waking up to the voice of a rooster and guinea pigs running in their small enclosed area in the backyard.

This time, however, Lupe woke up to desperate screams next to her.

Ellen had woken up to her own scream.

"Another nightmare, *amor mio*?" Lupe asked softly and patted her hair.

Ellen looked at her with wide pupils and Lupe could see the terror reflected in her eyes.

She nodded slightly.

Lupe enclosed her in her arms. "I'm so sorry *amor mio*, it will get easier, don't worry," she said. "It must have been terrifying what happened to you but eventually it will get better, trust me. I will help you, I will always be here for you."

She could soon feel warm tears wetting her white t-shirt front. Ellen was crying silently. "Thank you *mi cielo*, I don't know what I would do without you," she sobbed. "You are my hero and saviour. I would not survive without you," she whispered.

Lupe felt her heart miss a beat; it was just as she had pictured it, but for some reason, the picture didn't look so shiny anymore.

She knew Ellen would need her now more than ever after what had happened. The memory would haunt her for the rest of her life, and she would need a confidant to talk to and to hold her at night when the nightmares came. They would share her path towards recovery, and she would be her rock to lean on. It would bind them together forever. Ellen could never leave her after this, Lupe knew it but for some reason, the realisation only offered her slight comfort.

"*Amor mio*, you are never going to lose me, we are going to get through this," Lupe said and took her face in between her hands to dry her cheeks and plant small kisses on her swollen eyes.

Ellen closed her eyes and let out a satisfied purr. "I just keep thinking, why me? What did I do wrong to deserve it?" she said as new tears reached the surface of her eyes from the painful memory.

"Shhhh, *amor*, don't think about it now. We are together and I will always be by your side and take care of you. I will never leave you." Lupe hugged her tightly.

"I just think of how you must see me now: weak and stupid. I should have known better than to walk the streets alone and certainly not to stop like I did," Ellen said, her voice breaking in the silence.

Lupe looked her in the eye and gently touched her swollen bottom lip and the white clinical patch on her lower neckline; she didn't have to remove it to find out what was under it, she knew already.

The bruise underneath the clinical white patch had been made with a knife and took the shape of lightning. The bruise would leave permanent scarring, but even that could never take Ellen's beauty away; on the contrary, it would suit her, and Lupe would know she had left a mark on her, just like she had planned she thought as the growing guilt lifted its ugly head.

Lupe watched her silently and let her eyes run over her face, trying to memorise every single bit of her and hide it in the farthest corners of her mind.

"Hear me out, *mi vida*, because I'm only going to say this once. I could *never* ever consider you weak. You are perfection to me. No matter what."

"I just feel different, as if damaged and ugly," she said and buried her face in her hands.

As Ellen's sobs got louder as a result of her kind words, Lupe couldn't stop thinking of how sexy she looked at that moment. So fragile and broken, like an angel whose wings had been cut off.

And she would be the one to put the pieces back together.

She would recreate her again for *her.*

Lupe felt her breathing getting faster in excitement at her own thoughts; she could barely keep her hands off her.

For a brief second, a picture of her brother touching Ellen appeared in her mind, but she quickly shook the uncomfortable feeling off; her brother knew better than that and besides, he had been nowhere near her that night, Lupe thought and offered a tissue to Ellen. She took it gratefully and folded it in her hands. "Anyway, thank you *mi cielo* for being there for me. I knew you would," Ellen said as the tears dried up and she prepared to stand up from the bed, holding her left side.

Lupe could see she was in pain and gently lifted her white top. "*Dios mio, mi vida*, this looks painful," she said and lightly caressed the black bruise nearly the size of a football.

Ellen exhaled and grinned. "I know. At least I don't remember getting it."

"Still *mi vida*," Lupe said and stared at the black bruise, horrified.

Even though she knew Ellen bruised easily, she couldn't help the lump in her throat growing as she watched her limping towards the kitchen.

"*Amor*, where do you think you are going?"

Ellen turned in surprise. "I just wanted to get a glass of water," she said quietly.

"Let me get it for you," Lupe said and pushed the bed covers from her and swung her feet to the floor.

"OK if you want," Ellen said and limped back to the bed while Lupe assisted her back onto her back and tucked her under the covers. "There you go *mi vida*, are you sure you don't want something else, orange juice maybe?"

Ellen smiled. "Water is just fine."

"Water coming right up," Lupe said and bowed to her.

A quiet giggle left Ellen's lips and it was like music to her ears as she strode to the kitchen.

There was so much more she wanted to ask Ellen but she didn't know where to start. She knew Ellen was shy with her feelings and this was a very personal matter, but she was dying to know what had happened on the night. She hadn't been too specific and had only given guidelines about *what* she wanted to achieve; she had never mentioned *how it* should be achieved, as the whole conversation had made her stomach twist with guilt and disgust towards herself, but she had seen no other choice, she thought and glared towards the bedroom where Ellen lay with her eyes closed.

The funny thing was, Ellen could conduct endless conversations about politics, the weather and the housing market in London with total strangers, but she wasn't able to put her own feelings into words properly. It had taken time for Lupe, and almost driven her to madness, to get her to open up to her, which she had done little by little. She only hoped the events of the night hadn't done any permanent damage to their relationship, she thought as she strode back to the bedroom. "Your glass of water, miss," she said and bowed her head again.

Ellen opened her eyes slightly and took the glass from her hand and drank loudly. "Thank you *mi cielo*, I really needed it," she said and handed the empty glass to Lupe.

"Anytime *mi vida*, now move over," Lupe said and carefully slipped behind her in the bed and lifted Ellen's upper torso in between her legs, her back against her chest. "I have another idea about what you might need," she said, caressing her arms and massaging her tense shoulders before whispering in her ear, "I want to demonstrate to you that nothing that happens to your body can change my feelings for you. You are the sexiest and most beautiful woman I have had the pleasure to meet in my life," she said and slowly let her fingers touch her collarbone.

She could feel Ellen's body tense at first but then relax and melt under her touch.

She felt high and exhaled deeply, letting her hands wander slowly down to Ellen's hips. She knew she was playing with her luck and was scared to death that she would scare her away when the realisation hit her: she didn't know if she could ever bear rejection from her. It would destroy her.

When her hands touched Ellen's thighs and gently persuaded them to open, she felt her freeze and gasp. "I don't know if I can, *mi cielo*. I'm so sorry. I'm afraid I won't enjoy it and I feel disgusted," Ellen said and looked down, ashamed, closing her legs tight together. "I don't want to offend you."

Lupe lifted her face up, wanting to say something, but Ellen stopped her. "And just the thought of a man touching me ever again makes me want to throw up. Just the smell of men's perfume makes me sick," she blurted.

At that moment, Ellen didn't realise she had just given her world and life as she knew it to Lupe. She had no clue that those were the magic words Lupe had waited to hear that finally quietened the demons in her mind and made them fall into an endless sleep, just as she had planned.

Lupe felt her body react to her words as the familiar heat started building in her stomach, only this time there was something different. There was no sadness or panic in her head, she wasn't gasping for air as if she were drowning at the thought of losing her. She had never felt someone belonging to her as fully as she felt with Ellen and it was raw, dark and seductive, she thought as she closed her arms tightly around the blonde angel between her legs who had crossed her path nearly a decade ago. Her heart finally felt complete.

"Luckily, I'm not a man," she smiled and gently bit her ear lobe. "I will be gentle *mi vida*, I promise, just let me love you," Lupe said and let her fingers massage their path down to her navel.

Ellen sighed as the seductive pleasure surrounded her and she let her head fall back onto Lupe's shoulder. The stubborn brown curl from her forehead fell on Ellen's face, caressing her cheekbone like a feather.

Encouraged by her silent approval, Lupe opened her legs and let her fingers run up and down her milky thighs.

For a second, her hands stopped as she could see the shadow of a dark bruise on Ellen's inner thigh and the uncomfortable feeling returned to her mind again, but when Ellen lifted her hands and dug them into her hair, massaging her scalp with her fingernails, she let it slide but made a mental note to ask her in the morning. She ran her fingers up towards her lacy string underwear and massaged her entrance, gently pressing her index finger between her swollen folds through the fabric.

"Oh my God," escaped from Ellen's lips as her body writhed under her touch.

"You see, *mi princesa*, it's not that bad when I touch you, is it?" Lupe smiled behind her. "Do you want me to stop?"

"No, please don't stop," Ellen sighed and for a moment her words took Lupe back eight years ago to the large bedroom in Madrid where they had met for the first time, only this time, it was different as she was already hers, she thought as she increased the pressure and speed of her finger. The fabric under her fingers was moist and the familiar scent of desire Ellen's body produced when she was turned on filled the air. It was like a mixture of vanilla and hot rain that would leave the streets to steam afterwards, tempting and irresistible.

As the speed of her fingers increased, she could feel Ellen's body tense and hear her breathing get faster and just before her sex clenched, she let out a loud scream, calling Lupe's name in the air as her body jolted up and a lightning bolt ripped the dark sky in half and the sound of thunder and pouring rain hit the window pane.

Lupe smiled in the darkness as she pulled her body violently down against her chest and continued massaging her clit through the lacy fabric, causing friction between her tender flesh and the rough fabric until she could feel her body tense again as the second orgasm ripped inside her.

As the waves of the orgasm slowly faded, Lupe lifted her relaxed body in her arms like a child and caressed her breasts. They were wet. "You are dripping *mi vida*," she said and smirked.

Ellen looked lazily down at her chest. "Oh, I didn't realise – that's never happened before," she said and closed her eyes as she drifted into a peaceful sleep.

Lupe placed a tender kiss on her forehead. She didn't feel tired as the burning desire still ached in her body like a flame. She lifted Ellen's body next to her. Her figure glowed blue in the darkness. The heart of the flame is always blue, Lupe thought as she pushed the bed covers off Ellen's body and slid her own underwear down. She couldn't remember how many times she had envisioned her in her mind over the years as nothing else had helped to scratch the burning itch inside her, yet now she had the live show in front of her eyes, she thought as she touched herself with the same fingers that had just rubbed Ellen to oblivion. She smelled her fingers and felt their scents mixing together, her musky masculinity with her sweet vanilla and hot rain. Their scents complemented each other just like they did, she thought and quickly rubbed herself towards an orgasm and muffled her cry against a pillow so as not to wake Ellen up. She then gently covered Ellen's body and caressed her cheek and let her fingers stop under her nose letting her inhale the scent they had created together. Ellen snuffled in her sleep and Lupe smiled at her.

She adjusted herself next to her and closed her eyes. There were still a couple of hours left before the dawn would break the sky and the night would turn into morning again.

*

Lupe woke up before Ellen.

She was happy it was Saturday morning so she could just stay in bed and listen to the silence around them and watch her sleeping face.

Ellen looked so young and peaceful in her sleep. She had an innocent angelic face, which Lupe knew would take devilish shades under her touch. She may not have been the first, but she would definitely be the last one to see both of those faces she thought and lightly touched her cheeks and caressed her jawline. Ellen was simply everything she had always looked for in a woman. The realisation brought a lump of guilt to her throat, and she swallowed loudly.

The guilt would be something she would need to carry with her forever, but at the end of the day, it was a small price to pay to ensure she would stay happily by her side for the rest of her life. Sometimes one had to make dramatic moves in life to get what one wanted, Lupe thought and looked at the dawning sky, pulling Ellen closer against her body.

She parted her eyes. "You are not sleeping?"

"Guarding your sleep *mi vida*," Lupe smiled and placed a soft kiss on her forehead.

Ellen gently massaged her eye and smiled. "Thanks *amore*, is that all?"

"No, not really, there is something I wanted to ask you."

Ellen's eyes grew alert and she pulled the duvet to cover her chest as a protective gesture. "Well, what is it?"

"Will you marry me *mi princesa?*"

Chapter 52

The phone rang in the morning.

Ellen jumped. "Who is it?"

Lupe smiled at her. "Let me first answer and then I will let you know," she said and winked at her before grabbing the phone and pressing the green icon. "Hello, *digame?*"

After listening for a few seconds, she covered the speaker on the phone and turned to Ellen. "It's the police," she said.

Ellen's shoulders tightened and she grew tentatively silent, waiting for Lupe to end the call. She watched her nodding her head several times as if agreeing with what she was hearing.

"What did they say?" she asked the minute Lupe ended the call.

"They said that the crime record the hospital filed was comprehensive, however, they have checked CCTV in the area and can't find anything suspicious around the time of the attack. It seems like you were attacked in a blind spot," she said and held her breath for a second. "I'm sorry, baby."

Ellen sat down on the closest chair in the living room and allowed hot tears to build up in her eyes. Lupe knelt in front of her, massaging her shoulders. "*Mi vida,* try hard, is there anything you can remember from that evening? Smell, clothes, height, weight, tattoos, anything?"

Suddenly, a picture of the man on the bus with the gym bag and tattooed knuckles emerged in her mind but she stayed quiet. "No not really, everything happened so quickly and he only whispered once to me to stay before I took off and ran," Ellen said, her eyes frozen to a gaze as the painful memory surfaced in her mind again. "I should have looked back at once, you know. If I had, I might be able to recognise him at least," she said, covering her face in her palms.

"Shhhh, don't blame yourself *mi vida*, it's OK, you are here now at home and I won't let anything bad happen to you again," Lupe said clumsily trying to console her. She wasn't used to consoling anyone, but the pain in Ellen's eyes didn't leave her alone.

"There is something else, though," Ellen said thoughtfully.

Lupe stiffened and coldness entered her bones as she cleared her throat. "What is it, *mi vida?*"

"Just before I passed out, I could have sworn I was looking at you instead of the attacker," Ellen said and looked at Lupe. "How could that be possible?"

"Oh *mi vida*, you were running out of oxygen which makes you hallucinate easily. I wouldn't bother my head about that vision too much," Lupe said and sat down next to her and changed the subject. "Now, who would like to talk about the wedding?"

Ellen burst into a mix of a cry and laughter. "You know, you are definitely a crazy person," she said and punched Lupe playfully.

She laughed back and leaned to kiss her. "Correction *mi vida*, a crazy-in-love-with-you person."

The wedding was planned for a couple of weeks' time in a council registry office near their home. It was only logical as Ellen didn't want to leave the flat and couldn't really sleep due to the nightmares. They had managed to install a burglar alarm and sensor lights outside their flat and Lupe had even gone so far as to install double chains inside the flat just to put her mind at ease. Ellen had applied for emergency leave from the office for the next four weeks, and after the office heard what had happened, they had gladly approved it. The management team had sent a fruit basket and chocolates with a get well soon card but Ellen hadn't opened any of them. She was like a beautiful ghost wandering around the small flat, jumping nearly up to the ceiling every time she heard the lift ping. She didn't bother to put make-up on at all and wore only pyjamas after her shower. The worst part was, Lupe felt it only added to the raw beauty of her and made her see a new Ellen completely: fragile, broken, submissive, *hers*.

Lupe had asked for a couple of days off to stay with her, but she had then returned to the office but made sure she called in a couple of times a day and came home early. By that time, Ellen would have already cooked dinner and they would eat together before Lupe drew a bath for her and watched her bathe whilst telling her how her day had been. She would also ask Ellen about her day, but since there wasn't much to tell, she would continue telling funny stories of the people they both knew. She had tried to invite her friends over to see her, but Ellen had locked herself in the bedroom and refused to meet anyone, so she had cancelled at the last minute. She just needed a little bit more time, Lupe thought.

"What is this?" Ellen asked one late afternoon and caressed Lupe's inked skin as though it were the finest piece of art.

Lupe eyed the tattoo before taking Ellen under her arm on the sofa where they had been watching television. "It's a number seven."

Ellen giggled but didn't take her eyes off the tattoo.

"Yes I can see that, but what does it stand for? Is there a special meaning?"

Lupe released her hand, which had been around Ellen's back, and rolled up the sleeve of her flannel shirt to expose her full arm.

"Dice and playing cards?" Ellen raised her eyebrow.

"No *mi cielo*, look closer."

Ellen examined the drawing on Lupe's arm carefully before realisation hit her and she gasped. "Oh my God, the numbers on the dice equal seven. Same as the cards!"

Lupe smiled. "Exactly *mi cielo*." And kept rolling her sleeve up until Ellen could see her shoulder which was covered by an old Victorian pocket watch. "I also have a traditional watch stopped at seven o'clock."

The watch was resting in a bush of wild English roses. The thorns of the roses seemed to have scratched the metal parts of the watch, allowing rust to build up. The hands of the watch pointed to a seven in Roman numerals.

She could tell the drawing was well done as she inspected the mesmerising view. "Is there a special meaning hidden in the number seven?" Ellen asked again.

"It's my lucky number."

"Your lucky number, how?"

"It's difficult to explain," she said thoughtfully as she rolled her sleeve down. "It is something that has brought me luck throughout my life and trust me there haven't been many times that has happened, so I feel very grateful for it. I hoped that inking the number on my skin as many times as possible would make me even luckier." Lupe paused for a moment before continuing. "And it led me to you."

Ellen lifted her head to face her. "It led you to me?" she asked tentatively.

"*Cariño*, our first date took place on the seventh of June, we slept together for the first time on the 27th of June, and I asked you to officially date me on the seventh of July. You do the math." She paused for a moment. "And it is the number I couldn't see on the napkin you gave me when we first met in the hospital, which I then asked you." Ellen's face lost its colour.

"You see *mi cielo*, lucky number seven." Lupe smiled and waved her hand in the air.

Ellen stayed quiet for a moment digesting the information. "Do you think I bring you luck?" she asked with a serious expression on her face.

Lupe touched Ellen's cheek gently and looked at her green-blue eyes laying an entire ocean in front of her, like she had dreamt of so many times during the years.

"Every single day, since I laid my eyes on you the first time."

*

"Babe, we are going to be late for our own wedding!" Lupe yelled over the classical music Ellen was playing most days now.

"I'm almost ready!"

"Well get your ass here quickly because you know the judge won't wait!" she said and tapped her watch as the sliding doors to the bedroom opened: Ellen was wearing an all-white dress, which made Lupe gulp.

It was a basic strapless wedding dress with a mermaid hem. On top of the white silk, there was embroidered lace around her waist with Swarovski diamonds shining in the air. She didn't wear a veil but had her hair curled partly up and down, secured by a tiara with matching earrings and necklace. She had done her make-up herself with dark purple eye shadow and matching lipstick. She had brushed a couple of extra layers of mascara and eyeliner which made her eyes pop up in bright blue. These days she hardly had any colour in her cheeks but now she had a magical glow and pink blusher all over her cheeks. She looked like a dream.

"Are you ready to go?" Lupe asked huskily. A voice she didn't recognise even.

Ellen looked up at her from under her eyelashes, squeezing her tiny matching purse in her hand. "Yes."

Lupe approached and offered her arm to her. She assumed she might be more nervous about leaving the house for the first time since the accident than about the wedding; either way, it suited her – she didn't mind acting as her white knight, she thought as the irony of her actions made her blink.

Lupe had arranged a black Mercedes from Uber Lux to take them to the registry office. She had asked Ellen if she wanted to rent a car instead and decorate it with flowers, but she had said no, and Lupe had agreed. They both sat in the back of the black car and Lupe caressed the smooth leather of the seat and inhaled the new smell of the car. The driver looked at them with surprise but didn't comment on their attire. The journey wasn't long but it left enough time for Lupe to examine Ellen in peace.

She looked absolutely stunning, like no other. Her eyes stared into the horizon and looked big and troubled against her pale skin. She had lost some weight recently, but nothing to be worried about yet, Lupe thought. She had to pinch herself regularly to make sure she wasn't dreaming. She had never thought life could offer her something this sweet, but it had to be destiny that had led them together after all these years. A fact she wished she could share with Ellen, one day. She often compared them and previously had felt inferior to her, but after getting to know her, those feelings had completely disappeared.

She straightened her burgundy blazer and opened one of the top buttons of her dress shirt. She had chosen not to wear a traditional black suit for the day, instead she had spent the longest time of her life shopping for this special outfit and ended up finding a burgundy velvet blazer with black dress trousers with shiny faux-leather trimming on the sides. She had showered and let her hair curl naturally into big locks and fastened half of it back, just the way she knew Ellen loved. The clothes had been expensive but wouldn't break the bank for her, for which she was secretly happy. She felt like a million-dollar-girl for the first time in her life.

After many disappointments in life, she had sworn never to get married, and didn't know what it was that had made her change her mind in the end. Maybe it was just the way Ellen treated her and looked at her with lust and desire. How she lit her very soul and let her flames burn wild from the first moment, giving her a purpose in life, the rash she couldn't quite scratch.

Sadly, she had been forced to take drastic measures to keep her on her side. She had thought about it many times, but every time, she had ended up at the same conclusion and would do it again if needed. It wasn't about the trust issue, because she did trust her completely, but after the incident with her boss and then the new information she had learnt on the day they had met her friends and the side she had seen in Ellen, she hadn't been left with much of a choice. After all, she was like the devil's angel: looked innocent and sweet outside, but inside there was a blazing inferno burning the weakest soldier alive. Lupe knew, the combination would be her curse in this life for having her, but she wouldn't change it for the world. After all, it was those demons inside that made them equal and the same, which no one else would ever understand.

"I think we have arrived," Ellen said quietly.

Lupe jumped and Ellen placed her hand on top of her palm, smiling. "Are you OK *amore?*"

"Yes, of course. I was just thinking that's all," Lupe said and patted her hand reassuringly.

"I hope only happy thoughts?"

Lupe kissed her hand. "Always *me vida.*"

*

They had arranged a short ceremony in one of the meeting rooms on the third floor of the council offices. It was an old Victorian house, hidden from the main street of Kensington; Lupe hadn't had any idea of its existence until Ellen had brought it up. It was a majestic building to anyone from outside England and in fact, if known about, Lupe would have sworn it could be one of the main attractions of the city if only the council took better care of it; the concrete walls that had once been grey had turned a dirty blackish shade and the white window frames were so rusty, Lupe wasn't sure if they would even open anymore. There was nearly no light in the street leading to the building and the entrance signage had been covered by a wall of wild roses. They had walked past it once before and it had been exactly those roses that had caught Ellen's attention. "I have never seen wild roses growing like this before, it is magnificent, just like in the movie of *Beauty and the Beast*," she had said with a childlike smile on her face.

It had been the moment when Lupe had googled the address and recognised the front of it, and had made the decision they would get married there.

She helped Ellen to climb the stairs up to the main entrance and held the door open for her. Inside, it was cold and humid, but the air felt magical, just like in the movie of *Beauty and the Beast* that Ellen had referred to.

The entrance hall was majestic with two staircases leading to the first floor from where visitors were able to take the lift to the third floor where all ceremonies were performed. In the middle of the staircases, there was a big round wooden table and a large vase of lilies, artificial Lupe assumed since she couldn't catch the scent of lilies in the air.

They registered at the reception desk on the left side before going up.

Ellen handed her ID over and shivered.

"Are you cold *mi vida*, do you want to wear my blazer?"

Ellen shook her head. "No, I'm OK, just nervous I guess."

Lupe took off her blazer and placed it on her shoulders, which felt stiff. "That's OK *mi vida*, I'm nervous too but it is the right thing to do, we belong together, don't you agree?"

Ellen smiled. "I know."

They followed the receptionist upstairs and rode to the third floor, walking to the end of the long corridor before the receptionist stopped in front of an enormous wooden door and fished a giant skeleton key from her pocket to open the door for them. The door gave out a loud protest as if it hadn't been opened for years.

As if the receptionist had heard their thoughts she turned around and said, "The door is old and always makes that noise. I will ask the engineer to oil it after your ceremony." She nodded and left.

Lupe caught Ellen's hand and led her inside. It was a small room with dark mahogany bookshelves on the walls and a crystal chandelier attached to the ceiling. They had arranged for a red carpet to lead them to the end of the room to a table with some simple pink wild roses in a vase. Lupe knew they were handpicked outside and for a second felt irritated that the staff had not purchased decent flowers for the price they had paid for the 45-minute ceremony, but after seeing the approving expression on Ellen's face, she decided to let it go.

The celebrant was already in place waiting for them and the two witnesses quietly entered the room right after. Lupe had had to ask for unknown witnesses as she had no one she could ask to do it. She hadn't told anyone of their plan to get married and funnily enough, Ellen hadn't asked about it either.

The ceremony was quickly over, and after they had made their vows it was time to sign the marriage register.

"Which one of you wants the marriage certificate?" the celebrant asked.

"I do," Lupe said quickly and reached out for the paper before Ellen even had time to acknowledge what had happened.

They left the ceremony room and invited the two witnesses for a wedding lunch, but they refused explaining that they had other weddings that day. Lupe was secretly happy as she wanted just the two of them to fully enjoy the day.

Ellen had reserved a small room for the wedding lunch in a nearby restaurant. It was a fusion of Japanese and other Asian food, which included a private chef cooking show.

It wasn't the most traditional wedding lunch but Lupe knew Ellen had planned it playfully for her and she was thankful for it as she wasn't a big fan of traditional fancy lunches and felt rather uncomfortable, like a fish without the sea due to her modest background.

After their lunch, Lupe called the Uber service to pick them up. On the way, she asked the driver to make one more stop on the local street near their home.

"What is this?" Ellen asked in surprise but let Lupe help her out of the car.

"It's a wedding surprise *mi vida*, follow me," she said and opened the transparent door covered in flyers and posters of tattoos.

Ellen hesitated but grabbed her hand and followed her in.

A man with inked skin, pink hair and matching leather pants and jacket covered in silver chains approached them. "Which of you has an appointment?"

Lupe noticed Ellen grabbing her hand tighter and moving behind her. She was scared, how sweet was that, she thought.

"Actually, we have an appointment together."

Ellen's mouth fell open. "Both of us? But I don't want to have a tattoo," she whispered in her ear and licked her lower lip nervously.

Lupe smiled. "It's OK *mi vida*, this is a wedding gift from me. You don't have to have anything big, just something small to remember this day."

When the doubt didn't disappear from her face, Lupe continued. "Listen to me *mi vida*, you remember when you looked at my tattoos and I told you about the story behind my number seven?"

Ellen nodded suspiciously.

"Well I have a suggestion for you. What about you consider this as your own number seven, to protect you and bring you luck, are you interested?"

Lupe could see a light in her eyes. "I'm listening."

Lupe fished out a piece of paper from her trousers pocket. "What about this one around your ring finger?"

Ellen stared at the beautiful "Lupe" written in cursive letters.

"I will do the same of course but with your name," Lupe hurried to add nervously. She wasn't sure if she had gone too far this time with her. "Anyway, I asked already and you need to only wait a couple of weeks until you can put your ring back on," she said and waited for Ellen to respond but she stayed thoughtfully looking at the artwork on the walls. Panic started rising in her head as the tattooist grew impatient. "I mean I know it must seem stupid to you but I really think –"

"I love it, let's do it."

Lupe exhaled deeply. "Really, you like the idea *mi vida?*"

Ellen clutched her hand and crossed her fingers with hers. Lupe felt the rings clack together. "I love the idea." They stared each other in the eyes and, at that moment, Lupe thought she could have not loved her more.

"Great you guys – shall we get on? I don't have all day," the tattooist said and broke the spell between them.

"Sure, let's do it." Lupe nodded her head and massaged Ellen's shoulders reassuringly.

"OK blondie, you first."

Ellen stepped into a small room through a red velvet curtain. The familiar smell of antiseptic greeted her at the entrance and made her want to hold her nose, but she didn't out of courtesy. A lonely red leather chair stood in the middle of the room and the walls were covered in old rock star posters. She hesitated for a second and Lupe gave her an encouraging push on her lower back. "It's OK *mi vida*," she said and took her hand and pulled her deeper into the room.

The pink-haired man followed them. "OK, which of you sweethearts wants to go first?" he asked and pulled a metal table closer to the red chair.

"She will go first," Lupe said and pointed at Ellen.

Ellen frowned. "Since you have done this so many times before, why don't you do it first?"

She made a good point, Lupe had to admit, but she was too worried she would change her mind in the middle of the process, something she didn't want to risk.

"You go first, *mi vida* and it will be over for you sooner."

When Ellen didn't respond she added quickly, "I will sit right behind you and hold your hand still if you want?"

Ellen turned to eye the seat suspiciously. She was scared, Lupe could tell, but bravely sat on the chair.

Reading Lupe's mind, the pink-haired man pointed to the receptionist and told her to carry one of the chairs into the tattoo room. Lupe hurried to collect the chair and placed it behind the red leather chair Ellen sat on. "Now *mi vida*, I will hold you tight but whatever you do, don't move your hand; if you do, it will hurt more." Ellen nodded approvingly and allowed Lupe to embrace her from behind and together they leaned closer to the procedure table.

"Sweet," the tattooist said and rolled his eyes. "Can we finally start?"

Ellen inhaled and nodded.

First the tattooist drew the letters around her finger and after approval, started the needle machine. The buzzing sound filled the air and Ellen jumped. "*Tranquila mi vida*," Lupe said and grabbed her hand tighter to ensure it didn't move.

It wasn't necessary as Ellen sat tight on the chair, pale as a ghost, but with no intention of moving her hand during the tattooing process. Lupe was surprised but proud of her – she carried more inner strength than many she knew.

The tattooing process was quickly over as it was just four thin letters in cursive writing, however it would be noticeable even with the ring.

"Now remember blondie, you can't have your ring on until the skin is properly healed. You need to put this cream on twice a day or even more if you feel like it and don't worry once it starts itching, that's a normal part of the healing process," he said and turned to Lupe, forgetting Ellen's existence in the room completely. "Now, your turn *love*, yours will be slightly longer as you got more letters."

"It's OK," Lupe said removing her wedding blazer and rolling up her sleeves to expose her tattooed arms. "I think I can take it."

The tattooist eyed the artwork on her arms and nodded approvingly. "Cool."

One hour later, they both had each other's names inked on their ring fingers. Ellen admired the artwork around her finger. "I can't believe I have a tattoo now!"

Lupe smiled and placed a soft kiss on her lips. "Well, I guess there were many things you didn't anticipate you would have before me?"

Ellen smiled happily and shot a playful punch in her direction. "Stop it silly!" Lupe doughted and twisted her arm behind her back and pulled their bodies together. "Never as long as I live."

*

Three weeks later, Ellen returned to work and Lupe was secretly happy, as she had been suffering from sleepless nights due to the growing guilt inside her. She never thought seeing Ellen so scared and tormented would end up tormenting her very soul as well. Her mind had started to change after seeing the impact of what she had done to her beautiful wife. Even though she had looked ravishing on the day of their wedding, Lupe could now see the bags under her eyes, her paler skin and the hanging clothes that had once hugged her curves tightly. She still had her curves in the right places – it looked like she had lost the weight from her waist, making her hips create even more of an hourglass figure than before but Lupe could feel the pain in her every time she touched her body.

Ellen still refused to take public transport and insisted that Lupe take and pick her up from work. Lupe didn't mind at all and organised to be available whenever possible, or at least booked an Uber for her. She wasn't keen on travelling in the Ubers alone until Lupe installed a tracker on her phone to show her live whereabouts.

On the third day after Ellen had returned to work, Lupe was sitting in the office in the late afternoon when her phone rang. "Hello, *digame?*"

"*Hola hermana!* How are you doing?"

Lupe rolled her eyes at her little brother who had become a constant annoyance in her life, calling her several times a week asking about Ellen. He had also asked for wedding photos; Lupe had sent a couple but had felt too shy to share too many of the details. She understood his interest on Ellen but wanted to keep him at arm's length as he was still a man and she felt she owed it to Ellen to protect her.

Today, however, his voice sounded different. "Are you OK *hermano?*" Lupe asked.

"I'm OK, I just had a fight at home and Maribel threw me out again."

Lupe sighed deeply, knowing her sister-in-law, he would have a load of shit on his shoulders today. "I'm sorry to hear bro, what can I do for you?"

He hesitated for a moment. "I was wondering if I could stay with you guys for tonight?"

Red flags filled Lupe's mind. "Absolutely not," she said and stood up to close the door to the office which was nearly empty as most of her colleagues had called it a day early.

Deep silence filled the phone. "Why the hell not?"

Lupe hesitated for a moment. "Well, I don't want anything to upset Ellen, she is still not one hundred percent."

Jose-Luis laughed. "That's a lie!" he said and raised his voice over the phone. "I know this for a fact as I have seen her going to and from work for three days now."

Lupe's heart skipped a beat and the blood in her veins started to boil. "You have been following my wife you sick psycho?"

"Damn right I have, since you keep her hidden away in your small house. The whole family is interested to meet her, but no one can get through you."

"That's my business and it doesn't give you the right to follow my wife!" Lupe yelled but quickly calmed down, after all she was talking to her baby brother. "Look Jose-Luis, I'm sorry you have troubles with your wife, I truly am, but I don't think this is the right moment to share a flat with you and my wife, especially after we planned the attack on her," Lupe said and lowered her voice. "She is terrified of men in general at the moment and wouldn't want to sleep in the same house with any of them."

The anger in Jose-Luis's voice died but he remained tense. "Well, that's exactly how you wanted it, isn't it?" he said and sighed in frustration. "I just don't get it, what's so special about her? Why all this trouble and marriage with her? You don't even like European people – in fact I always remember you being very clear saying they are intelligent but their heart is pure ice that could never satisfy your needs."

Lupe debated whether to open her heart to her brother, after all he might not understand it at all. "Look, I don't know, but she is different OK. Her heart is pure gold and passion boils in her veins as though she were Mexican, so much so that sometimes it is almost too much for me to take. She has a twisted but open mind that matches mine, what more can I say?" Lupe said and opened her arms out of frustration.

Jose-Luis listened silently. "I feel there is something familiar in her eyes. I can't put my finger on it, but it's as if I have seen her before."

Lupe inhaled deeply. "OK, I need to tell you something, but you have to promise you won't tell a soul."

A long silence filled the phone before her brother responded. "OK *dime*."

"Remember the robbery gig I did about eight years ago in the *barrio* of Salamanca, with the two dickheads we met in a bar fight some years before I sent you to England?"

Jose-Luis stayed quiet for a while and Lupe could imagine his brain working. "The Picciani mansion – I spent months figuring out how to pass the security alarm system?"

A light lit in her brother's brain. "OK, yes I can, so what?"

"OK, it's *her, hermano*."

"What do you mean it's *her*? Talk to me clearly, *idiota*, I can't stand riddles."

Lupe sighed in frustration. "*Her*, the girl who almost busted us on the day."

A long silence fell over the line before she heard a loud scream. "WHAT?!"

Lupe pulled the phone further from her ear before responding. "That's right *hermano*, the girl I chased upstairs to make sure she wouldn't talk and call the police."

"I can't believe it," Jose-Luis said. "Are you sure? Maybe she just seems like her?"

She knew her brother couldn't see her gesture over the phone but she shook her head anyway. "No, you don't understand, she told me the story, how she saw us. I still don't know why she didn't call the police, but it is *her* Jose-Luis, I swear."

Her brother stayed quiet on the phone and for a second Lupe thought he had hung up on her.

"Bro, are you there?"

"Yeah, I'm. I'm just trying to figure out how all this happened."

She could almost see him scratching his head.

"I mean, she is your wife now and you planned an attack on her even though you knew she had gone through something similar previously. I mean, didn't you tie her up or something?"

I wish it had been only that, Lupe thought. "Look, I know I messed up planning the attack on her and then marrying her but I didn't have a choice, she was made for me. We met eight years ago and I marked her mine then; ever since, she has haunted me in my dreams and I haven't been able to find anyone else who would hold a candle even close to her." Lupe sighed in frustration and ran her fingers through her curly hair. "Every single relationship I have had ever since feels mediocre and wrong, it has been a torment for me for *years*, until the destiny joined us again" she raised her voice.

"OK, calm down *hermana*, you are not thinking straight. Shall we have a quick beer and talk?"

"*Vale, hermanito*, let me check if my lovely wife got home safely and I will call you back, OK?"

She didn't hear her brother's response as she heard a small voice behind her. "Lupe?"

The echo of the phone dropping on the floor filled the silent room.

Lupe froze in her place. "*Mi vida*, I thought you took an Uber home."

Ellen shook her head. "It never arrived. I came back to ask if you would be ready to leave with me," Ellen said and stared at the phone on the floor. "Who was that, your brother?"

Lupe started approaching her. "Look, whatever you thought you heard is pure nonsense *mi princesa*, let's go home," she said and tried to grab her wrist but Ellen pulled it away.

"No, I heard it very clearly Lupe," she said as the tears filled her beautiful blue eyes. "How could you, after all that I told you? After all that has happened between us?"

Lupe approached her and placed her hands on her shoulders. "Sweetheart, don't take things out of proportion. Yes, I might have not mentioned one or two things, but that doesn't mean…"

"One or two things?" Ellen raised her voice angrily and took a step back out of her reach. "Not mentioning your last name or your brother's second name would be one or two things, but arranging an attack and forcing me to have sex with you eight years ago is not one or two things!"

A sweat broke out on Lupe's forehead and she used her hand to wipe it quickly. "So you heard it all?" she said. "I thought you told me the night eight years ago felt magical to you too, you said it yourself."

Ellen shook her head. "I don't know what I felt on that night and it doesn't matter anymore. You organised someone to *attack* me and *abuse* me. Your own wife! What kind of person does that make you?"

Lupe grew silent. "I did the only thing I thought was right for us. Besides I was very clear not to do you more harm than was necessary."

Ellen pulled her turtleneck sweater down from the collar exposing the red scar leading down her neck. "Does this look like nothing to you?"

Lupe couldn't bring herself to look at her, she felt ashamed. "Consider it a war wound and wear it with pride."

Ellen shook her head. "You are insane," she said and started packing her bag.

Lupe looked at her and panic started to fill her body. "What are you doing?"

"What does it look like? I'm out of here," she said and closed the zip on her bag.

"Fine, I will get you an Uber home then," Lupe said and picked up the phone from the floor and started typing.

Ellen laughed. "I'm sorry. I don't think you understood me. I meant I'm out of here and I'm not returning home tonight."

A dark shadow started seeping into Lupe's mind and a muscle on her lower lip started twitching. "We will go home together, and there you can kick and scream all you want. But we go home first."

Ellen shook her head again with a fake smile on her face. "Home? Are you kidding me? The home you created for us was a lie all along, you just used me the way you wanted like you did eight years ago." She backed towards the door. "Silly me – I didn't even consider reporting you to the police because I felt there was something more in the air on that night, but now you have made it all dirty and damaged!"

Her words stabbed Lupe like a knife, but she wasn't willing to lose her, not now, and not ever. "I understand *mi vida*, this is a shock for you and trust me it was for me as well when I first realised who you were, but can't you see it was fate? We are meant to be together," she said and tried to grab her hand again but Ellen jumped as if her touch would have burnt.

"Right, so only for that reason, you arranged for someone to attack me?" The hot tears dropped on the floor. "Haven't you seen how much I have suffered since then? I can't go out alone, I can't eat, or sleep without nightmares, thinking it was my fault and I did that to myself when all along, it was planned by you." She swallowed her tears. "You broke me for anyone else but you."

Lupe tried to hold back her own tears but seeing the pain in Ellen's eyes, knowing she was the single cause of it, made her swallow hard. "*Baby*, I did it not to lose you, you mean the world to me. I can't lose you now that I have found you again, you belong to me."

Ellen shook her head. "Lupe, don't you see? I don't belong to anyone except myself. I *let* myself belong to you voluntarily and I would have been there for you always if you would have just let me," she said and opened the office door behind her back.

"Don't do it, Ellen," Lupe said in her most authoritative voice. "I won't be responsible for the consequences, you know it."

Ellen's hand stopped for a second and she raised her head to face her. She was smiling. "I know *amore*, but it is not in your control anymore now, is it?" she said and before Lupe had time to reach out to her again, she swirled out of the office and closed and locked the door. Lupe knocked on the door hard with her fist, cracking the glass. "Don't you dare leave. I swear to god I will find you, you will never ger rid of me."

Ellen smiled and her eyes flared with fury so hot it was as blue as the centre of a flame. "Something you never knew about me is that I'm good at running, I have done it already several times. Why would you think this time would be any different?" she said and threw the office key across the entrance hall, turned around and ran.

Lupe banged and kicked the door, causing the security alarm to go off. As she waited for the security team to attend the office and unlock the door, she felt something warm and salty dripping from her face and for a second she thought she had hit her head trying to open the door, but when she touched her face she realised they were tears. She was crying for the first time since her childhood.

Chapter 53

The rain hit hard on the concrete pavement outside the hospital. The sound of the emergency vehicle sirens travelled to the closest underground station in Central London. Lupe was running, hoping to catch Ellen but she knew she wouldn't have waited for her. It had taken more than an hour for the security team to arrive to open the office door Ellen had locked her in to give her good head start of running. The team were significantly understaffed and couldn't care less about any low-priority emergencies.

"Lupe, what the hell happened to you mate, you got stuck in your own office?" Steven, one of the black security guards asked and winked at her.

"Yeah, something like that. See you guys later," she said and passed them quickly to reach the main entrance. Steven's laughter filled the empty corridor as she ran towards the main entrance.

She looked both ways, protecting her eyes from the vicious rain but couldn't see anything except the emergency vehicles arriving with blue lights on when Giuliana ran towards her, breathing heavily. "Have you heard already?"

Lupe looked at her and raised her eyebrows. "Heard what?"

"Terrorist attack, Westminster Bridge, lots of victims."

Lupe exhaled. "No, I haven't, but I can't stay here, there is something I need to do right away," she said and was about to hail a taxi instead of collecting her motorcycle when Giuliana grabbed her shoulders. "It is Ellen, Lupe, she is one of them."

Lupe's blood froze in her veins. "What?"

Giuliana tried to catch her breath. "Her, Ellen, victim, terrorist attack."

"Are you sure?"

Giuliana nodded vigorously. "No question about it. I just saw the emergency team take her to the new A&E majors, I think…."

Lupe didn't wait for further details, instead she sprinted off towards the Emergency X-ray and Scanning Department, shortcutting directly to A&E majors. She saw an incoming patient in her wheelchair cutting her path unexpectantly and hit her leg on the wheel, almost making them both fall down.

"*Mierda!*" she cried and felt a sharp pain on her injured knee and pushed her curly hair back. The ponytail from the morning had loosened almost to nonexistence letting her wild hair run freely. Suddenly, a picture of Ellen appeared in her mind: laughing softly and running her fingers in her curls like she always did. She could almost hear her voice.

Lupe looked to the right before touching her identification badge on the card reader to open the door. They were not supposed to use shortcuts unless they were performing hospital duties. She knew it but this time she couldn't care less as she entered the A&E majors and started peeking inside the cubicles.

"*Ma'am,* you can't enter here, we have a medical operation in progress," a nurse said and tried to push her back behind the curtain but Lupe resisted. "No, please, let me go, I need to see her!"

"*Ma'am,* back off, now!" the nurse said and signalled to the nearby security. "Security, a little help here!"

Two of the security officers jogged to the scene and hooked their arms under Lupe's armpits.

"Let me pass, please," she panted and desperately gasped air into her lungs. "Let me go. You don't understand, I know her!"

The loud noises attracted the doctor's attention and he lifted his gaze. "Get her friend out of here!" the doctor yelled, annoyed. "We are trying to treat a critical patient here."

Lupe tried again, tearing her limbs from the security officer's grip, but it was pointless: two against one, there was no competition. "No, she is not my friend! You don't understand. Please let me see her."

Suddenly, the cardiac and pulse monitor came to life and an alarm went off.

The nurse quickly placed her fingers under the patient's jaw looking for a pulse. "Doctor, I can't feel the pulse, we're losing her."

"Fuck, bring the defibrillator, now," the doctor said and turned around ready to receive the defibrillator machine. "On three. Get another adrenaline shot ready," he said and charged the defibrillator. "Clear!" the doctor said and gave the first electric shock.

"Noooooo!" Lupe cried out loud as she helplessly watched the doctor trying desperately to shock life back into Ellen's body. When the defibrillator went off and her body jolted up from the bed, the physical pain ran through her, bringing stomach acids up to her throat.

The cardiac and pulse monitor continued alarming.

"Doctor, still nothing."

The doctor nodded. "Reload again and... clear!" The doctor gave a second shock on her chest.

Her body lifted from the bed like a rag doll.

The doctor motioned one of the nurses to wipe the dripping sweat from his forehead and looked up to see the security officers and Lupe frozen in their places watching them.

"For fuck's sake, get the friend out of operation room, now!" he yelled and angrily swung his hand toward them.

His outburst brought life back to them all and Lupe fought back fearlessly. "You don't understand, she is my life. I have nothing else!"

The nurse came to her, "I understand *ma'am,* but we need to let the doctors do their best now without distractions. Everything else is in the hands of God," she said and squeezed her hand before closing the cubicle curtain and leaving the security officers to escort Lupe out of the A&E majors.

When the door light turned red again signalling it had been locked, the security officers let go of Lupe's hands before a bleep on the radios attached to their uniform belt told them another emergency required their attention and they left Lupe in the corridor.

"I'm really sorry mate." Steven, one of the security officers, murmured before leaving her alone in the corridor.

She stood in silence for a moment listening to the sound of her own heart pumping quickly against her rib cage as if trying to escape. If she could, she would gift it to her, she thought as tears emerged in her eyes. She hardly ever cried as she saw it as a sign of weakness, something that had never been allowed in her world, but this time she couldn't stop it.

She gently touched the door separating her from Ellen lying inside the operation room. They were only ten feet apart, but somehow it felt like an ocean. She looked at the light above the door, which was lit up red: *Occupied.*

It meant there was an emergency operation in progress and no one was allowed to enter except medical staff. Lupe knew it, but she had never expected the room to be occupied by someone who held this much importance in her life, it felt too personal.

What if she hadn't gone to work today? What if she hadn't heard the conversation? What if she hadn't let her go? she thought as the pool of questions occupied her mind. Letting the anger get the best of her, she punched her fist to the wall so hard her knuckles burst open and left a trail of blood on the white wall but the physical pain didn't release the searing pain in her chest that threatened to rip her heart apart.

She had wanted to tell her so many times, but in the end, she had run out of time. The fear of her reaction had held her back and as the time had passed, the events of eight years ago had become only a distant memory. Especially after Ellen's confession of how she had felt about the whole night, it had made her confident and released her from the guilt she had felt since the start of their relationship, it had given her hope for the future, she thought.

She started wandering the hospital corridors and soon, without realising, she was standing in front of the chapel door on the lower ground floor of the hospital. She noticed the construction team equipment nearby and quickly snatched the "work in progress" signage and placed it in front of the chapel door before entering. She didn't want to be disturbed.

She hesitated for a moment before sitting down on the bench crossing her hands for a prayer. "God, I know we haven't been in touch for a while," she started, "I know I lost my hope at some point, because I couldn't understand why you put me through so much *shit*." She winced as her hard words echoed in the small chapel. "I still don't, but it doesn't matter anymore because when I was in a thousand pieces you sent *her* to put me in one." Lupe felt tears surfacing again and sobbed out loud. "But I can't understand why you are taking her away from me now. It doesn't make any sense, haven't I suffered enough?"

She heard someone trying the handle of the chapel door and waited in silence until she heard footsteps walking away from the door before continuing. "But I tell you this, if you take her away from me, I swear I will take my own life and I will hunt her down, I will travel through hell and heaven to find her if I have to because she is the blue heart in my flames. She belongs to me."

"Lupe?"

She turned around so fast her neck ached. "Danilo, what are you doing here?"

"I heard you might be here," the ginger-haired Italian doctor said and sat down next to her.

They had met in the hospital when Lupe had started working there. One evening, after a twelve-hour shift, he had seen Lupe holding a mop while a brown-haired lady with a supervisor badge yelled at her in the corridor.

He had approached them both. "Excuse me, what seems to be the problem here?"

The supervisor had turned around surprised. "Oh, sorry if I'm being loud, it's just it's difficult to find good staff these days who understand basic English," she had said and rolled her eyes towards Lupe.

Danilo had looked at her and changed the language to Italian. Lupe's face had immediately lightened, and she had burst into loud Spanish patter. Danilo had quickly discovered the problem and translated it into English for the supervisor who had thanked him politely, given Lupe a murderous look and disappeared from the scene.

Ever since, they had been friends and even though they didn't share a language, they had shared more thoughts than he had with many of the colleagues he worked with on a daily basis.

Lupe didn't bother to answer.

"Well, it's a good thing that I found you, because I just happen to have lost this very important patient file," he said and waved a patient report in his hand.

Lupe lifted her gaze but didn't make a motion to take the report.

"Well, I guess I *accidentally* left it in the chapel on my way to a toilet break," he said and placed the report on the bench before standing up. "Oh, look at that, how sloppy of me, I hope nobody *reads* it before I come back in five minutes to look for it," he said and walked away.

Lupe waited for him to disappear through the door before grabbing the file with both hands. She caressed the patient number on the cover of the file "345777".

Lucky fucking number seven, she thought and glanced behind her before opening the file.

She quickly scanned through the file before she gasped out loud and let the papers fly onto the floor like feathers. The time seemed to stop at that moment and create a time capsule. She couldn't stop staring at the blood test results.

Ellen was pregnant.

Dear Reader

It's always a pleasure to write a novel inspired by real-life events, so much I've even lost the track of what is reality and what is fiction as any good book should do. I've tried to stay true to the language, cultures and countries the novel takes you. Any mistakes are all mine and not meant to offend anyone. Even though, I enjoy writing sexy scenes and mature content which are part of the book, they don't represent my ideology of life or my opinion at any way.

The sequal Her Obsession is in the works.

Did you enjoy Her Salvation?

Please leave me a review! Just one sentence, even a word will be enough for me as it really helps other readers to decide whether my book is for them. You can also find me on:

Website: www.elleneauthor.com

Instagram: @ellen_e_author

Facebook: https://www.facebook.com/HerSalvation/

Twitter: @author_ellen

ABOUT THE AUTHOR

Trilingual Ellen E. was born in Scandinavia but currently resides in London, UK, and over the years she has travelled all over the world and lived in places such as Estonia and Italy. She started writing at a young age but still pursues her 9-5 corporate job although she dreams of being a full-time writer, one day.

Printed in Great Britain
by Amazon